SCORCHED

THE LINKED TRILOGY
BOOK ONE

CASSIE SWINDON

Scorched

ISBN for Scorched eBook- 978-1-7373469-6-8
ISBN for paperback: 9798430810474
ISBN for hardcover 978-1-7373469-2-0

Cover Design by Christian Bentulan
Editing by Kirsty McQuarrie at Let's Get Proofed and Kelly George at Polished Proofreading
Interior Formatting by Jennifer Laslie

SCORCHED

Kyra Kozelski

"All men deserve to burn in eternal Abyss."
Every male disappeared.
Turns out, I did that. Who knew I possessed Magik?
However, Jadox Griffin—a quiet, annoying soldier who definitely doesn't have eyes to die for—is still here. I need his help to return my nephew before it's too late. But Jadox is hiding something, and a whispered threat is creeping closer with each passing moment.

Jadox Griffin

Kyra is gorgeous, powerful, and a pain in my ass. Her wish turned the world upside down.
Teaming up with her is necessary to find the answers I seek. I'm not her only option, so maybe she won't choose me. If that's the case, I might be the next to disappear. But time is running out.

READER REVIEWS

"Kyra is an extremely powerful heroine but still not perfect in any way."

"You will absolutely fall in love with Jadox, this handsome sweetheart."

"Get ready to be frustrated, happy, tense, angry, and heartbroken!"

"This book is more than their relationship; it's a journey for their souls, filled with grief, failures, even death."

"I cannot put into words just how much I love Isaac."

"This intense romance will make you fall in love."

Dedicated to:

The biggest butthead of all time
who lives off of skillet cookie desserts and ridiculous playlists.

ALSO BY CASSIE SWINDON

LINKED TRILOGY

Scorched

Severed

Shattered

GOLDEN CHAINS TRILOGY

Break the Stone

Hunt the Storm

Stop the Clock

ACKNOWLEDGMENTS

Developmental and copy line editor: Kirsty McQuarrie at Let's Get Proofed
Map Designer: Adriana Pausenwein
Character Illustration Artist: Claudia Hopkins
Proofreading: Kelly George at Polished Proofreading. Kelly is also my personal cheerleader and the best supporter! Thank you!
Trilogy Covers: Christian Bentulan at Covers by Christian
Beta Readers: Aubree Anderson, Ana Maria Tufescu, Aimee Harrison, Janete Lawson, Paula Lloyd, Michelle Richardson, Arceli Friage, Vicki Chow
Short Story Covers: Anna Cackler

Thank you to everyone involved for their hard work and dedication devoted to improving the quality of Scorched. Y'all make my job easier. Thank you to my parents, Dan and Kathy, for giving me a solid foundation and remarkable education that eventually guided me toward this path of writing. Always keep the dad jokes rolling and the plate of Mom's frosted brownies full!

TRIGGER WARNINGS

Recommended for age 18+ due to profanity, violence, sexual content, and other sensitive topics that could potentially trigger the reader. Read at your own discretion.

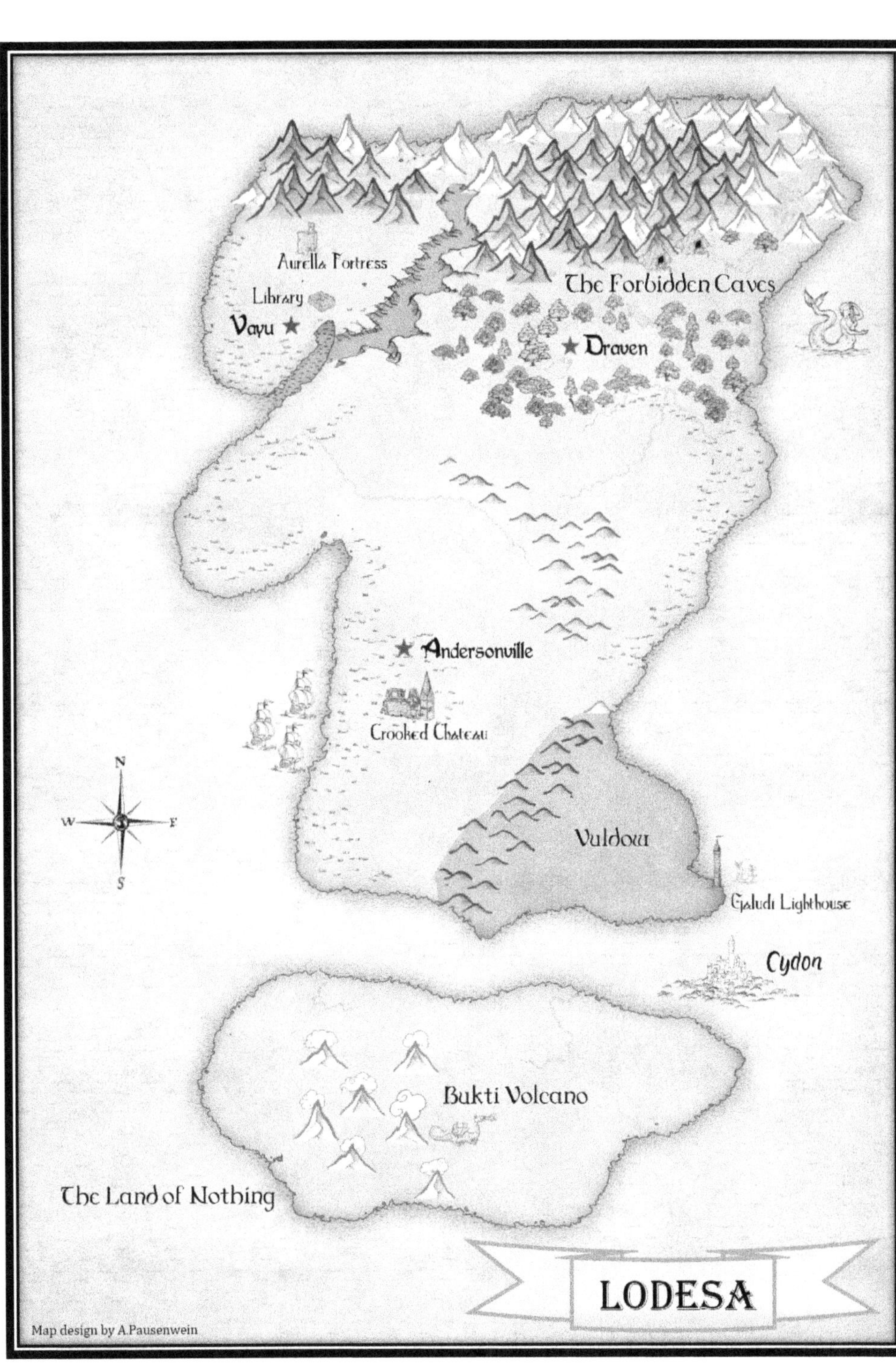
Aurella Fortress
Library
Vayu
The Forbidden Caves
Draven
Andersonville
Crooked Chateau
N
W
E
S
Vuldow
Galudi Lighthouse
Cydon
Bukti Volcano
The Land of Nothing
LODESA
Map design by A.Pausenwein

I

KYRA

Hard beats blared from the speakers that caged me, and the bass punctuated my intense longing for freedom. Thirty hours per day, seven days a week, for six months, I have longed to escape. Our band was already late going on stage, but Quamir demanded an emergency meeting with the entire staff. A bartender to my right plucked a hair off her shirt, then crossed her arms, waiting for the club owner to begin.

Quamir's glare lingered on us for a few seconds too long. "One of you knows where Tanya is. Please come forward with her location. She needs my help."

The tension was so tangible in the air I could almost taste it on my tongue.

I rolled my lips in and stayed tucked in the shadows. If Quamir knew I covered for Tanya last night while she fled, I might end up with a broken leg. He paced in front of us, trying to keep his face calm while his fists flexed into balls by his side.

"You all know I want what's best for you." He stopped in front of a waitress, their noses almost touching. "Where is she?"

The waitress gulped and fidgeted in her pockets. "I don't know, sir."

"One of you knows. And until I find out, there will be...consequences."

The fact that he didn't elaborate only increased the fear of the unknown. I stepped back quietly, away from Quamir's circle of attempted coercion. I knew, of course, that not one of the bandmates or bartenders would have my back if I confessed that I helped Tanya leave. There was too much at stake, and they'd get extensive praise and rewards for turning me in.

My solar watch blinked tiny red lights, warning me of only three minutes remaining. I was lucky to notice them with the strobe lights from the dance floor competing for attention. My bandmates would have to search for me a bit longer before we took the stage. I hid behind the backstage pillar and quickly dialed my sister's number. I had to push away my pride and contact Hallie. She was never up past midnight, but I had waited long enough to ask for her help.

My watch flashed faster. Two minutes and forty-five seconds remaining.

"Hello?" Hallie's voice was so quiet compared to the club that I had to bring my watch's video screen closer.

"Hey! It's me." I screamed over the chaos surrounding me.

"Kyra?" Hallie squinted her eyes, peering into the screen. "Holy shit, sis! You look so different with that hair."

Now that there was a chance for my band manager slash boyfriend to find out what I did. I needed to talk to Hallie to focus. I scanned the dance floor for him, then stumbled into a couple making out in the corner. "Listen, I don't have much time, but—"

Hallie smiled on the screen. "I mean, if you'd returned my calls in the last three months, maybe I wouldn't be so surprised that your hair is *red* now. And is that a new piercing?"

How did she have so much energy at this hour? That wasn't like my older sister. Pausing, I glanced behind her as a shadow moved across her room. "Uh, Hallie, is someone there with you?"

"No, well, yes. Look at these adorable kittens I found." She stepped out of the frame. Damn it, I didn't have time for this. The music blared louder, and a beeping sounded from my watch every few seconds, cutting off half of her words. "You…come tomorrow… kittens…adopt."

My foot bounced faster with each passing second. As much as I'd love to adopt one, Quamir would never let me keep a kitten in his apartment. He'd probably end up cooking it on his grill just for fun. But obviously, Hallie didn't know any of this. My sister was completely unaware of my predicament.

"Look at this little smushy face." Hallie held up a tabby with entrancing eyes and ears three sizes too big for its body.

One minute and thirty seconds left until my watch battery ran out. There wasn't enough time to tell Hallie that my boyfriend was the villain. Quamir had refused to help with my last watch bill, and since he was my band manager, who also refused to give me a paycheck, I barely had any money left.

"Hallie! Listen, I need your help."

"What? I can't hear you. Wait, Kyra, where *are* you?" She finally put down the kitten and started paying attention. I'd been so stupid waiting this long to call my family. In less than a minute, I'd have no outlet, no way to communicate if things got worse—no means of escape.

The DJ started introducing our band on the mic, his voice crackling louder than the music, so I crouched down on the floor, trying to block out the noise.

"Hallie! I need you to pick me up downtown Andersonville at—"

"Kyra?" Her face blurred in and out of focus. "I can't hear—"

The call dropped.

"Shit!" I dropped my arms to my side, my heart pounding.

"Kyra! There you are," Quamir roared from the shadows, racing footsteps thundered after his voice. "You're ten minutes late! I was so worried."

Fuck Quamir and his fake charm. He lifted me from my crouched position, crushed me in a suffocating hug, and kissed my forehead.

"I don't know what I'd do if something happened to you." He scanned my outfit, a red tank top with black shorts, and for just a moment, his eyes narrowed with possessiveness. "They're waiting for you. Get on stage, babe." He handed over my drumsticks and spanked my butt while pushing me toward the stage.

If only I could punch the drumsticks into his eyes. As the lights blinded me, the raging crowd burst into applause and screams.

I pounded my drumsticks together, yelling, "One, two, three, four."

Soon, we were creating the hypnotic rhythm all the hopeless couples craved. Scarlet-red and atomic-orange beams from the strobe lights sliced through the fog to the mosh pit below our stage. For a few moments, true passion struck deep in my core, with every beat thudding faster on my drums. The smiles of my bandmates mirrored my own, though theirs probably weren't layered with pain.

Even though our lead sang the routine lyrics, I hummed a verse of the words I had written in my journal, matching them to this beat.

You ignore my soul that could've shined so bright,
You've swallowed me whole and stolen all my light.
I'll soon find my violent spark,
So watch your damn back, cuz I'll put up a fight.
And one day soon, my soul will ignite,
No one can trap me in the dark.

I wanted freedom from this bar, this band, my 'boyfriend,' AKA captor, and rid of Lodesa. At this point, I'd even live in abandoned Vuldow if it guaranteed that I'd never have to see Quamir's face ever again—or any man, for that matter. But that'd never happen. I was so devastatingly trapped. I stared at the neon sign flashing on the wall, mocking me with the name of the run-down bar which had imprisoned me in the capital city for the last few months.

I caught Quamir's eyes through the crowd. When a guy leaned in to whisper something in his ear, Quamir's features turned from cold to deadly. My heart rate instantly tripled. What secret passed between them? Did he know I helped Tanya escape from his clutches? Or maybe someone had caught me stealing money from his usually thick, but now lighter, wallet.

My stomach coiled from the memory of Quamir's fists hitting my stomach last week. Screw all men. There wasn't one good one left. My time to act was running out. One week—if I could survive seven more days under Quamir's slimy fingers, I'd finally have enough hidden cash to flee.

He stepped forward, parting the sea of sweaty bodies, and headed straight toward me. Shit, whatever that guy had told him made him snap. The prospect of a week rapidly disappeared. I needed to leave tonight. Now.

Someone blocked me from Quamir's predatorial eyes in the knot of swaying bodies. I leaped out from behind my drum set, jumped offstage, and bolted into the shadows.

"Ky-ra! Ky-ra! Ky-ra!"

The crowd's chanting of my name faded into a blur. As I jogged away, every hair on the back of my neck prickled in warning. I broke into a run down the dark hallway when I was free of the crowd, yet Quamir's gaze burned a hole in my back. My heart thudded with each clomp of my boots that echoed off the walls. I needed to grab the stolen cash; otherwise, I'd never survive. The terrifying thought that someone may have found my secret stash made my legs push harder.

As I sprinted down the long hallway, my ruby necklace slapped between my breasts. I prayed to whatever goddess above for the elevator doors to magically open. Too bad magic didn't exist.

Panting, I used my drumstick to jab the elevator button repeatedly.

Jab.

Jab.

Jab.

"Come on!" Bouncing on the balls of my feet would surely make the elevator appear faster. "Let's go!"

Finally, the elevator doors screeched open, and I released a breath. Inside, mirrors surrounded me on each side. My long, brown locks fell down my chest, with the red highlighted streaks matching my crimson shirt. My face showed the similar edges of Mom's jaw and the soft curves of her nose. Maybe I should've called her instead of Hallie—too late now.

I had two options: head up to my cash hidden on the roof or down to the basement tunnel exit. But there'd be no point in fleeing without the safety net of money. Loud thumping footsteps triggered a glance over my shoulder. A dark silhouette loomed from down the hall.

Quamir had caught up with me.

Thankfully, the elevator doors swished shut between us just in time. I pressed "R" for the rooftop and nervously fiddled my drumstick between my fingers.

It lifted. Up. Up, rising higher. I gulped as the elevator doors opened to the roof, revealing the onyx sky. Darting forward, my feet followed the path straight to the loose brick in the corner. A bluster of wind flung my long hair across my face. I wiped it off, careful to avoid the tender spots hidden by makeup. Lightning splintered the darkness like a spiderweb. With a steadying hand on the side of the roof, I checked the fire escape ladder. Gone.

Shit! My plan was doomed from the start. I quickly peered ten stories below to The Crooked Chateau's graveyard, where my father's bones lay resting. Another man I used to run from.

"I hope the Divinities burn you a thousand times over, Dad, and melt the skin off your face for eternity," I spat into the wind, hoping it landed right on his tombstone. Unfortunately, Quamir was just like Dad, an abusive asshole—like all men. They should all just disappear and make our lives much better.

Crouching with trembling hands, I twisted the loose brick to the side and reached into a hole. Something sharp jagged into my forearm, and I gasped from the pain.

"Keep going, Kyra," I whispered to myself, "Don't stop."

Finally, I grasped the wads of cash. Hopefully, I'd have enough for a hoverbus ticket out of Andersonville and a place to stay. Heart pounding, I pulled out the money and clutched it to my chest for just a beat. Blood dripped onto the top bill from the gash on my forearm. One more injury wouldn't hold me back—not tonight. I'd rather slowly bleed out than stay near that sociopath for one more minute.

A heavy sigh puffed out behind me. "You'll learn to trust me one day, Kyra."

Rising, I spun on my heels and stared into Quamir's monstrous eyes. He leaned on his stupid cane, a tool he used for power, but I only saw weakness.

I gritted my teeth together and hissed, "If you try to make me stay, you'll regret it."

"Is that a threat?"

"It's a promise." I shoved the money into my purse.

He closed the gap between us, stretching his snakelike smile across his cheeks in a way that had charmed me once before. "Let's get you back on stage. The band sounds terrible without my star. No one uses their hands as good as you, Kyra." He winked. "I'd know."

The edge of the rooftop crept closer. If I jumped, I wouldn't survive, so I faced him directly. Bile rose in my throat at the reminder that I used to trust him, like him, maybe even love—no, I couldn't love any man—never again. I eyed the rooftop elevator behind him. But Quamir pulled up his shirt, hovering his hand over a gun—a rare weapon and outrageously expensive.

"Give me back my money," he growled, "And let's get you downstairs where you belong."

Thunder rumbled, followed by another crack of light above. As I backed into the brick wall, rain splattered, drenching my hair. If only I could harness the downpour and strike Quamir down where he stood.

"Don't test my patience," he snarled.

If I gave him the money, I'd live at least another day. If I ran for it, I might last four seconds until he shot a bullet into my back.

"Kyra, don't make me hurt you."

Those words stoked a flame deep within my soul. He had already hurt me. It was too late for that. Instead of running toward the elevator, I rammed my head straight into his gut, and we toppled backward. His gun dropped onto the rooftop.

"Bitch!" He scrambled toward me, but I crawled faster, kicking his neck.

I grabbed the gun and rolled, but his firm hand clutched my ankle, pulling. Hard. My back scraped against the concrete. Rain blinded me.

I squeezed the trigger. Sound erupted from the weapon and jerked my body. I wouldn't miss the second time.

"Hey! What's going on?" A sharp, deep voice yelled from the elevator.

I glanced over to where a man stood between the opened doors, a dog by his side.

In the distraction, Quamir kicked my leg. A scream burned my throat from the searing pain, and I dropped the gun.

"Hurry, get over here!" The man beckoned me forward while holding the elevator open. I swore the rooftop shook for a second.

Through the pummeling rain, I crawled. Gunshots blasted louder than the thunder. I didn't dare look behind me. Fear clawed at my heart and sliced its way into the roots of my soul.

Six feet to the elevator. My breathing turned ragged.

A sound like cracking stone split the night air. Was the roof moving? The dog barked frantically, urging me on. I couldn't see through my sopping hair.

I was only four feet to safety.

Pebbles dug into my knees and palms. *Faster!*

"Hurry!" the stranger hollered.

Two feet.

I collapsed inside after another blasting gunshot. The elevator's mirror cracked and split like a painting of silver veins. Before the doors clamped shut, a bullet had flown between them.

"You okay?" The man reached his hand to help me up.

"I'm…I'll be fine."

Silently, the stranger stood before me with a posture so straight that he might have a rod for a spine. His brown complexion was a shade darker than my golden tan, and even though he looked to be only a few years older than me, his expression reminded me of cold, ancient tombs. Those near-black eyes were so harsh that they could've been made of stone.

"If you touch me, I'll carve your damn eyes out." I gulped down my fear of his titan size towering over me.

"Woah, it's okay." He stepped back and leaned against the shattered mirror, his eyes fixated on his dog, who sat calmly by his side. I tilted my head and squinted at the tiny cloud patch between the chocolate lab's brown eyes.

"Have we met before?" I pointed my drumsticks like daggers which didn't bother this giant in the least.

"No, but you look cold. Take my jacket." Those dark eyes held no spark of life, and that thick, messy, brown hair gave him a look of not-giving-a-crap that couldn't be faked.

I was about to refuse when he draped it over my shoulders. Now, I could see his camo cargo pants, military-looking boots, and a tight brown tee that hugged his sculpted chest.

"I'm hitting the emergency button," he said quietly. "Please don't stab me with your...um...drumsticks." A hint of a smirk quivered at the corner of his lip, but I probably imagined that too. This guy didn't seem like he had smiled a day in his life.

"No, I need to get *away*. Don't, for one second, think that you're trapping me here."

"I'm helping." His voice was sharp enough to cut straight through bone.

"Sure, *every* man thinks their ideas are the best ones."

The elevator shook fiercely. "Crap!" My side slammed into the shattered mirror, and glass pieces cascaded into my hair.

He stared down at me from his six-foot-something with a practiced scowl meant for enemies. His hand reached for my face.

I flinched and squeezed my eyes shut, ready for a slap to the cheek.

"Hey, calm down. I'm never going to hurt you, Kyra," he said, then plucked a piece of glass from my hair.

How does he know my name?

"This is Chocolate, and I'm Jadox Griffin," he said, with a voice like sin.

I studied his features—bone structure that looked cut from an edge of quartz, but his thick, long lashes didn't match the rest of his masculine features.

His large hand pinched his stubbly chin, and he took a deep breath. "Why was that man shooting at you?"

"Does it matter ... Jade ... Jay?"

"It's Jadox. It's a native name from my village, Draven." His deep baritone mumbled the words together.

Draven must've been outside of Lodesa. I hadn't heard of it.

This time when Jadox shifted his weight toward me, I stayed firmly in my spot. I still waited for an impact, not trusting him, but his hands wiggled a lever in the ceiling. "Let's go, climb up," he said.

I looked up into the dark space above, refusing to tell him about my fear of heights.

"We don't have time to chat. Your rooftop friend might be waiting when these doors open...and his gun might be aimed straight at your heart."

With that last word, his gaze scanned my chest, my tight, wet top with my breasts squished together. Typical male—only three possible things on his mind: sex, power, money.

"I'll go up alone," I said.

"No, I'm not leaving you."

His dog's wet tongue licked raindrops off my calf. Something about his pet looked familiar. I bit my lip and let my mutinous gaze skate down his flat torso.

"You make a hideous first impression with that alpha attitude."

A devious flicker sparked in his dark eyes as he stared at the elevator ceiling. "So, when did you receive your tattoo?"

"Receive? That's a strange way of putting it." I flipped my forearms over. "Which one? I got this feather during the Snow Moon of year 80T. Or did you mean this rose? That was earlier, I think, in 76D."

"No...your Circle." Jadox's eyes raked over my face.

"Uh, I have no idea what you're talking about."

"You...don't...have a...?" One of his thick eyebrows almost met his hairline. "You don't have one," he said, not as a question this time.

"Um, this has been lovely. Thanks for the thrilling conversation, but I'm leaving now."

His mind seemed far away, like we weren't in the same place. Of course, he was probably just another egotistical asshole who thought the sun revolved around him even though I was literally running for my life.

"Um, actually, can you please lift me?" I reached into the darkness.

Jadox laced his calloused fingers together, and I placed one boot in the center. With the ease of an athlete, he projected my one-hundred-and-thirty pounds straight up through the hole. One wad of cash thudded to the floor, landing by Chocolate's paw. Jadox shoved it in his cargo pants. "Thanks for the tip."

"Hey! I need that money."

I turned and surveyed the dark elevator chute. A thick, long cord was hanging down and swaying. Next to it were divots that formed a ladder on one wall.

A pounding sound came from below against the closed elevator doors.

"He's trying to get in," Jadox said. "Move so I can climb up."

"No, you stay down there," I hissed. "Your dog can eat him."

Ready to dig my boot into the narrow ledge, I suddenly heard heavy breathing directly behind me. A landmine of goosebumps sprinkled my neck. Holding my breath, I turned slowly, so slowly. Silent as a ghost, Jadox had somehow magically appeared next to me, his deep oak eyes boring through me. I didn't dare make a sound. This man just rose seven feet while holding his dog without making a sound.

"What the? How did you get up here already?" Chocolate wagged her tail beside him. "Maybe I'm dreaming. Or I must be in the afterlife."

"Kyra—"

"And stop acting like you know me. It's creepy. Are you a stalker?"

"No."

Quamir's pounding below grew louder and louder until my head buzzed intensely.

"I have to get out of here," I mumbled to myself, absolutely frantic.

One of the dim lights overhead burst into a shower of sparks. I climbed the steep wall, slipping with each attempt.

"I'll help you up. Step on my hands again," Jadox insisted.

The divots were too shallow, and I wasn't strong enough. I struggled, trying to pull up, but slid down with each try. Gripping a tiny indent, my fingertips turned red from pressure, and my arms shook. I groaned and pushed up with my legs. I fell. Useless.

"Fine, help me up, but only because I asked you. This is *my* idea," I said, seething at having to give in.

"Okay, and when we're out of here, there's something I need you to do for me."

"I don't owe you anything."

"It's not really an option." His eyes grazed my chest again, his irises lit from the inside, full of mystery. This time, I realized he wasn't soaking in the view of my cleavage but had his eye on the necklace draped between my breasts.

"I need your ruby."

2

JADOX

Kyra Kozelski wasn't what I expected. It had taken me eleven grueling months to find her again. About this time last year, I had her just out of reach. Instead of politely introducing myself and explaining why I needed her necklace, I managed to murder the man who raised her. And I was ninety-nine percent positive that Kyra was still unaware that her dad was actually her stepfather. Hopefully, I'd never have to tell her any of that, and we'd go our separate ways.

I definitely didn't expect this outrageous attitude from such a little thing. But that didn't mean I'd let her suffer when I could heal that bloodied scratch on her forearm. When I leaned in closer to inspect the cut, strands of her chestnut hair streaked with red tumbled over her face.

The banging below escalated. The man chasing Kyra would soon find a way to smash through those doors. What had Kyra done to piss him off so badly?

I hoisted her up the side of the chute's wall. "I can't see in this darkness. Let me know when you reach—"

"I got it. I'm up!" She pulled herself to the higher level, then glued her shoulders against the wall. "Are you gonna do your voodoo thing again to get that lab up here?"

Her sarcastic voice sent my nerves into a chaotic frenzy. Why did people have to talk so much? She had better agree to give me the ruby because the thought of spending time with someone other than Chocolate felt like being trapped in a suffocating coffin. My dog was the only companion I ever wanted or needed.

I had three rules in life: one, only trust Chocolate. Two, never make friends with an Ordull because those without Magik could never be fully trusted. Well, apparently, Kyra was an Ordull, which made no sense. My third rule was never to rely on another Mystier, thanks to what my tribe decided. Basically, only dogs I could vouch for, and that included family. I definitely didn't miss my grandma or sister.

When we were little, Gemm told Alaska and me the haunting history of The Fall. About eighty years ago, entire cities were ripped to shreds, most Mystiers were slaughtered in the night, and it was all covered up by the Ordulls blaming it on terrorists. Thankfully, most of society didn't even know that we Mystiers lived among them, which is why we continued to live in hiding, protected behind our village's invisible shields. At least Gemm and Alaska were still safe in Draven.

If Kyra hadn't received her tattoo yet, did she not know any of this?

"Hey, pay attention, and someday, you might win a Lodesa Peace Prize for your fantastic listening skills."

Her amber eyes looked like they could crush metal, challenging me with the world's most epic stare. The golden flecks sprinkling and swirling looked like another universe full of adventure. I didn't dare bat an eye.

"Make yourself useful and separate those elevator doors." I pointed behind her.

Her exasperated huff echoed through the shaft, but she wedged her drumstick between the two metal doors. I wanted to help, but the electricity sparking around us dampened my Magik to weak flickers, so I had to resort to the old-school methods. Quickly, I reached into my pocket, pulled out a fistful of dirt, and multiplied it to form a ramp of soil. I sprinkled the last few pieces on Chocolate and tugged her collar.

"Come on, girl." We climbed the makeshift ramp in one breath and stood behind Kyra on the ledge.

"This can't be real," Kyra stiffened once my breath brushed against her neck. "Someone must've drugged my drink before our show."

"I'll explain later."

If she truly didn't know about Magik, then here and now was not the time to spook her if I wanted any chance to convince her to hand over the necklace. I squeezed my fingertips between the doors and pulled. My shoulders strained. Gritting my teeth, I yanked with every ounce of energy.

Animalistic grunts came from both of us. Our elevator doors finally screeched open, and a bright light temporarily blinded me. I squinted into a long, clean hallway.

She jogged ahead, Chocolate chasing her heels. From over her shoulder, she asked, "Why were you on the roof?"

"Why is your tone always so harsh?" I spat back.

"You have a slight accent. Where are you from?" She rushed forward.

"I already told you...Draven."

"That's not a place."

Frustration coiled tight in my gut. "It doesn't matter. I need your necklace."

Kyra turned so fast that I almost ran right into her. Her stubborn scowl glared at me with the intensity of an Elidian, her lava eyes liquid like honey. But she didn't possess Magik—yet. How was that possible? I knew she was Kyra Kozelski. She had to be.

"Are you always so serious?" Her question cut through the silence.

"Are you always so stubborn?"

"Are you always so grumpy?" she hissed, her words tighter than any noose.

I eyed the one-of-a-kind ruby hanging over her shirt and didn't mind the rest of the view either. I couldn't even remember the last time I'd seen a woman's—

"Eyes up here." Kyra glared at me and followed it with a scalpel-sharp threat.

Her snappy tone sent me into a frenzy. Normally, I had no trouble maintaining an expressionless face, but my entire body battled with my mind.

Desperate to flee this confusing feeling and create as much distance from her as possible, I grabbed the necklace, breaking the chain off her neck. A raging heat burned through my skin from the gem and tore through me. Screaming in pain, I shoved it into my pocket.

"Hey! Asshole, give that back!" Kyra swiped her nails like claws.

I ran. Kicking the stairwell door open, I flew down, three steps at a time. Chocolate barked and sprinted ahead, her nails clicking against the hard surface around each bend.

"Faster, Chocolate!"

"Stop!" Kyra screeched, then cursed nonsense that I couldn't understand, making this far more enjoyable than I expected.

I descended faster.

Fourth floor.

Something hot pressed against my thigh. The necklace emitted an overwhelming temperature through my pants. Damn it!

"...Rip you...to pieces!" She was panting between breaths.

I could smell her sweat from above, mixed in with her intoxicating lotion.

Third floor.

"You filthy bastard!" Kyra's voice echoed in the stairwell. "Give it back!"

Second floor.

My heartbeat hammered under my ribs. For the first time in years, I felt alive again.

With a thud, I hit the first floor, hoping that guy chasing her wasn't waiting around the corner.

The heat from the necklace grew more intense, burning a hole through my pocket. The ruby clattered to the floor, thankfully, still in one piece. Chocolate stopped and pointed her nose at the necklace, whining. How had Kyra kept it wrapped around her neck without pain?

Just as she rounded the last bend of the stairs, she barreled her foot into my shin with the violence of a tigress. "You piece of trash!" She swiped the necklace from the floor and wrapped it around her neck without getting burned. "Don't you ever steal from me."

The room spun, and my vision blurred. I stared down at my red finger, and the violent burn traveled quickly over my hand, scalding my palm, wrist, forearm, and elbow.

What kind of curse is in that gem?

Unaware, Kyra still rambled, but all I could process was the agonizing pain. I sank to my knees by the pile of dirt on the floor that had fallen out of my pocket, then covered my injured hand with it.

"What...what are you doing?" Her voice sounded miles away, muffled and incomplete.

Closing my eyes, I chanted a healing spell, *"Terra angakok. Terra angakok."*

Quickly, the pain faded, and the boiling blisters healed, turning my skin back to my treasured brown Dravian shade—good as new.

Only then did I notice the utter silence in the stairwell and two black boots pointed in my direction. I followed them up to Kyra's toned thighs, her black leather shorts, pierced belly button, the tattoos crawling out of that strawberry-red top harboring the demon necklace, and finally, her face. Kyra's jaw was made of sharp corners of mistrust and a bone structure sliced from betrayal. I was stupid to want to memorize every detail of her thick lips and high-planed cheekbones. Dark eyeliner framed her top and bottom lids, making her golden eyes pop. Shit, Kyra Kozelski really was sexy as fuck.

"How did you fix your hand?" she asked, wide-eyed. "Was that some charm or spell? Are you a magician? Am I dead? I'm dead, aren't I?"

"I'll explain when we're safe." I cleared my throat. "Let's get out of here."

Looking awe-struck, Kyra tucked a long strand of hair behind her ear.

My grandma was never wrong about her visions. If I couldn't touch the ruby, I still needed to convince Kyra to bring the necklace to Gemm. "Follow me."

She looked unsure, finally at a loss for words.

Together, we marched through the stairwell's door. Music attacked us from all angles and strobe lights danced.

With each step, the electric base of the music thrummed through my bones. The smell of beer and sex assaulted my nostrils, igniting a flashback of my days in the army. All my teammates would party without me, knowing I liked quiet nights, just another way people left me behind. No wonder dogs were called a man's best friend.

"I'm not going anywhere with you. Give me back my cash, then leave me the Abyss alone."

I had forgotten about teasing her earlier, so I pulled it out of my pocket. The top bill was a two hundred with President Giselle Dominia's face on the front, the leader during The Fall. Those bills were hard to come by. Kyra buried the cash in her purse, then tied her hair in a high ponytail and stuck both drumsticks out of the top.

"Why do you need all this money?" I asked.

"Doesn't matter. Bye." Kyra paused. "Why are you looking at me like that?"

"I'm not looking at you."

"You're a bad liar." When she rolled her eyes, that rotten smirk threatened me with pearly white teeth. "I said bye. You can leave now." Her little wave to send me away instigated so much irritation I had to bite my tongue.

Cheers escalated from the dance floor. Kyra glanced in each direction, eyes wildly searching for the threat. A fog machine hissed and blocked out the swarming bodies in a sea of mist.

"I don't see Quamir." Her voice had turned from lioness to mouse.

"I'll help you escape safely. Please follow me."

"No, I don't need a man's help for anything. Especially one who just tried to steal from me."

I ran a hand over my stubble, taking a deep breath to lessen the frustration she had caused me. "So, *who* do you have to help you?"

Her mouth opened and closed, paused, then said, "My sister, Hallie."

"Hhm, and where is this, Hallie? Is she the one singing on stage?"

Her eyes widened, fixated on something behind me. "Watch out!" She ducked low, grabbed Chocolate's collar, and tugged my pup behind the corner.

A bullet pierced the wall where my lab had just been standing. My heart raced as I glanced at Kyra hiding behind the wall. She had saved Chocolate. I owed her everything just for that one action.

No one fucks with my dog!

Quamir's nasty grin was plastered across his face as he trained his gun on me. "What are you doing with *my* girl?"

"He hits me," she whispered from behind the corner. "No one would ever believe me, but if I'm about to die, I can't hold the truth in any longer. Someone needs to know. He hurts me, so get the other girls in the band out of here."

My whole body went rigid, and I clenched my fists. I'd gladly kill the motherfucker who laid a hand on her.

"Ah, I see. You're a fighter," Quamir snarled. "But you'll need a whole team against me."

Next to me stood pots of Ming Aralia trees, helping me form a plan. I peeked around the corner of the hallway at the oblivious dancers grinding against each other. I no longer cared if the Ordulls would notice my next move.

"Hey, I'm talking to you." Quamir stepped forward in the hallway, finger hovering over the trigger. "You ignoring me?"

I took a deep breath and summoned my Magik. Tension clamped in my stomach, and energy circulated in the Circle tattooed on my hip. It surged a pulse to my fingertips. Power flowed through me, desperate to be used. Strength coiled in my head, turning to a substantial pressure until it spiraled up and out of my skull.

"Dehano huc."

One of the plants obeyed my summoning spell. It flew from the pot and into my grasp.

Quamir's jaw dropped. He squeezed the trigger. Shots fired. Kyra screamed. I gripped the tree trunk tight, then threw it at Quamir. The tree slammed into his chest, crashing him to the ground.

I concentrated on the next plant, and a ping of power slashed through my tattoo.

"*Digati impetu*!" I yelled.

The remaining four trees attacked on command, soaring through the air like a spear. A sharp branch speared Quamir's chest. It stabbed straight through his body and pinned him to the floor.

Dead.

Blood drained and pooled under his back.

Protectiveness tangled in a mess inside my throbbing tattoo, urging me to move Kyra to safety. When I glanced over, she lay flat on the floor, clutching her side, screaming.

"He shot me!" Her eyes squeezed shut, and she held her side with both hands.

"Don't worry, I've got you." I hovered my hands over her.

She moaned and curled into the fetal position. "It burns!"

"Hold on, I can help." Breathing heavily, I reached toward her stomach, searching for any sign of blood. Nothing. "Can I touch you?"

She barely nodded, tears falling from her eyes, soaking her cheeks. "Please make it stop!"

I gasped when I rolled her shorts lower and scanned the site of her pain. "*That's* not what I expected to see."

3

KYRA

"Please. Please make the pain stop!"

I squeezed my eyes shut as pain pierced my abdomen. It felt like a thousand needles stabbed me from the inside again and again. A surge of energy scorched under my belly button. Light filled my head, blinding me, drowning me. Another fresh wave of pain shot through my body.

"It's okay, Kyra…you weren't shot," a male's voice said.

"Ahhh!"

Someone was screaming. Who? My breath turned ragged.

"*Ahhh*!"

It was me. I was the one screaming.

"It'll be over soon…breathe through it. Breathe, Kyra. Listen to my voice. In and out."

Then the world stilled, and the pain finally ceased. A sea of oblivion. Then snippets of sound. The room held its breath. No, I was holding my breath. I gasped, sucking in air, and sat up straight. Frantically, I clutched my side and groped my stomach and hip. No blood. No gunshot.

"He shot me." I wasn't even sure if I spoke the words aloud.

"No, you're okay. You're safe, and that asshole chasing us is dead."

My fingertips grazed over the sore spot where a bright gold circle glowed on my skin. The symbol looked alive, like a trickle with lights.

"What is this?" I locked eyes with Jadox, who had summoned fuckin' trees with the flick of his wrist.

"Take a deep breath."

I rubbed at the golden circle. "Get this thing off of me!"

"I can't; it's a tattoo." His tone was laced with fact and certainty. "It's what I asked about earlier."

"What? Why is it on me? Where did it come from?" The high-pitched sound of my voice sounded foreign. "I don't want this! Take it back."

I rubbed my pale skin over the area that would be half covered by a bikini. A monsoon of strange energy catapulted into my chest and swam through my veins. Power spoke to me with uncontrolled energy. Fire. Heat. Steam. Smoke. Blaze. Strength. They all lived inside my fingertips. Inside my soul.

I eyed the door. If Quamir was dead, this was my chance to run to Hallie. But how could I explain to her what just happened to me?

"You did this to me." I shoved Jadox. "Get this tattoo off of me. I don't feel right."

"Kyra, I can explain." Suddenly, his voice contained a dozen layers I hadn't heard before and felt like a drug, resonating deep within me.

"I can feel the...the energy. It's everywhere. What happened to me?"

"I'll tell you after you calm down." He lifted me like I was lighter than air and carried me outside through a side door.

"Put me down!" I yelled, thrashing in his arms.

Rain pelted my face, smothering my vision. Every single raindrop, thousands and thousands, plunked a chaotic beat. My ears lasered in, and I could hear every single one like a thousand different pitches. My heart slammed in my chest. No, *his* heartbeat. How could I hear Jadox's heartbeat? How? With every shift of his feet, I could hear the faintest scuffle of his boots on the pebbles. Chocolate was exactly ninety degrees to my right, obvious from her soft inhale.

Jadox set me down by the alley dumpsters, where boxes and debris were stacked in piles. "It'll all make more sense if—" he started.

"Get away from me."

"Fine, if you don't want to listen…." He raised both hands in the air calmly. "Then, at least, please go to Draven. Gemm can help you understand."

"Who? What? Where?" I pulled my drumsticks from my hair and brandished them like daggers. "I said stay back."

"Draven is a secret city, shielded by a protective bubble of sorts."

"You're crazy. You killed someone, and you're a murderer, and you're insane, and…maybe I'm dreaming." My chest tightened to the point of terror. "This isn't real. I'm having a nightmare."

"This is real." Jadox lowered both hands slowly. "You have Magik, Kyra. Your great-grandma was a Mystier."

"Very funny." Laughter made no sense at the moment, but it bubbled out of me anyway.

"You're a direct descendant of hers. The man you thought was your father, the man who raised you, did not share any blood relation with you."

I clamped both hands over my ears, trying to block out Jadox's words. What he just said was a wish I had made every day since the first time Dad hit me. But, Jadox had no right to steal my rage associated with that man. If he wasn't my father, then…then what? Where would my anger go? To him—yes, to Jadox— he had started all this insanity.

"Stop it! You're a lunatic, and none of this makes any…." A creaking sound from far off, followed by the skitter scatter of tiny animals cracking open an acorn, jolted my ears as if they were directly next to us. "What was that noise?"

"I didn't hear anything." Lines of worry painted deeper shadows on his expression. "Kyra, you're…different than the rest of us."

Confusion turned my bones to water. "Different? What do you mean?"

"You're the only one I've ever heard of to have a *gold* tattoo. All Elidians have red ones. My Circle is the color of pines in the woods like all other Dravians, see? He lifted his shirt, showing impeccable abs and a mesmerizing V shape down to his...

"Kyra, are you listening?"

"Uh yeah," I had no choice, because somehow my damn hearing had gone on overdrive like a superhero, and every sound was magnified, a cacophony of melodies combined with rambunctious noise, all mixed in a pile of notes and beats.

"Are you joking? I can hear *everything*. I just heard that leaf detach from that branch." I covered my ears which didn't help. "Everything is *so* loud."

"Hmm, interesting," he whispered and stepped closer. "It means you have an enhancement. You'll eventually be stronger than most Mystiers."

"What is a Mystier?" I paced in chaotic lines, splashing through puddles. "I'm still hallucinating; someone drugged me. My sister is a nurse. She'll know how to get the drugs out of my system."

"Kyra." His voice turned stern. "I'm taking you somewhere safe."

I froze and stared at him. If this asshole thought he'd control me, he had another thing coming. I let a wicked smile bleed onto my lips. Jadox would pay for all this—for branding me and lying to me. I'd do to Jadox what he did to Quamir.

I widened my stance and held both arms out. "So, if I have power in me, how do I use it?" I screamed at him. Clenching my muscles, I tried to summon magic. Nothing.

He crossed his arms. "You don't understand your Magik yet. Let me take you somewhere, then I can help teach you."

"Help? You just turned me into a witch!"

"You're not a witch, and we need to leave."

I grabbed a rusty barstool from the stack of trash by the dumpster and threw it at him. Hard. The metal rocketed toward his face, but he blocked it easily.

"Stop it. You're gonna attract attention." He frowned. "We need to leave."

A storm of rage whirled in my chest. If I could learn to summon magic, I'd shatter him to pieces. He was to blame. Everything had worsened when he stepped into my life tonight.

I picked up a wet pipe from the trash and slammed it against the metal dumpster to try and intimidate him. "I'll destroy you if you don't get out of my way!"

His eyes flickered to Chocolate, then a dark cloud passed over his striking features. Those brown eyes turned hard as stone and his fists balled up tight. Under the downpour, Jadox's whole body flexed, then he held both palms out. A smatter of insults stung the tip of my tongue, but before I could toss one at him, mud rose from the ground and splattered my face.

"You think I care about getting dirty?" I yelled. "I love mud. Bring it on, soldier."

I spoke too soon.

Jadox thrust more mud toward me. It crawled up from the puddles under my boots and glued my shins to the brick wall in the alley. Trying to kick myself free was useless. I bent, tearing at it with my hands, caking my skin in filth. It rose. Higher. Higher. My waist. My chest. Like it was alive, a wall of mud stuck me solidly to the building.

"Let me out!" The scream that pulsed inside my throat poured out of me hard and fast as the sky opened wide and fierce rain slammed down. Writhing against the thick, heavy mud restraint, I could hear my heartbeat slowing from the lethal pressure on my lungs.

"Let…me…out!"

"Take a deep breath, Kyra. If you won't leave with me, then at least listen. You need to know the basics if you won't let me help you. There are four types of Magik. Those of us from Draven control rocks, dirt, and trees," he spoke quickly. "That's where I'm from."

"I don't give a damn about you. I just want to go back to normal!"

Now, he stood an inch from my face, covered in the scent of rain. "Don't lie to me. You hated your normal life."

"You don't know me," I whispered.

Without a blink, he glanced over his shoulder, then continued, "Mystiers with Elidi powers, like you, manipulate fire, steam, and heat. You're strong, and you'll learn how strong over time, just like your relatives did."

"Stop talking!" I said, but when he was this close to me, I had a hard time focusing on anything other than his eyes, speckled with stars.

A haunting thought consumed me that Hallie or Mom had been through this and kept it a secret from me. Images of Hallie, my sister, my best friend flashed through my mind. Did she have these powers too? Had she hidden them from me? I recalled her terrified expression when we were both young, hiding in a closet from Dad when he arrived home from work. My whole life had been about survival, making it through to the next day, protecting her, and suffering the consequences.

Fear clotted my heart. "Does Hallie have this too?"

He sighed, and his expression finally softened. "No, Kyra. Hallie isn't related to you, either. The man you thought was your father was actually *her* father. You share no genes with Hallie."

It felt like bowling balls crashed into my skull. "You're lying."

He stepped closer.

"Don't touch me!"

"I'm never going to hurt you."

Except he already had. In one night, this stranger managed to turn my world into chaos, curse me with magic, stain my skin with a ridiculous tattoo, and shatter every precious memory I held with my sister, who apparently wasn't even my sister, after all.

Tears threatened to spill, and I stopped struggling. "Too late, soldier, you've already destroyed me."

Jadox stepped back, mouth agape, and let the mud slide down my front. I was finally free. But not really.

Raindrops showered my temples, sliding down my cheek. Tears would blend right in if I let them fall. But I couldn't even recall the last time I cried. I didn't cry at my father's—or fake father's—funeral last year or when Quamir smacked me around day after day.

Patterns from the past emerged and flooded my vision: male professors speaking down to me, boyfriends treating me like trash, managers paying the male musicians more than me, then, of course, Quamir. I never played the victim card; I fought back with claws out, but it didn't do any good. I always lost, but at least I kept Hallie safe.

As a child, I had distracted Dad away from her. When a male teacher tried to manipulate me, I reported him, then convinced Mom to move Hallie to a different school. As an adult, whenever I made more than minimum wage, the extra money was sent to Hallie to help raise her son, Landon. Not once did I play the damn damsel in distress. I was a warrior–for my flesh and blood–my sister. Except, she wasn't my flesh and blood.

The person to disrupt my entire identity, the root of all this pain, stood directly before me—Jadox. No, I wouldn't let this stranger have so much power over me. I wouldn't cry from the pain he created. This man didn't deserve my tears.

I glared at my enemy—Jadox Griffin.

"Fuck you!" I yelled. "Leave me alone."

Pure hatred for him tornadoed inside me. I never wanted to see Jadox again, or any other man for that matter. I never wanted to be abused, talked down to, pushed aside, or belittled again.

Energy rushed through my body, vibrating with years of built-up resentment. Into the night air, I screamed. Rain poured into my mouth as I craned my neck to the sky. Then I screamed and screamed again, fury bursting from my fingertips.

A man bolted through the club's door and glanced between us both. "Hey! What's going on out here?"

Jadox ignored him and stared me down with something like pity claiming his face.

"I wish…"

"What do you wish, Kyra? I can help you," Jadox said softly.

"I wish…"

Pause.

"I wish for every fuckin' male to DISAPPEAR!"

A sudden buzz singed my insides below my new tattoo and swirled through my core.

The man hovering in the doorway erupted into a ball of fire. He disappeared in an instant, embers floating down to the ground right where he had stood. Shock racked my body. Was I still hallucinating?

"What the?" I gasped.

A loud screech assaulted my ears, then metal on metal crunched as a car crashed into something on the other side of the alleyway.

Through the club's walls, a shriek pierced from the dance floor. Then another. High-pitched, blood-curdling scream after scream.

Jadox's eyes turned wild, and his head whipped in each direction.

He ran toward the club. I chased after his long footsteps, Chocolate by my side. Jadox pulled at the back door to the club, but it was jammed. I followed his scrutinizing eyes to a side window. He grabbed the stool I had previously chucked at him and slammed it through the window. Glass shattered. Rain splattered against the sharp pieces underfoot. More frantic cries burst from inside the dance floor.

He climbed through the window. I followed. The music and fog machine had stopped, but the strobe lights still flashed, sending beams of confusing lights in all directions.

Women were spread around the dance floor, either hugging each other or dropping to their knees. Another single scream assaulted my eardrum, and a young woman rushed out of the bathroom.

"Someone, help! He disappeared!" Tears streamed down her face. "My boyfriend, there were flames, and then he vanished!" Her voice shook as severely as her hands, and she collapsed to the floor in a heap.

Another woman stepped forward, panicking. "My fiancé is…gone. What happened?"

I looked around. Some women were tapping their solar watches, probably to call for the Andersonville Police.

Sobs and whimpering sounds surrounded me, and I was sure I could hear a dozen distinct conversations throughout the bar. I turned, and Jadox stood hidden, his ghost-like face ashen as he backed into the shadows.

"Kyra. What. Did. You. Do?" His whispered accusation cracked like a whip.

"I didn't *do* anything." I stepped back and joined him in the darkness.

I gaped at the mess of women standing in terrified huddles. In response, my tattoo flared, confirming what I already knew. The power had felt *so* strong. It was me. I made the men disappear. How? They were just *gone*. I finally had real freedom. But all the women's distraught faces tugged at my heart.

Shit, what have I done?

One woman ran in from down the hall and pointed to where Quamir's body lay. "There's one man here still, in the hallway, but he's…he's dead."

"Is it Carlos?" One woman sounded manic.

"Is it Hunter?"

The mass of women rushed to see Quamir, and more screams filled the club when they spotted his bloody body impaled by a branch.

"How is *Quamir* still there?" I spun on my heels and squinted at Jadox, still hovering in the shadows. "Wait, how are *you* still here?"

He opened his mouth, then closed it again, shaking his head in clear confusion.

Sirens wailed in the distance like a call from the wild: menacing, real, and closing in.

Jadox rubbed the back of his neck. "We need to go. I'm not taking no for an answer this time." He wrapped a large hand around my waist.

"Wait." I pushed him back.

As someone turned off the strobe lights, a woman pointed a remote at a TV hanging from the wall and turned it on. She flashed through channels, most of them full of fuzzy static, then one finally came in crystal-clear. Two women news anchors sat behind a desk, dread oozing from their expressions.

"We have received numerous reports that multiple men have… disappeared. A doctor vanished during surgery at Lodesa's hospital at Wake Memorial. A policeman making an arrest evaporated into thin air. Our network here in the studio just confirmed that all male employees in our office have disappeared without a trace—" The woman on the screen stopped reporting as her watch rang. She glanced at her female co-anchor, who nodded, then projected the image of a young girl on the wall.

"Mommy...come home...Daddy's gone. I woke up from thunder and went to get him, and I couldn't find him anywhere."

The reporter's jaw dropped, and she stared at her daughter on the video call. "I...I...I'll be right there." The chair scraped against the floor when she stood, and she walked off camera.

I glanced around the silent club. Almost every woman had covered their mouth with one hand. Whimpering sounds crept into my ears like a ghost. I could hear my own blood rushing with dread. My gut twisted into a tight knot, and I feared what came next.

On TV, the remaining anchor shook her head, then spoke like a robot. "We have just received dozens of videos of numerous plane crashes, electrical blackouts, and...."

She stared at something off-screen. "I can't do this." The screen began flashing the videos she had mentioned, and I had to look away. Maybe my wish only spread locally, in Andersonville. "Everyone, pray that this is a nightmare."

A quick tug on my wrist snapped me back to my surroundings. Emergency sirens grew closer to the club. Jadox pulled me into the hollow midnight air. Too stunned to fight back, I let him. A flickering light flashed high in the alleyway. A camera. Crap. My sights darted from the camera to Jadox, back and forth.

"They caught everything out here on tape," I said, my voice shaking.

"I'm sorry, Kyra, but we don't have time to argue." Jadox did some crazy magic thing, and twigs flew toward us. They wrapped around my wrists like cuffs. Then mud packed over my mouth, silencing me.

He flung me over his shoulder and ran through the puddles in the parking lot. I'd murder him for touching me again. I writhed and struggled but could barely breathe, with only my nose available to suck in oxygen. In the shadows, we passed a grocery store where a group of women had gathered and begun to throw carts through the windows. One woman ran straight to another, shouting about her missing son.

I hadn't meant for this to happen.

Jadox jogged by the art gallery I knew as "The Crooked Chateau," with climbing vines choking its exterior. Near the side of The Crooked Chateau, a hoverboard lay tucked behind a tree. While holding me tight, Jadox hopped on, straddled it, then placed me in front of him, his chest to my breasts. Naturally, I recoiled, hating when men initiated touching me, grabbing me, and owning my body. It wasn't something I'd ever get used to.

"Come on, girl." He tapped his thigh for Chocolate to jump behind him. Holding the collar with one hand, he leaned forward, zooming us up. Higher. Higher. To not fall off, I stilled so I didn't have to press my body against Jadox's firm chest. It wasn't like I could hold onto anything with my wrists bound.

We swiftly zig-zagged around the castle and other buildings. I could hear every doomsday sound of the city. Gunshots. High-pitched screams on the side of the road. Young girls cried. The crackle of fire billowed on burning buildings. Fire! My tattoo surged with wanting, a longing deeper than I could express, desperate for the nearby flames. My nerves flared to life as I reached forward. This time, a tingling sensation brushed over my skin like a microscopic spark of heat waves.

"Kyra, focus! Fight the urge." Despite the multiple alarms blaring below, Jadox's tone was calm and centered as he latched onto me tighter. "If I untie you, you need to calm down." The vines released my wrists.

We flew faster over the frightful scene on the streets. A buzzing zapped my ears, reminding me of the watch in my purse. Awkwardly, I unzipped it with trembling fingers and pushed a button. There was still one minute of power left. Hallie's blotchy face with puffy eyes stared back.

At that moment, all the thousands of sounds competing for my attention hushed into nothingness. My sister's voice was the only thing I registered.

"He's gone. Landon isn't in his bed." Hallie's porcelain face looked broken beyond repair. Stones were stacked against my chest, weighing me down. Burying me.

The thought of my nephew gone stripped me raw.

"Kyra, what should I do? I can't breathe. I can't...Landon...he's gone." Anguish layered her every syllable.

"I'll be there soon. Just hold on. We'll fix this."

The call dropped, and I let the tears flow, imagining little Landon's mop of sandy curls. Gone. Agony and remorse rushed at me in a whirlwind.

"What have I done?"

4

JADOX

Cloaked by night, I landed our hoverboard in the shadows behind Kyra's apartment complex. I'd been tracking her for months, waiting for an opportunity to approach her, so I knew exactly where she lived. I was a certified asshole for restraining her.

Her apartment building was eerily quiet compared to downtown, but somehow, it smelled worse. Rotten meat wafted through the darkness. A few faded emergency sirens still rang in the distance. But the citizens slept here, unaware of the horrors they'd find in the morning. Half of their families were gone. Empty beds. I felt in my gut that this phenomenon was global, spreading further than the borders of Lodesa—not that I cared since Kyra's death wish hadn't affected anyone I cared about.

My grandmother, Gemm, and my sister, Alaska, were the only people who mattered. I'd have to call them soon to see how the Draven women were holding up. Gemm's husband died years ago, and Alaska was queer, so thankfully, neither had lost a partner from Kyra's Magik. Did that mean I was the only man left?

"I can't believe this is happening to us," I whispered to Chocolate.

My pup stayed at my heels; her heavy steps showed obvious fatigue.

Kyra shot me a threatening glare that I only caught thanks to the streetlamp flickering above. Her eyes held curled tendrils of secrets with an energy I had never felt in all my twenty-eight years. The feeling gave me a sense of belonging that I needed to ignore and bury.

She had clearly been through her share of trauma, and here I was, barking orders and manhandling her. Of course, she wouldn't trust me. If the roles were reversed, I wouldn't either. In fact, I wouldn't blame her if she attempted to murder me. Fuck, I was an idiot. I needed to untie her quickly and explain myself.

When I glanced at her eyes again, the magnetic draw to her convinced me to stay as long as humanly possible. Even though I wasn't a hundred percent human.

I ignored her confused look when I punched in the password to grant us entrance to her apartment. The door scraped against the hardwood, adding more scratches to the dingy floor.

Once inside, I braced for the worst, expecting a full explosion of curse words from her witty lips. But Kyra marched off into a room and slammed the door shut. Shit. I was an awful, despicable person. I need to apologize. Except Kyra might not want one. She wasn't like any other woman I'd ever met. She was full of such...something. Spunk? Life? Determination? Passion?

Flicking on a light switch, I scanned her apartment. Her creativity and unconventional lifestyle were evident in every corner, suffocated by the obvious signs of a man. A three-piece suit was draped over mismatched furniture, assembled by a rookie. Four pairs of men's dress shoes lined the wall, next to her heeled boots.

My heartbeat accelerated—betraying me with a need to learn more about this intriguing woman— who did she live with? Why would she wish all males away if she had a boyfriend? Why wasn't she calling out his name? And lastly, since I've been tracking her for months, how had he slipped under my radar?

I turned and spotted a dozen dead plants framing the side wall. No amount of her delicious spunk could make up for the irresponsibility displayed in front of me. Fiddleleaf figs, rubber plants, and calathea plants drooped in crusty browns. Sudden rage fumed in me at the disrespect toward Mother Nature Draven. Any hope of ever understanding this woman immediately faded. She was raised by wretched Ordulls and lived a life just like them. I shouldn't have expected her to have any empathy toward life or what mattered.

I held back the growl climbing up my throat. All I needed was to convince Kyra to go to Draven, then my debt to Gemm would be repaid, and all would be forgiven. I'd finally be allowed to return to my tribe. No one was meant to live in solitude for as long as I had. During my childhood, every villager's fingers turned raw with blisters on weaving days. Yet, at the ritual feast, not one Dravian had ever asked me to use my enhancement to heal their bleeding wounds—a symbol of their work. We had suffered together, worked in unison, relied on each other, and lived as one. Until I made a pivotal mistake and was no longer welcome.

I crouched in front of the plants, laying my palm flat on the dried-up soil. Closing my eyes and lifting my head to Divinity above, I invited my healing gift. Nothing happened to the plants. I couldn't save a life that was already gone. With fatigue raining down from the night's events, I tried the next plant. A quiver shifted inside my pulse like a single breath stolen from my lifespan. Before my eyes, a thin twig sprouted out of the soil and grew a few inches tall.

Tears pricked the back of my eyelids. Or maybe that was my body demanding rest at this hour. Only creatures of the night should be awake this late. Just like that, the joy from growing life from my very hands was clouded over by memories of my time in the army.

I hated patrolling in the middle of the night. Nothing good happened after midnight, hence the stranger lurking in the shadows. Gunshots followed. Blood. Broken bodies. Flesh carved to pieces. Bones snapped. Friends fell. Death everywhere. So much death.

. . .

In war, it didn't matter if I was a healer. My Ordull comrades could never learn about my Magik. It was an all-time low when I was forced to watch my friends die in front of me. My healing gift could've saved some of them, but the inability to act was torture I'd never recover from. It served me right for ever making friends at all. A loner life was best.

The room spun with ghosts from my past until Chocolate licked my fingers and centered me. Only my pup understood the memories that haunted me.

"Thanks, Chocolate."

After patting her head, I brushed my fingertips over a drum set by Kyra's window, which was smudged with stains. To my right, hundreds of pages of sheet music were plastered like wallpaper from floor to ceiling, all hung artistically at various angles and overlapping. This was Kyra's obvious sanctuary. Wait, no, hold that thought: red ink in different handwriting scratched over her lyrics and crossed out lines in fury. Who wrote over her words—a harsh music teacher or the guy she lived with?

I heard frustrating grunts and stomping from the other side of the bedroom door. Maybe she was already attempting Magik. Never in my wildest dreams would I have expected that Kyra held no knowledge of her powers or Mystiers. Why didn't she get her tattoo as a teenager like the rest of us?

In three easy steps, I made my way to the kitchen and found a bowl to give Chocolate water. She lapped it up, then comfortably claimed her spot on a couch in the center of the room.

I searched for a TV—nothing. Usually, I'd be grateful for the lack of electrical current that weakened my powers. Resorting to my solar watch, I displayed projections of the local news on Kyra's wall. I flipped through solely static channels, which sent unease through my veins. I stopped on the only channel still broadcasting.

On the screen, Vice President Syvonne Stirk sat in her hoverchair at a microphone. Her silky dyed-white hair fell over the presidential robes that hid her amputation sites, just above the knee. She sat tall and proud, no doubt wearing a bulletproof vest underneath. Her lavender eyeshadow made her look even younger than her age of thirty-eight. She'd be my new Commander-in-Chief if I were still in the army. How were my past comrades dealing with the shift in leadership? Wait, most of them were males. They'd be gone. Where did they go? A sinking feeling gripped my heart. Lodesa would never be the same.

I shook my head and focused on President Stirk's face again. Her confident posture disguised the fact that her hoverchair was necessary since she could no longer walk. An explosion in the capital years ago had resulted in her losing both legs. Her tenacity through that crisis only made the people of Lodesa adore her more.

Stirk was only ten years older than me and probably not ready for the task at hand. A banner showed captions along the bottom of the projection. Stealing a breath of confidence, I turned up the volume.

"And Crimble's factories have crashed, the southern cities of Lodesa have no electricity, and Minister Rustal of Topell is threatening to launch a bomb within the hour. I don't bring you this news to frighten our country but rather to prepare my beloved citizens for the truth. Prepare yourselves. The next couple of weeks will be a massacre unless we women work together. I understand your pain, confusion, and shock. We have lost 60% of the planet's population in less than an hour. Not only did we lose our men, but women patients on the operating table died during surgery when their doctors vanished. Male drivers smashed their hovercars into women, killing them on sight. The list is extensive, the loss is…." Vice President Syvonne Stirk looked up at the ceiling of wherever her guards had hidden her.

"This speech hasn't been planned beforehand; I apologize. So many citizens are gone. Our late Commander-in-Chief is gone, as are so many of our front-line emergency workers, including my brother and fiancé–all gone in a snap. There have been zero reports of any surviving males. Our loss is substantial." She paused and rolled her lips.

I didn't even want to listen to the rest. Every one of my muscles clenched tight when I whispered to Chocolate, "She said, 'Zero reports of any surviving males.' Am I seriously the only one left?"

Syvonne Stirk's hoverchair shifted as she continued, "But, I'm begging you to work together. United, we will survive this. As your new leader and president, I promise to figure out why this happened and find a way for the rest of us to prosper. This is not the end if we women come together as a team."

I tuned out her speech, turned off the feed, and sunk into an old flat armchair.

"Why am I still here?" I asked Chocolate. "Why?"

It didn't make sense. After all the mistakes I had made and the people I had pushed away, it was completely ironic that a lone wolf like me would be spared. Of all the men, Ordull or Mystier, I was the least deserving to live. There had to be a reason.

Swallowing the lump stuck in my throat, I made a gut-wrenching call on my watch to Grandma Gemm. I had never needed her more than now and had to trust that someone from Draven would finally be there for me.

"Pick up, come on, pick up."

No answer. On my next exhale, regret thrust itself out of my lungs. My finger hovered over Alaska's name in my contacts.

"What do you think, Chocolate? Has she forgiven me yet?"

Before I had the chance to find out, Kyra burst through her bedroom door like a crazed buffalo, freshly showered and wearing long black yoga pants and an extra-long tee that fell off one shoulder, exposing her freckles. I averted my gaze and cleared my throat.

"I tried to call Hallie from the home system, but all the watch lines are down." Her voice softened.

She bustled around from drawer to cabinet to storage trunk, grabbing items and shoving them into a big backpack. "I'm going to Hallie's. I can't leave her alone after my nephew—"

"What about me?" I wasn't sure if the words left my lips.

"You?" Kyra didn't even look up. "What about you? You can take care of yourself with all that...." Her hand waved over my physique.

Heat rushed to my cheeks. I had been taking care of myself for years, ever since I was separated from the army. The Code of Military Justice didn't believe my side of the story, so my punishment split me from every friend and teammate I had ever made. Like I said, only rely on dogs.

"I might be the last man alive," I whispered, "that's a big deal, Kyra."

A tightness formed inside my chest, considering what that could mean for my future. I wasn't even sure why I was reaching out to Kyra as a lifeline. But I had sworn to Gemm that I'd bring her to Draven, and I wouldn't break promises just because Armageddon knocked on our door.

Kyra halted her packing and glanced up. "Actually, you're right. I should turn you into the cops."

She had a valid point. I *had* just abducted the poor girl.

"They'd probably give me some huge reward since they'll need to know why every man disappeared except for you. Unless..." Kyra's gaze dropped to my crotch. "I might need proof."

There was no way I'd grant that request. She could stare all day. Or maybe I'd take a shower, then walk around naked just to piss her off. I folded my arms and waited patiently for her eye contact once more.

Her cheeks flushed salmon-pink, something I wouldn't believe possible from this fierce spitball of a bull. "Never mind, you... um...pass."

I tracked her sudden movements from one side of her apartment to the next, wearing lines into the carpet. She shoved snacks from her pantry into the pack, but I noticed her hands shaking.

"What did you feel when you made everyone disappear?" I asked.

"Almighty Abyss, I didn't do it. Not my fault. Case closed."

How much of herself was she hiding behind an armor of steel? It didn't seem like Kyra lacked the inability to see her own faults, so what was the thing she was truly afraid of?

She showed a flicker of uncertainty, and her voice tremored for just a moment when she said, "Don't you dare put the blame on me. *You* did all of this. When you showed up, the world imploded, so it's my turn to ask questions. Why did you come searching for me on the roof in the first place?"

I shook my head, reached into her backpack, plucked out a water bottle, and guzzled it. The frigid liquid glided down my throat inch by inch. After I finished the whole thing, I crunched the plastic between my hands and tossed it into the recycling. Saving the environment one day at a time.

"I was looking for you because I need your necklace," I said.

Like a dragon, she could've breathed fire from her nostrils. She pressed on, demanding, "Tell me why you want it."

The less I told her, the better. Maybe the librarian from Vayu would have information about harnessing the necklace's power without burning my skin again. Other than Gemm, he knew more about Mystier history than anyone. Wait, he would have disappeared too. Maybe his disappearance was for the best. I hated Isaac Nilson. He contained more arrogance in one fingertip than all the ancient Mystiers who created the spell book in his vault combined.

"Well, it's obvious you don't want to work together, but before things get too dangerous on the streets, you need to head straight for Draven. I'll draw you a map. When you arrive, ask for Gemm."

She laughed an entranced, Luna-Festival laugh. For a second, I paused and absorbed the youthfulness on her face.

"You think you can order me around or tell me where to go?" Her taunting smile disappeared in the blink of an eye as she stepped forward, conquering the space between us. "Get out of my way, soldier."

"How do you even know I was a soldier?"

Kyra rolled her eyes as her hand waved at my body again. "Am I wrong?"

I crossed my arms. "You're seriously gonna make me drag you to Draven?"

She immediately straightened, and her height increased an inch or two, not that it made much difference as she was a foot shorter than me.

"I need you to cooperate with this plan," I begged. "It's the only way, please. It's not like your boyfriend is coming back here since you wished away all men."

The moment I released the words, regret piled over me. Her face turned to ash, and her gaze darted to the door as she said, "You said Quamir was dead."

My breath hitched. "Wait, the guy you were running from was your boyfriend?" Suddenly, all the pieces clicked into place. "I'll never hurt you, Kyra. I'm not like him."

A hundred thoughts were written across her face. She snorted genuinely, then crossed her arms tightly, mirroring my stance. I could see those wheels spinning.

In a staring contest, I'd put every penny on her winning, but that didn't mean I'd go down without a fight. "I'll guide you to the Draven wall, drop you off, and leave. You'll be safe there."

"I've had enough of this." Kyra grabbed a knife from the kitchen counter and pounced toward me, pointing it straight. "You *cursed* me with a tattoo, manipulated, stalked, restrained, and abducted me. Give me one reason not to kill you."

I sighed, unsure of what exactly to say, but my words slipped out anyway, "You couldn't if you tried."

She lunged, the gleam of the kitchen light reflecting off the shiny metal blade. Chocolate jumped up from the couch.

"No, girl!" I gestured behind me. "Go lay down."

She barked.

"I guess dogs don't like being bossed around either. You should listen to her," Kyra spat out, but her voice trembled.

How much has she had to fight in her past? Was it only Quamir who had traumatized her?

Sidestepping her, I raised both hands in surrender. "Can you put the knife down, please?"

"Even if you're the *last* chance of human survival, I don't care if humans can't repopulate. I'm killing you here and now."

That unexpected revelation struck me hard. *The last surviving man. Repopulation.* But I wouldn't let her see the concern crippling me from the inside. Slashing the knife in the air with every step forward, she chucked curse words my way. The sight of her knightly attempts to murder me in cold blood nudged my powers awake again.

Swiftly, I stopped her wrist high above her head. Kyra continued to push forward, but I twisted the knife from her grip and let it clatter to the floor. The scent of her passion only excited me, which made no sense. This girl would be my ruin.

I wrapped her close, holding her tight. For once, she stopped struggling, and our chests fell and rose fast against each other.

She looked genuinely confused, baffled. "You're…different. When I touch you, I…." Her voice became barely a whisper but didn't compare in sweetness to her silky, golden eyes looking up at me through thick eyelashes. My tattoo singed with longing for this devil before me. She bit her lip. All I wanted was to lock our mouths in a feverish battle. Why?

I whispered to her, "I can handle your pain," matching her intensity, making sure she understood loud and clear, "I can take it. Keep spitting it out. Eventually, you'll realize you don't hate me and that I'm on your side."

She raised up on her tiptoes, moving those plump lips closer. Now it was my turn to feel baffled. Kyra leaned into my ear. "I dare you to show me exactly what you mean."

My grip around her tiny waist tightened, but when I heard a truly terrifying squeal from her small frame, I loosened instantly. I had two choices: empower her or deal with the outrageously frustrating sass that belonged to Kyra Kozelski, Queen of Fire and Flames.

She spun free, the knife laying directly between us. We both glanced at it, but I summoned a bowl of acorns decorating her counter. They flew and covered the top of the blade in a messy pile.

"Fine!" I yelled. "I'll help you travel safely to Hallie's under two conditions."

"Oh, your highness, please tell me *all* the ways I can please you." She rolled her eyes.

"First of all, you'll give me that necklace once you arrive safely at Hallie's."

"Nope. This is my special, one-of-a-kind, awesome-sauce necklace. My heavenly treasure, especially because of how much you want it."

"And the second condition—I need to teach you how to control your Magik."

Her eyes widened with interest at my proposal for only a beat. "Nice try, but I get to set the terms."

The spark in her eyes told me I was in for an adventure if I stayed by her side. I still had the option to walk away and bunker in the deep woods where no person—woman—would ever find me again. Chocolate and I would happily live off the land in solitude. No repopulation responsibilities would be on my shoulders. No need to heal the relationships with my Draven tribe and family. No friendships. No army. No Kyra. For. The. Rest. Of. My. Life.

Kyra paused. "Could your infamous Gemm get rid of my tattoo?"

"We could ask. Anything's possible."

She turned and grabbed more food from the cupboard. "How far away is your Dravie town?"

Her lips curved at the edge, showing me how purposeful she was in botching the name of my cherished village. Someone like her would never understand what it meant to have the connection of a close-knit tribe—the love that flourished inside the protective walls of Draven, the pain to be cast out and forgotten.

When I leaned forward with both arms out wide, grasping the cold granite counter, it paralleled the message deep within, reminding me of my reasons to stay cold and stone-like to everyone around me. Self-preservation. Protect my heart. Put up the walls. Never form bonds with an Ordull, never befriend another Mystier, and never show anyone who or what matters to me. This woman had the potential to shatter all three before the sun rose.

"Well, if we have a trip ahead of us, let's fuel up." She looked around the kitchen.

What had made her change her mind? My little white fib? There was no way to erase a formed tattoo. She was a Mystier now, whether she liked it or not.

"I'm guessing you like protein, so do you prefer chicken or peanut butter sandwiches?" She held me by a wicked spell as if leading me to an early grave.

"If you're offering...then chicken. Thank you." I sniffed the pleasant aromas from the leftover food heating in her solar oven.

"Is that one plugged into anything?" I pointed.

"No, why?"

"Electricity will weaken your Magik."

"Hmm, you should probably elaborate on that just a bit."

"Well, as you know, most of what Ordulls use is solar-powered, so it won't often be an issue unless we're in a highly populated city since more of the old electricity is used downtown. This is one reason why many of our villages are in remote areas." He paused and scanned the appliances in the apartment again. "Depending on the voltage level in the surroundings, my Magik will weaken, but sometimes my enhancement still works. Since you're different than the rest of Mystiers, I'm not sure if you'll react the same."

While she chopped chicken, I slid toward the bay window. Light from the red moon shone through, bouncing off the metal rim of her largest drum. Below, the streets slept, and my heart plummeted at the knowledge of the grief the rest of the city would awake to in the morning.

My watch pinged, snapping me back to attention. Expecting the message on my phone to be from Gemm, I sucked in a hasty breath in surprise when I read the sender's name. I checked over my shoulder to confirm that Kyra's back was turned, then muted the sound. The text showed at the bottom of the screen. After reading the jarring message, I let out a long breath.

Well, plans have changed.

5

KYRA

I'd marry my bed and sing vows to its blissful comfiness. I arched my back and stretched my legs under the soft sheets, then rolled over and hugged a pillow tighter. I thought of the other things in this world I adored: dessert, drums, or any music for that matter, animals, adventure, and, did I say, music?

A little melody tickled my ear in the key of G. A bird outside my window? The different hues of the sunrise sang a tune to me, mixing notes with the swirling ice cream shades of mangos and magentas. But other new colors also popped up that I had no words for—I'd label one "Fabre"; it sounded classy enough.

Morning sunlight streamed through my window. One of these days, I'd have to hang a sheet as makeshift curtains. Adulting sucked. Even though I'd lived away from Mom's for eight years now, my few things in this shabby apartment totaled three hundred bucks, except for my drum set. My nephew hated the single rule that he couldn't play my drums without me supervising. *Landon.* Wait.

Landon. Did I have a dream about my nephew?

A strange feeling swarmed me like I was stuck in a hazy nightmare. Suddenly, a wet nose nudged my palm. My eyes flew open to a pair of dopey dog eyes.

"Chocolate?" Sitting upright fast, I glanced around. "No, no, no. Last night was real?"

I clutched the necklace draped under my shirt, then glanced at my clock: seven am. When did I fall asleep? Last night's events crashed into my heart. Patting myself down, I realized all my cuts, scrapes, and bruises were healed. Memories of Jadox sent an undeniable tingling down my hip. After rolling down my shorts, I stared at the golden circle that radiated a faint light from my skin, humming with power. At least Quamir would never bother me again.

"What am I going to do, girl?" I patted her fur.

I should never have made that wish.

"Stupid!" I palmed my forehead and hissed, "Stupid, stupid!"

Outside my window, silence haunted the neighborhood. City buses didn't pull up for the morning commute to work. My neighbor wasn't unlocking his hoverboard from the rack at the corner street. Half the world had died. And it was all my fault. I would never have knowingly wished away all the males. How was I supposed to guess I had that kind of power? Because of my impulsivity, all of Lodesa could fall into chaos. I gripped a pillow, shoved it over my face, and screamed as loud as possible.

There were mothers, daughters, sisters, and wives out there who must have had a positive relationship with a male. Now, all those women would come after me if they found out I was at fault. A bigger person would turn themselves into the authorities. Maybe I deserved to rot in a cell for eternity.

Goddess, I needed Hallie. We had been each other's rock throughout our childhood, ensuring we had one another's backs in times of need. I remembered how she'd hide heavy or sharp objects when our father wasn't looking, then I'd convince Mom to drive us to the park so he'd be passed out by the time we returned. Not all memories were awful, though. Eventually, both parents started to avoid me, but Hallie's loyalty never faltered. She had taught me how to bake banana bread and bought my first pair of drumsticks.

Soft footsteps treading around the next room snapped me back to reality, and the sound of knuckles cracking crept up my spine. Jadox's movements formed a canvas of harmonies on the other side of my blanket fortress. His steady heartbeat created the base. The faint scratch of his shirt rustled against the doorframe. Maybe, deep, deep, deep, super deep down, he wasn't such a bad guy, but I had no proof of that so far.

"We need to leave," he said casually, like we had plans for Sunday brunch.

Moaning into the pillow, I shook off the thought of him carrying me into my bed last night because I surely didn't fall asleep here. I'd be perfectly content if that man never touched me again. Or I could use him as my personal bodyguard through whatever chaos awaited outside. That was food for thought.

"Go away." I threw the pillow across my bed.

Looking up, the sight of him shirtless caught me by surprise. His chest looked carved from stone, and his abs screamed the opposite of mushy Play-Doh. The man belonged on the front of a magazine or on top of me. No, definitely not the latter. If I let my guard down, it'd further prove my level of absolute stupidity. When he ran a hand through his thick, silky brown hair, it sent butterflies through my stomach. Or maybe I was nauseous.

Jadox smiled for the first time. Beautiful and hideous, breathtaking and cruel like how the knife's edge gleamed and reflected. I inhaled sharply at the curved arch of his corrupting lips. His insufferable face deserved a punch to the nose.

"Where is your shirt?" I asked.

"Good morning to you too."

Under the blankets, I patted my body down to ensure he hadn't removed any of my clothes last night.

"I get hot when I sleep." The mug he held was dwarfed in his large hands as he raised it to his thick lips and sipped.

As the steam rose from the rim, a spark ignited inside my Circle, begging and longing.

"Have you figured out a master plan yet?" He held back an obvious smirk.

Even though his words sounded like he whispered them an inch from my ear, I tuned him out, hypnotized by the steam rising. Amazing heat. Bolting out of bed, I rushed to his side and held out my hand.

"Give me that," I commanded.

One of his bushy eyebrows rose, but he did as I asked. When the scalding mug sat in my palm, my tattoo throbbed with such pressure that dizziness overtook all of my senses. Crazed energy started in my stomach and spread to the tips of my toes and fingertips. My dresser swayed, and the room zoomed in and out.

Heat.

Amazing pressure pushed me from all angles. If I contained it for one second, I'd faint. The mug shattered in my hand, and scorching tea ran down my wrists. Relief. I closed my eyes and relished in it, absorbing the heat and power.

"Uh, Kyra?"

I snapped open my eyes to the sight of Jadox hunched behind the doorframe, only his eyes and nose peeking out.

"What'd I do?" I checked around for Chocolate. "Did I…did I hurt her?"

Jadox sighed and came out from the world's most terrible hiding spot. "No, but we need to work on controlling your Magik."

"Why do you pronounce magic like that?"

"Because it's a different power that Ordulls don't know about. Whether you like it or not, you're one of us, so get used to it and show our kind some respect by calling it Magik."

"Sir, yes, sir." I saluted him sarcastically, making my shirt fall loose over my shoulder.

His eyes briefly landed on my bare skin, and he mumbled softly, "By the way, I'm sorry I've been a jerk."

"Say it again."

"You heard me." He reached his hand high on the wall, leaning his weight against it like a gorgeous model. The pose deserved the world's biggest eye roll.

So, I rolled my eyes and said, "I need to hear you grovel."

"Fine, I should be writing you poems of apologies at this point."

"Yes, I'll expect a *sonnet* on my desk in twenty-four hours."

His jaw tightened. "I'm gonna go take a shower."

"Excuse me, this is my house. You need to ask permission."

Jadox had the nerve to ignore me and slam the bathroom door in my face. The lock clicked with forcefulness on the other side. My entire body wanted to pound on that door, kick it down, slam it, and bring all sorts of fury, but Chocolate whined by the front door.

"He probably didn't even take you out, did he?" I grabbed a scarf from my coat rack, looped it around her collar to use as a leash, and walked her outside. "Or...wait...he couldn't because if any woman saw him, he'd probably be killed or taken."

Outside, the wispy cerulean sky contrasted with the autumn leaves as if today was the same mundane day as yesterday. On the ground level, sounds of nature exploded instantly, and frogs over a mile away chirped in melody with birds tweeting in the distance. Why did enhanced hearing come with this Magik power?

Muffled voices of neighbors speaking in low conversations vibrated through the walls of my building, with every sound magnified. I'd need to adjust to this new sensation or buy some damn earplugs. Although, after all the men had vanished, most of the factories had probably shut down. Inventory would have crashed last night. Many truck drivers who delivered packages were probably males, so all package deliveries would be delayed. What'd happen to Lodesa's food supply for grocery stores?

A heaviness weighed on my chest. "I'm sorry, Chocolate. I ruined our world. Nothing will ever be the same."

Regret tore through me, and I felt like someone was ripping me in half. Part of me wanted to celebrate that I'd accomplished the impossible—freed myself from Quamir—but what about all the others who had been in not-so-terrible relationships? What if there was a single sweet grandpa out there who I had just stolen away from a little girl? There was a small chance that one brother might've made his sister smile somewhere. And I ruined her life.

The power running through me wasn't natural. What if I accidentally did something like that again? The safest thing would be to turn myself into the authorities. Except, I wasn't that noble of a person since they'd probably use me for science experiments.

Chocolate looked up at me with no judgment in those adorable eyes. Her ears perked, and she shoved her nose between my knees, knocking me off balance. "I've got to get away from here if I have any chance of getting to Hallie's."

Above, flashing lights on a solar billboard stole my attention. Vice President Syvonne Stirk's face twisted into concerned knots. Her strength after a double amputation made her increasingly popular among Lodesa, but she always had a look in her eye that I didn't trust. At the bottom of the screen was a contact number for emergencies. Well, I had possession of the last-living male. That was definitely an emergency.

"Should I call the cops on your owner, girl?" I asked Chocolate.

The sun peeked out from behind a cotton-ball cloud and immediately slaughtered my skin with heat as if I were baking in the oven. New, fresh freckles sprinkled my forearms, and a sharpness erupted along my Circle.

I jumped into the layers of a shadow, tugging Chocolate alongside. "This is all too weird."

My heart beat wildly as I checked the old solar watch. Thirty seconds of call time still remained on my charge. Just as I was about to call the emergency number, a message came in from an unknown source.

> Recipient: Ms. K. Kozelski
>
> The representatives of Andersonville, Lodesa, regret to inform you that a biological relative,
>
> Maria Berlusconi Kozelski [mother]

> has been identified and labeled as deceased from vehicle collision #4796 in the aftermath of the international phenomenon on red moon, day 15 of year 82T. Remains and viewing open for 48 hours before cremation. Pick up deceased's personal items by that time or they will become property of President Syvonne Stirk.
>
> Condolences on your loss.

What? Mom was dead? No. Did I read it wrong? My ears were ringing, and a gaping hole opened inside my chest. I struggled to take a breath as it hit me. A violent shudder ripped through my body. We were never close, and I hadn't spoken to her in months, but the reality was hard to swallow. Did Hallie already know? At least Mom wouldn't have to suffer through the news that I singlehandedly destroyed our world. The mess was all my fault. All I ever did was create havoc for those I cared about. I had to fix one thing at a time.

I pushed other buttons on my watch in a daze as a thousand questions whirled in my mind.

"Wake County Authorities, what's your emergency?" a tired female voice rushed out her words on the other line.

I bit my lip and avoided looking at Chocolate. "Uh, there's been a break-in at my apartment."

"Given the international crisis, your dilemma is number forty-two priority on our current list, and you most likely will not receive any assistance. I advise you to find a neighbor to stay with— it's the safest location—lock the doors and keep all lights on."

The fact that Jadox would be stuck with me longer sent panic surging through my blood. Would I be able to hold my emotions together about Mom in front of him? Did I even have any grief? She might be blessed with an early exit from this disastrous world I created.

Desperation hit me like a grenade, and I rushed out an explanation to the emergency responder. "But the burglar was a man. He's still alive, and I have him trapped."

"Miss, we don't have time for pranks. Please—"

"It's not a prank. My address is 222 Sycamore Street. Hurry, he might bust out of my closet soon."

If this was what it took to get rid of Jadox and get to Hallie faster, so be it.

She sighed, obviously not believing me. "I'll send a team your way. Keep *him* contained for eight more minutes."

My heart pounded fiercely, and I imagined holding my drumsticks, trying to slow down the beat. If the police showed up, I'd need to be prepared. Turning, I sprinted up the stairs, Chocolate racing ahead. By the time I reached my floor, my lungs burned, and my calves twitched. I punched in the door's code.

I lunged inside and headed straight for my backpack, grateful I had already packed Quamir's backup solar watch, food, and water last night. Slow drip drops of the shower plunked in a steady rhythm behind me.

"Thanks for taking Chocolate out," Jadox's voice thrummed through the bathroom door.

"Uh, no problem." I cringed, hoping he didn't have x-ray vision to see my lying face. "We have to work together now, ya know?"

Silence.

The door flung open, and Jadox stood gloriously nude right in front of me.

And...that's a penis.

As he braced each hand on the sides of the doorframe, tendons stretched in his arm. Well, that sight sure didn't help my heart rate. His deep brown, fudge-me bedroom gaze ran over me with a sour glance. An unspoken promise hovered in the air between us like a beautiful decay. I used every inch of willpower to not drop my eyes—but failed. I swallowed my thoughts. There was no time for this. The seconds were ticking down. And I hated men. *Hated them.*

He analyzed me, then asked, "You look guilty. What'd you do?"

"Nothing." I threw him an extra-large sweatshirt from Quamir's side of the closet. "Cover up your dick. No one wants to see that."

Chocolate barked and jumped by the windowsill, placing both paws to look outside. I glanced at the clock.

Jadox dropped the sweatshirt on the bathroom tile and walked past me to my dryer. Suckable droplets raced down his long arms. Damn it. And his back could've been sculpted by a professional artist. Not that I looked. Because I hated him. *Hated.*

I glimpsed at Chocolate for reassurance, but her head rested on both paws. I groaned as my eyes went back to his ass.

"So, I'm gonna…um…need to lock you in my bathroom." I cleared my throat.

He laughed. "I don't think so."

"I don't have curtains. If you're seen by anyone, half the women would want to capture you for boinking purposes."

"Did you just say '*boink*'?" He threaded his long legs into his freshly laundered briefs and cargo pants. I'm glad he wouldn't have to squeeze into Quamir's clothes. Built like an oak, Jadox was sturdy, wide, thick, tall, and…probably scratchy…obviously uncomfortable to the touch. A barren tree in winter with rough bark. The absolute worst.

He eased into the tee that hugged his despicable shoulders, then ran a hand through his putrid hair. I glanced at the clock. Three more minutes.

"Let's check the news footage."

Jadox flipped on a live feed on his watch and projected it on the wall. A video showed broken store windows, empty shelves, and women running around frantically. An interruption stopped the broadcast, and Syvonne Stirk addressed the nation.

"I speak to my fellow women, the survivors. We are strong together, and we will get through this devastation. But shocking evidence has now been found that we have an enemy hiding among us. My top advisors have led me to believe that witches exist and that those who live here in Lodesa are to blame for the horrific terrorism last night.

After the power outages, multiple small towns popped up on our radar that were previously never recorded in our data. What's left of our military has invaded one of them, a small witch village by the sea called Cydon."

Jadox sucked in a fearful breath. Nerves wrapped around me tightly like the vines he had tangled me up in last night. His drastic unease made me genuinely worried. And now it was only two more minutes until the cops came.

"...If anyone has information about *any* of these witches, contact the number on your screen with their exact location," Stirk continued, "all these witch creatures are considered highly dangerous criminals and are not to be trusted."

My jaw fell to the floor. I didn't know anything about these powers or how they worked. Now I needed to learn my Magik just to protect myself. My only chance at survival was Jadox.

"We need to leave. Now!" I yanked away and shoved him away from the front door, making the newsfeed fall out of focus and off the wall.

"That's what I've been saying all along."

A hard pounding slammed on my door. "Miss? It's Officer Wiley."

Jadox's glare could've frozen the sun when he hissed, "What. Did. You. Do?"

I threw my backpack on. Pulled his wrist toward my window. Tried to thrust it open. It was lodged. Adrenaline surged, and my heart raced.

"Try that one!" I pointed as I ran to a different window. The next was locked and jammed too.

Jadox grunted while prying a window open with such force the seam in his sleeve split. "I got it."

A fresh breeze flipped my hair all over my face. "Let's go!"

Jadox scooped Chocolate in his arms, and she flopped awkwardly against his chest. The pounding on the door felt like firecrackers in my head. *So loud*. I winced, ducking and covering my ears.

Jadox rushed by me and leaped out my window, landing on a thick branch outside.

"I can't make that jump!" I hollered after him.

A clinking sound rattled my locked door. There were mere seconds until the cops were inside. Calling them was stupid. If they found Jadox, they'd ask why he was with me and how.

Ten.

Nine.

Eight.

I climbed onto the windowsill, gritted my teeth, and right before I jumped, a branch jutted out, unnaturally growing longer. It made a natural plank, bridging the space between the window and trees.

"Hurry!" Jadox called out and waved me over.

Maybe he wasn't so awful after all.

"Asshole." I tiptoed across.

"You mean the perfect gentleman." He scaled down the trunk like he was an extension of the tree, completely at ease.

The moment our feet hit the ground, we were running through the streets. "Where are we going?" I panted, and a cramp split my side as we ran.

"Those woods. Run faster."

My boots splashed in the puddles from last night's rain, coating my shins with mud. The sounds of the promise of nature sang a siren's song, egging me to sprint.

Sunrays beamed down, drenching me with warmth. This time, I allowed the sensation to take over my body like a soft blanket. Bliss. Heaven. Heat radiated through my core. I could do this. I could harness and learn my Magik.

He cast a hand out. Immediately, an army of roots broke through the ground behind us, forming a dozen obstacles for the cops. Magik might actually be helpful. A smile plastered my face until I noticed all the cameras lining the exteriors of the ramshackle apartment buildings, filming our every move.

Before the opportunity arose, Jadox whispered into the watch to someone, "No, I'll find you…and she can't know."

Effing Divinity! Of course, he was lying to me. And Jadox Griffin would burn for keeping a secret from me. But there was no turning back now. I was a witch fugitive, paired with the only surviving male on the planet. I needed Jadox for answers.

But what was he hiding?

6

KYRA

Left foot, right foot. Autumn leaves crunched with every step. Step after agonizing step. My thoughts spiraled out of control on our silent trek through the forest. Oh, Goddess, did Marie disappear too? How were trans women and trans men impacted by my wish? Who remained? And what about those who used "they" as their identifying pronoun? Fuck, I messed up. How could I return the males? We were wasting too much time.

I checked over my shoulder, awaiting the sound of cracking twigs under a pursuing cop's foot. But no one had followed us from Andersonville. Only a silent presence stalked us, its energy growing stronger the deeper into the foliage we journeyed.

"What time is it?" I asked and reached down to stroke Chocolate's back.

"Thirteen o'clock," Jadox mumbled.

After trudging through the dense woods for eternity, it was a miracle that Jadox spoke a word. I wanted to ask more questions, but it'd only bite me in the ass.

"What time is it now?"

Jadox sighed. "Exactly ten seconds after I said thirteen o'clock."

"How long does it take someone to die from walking?"

"How long does it take for you to die from asking questions?" His voice was sharp, but when I looked over, Jadox's slight smirk had finally returned.

He marched without breaking a sweat. His arms dangled leisurely until he wiggled his fingers, prompting a stick to jump from the forest floor straight into his grasp. He threw it impressively far, and Chocolate chased after, smushing leaves under her paws along the way. Jadox's rigid shoulders had finally eased to a normal-person calm. But the man leading me was anything but human—he was an obvious robot soldier who never tired.

Maybe Jadox had experienced too much seriousness in his life. Maybe the only way to crack his stern demeanor was to pretend to be some jolly damsel to make him feel more macho.

Against my better judgment, I skipped to his side ridiculously, grimacing at the thought of curling my hair around my finger like a naïve schoolgirl. Maybe if I played the part, his energy would shift. I'd try this once, and if he didn't give in, I'd return to our sulky trudging. I tapped an upbeat rhythm on my thigh and imagined all the thousands of cat videos I had scrolled through last week: kittens playing in boxes, cats standing on their hind legs, kittens attacking a puppy. Yup, that'd work.

"Why are you smiling?" Jadox asked condescendingly.

"Cats."

He grunted. "I'd rather not know."

"You don't like cats?"

"They're little demons," he grumbled.

"I was supposed to adopt a kitten from Hallie today. It looks like the goddess above had other plans."

Silence. He marched on.

"*Okay,* um, so I was thinking of reasons why my tattoo came yesterday. Why didn't it happen sooner? Maybe it was because I was under a lot of stress? Maybe it was fate?"

"I bet it's because you're Golden," Jadox mumbled.

"What?"

Without looking at me, he stomped over leaves and said, "Golden tattoos are rare, basically nonexistent. You probably don't adhere to the typical Mystier rules of maturation like the rest of us do."

"Ooooh, maturation. That's a college-worthy word. Did you go to a university near Andersonville?"

Silence.

"Let me guess, I bet you majored in debate. No, public speaking."

The smallest curve to his lip tilted up in the corner, and I pocketed my success quietly. "Hey, let's make a deal to protect each other until we arrive at Hallie's. Does your Mystier culture need a blood oath or something to seal the deal?"

He marched on.

"Okay, well, now that our oath is official. I'll forevermore save you with my karate chop maneuvers." I pulled the drumsticks out of my ponytail and stabbed the air high, then low.

Under his breath, he grumbled, "At least this deal isn't like Linking."

"Linking?" I kangarooed to his side again. "What's that?"

"Nothing." Jadox rolled his eyes. "You have too much damn energy."

No amount of my endearing, adorable, fake giddiness would unwrap his stone-cold heart. This man was a locked box of grumps.

Maybe if I just focused on this gorgeous forest, I could forget about him completely. Grasshoppers chirped as a chorus of birds sang falsetto. The animals needed my steady beat. As I walked along, I gently tapped my sticks against different trees. Scratchy bark, narrow trunks, wide, tall, flimsy trunks, and hollowed logs. Each beat sounded different. It felt like magic, no, more like—Magik. But, still, too quiet. I was used to the city, the rush of hoverboards flying outside my window, and music at all hours of the night. Hearing Jadox's heartbeat so clearly was just too creepy.

"Wanna play a game?" I asked.

Jadox's square chaw clenched, and the veins in his neck popped out.

"Fantastic, I'll go first. What's your favorite color?" I asked.

Silence.

"Come on, it'll make time go faster with all this walking."

"If I answer one, will you stop asking?" he asked, the grass somehow turning greener with his every step, like it awoke with his presence.

"Probably not," I replied.

A deep groan vibrated from his throat and sounded almost yummy. I shook my head. "Okay, your favorite color?"

"This is stupid."

"You're wasting words and seconds of your precious life. Just answer."

"Brown."

I laughed. "Brown? I don't think anyone in history has given that answer. Who likes brown?"

He rubbed his temples and walked faster.

"Fine, favorite food?"

"The vegetables from my Gemm's garden, but I haven't eaten any of those in years."

"Ooooh." I poked his side. "You just volunteered information about yourself! That deserves a trophy or something. Okay, okay, I got one. Why do you say those weird incantations out loud sometimes, but you're silent other times?"

"All spells are different. Some require more focus, so you get more distracted if you say them out loud. But the opposite is true for others. Others bring more power to the punch if you say them out loud. It depends on your level of exertion and what you're trying to do."

"Wow."

"What?" He eyed me worriedly.

"That's the most you've ever spoken at once, isn't it?"

"Okay, we're done with this."

I nudged him playfully and asked, "Don't you want to know all 1,568 quirks I have?"

"No."

I tried to contain my smile, failing miserably. This guy wasn't totally despicable, but I huffed out a puff of air anyways. "Ugh, you're insufferable. At least tell me more about this magical land full of fairies and stuff."

He side-eyed me. "I could kill anyone with my powers because I know about every plant. If I tear that thorn through your flesh, the poison will only take fifteen minutes to kill you, but it would be the most agonizing way to die. No one should have to leave this life with blood spurting from every orifice while seizures overtake your nervous system."

"Yikes...you're a bit intense, huh?"

"I've been told." Jadox faced me. "Okay, listen, you're right. You need to know about your Magik to survive. There are four elements. Each tribe controls one element. Draven is connected to the earth. We're villagers who are natural with what matters; plants, soil, rocks, roots, you name it."

I was intrigued by how his eyes lit up when he spoke about his village.

"Vayuians control air or wind. People from Cydon control water. Elidi power is supposed to be you, Kyra, fire, and heat. But I've never met anyone with a Golden tattoo—you're made of legends. Also, everyone gets their power as a teen, not in their twenties. Maybe you're ₵sµwi."

"What's ₵sµwi?"

"Dark Magik." He turned away. "Some Mystiers don't think it's just myth."

"Do you believe in ₵sµwi?"

Silence. We walked some more. Chocolate was panting by our sides and slowing her momentum considerably.

I replayed his answers, committing them to memory, then asked, "Where did those four names come from?"

Jadox sighed as if simply talking stole all his energy. "The tribes are named after the most powerful ancestors in our tribes. Before The Fall, eighty years ago, the tribes were spread out over more than fifty Mystier villages, but now only three remain. That generation of survivors joined forces to form the Mystier villages that exist today, Vayu, Cydon, Draven, and...well, Elidians are all nomads."

I shook my head, trying to remember all of it. "What was *The Fall*?"

Jadox shook his head. "Sorry, I forgot Ordulls don't know. What do your history books tell you about our calendar years starting over at 00-00?"

"You mean the Topell war when the terrorists bombed Lodesa? The leader of Ebovtus wasn't happy that we elected our first female president, so they bombed a bunch of our eastern cities. It was the only time we had been attacked on our soil. We called that Vuldow Glory. We even have a holiday for it."

"A holiday for mass murder?" Jadox asked.

"Mass murder? Giselle Dominia proclaimed it as a holiday to remember we can't be broken."

"Listen, your government is lying to all of you. That story is a cover-up for what really happened."

"*So*, what really happened?" I registered the pain in his eyes.

"The Fall happened because *your* great-grandmother, Elana Elidi, Linked with a man from a different element. Doing so has risks, such as decreasing the protective shields around our villages. Ordull governments discovered us. When they realized our powers, it was a massacre of thousands of Mystiers. We went from fifty villages to three."

"Why would two Mystiers do that Link-thingy if it'd crash their shields? There was a reason they Linked, wasn't there?"

"You catch on quick," Jadox said. "Yeah, they Linked to be more powerful."

I turned and kept walking while processing this explosion of information. How many Ordulls secretly knew about Mystiers? Secrets must have been passed down over generations through government officials. It was a lot to consider. I was getting a headache, and my stomach grumbled. I needed a distraction.

"Mister Grumps, I owe you a trick." Before I lost my nerve, I reached into his pocket and pulled out the matches I had spotted a few hours ago.

I expected a reprimand or snarky comment, but Jadox only picked up the pace.

Allowing him to brood like a teenager, I fell back again. With a flick of my wrist, I lit a match and stopped suddenly, cemented to the spot. The flicker of the fire felt like an extension of my finger, wholly entrancing me. I thought of his story of The Fall.

Inside the wild dancing light, images begin to swirl.

People collapsing by the masses. Men, women, and children—alive and smiling in one moment, then dead the next. A heap of bodies dumped off boats into the ocean. Time slipped by in seconds, minutes, days, eternity.

Then the light went out. Panting, I shook my head and scanned the enveloping forest, grounding myself in the present moment. What just happened? Behind me, soft rustling scuffed by an oak. I whirled around and ran straight into Jadox.

"Open fire in a forest isn't brilliant, Kyra." he scolded. "It's dangerous."

"Maybe later. I got this, Mister Grumps." I lit another match and skimmed my hand through the heat. My skin prickled with power, so I closed my fist over the flame, hoping to contain it, but the light faded out.

"You're not using your Circle. Here, let me show you," he snapped.

"How about telling me instead?"

An eerie warning whistled in the breeze. I spun on my heels toward the sound, searching the high branches. Nothing. Not even a bird; they had all quieted. Then Chocolate hopped closer, shoving her nose in a pile of leaves.

The warmth of Jadox's body brushed against my forearm as he walked by my side. "We still have a mile to go."

"If *only* someone had a remarkable game to pass the time."

"Fine. I'll play."

"Oh, goody goody-joy-joy." I rolled my eyes but agreed to pass the time faster since my feet were growing sore. "No topic is off limits, though."

"Wrong, don't ever ask me about my family." His eyes were the color of loneliness when he glanced over, resonating deep within.

"Name a toxic plant."

"Are you quizzing me?" He smiled. "Ragweed or jimsonweed."

"Favorite flower?"

"Tulips."

As we walked, I lit another match and set my arm hair on fire. It reminded me of dipping into a refreshing, boiling hot tub that melted away my worries. The flame of the match continued even when a breeze blew through.

I misstepped, tripping over a bush. Like an action hero, Jadox caught me in mid-air. While hoisting me to my feet, he relieved me of my backpack by looping it over his shoulders in one single motion.

"My turn. How old are you?" he asked.

"Twenty-five. You?"

"Twenty-eight." He frowned. The maturity of his expressions had me guessing thirty, so I was glad we were closer in age—not that it mattered for any reason. "Are you allergic to anything?" he asked.

I smiled. "Really, you're going to use up one of your questions on that?"

"I'd like to know if I need to heal you in case one of these plants makes you break out in hives."

"Oh." I moved closer to him and further from a vine crawling up a trunk. "Uh, I'm allergic to men." I shrugged. "What's the hardest thing you've ever healed?"

"Chocolate."

A gasp shocked my lips, unwilling to imagine any harm to any animal. "Did she die?"

"No, I can't bring anything back from the dead."

"When did it happen?"

"Last year. I tried to get the Unetlo Book from a vault…never mind." Jadox chucked another stick for Chocolate, and I couldn't help but follow the swing of his bulky arm through the air, wondering what it'd feel like to use that muscle as a pillow someday. Ugh.

"I'm glad you have her. I worked in an animal rescue center as a teenager and almost stole each and every one to bring home. What were you like in high school?"

He huffed, but his eyes were trained on me as we kept walking. "Have you ever manipulated fire before we met?"

"Nice topic shift. Super smooth and not at all obvious."

A low guttural sound reached my ears, and I let him get his way.

"I think I used fire once, but I'm still not quite sure what happened. It was the day my dad died," I responded flatly without missing a beat.

"Sometimes, I tried to replicate the feeling and use it against Quamir, but I had convinced myself it was all an illusion based on the shock that one time." I didn't meet Jadox's eye but continued, "I know you probably think I'm stupid for being manipulated by Quamir, but I swear, he started out nice."

"I don't think you're stupid, Kyra."

"Over a few months, he slowly took my freedom away without me even realizing it. He convinced me to sell my hovercar, made it seem like my idea to invest my savings in the nightclub, and took over small chores like buying groceries to control my bank accounts. I should've seen it all coming."

Jadox listened patiently, surprisingly allowing me to feel free to open up. The things I was telling him Hallie didn't even know.

"I didn't realize how deep into it I was until it was too late, but by then, I felt so foolish I didn't want to contact my mom or Hallie." I kicked at the dirt. "I'm such an idiot for finding a guy so similar to my fake dad.

He rubbed his black beard. "Are you gonna call him 'fake dad' now?"

"Definitely." I chewed the inside of my lip.

Jadox patted his leg for Chocolate to return the stick. "Kyra, some men suck, and some women do too. We all have faults, but no one in their right mind would blame you for what that creep did."

"Which one? Fake Dad or Quamir?"

"Both."

"Yeah, well, they're both gone now." I gulped, feeling too vulnerable. "So, do you think I sparked a fire for the first time because my fake dad died? Maybe from the high emotions? Actually, my fake dad was killed in that building we passed last night in Andersonville, in The Crooked Chateau. That's the place I manipulated fire before."

Jadox stopped in his tracks.

I turned around. "What's wrong?"

"Nothing. I thought I smelled something." The strangled sound of his voice kind of spooked me.

For some reason, when he mentioned smell, I immediately imagined Mom's apple pie. Why wasn't I thinking about her more? She was gone too. Everything was falling apart, and I was playing nonsense games in a forest.

"Why is your face doing that?" He pointed to the bunched line between my brows.

"If you must know, as of a few hours ago, I'm now an orphan," I tried to say it like I didn't care.

Jadox's jaw dropped. "Kyra..."

"Yeah, um..." My hands shook, so I hid them behind my back. "My mom died last night in a car crash."

He stepped toward me, both arms extended. "Shit, Kyra. Why didn't you say something earlier? We've been walking together for hours. Were you close with her?"

"No. She was an addict, abusing every drug possible, Venicke, Cratee, even Mithilim."

"Did you try to get her into rehab?"

I rolled my eyes. "Shucks, I hadn't considered that."

"I'm sorry, Kyra."

"She's gone now. No more suffering." It still felt like a thousand bricks stacked on my chest, the regret almost overcoming me. "I don't want to talk about it anymore. Let's just keep going. I need to see Hallie." I swept past him and sidestepped a sharp branch sticking out into the path.

His footsteps were softer than before, as if stomping too loudly would make my body crumble. My family was falling apart. I desperately needed to focus on anything other than my mom. And Landon.

Birds flew from branch to branch as if spying on our conversation. Now that Magik existed in this world, I guess anything was possible. I struggled to put all the pieces of the Jadox-Griffin puzzle together. The man somehow knew the code to my apartment, where I worked, and the name of my great-grandma. I should be sprinting away from him, but a strange spark zapped my new tattoo when I considered running. There must be a reason we were shoved together on this path. What was the reason he said he was following me? *The necklace.*

"Why is my necklace so important? Why do you want it?" I asked.

"It's rare protection, like a shield. Mystiers' powers weaken around electricity. Someone who possesses one of the four necklaces is more immune to the electrical currents, and their Magik remains strong. I hope to use it to strengthen Draven's shield."

"There's more than one necklace?"

"There used to be four, but now, the Elidi Ruby is the last one... and it's wrapped around your neck."

"What happened to the other three?"

"The Vayuian Crystal, Cydian Pearl, and Dravian Emerald were all destroyed in The Fall." His voice deepened, full of a grave tone I'd rather not hear again.

My toes tapped a moldy log, and I jumped over it.

He ran a hand through his dark, wavy hair. "So, what do you plan to do when you meet up with your sister?"

"Find a way to bring my nephew, Landon, back."

He turned abruptly, shock covering his dark features. "What? You think that's possible?"

"I have to hope. There's always a chance if someone hopes."

"I wouldn't have considered you such an optimist."

He studied me and admitted, "I've been fighting all my life. Whatever I want most, I can get if I don't lose hope. The moment I give up, the dream dies along with it."

"Hope sounds like a fantasy."

"Well, until last night, I didn't know Mystiers existed or that I had Magik. Now, I'm living in an alternate world. Maybe Landon is stuck in some lovely dimension with unicorns and floating gumdrops, and he just needs me to rescue him."

"Well, if anyone could pull it off, I bet it'd be you."

"Exactly, I don't need...Wait." I poked his chest. "Did you just compliment me?"

"No."

"Yes, you did." I smiled, then kept walking, walking, and more walking. We matched each other's strides step by step and even exhaled in sync. The melodies of the forest would've been beautiful if it were any other day.

"I'll do it. If I train my Magik, I can bring them all back. As you said, I have a Golden tattoo, so that must mean something."

He worked his jaw and ran a hand through his thick dark hair. "Why do you hate men so much?"

"Next question."

"Tell me, Kyra."

A phantom voice whispered in my ear again like an ancient siren, pushing me to open up to him.

"I used to have a brother." I drew in a breath of confidence. "...A really long time ago. But I guess after what you told me about my fake dad and Hallie not being related to me, I'm not even sure if he was my brother or not." My lungs compressed on one another in grief. "We looked alike, though. He had brown hair and my medium skin tone."

"What was his name?"

"Caldo." The emptiness in my chest stayed for years as though Caldo was carved out of my soul. "It doesn't matter, though. He's gone like all the other boys. I guess it was better to lose him as a child rather than now."

Jadox glanced to the north, the same direction he had been nervously checking every other minute. I followed his focus and only heard the wisp of the wind, though my gut agreed with his tense posture. Something or someone was out there. Close.

Jadox held a finger to his lips and gestured for me to stay put. Slowly, he crept behind a thick trunk and leaned around the side. Ignoring him, I snailed after him, step after step. My Circle pinged with inhuman awareness, alerting my senses.

Jadox sighed. "It's just a couple of foxes going at it."

Sneaking a peek confirmed that he was right. "Well, at least we know male animals didn't disappear. Chocolate might still become a momma one day." I smiled and nudged Jadox.

He crossed his arms. “You think someone like me would take care of puppies?”

I skipped around his statue position, poking at his side, and teased, “Oh, come on. You’d be a total sucker for teeny-tiny paws, those itty-bitty little ears flopping around. I can totally see puppies melting you like ice cream on a summer day.”

A real laugh burst from deep in his belly. “Kyra, do you even know—”

“How much you adore me? On a scale of one to ten, you’re so fond of me, you’d rate me as a twelve—no, a fourteen!” I teased.

In a swift motion, still laughing, he picked me up and looped me around his side, but I screamed so loud that birds flew off the branch above. My instincts took over, and I slammed my elbow into his nuts. Grunting in pain, he instantly collapsed to his knees, dropping me into a pile of soft leaves.

“Don’t touch…me…like that!” I forced the words through panting breaths.

“I didn’t mean to scare you.”

We lay next to each other, staring up at the canopy. A crisp collage of red and brown leaves mixed on the branches like a forest aflame. Two elements that didn’t mesh well yet looked beautiful all the same —a beautiful tragedy. I tapped a soft, steady drum beat on my thigh to calm down my nervous heartbeat.

“I’m sorry,” he groaned with one hand still cupping his crotch.

“I’m okay with initiating contact …like this.” I laid my hand on his. “But my body freaks out when a man touches me without asking first.”

“I’ll do better.”

I petted Chocolate, who always seemed to know when to stay close to me. “We only have like a day left together, then you’ll never have to see me again.”

“Right.” He pushed himself off the pile, biceps flexing.

My eyes lingered a second too long, and he caught me scanning. Immediately, my cheeks flushed warm. “Thank you, Jay, for helping me last night.”

"No problem." Furrowing his brow, he brushed off his cargo pants and said, "If you want to learn Magik quicker, envision your Circle. Concentrate on the shape and loop of the Möbius, almost like meditating. If you can picture it clearly, the fire is more likely to appear.

"Okay, right. I'll try that." I swallowed and pushed myself to my feet. "But what the heck is a Möbius?"

"The never-ending loop." He drew in the air. "You know, like this, around and around."

"Oh, okay. Got it."

I closed my eyes and tried to summon fire, but only images of Mom lying on the roadside haunted my visions. Then it switched to Landon burning in flames, then Hallie screaming at his empty bedside. My eyes snapped open.

I fiddled with the buttons on a spare watch I had stolen from Quamir's drawer and cast the projection onto a wide tree trunk to call Hallie. At least I still had her. Would she have gone back to work since nurses were necessary right now?

Hallie answered the video call on the first ring, "Hello? Is this Officer Prim? I filed a missing—"

"Hallie, it's me."

"This isn't your number," Hallie said.

"I know. I stole one. Are you okay?"

"No, I'm not okay. Landon is missing." Her breaths came heavily between each word. Pristine walls with lavender and silver streaks of paint rushed by behind her. That didn't look like the wing of her hospital.

"Where are you?" I asked my sister.

"Syvonne Stirk's headquarters."

"What? The vice president?"

"She's the president now, and I just enlisted in her army."

Images flooded my mind of Hallie as a child, playing tea party and refusing to climb a tree with me. She was a nurturer, not a fighter.

"Hallie, no! What are you thinking?"

"The witches need to pay for stealing, Landon. I won't stop until each of them is dead and he's back in my arms." Her face flushed red. "Did you hear the news? Our soldiers have already arrested thirty witches. I bet there are tons more hidden somewhere. I can't believe we didn't know about it until now. It's like we're in some twilight zone." Hallie's head bobbed in and out of focus as she ran down a long hall. "Stirk says she's going to make them return all the males. I'll do anything to make that happen."

"Hallie, you can't enlist."

"I already did. Join me. We've always made each other stronger."

Jadox violently waved his arms and shook his head no.

While imagining Landon's mop of sweet, sandy curls, I nodded into the screen. "I'll be there."

Jadox dropped his head.

"I knew you would. We'll make them all suffer." Hallie didn't sound like herself.

Tears pooled behind my eyelids. "I'll be there soon."

Instead of her usual parting joke, Hallie only nodded and hung up. Uncertainty wrapped tight ropes around my frame and squeezed the life out of me. I had to fix what I had broken. No matter the price. Turning to Jadox, I leaned against a tree trunk. "Okay, soldier, teach me how to control my Magik. I'm ready."

"Kyra…I need to tell you something," he said. "We're not headed to meet your sister."

The small amount of friendliness I allowed toward him suddenly snapped in half.

"*What?* Have you been leading me the wrong way?"

"Yeah, and there's something else too."

I threw my hands in the air. "How could there possibly be more?"

"I'm not the only male left."

Surely, my face must've blanched. There was no way I had heard him accurately. Just as I was about to ask him, a loud crack snapped behind us. Jadox twisted around fast, sniffing the area, and said, "We're not alone."

7 JADOX

A sharp pain shot through my fingers as Kyra's wolf-like teeth chomped hard through my skin.

"Ow! You bit me," I whispered with a hiss.

"If you ever cover my mouth again, I'll rip your balls off." Kyra spiraled out of my grip.

"Well, it's a good thing you'll never be granted access to my balls or anything attached."

Chocolate didn't bark at the incomer, confirming my suspicions. My pup always took the woman's side. Just like when I erased Paola Perez's memory years ago, my dog had stayed by Alaska's heels for months as she grieved the loss of her girlfriend and the future they could have had.

Goddess above, my sister didn't deserve to suffer though.

What right did I have to control her relationship? Chocolate was right. I had made a terrible mistake before, so maybe I was wrong now too. Maybe each of my decisions only hurt those I cared for instead of protecting them. My duty was to protect. If I couldn't even do that, well, what purpose did I serve? And now, I was making the same mistake with Kyra.

"Did you just say other men are alive?" Kyra asked, "Why would you lie about that? It's not funny."

"I'm not lying. A librarian from Vayu sent me a message. And he's tracking us."

Her shoulders went stiff. "Maybe your watch is faulty, and it was an old message."

I sniffed the forest air, pines, oaks, and ferns mixed in a soup of heavenly scents, but two other ingredients didn't belong, one of which racked a paralyzing skitter through my spine.

Isaac was definitely alive and nearby. Kyra's wish must've only worked on Ordull males.

"Do you hear that?" Kyra grabbed my hand for a moment before realizing what she had done.

"It's okay. It's not the man." Relief cascaded over me at the familiar scent. "I know you're there, Alaska. Come out."

"Who's Alaska?" Kyra asked, dropping into a fierce knightly pose with both palms extended out. Apparently, miss sassy-pants believed she could take down my sister with no training in her Magik.

Alaska stepped out from behind a wide redwood. Her frown mirrored mine, and when she crossed her arms over her outfit that camouflaged into the trees, it brought me back to a time when my sister was only seven years old.

"Long time no see, bro." In the wind, the tips of my sister's raven hair brushed below the sheath hanging from her belt loop.

"You're his sister?" Kyra eyed Alaska's bare feet, brown shorts, and matching tee that blended into my sister's skin.

Alaska's brow perked up at the sight of Kyra. "She better not be an Ordull, you hypocrite."

Great, she hadn't forgiven me yet. I held in a sigh. If I had never caught Alaska in that cabin—kissing an Ordull—we might still be best friends. If I had never used a memory spell on the woman my sister loved, I wouldn't have been cast out of my tribe. But I was trying to protect her. She couldn't be with an Ordull because they would never understand our Magik.

Alaska's brown eyes weren't the same as the last time I saw her.

Layers of mistrust, pain, loss, and resentment stacked high in her irises, hiding the spark I had memorized from childhood. And it was all my fault.

"So, if you truly are his sister, then I suppose you're here to take me to some mystery land I've never heard of, but too bad, chica, because I need to return my nephew—" Amid Kyra's babbling explanation to Alaska, my sister interrupted.

"What makes you think you can return the other males?" Alaska asked.

"The other males?" Kyra straightened. "So, it's true? Some survived?"

Alaska nodded.

Kyra turned to me. "You were telling me the truth?"

"Don't be so surprised," I said, "I'm an amazing person."

Alaska laughed, and despite the circumstances, it made my heart leap at the sound. "Oh man, you two will be the death of each other."

Kyra crossed her arms and scanned each of us, asking, "Are you two close?"

I responded with "Yes" at the same moment Alaska said, "No."

We stared each other down like in our childhood until Kyra interrupted our silent battle by clearing her throat. "Okay, well, I'm on Alaska's side then."

"I don't want you on my side," Alaska hissed. "My brother may be some things, but he's your best bet for surviving this mess."

Finally, my sister had my back again. I could've reached out then and there and wrapped her in a tight hug, but the quick joy faded when I smelled Nilson's shampoo. "Alaska, we need to make the jump. Now!"

Showing understanding with a single look, Alaska pointed up a tree. "You know how teleporting works. Climb."

Kyra's head tilted to the side. "How *what* works? Excuse me? Teleporting?"

"If you ever close your mouth, *Keyrah,* I can explain." Alaska rolled her eyes.

"My name rhymes with Myra or Tyra. It's not so hard, but people manage to butcher the pronunciation all the time."

"There's no time for this argument. Get up." I had every intention of pushing Kyra up the damn tree before Nilson arrived, but I remembered her fears about men touching her. "Please, Kyra, climb."

"Seriously? Teleportation? Is my body gonna be split into a million pieces?" Kyra asked.

"No, you'll be safe. Those of us that are directly related to the strongest ancestor in our tribe have extra powers. I am a descendant of the original Draven leader, so I can heal others. My sister shares that DNA, and her gift is teleportation."

"Our Grandma Gemm has prophecies," Alaska said proudly.

My watch dinged, showing me a message from Nilson. My heartbeat spasmed in my chest. I swiped the message away so Kyra couldn't see it. This was one situation where using Magik wouldn't necessarily help since he had strong wind powers.

Heavy sweat and the scent of Nilson's rage wafted closer, stalking in the shadows, sprinting to us. I knelt in the dirt, giving the women a way to step up to a branch. Alaska leaped up in a single bound, her weight barely registering on my thigh when she pushed off like a nimble raccoon. She scurried higher with such grace that her moves mirrored a circus act.

Struggling, Kyra stepped on my leg and pulled herself up, grunting like a drunk bear. I crouched and scooped a handful of dirt into my palm, then rubbed it over my biceps, forearms, face, and under my shirt for protection. My personal shield. The comforting scent of soil calmed my racing nerves.

"Chocolate, stay."

My dog lay on overgrown grass and rolled over onto her back without a care in the world. She sure didn't know how to perceive danger if it hunted her down.

"What? You can't leave her!" From a higher branch, Kyra peered down at me with those amber eyes full of concern. Surprise coiled through me that she cared about anything involving my dog or my life.

"Trust me," I said.

"Doubtful," she mumbled while reaching higher.

The branches thinned, sending a jolt of adrenaline through my tattoo, ready to fight.

"This is too high!" Kyra's voice shook above.

"You don't seem the type to be scared of anything." I needed to keep her moving.

"Well, you'd be wrong."

At the top branch, thousands of trees stretched for miles, the apple colors blurring together with shades of oranges and lemons.

Alaska reached out to her. "Okay, this is going to feel weird, but you'll be okay…probably."

"Just do it, hurry. We have maybe one minute," I said to my sister, "and get Chocolate second. I'm last."

Alaska huffed, but I knew from that look that she'd do as I asked. "Okay, Keyrah, on the count of three, we jump off the branch."

Kyra backed into my chest, her whole body curling in on me. "Are you crazy? We're forty feet high. What are you talking about?"

"You won't reach the ground. Just hold my hand tight." Alaska twined her fingers with Kyra's. "One…"

"No way. I gotta pee! Let's climb down."

"Wow, you're a piece of work," Alaska said. "Two."

Kyra's expression pleaded, and, for a moment, I wanted to save her from her fears when she begged, "Jay, I don't want to."

Alaska jumped, pulling Kyra with her. A squeal soared through the afternoon air until both women disappeared. I waited for Alaska to reappear and grab Chocolate next. Teleporting would be harder for her from low on the ground.

My watch beeped again. Swiping the buttons, a name on the screen flashed. I gritted my teeth when the Vayuian man's face popped up—Isaac Nilson. The live stream showed his blond beard and matching hair pulled back into a high bun. His expression twisted in torment.

"Scared of me, Griffin?" Nilson's voice was laced with venom and clear enough that it sounded as if he were standing right next to me instead of speaking through my watch's screen.

The veins on Nilson's forehead bulged on the screen and spread like a lightning bolt across his pale skin. I sniffed the breeze, trying to determine how far away he was.

A soft zip sound swooshed below. Alaska appeared from thin air, wrapped her arms around Chocolate, and disappeared again. Two down, one to go. But I wasn't the one who mattered; if those three were safe, what pain Nilson had planned for me wasn't important.

"You're gonna die, slowly and painfully, Griffin, for making my son disappear," said Nilson.

"No, thanks. I enjoy the forest too much to die before I'm thirty."

"Shut up! I know you did it. I know you *hate* Ordulls, so you found a way to eliminate all their males. Now my Wes is gone too."

Genuine confusion tore through me. "I thought your son had Magik."

"His mother was Ordull. He was a half-breed, a hybrid. And you took him from me!"

Understanding slapped my body to high alert when I realized he blamed me—not Kyra. This was my chance to set him straight and let Nilson know the truth. Or, I had a chance to protect her. My mind see-sawed for only a moment before sealing my fate.

"Well, I've always bragged to everyone about how brilliant you are, Nilson. Congrats on figuring out my plan quickly, man. You're right. Hybrids are just like Ordulls: useless and a threat to our kind. I'm glad they're gone. I'm glad your son is gone. Unfortunately for you, I don't plan to die today."

"Oh, it won't be today," he snarled. A vicious smile crept up his face on my screen and his shirt flapped in the wind.

His scent grew stronger below. Closer. I only had seconds left.

"First, I'll torture you one limb at a time, then test out a few different ways to kill you but not quite finish the job."

"Sounds like a hot date. You've got me picturing restraints and whips, but you're not really my type. I need to head out now. My favorite team is playing—you know how it is. Game time and nachos."

"Griffin!" His bloodthirsty scream shook the forest. "I'll kill your whole family, then hunt your little girlfriend. The one with the red streaks in her hair. Maybe I'll let her fuck me too. And I'll even let you watch."

A pounding throbbed through my temples, and ice ran through my veins.

"Peek-a-boo, Griffin. I see you." Nilson's voice was nearby and clear at the base of my tree.

My Circle awoke, sending a crash of pure energy from my core to my fingertips. I pulled on the strength from my tattoo, and tension swirled inside me, ready to burst. I pointed straight at a giant thicket from the top branch and coaxed it, seducing the wiry roots up and out of the ground.

The corpse of tangled branches obeyed, rising and stretching into a mass of impenetrable vines and branches. It stood on sturdy limbs and moved toward Nilson like a puppet under my control. The spindly upper appendages flailed in wide circles. Each heavy step crunching the ground pounded a hole into the soil. Sap seeped from the cracks of the bark like little battle tears.

Nilson backed up a foot before a crazed smile covered his snakelike face again and reached his disgusting eyes.

"Griffin, you're slacking. At least give me a challenge this time."

Instead of attacking the thicket monster, Nilson turned and gazed up at me. Using the moment of his distraction, I commanded the thicket. Its seven gangling arms crashed to the ground like it was playing a game of whack-a-mole.

Nilson hopped, jumped, and leaped like he was weightless, bouncing mid-air and out of reach with each swing. Damn it, my monster was too slow.

The arrogant asshole tore off his shirt like a soccer celebrity and chucked it to the ground. "Is this all you've got?" he screamed. "I have nothing left, Griffin! Rajitha was on a plane when the pilot disappeared. It crashed, and she's gone! Wes is gone! Both were ripped from me. How could you do this?"

Nilson raised both hands to the cyan sky like he was praying. A horrific scream scraped out of his throat as the puffy marshmallow in the sky turned gray and ominous. Shit. He was stronger in his rage. But I had my dirt shield still caked over my skin for protection.

Veins popped from his forearms and biceps. The top arch of his blue Circle poked from his pants and glowed with a white hue. Another cry from deep in his soul, and I could practically smell his pain. But I wasn't dying today. I still had to make up for my mistakes with Gemm and Alaska.

His wind accelerated, shifting my branch. It quaked underfoot. Tightly, I wrapped my arms around the trunk. If I survived the fall, I'd be in a vulnerable position, tumbling to the ground. Nilson would have the full advantage.

The branch holding my life in its grasp swung brutally. My foot slipped, and a gasp shocked my lips as bark sliced into my skin. Using every ounce of energy I had, I forced another command.

The skeleton of chorded vines twirled toward Nilson, pinning him against a tree. I pulled myself up to the branch again. The wind whipped my hair. I could tell the thicket monster to stab Nilson through the chest, the same ugly demise as Quamir. But I had sworn an oath to myself—never take another Mystier's life. There weren't enough of us left to waste. Ordulls would always be the true enemy.

"I'm going to release you now, and you'll leave this forest, go back to Vayu. It's what Wes would've wanted," I silently commanded the thicket to loosen its hold on Nilson.

His deep voice boomed, "Don't you *ever* speak for my son!"

A body collided with mine, sharp and sudden. "I'm here," Alaska whispered.

Before Alaska whisked me away, Nilson shouted, "You have twenty-four hours to drop Kyra off at the Vayu border, or your entire village will suffer."

My heart pounded. Kyra? Why? What did Nilson want with Kyra?

8

KYRA

The sinister forest surrounding me had a living, breathing heartbeat. Each time the leaves swayed, it felt like a direct message to return to where I came from and never look back.

A soft breeze blew my shirt up, and dry bark scratched my skin. Chocolate's chin rested on my leg as she recovered from Alaska's dizzying ride. Together, we awaited Alaska and Jadox's return. At least my outfit was perfect for the wilderness.

The shaded forest I sat in held the same deciduous trees, which dropped red and orange leaves like rain, smattering the forest floor. Twigs poked into my thigh, so I picked a few up and twisted them together in the same way I used to braid Hallie's long hair.

As children, she was the one with delicate bows in her hair, and I'd have dirt stains all over my hand-me-down outfits. There was no way I'd let her fight in Syvonne Stirk's army.

"This is goodbye, girl." I swept a hand through Chocolate's brown fur. "Don't look at me like that. I'm going to Hallie's. I need to be with my sister right now."

"We're here." Alaska's voice suddenly projected from behind me.

I rushed around a trunk, tripping on roots in the process. When I saw Jadox, strange relief washed over me in a heavy wave. The pressure coiling in my chest soothed into a dull fizzle.

"Are you okay?" he asked.

I nodded. "Why do you look worried?"

"My face always looks like this."

I studied the concerned furrow of his brow, not convinced. "So, you can heal, and your sister can teleport. Are there any more surprises I need to know?"

Jadox nodded. "Special skills run in one family over generations, so, usually, a member of that family takes on a leadership role in their community."

"You two go inside, and I'll be there in five," he said. "I need to give Chocolate a pep talk. She hasn't been back here in years."

Alaska sighed. "Fine, I'll come back for you in six minutes if you're not in there. Come on, Keyrah."

"Her name is Kyra," Jadox said and pulled me aside. "When you go through the barrier, you should feel a sharp zap in your tattoo. Expect it to shock you like an electric jolt."

I tapped my fingers on my thigh, using them as drumsticks. "Sounds super pleasant. But I can't go to your village. Remember, I need to find Hallie."

"I know." Jadox nodded. "Once we're safely inside, we can figure out the best plan to get you to her. You need food after our long walk."

"Okay, fine. Only a quick snack. How far is it to Draven?" I glanced around at the hundreds of trees circling us.

Alaska smiled, joy spreading to her brown eyes. "We're here. We have an invisible shield around our village." She stepped forward and disappeared.

I gasped, then met Jadox's eyes. "Did she teleport again?"

"No, she went through the barrier. Go ahead; it's safe," he reassured me. "Actually, wait."

"What's wrong?"

"So you *do* care a little." His smirk rose slowly. A zing went down my spine. Was he flirting?

"Ugh, you're the absolute worst."

He chuckled. "Listen, once you're in Draven, never accept a gift offered by a gorula."

"What's a gorula?"

"A big, furry, golden primate with six limbs." He flailed his arms around like in a game of charades.

"Sounds like you're messing with me. Are there elves too?"

All he did was shrug, so I held my breath and stepped forward into the unknown. A sharp shock pinged in my tattoo and zapped my whole body from head to toe. I landed on my hands and knees on the other side of the seal.

Awe raced through my veins at the impossible forest scene before me. Branches rippled and curled as if they were arteries projecting from a beating heart. An iridescent orchid-butterfly, the size of my head, flapped by. Vivid green hues somehow sang a harmony. Gorgeous hunter-green crooned the base, lizard-green hummed the tenor, and mint-green purred the soprano: all of them spiked with heavenly sounds like a drug.

"Am I hallucinating?"

A thrill raced through my blood. I could feel the heat of a campfire in the distance and desperately wanted to suck the flames closer and harbor the energy. Magik swarmed in every spec of the air. This place was real. How? A childlike swarm of glee and joy frolicked inside me, bursting with impossibilities and awe. Every inch felt like a fairytale—a world promised to only those who deserved this wonder.

A tear coated in sweetness slid from my eye at the sight of this beauty. The village had a living pulse, a native texture to the soil as the dirt coated my fingers. Unfathomable trees that I couldn't ever describe towered in various thicknesses, textures, and heights. And half the trees were horizontal, floating parallel to the ground somehow.

Magik peppered my soul. My hearing zoomed into the cacophony of a forest orchestra as it buzzed to life. I listened to the subtle movement of the soil, and whimsical notes of the woods swelled, clanging like wind chimes. Birds chirped, singing an afternoon song. Above, children's laughter caught my attention, and my gaze rose to hundreds of elaborate, camouflaged treehouses. I placed both hands over my heart and savored this feeling, knowing I'd never forget it for as long as I lived.

A wet nose rubbed against the back of my knee as Chocolate nudged me forward. Then, Jadox's silent, intense energy pulsed next to me. I watched him scan the gorgeous view; it was obvious that he hadn't stepped foot in Draven for years. Jadox's face showed a buffet of feelings, and I wondered what about his story had caused him such longing.

Across a clearing, women stopped their gardening and looked over, taking in the sight of Jadox. I didn't see any men. Maybe he was wrong, and I demolished their loved ones too.

"Any of those your ex-girlfriend?"

"Wouldn't you like to know," he grumbled, his eyebrows pulled together tight.

Jadox stepped toward a giant boulder embedded in a moss-covered hill. The further I inspected it, the more certain I was that a door and windows were sketched into the side.

"I have someone I need you to meet. Grandma Gemm might be able to explain why you have that golden tattoo."

"Fine, but after I meet her, I'm leaving."

Mushrooms as tall as my knees lined our path to her den door. A drumstick slid from my ponytail and clattered onto a stone.

Jadox swiped it up and hesitantly held the drumstick over my hair. "May I?" The warmth of his face surprised me.

"Um, sure." Locking onto his deep cocoa eyes, I held my breath as he slid the drumstick back into my ponytail.

We were so close that if I rose on my tiptoes ever so slightly, my lips could brush his bottom lip. Not that I wanted to, of course.

He nudged my side while trying to hide the tiny smirk. "Let's just go in."

Inside, plants and apothecary bottles covered the numerous shelves of Gemm's cozy den. Containers of herbs and spices were stacked to the ceiling, and recipe books lay scattered and open on the surface of the rock floor.

I caught Jay's one-of-a-kind, heartbreaker smile when he picked up a ladle from the counter coated in something sticky. But I couldn't focus on him for long when the burning stove called to me. The flames flirted with a slow and sensual rumba, asking me to dance.

Magnetized by the heat, I grasped the scorching stove with my bare hands. A current spiked through my body, and savage power raged within, begging to be used. Before I could try, something whistled, snapping me into focus.

"Kyra, you need to harness the urge. It's dangerous." Jadox reached out, but my body needed the heat. The next thing I knew, we were tumbling together to the floor. A chair snapped and cracked as it crashed against the wall. Jadox and I grappled on the floor like crazed animals until he pinned me.

Chest heaving, I stared up from under his strong body. The view riled me. Those arms. That wide chest. His eyes. One piece of his thick, silky brown hair that was a bit longer than the rest flapped low over his forehead. I had half a mind to comb it back from those addictive eyes. My heart pounded harder than ever, and my breaths came out in strange stutters. He reached down slowly to cup my face as his weight covered my body. I stared into his eyes.

I could write songs about the brown speckles in his eyes. They swirled with a perfect balance of loyalty, protectiveness, and dedication. But I'd been fooled before. A man won't fool me again, no matter how decent he proved himself to be.

"You can get off me now." Trapped between his strong legs, I started to scoot out, but the den's door swung open.

A short, round woman with gray, knotted braids cascading to her abdomen sauntered in holding a watering can. When she spotted us on the ground with Jay accidentally pinning me, a brief smile flashed across her wrinkled face.

Jay jumped up quicker than a rabbit and leaned against a long wooden table. "Hi, Gemm. I'm sorry for...barging in."

While setting the watering can down, she lowered her chin. "Once, there was a lady who lived on the beach with her turtle. Her turtle left one night for a midnight swim. The current took him miles away, and he was lost in the open sea. After struggling for years to find his way home, he finally made it. The lady was waiting in the same place for him on the sand."

"I understand, Gemm. I know I took too long to return."

Both of her arms spread wide, and Jadox glided into her embrace like it was a gift. All of his toxic energy oozed away and out the window, releasing him from whatever burden he had been carrying. Instead, he melted into her arms like ice cream on a sunny day.

Gemm's brown eyes met mine, and she held out one hand. "Once there was a special child who beat drums with the fierceness of the divine, but that girl held a secret." A dimple showed with her smile, making me instantly fall in love with this treasured woman. "Once, there was a girl born of Elidi fire blood. Who received her powers later than the rest."

Tapping a tempo on my thigh with my fingertips didn't calm me this time. Every woman in my family had blessed me with acceptance. But would Gemm realize I didn't belong here with the Dravians? Did she know I was to blame for the males' disappearances?

Gemm's small hand reached for my ruby necklace. When her fingertip brushed over the jewel, a bright red light shot out, then disappeared. Her entire body went as rigid as a wooden board. Fogginess spread over her face, and her eyes rolled to the back of her head. She teetered back, pulling me with her.

"What the?"

Jadox lurched out, catching us mid-fall.

A cryptic voice several octaves lower forced itself from Gemm's throat. "She must Link before dawn on the Luna Festival, or Draven will perish."

Terror crashed together in Jadox's eyes, reflecting my own confusion.

"What?" I attempted to pull my hand from Gemm's, but she had a death grip.

"She must Link with the man who hunts her soul before dawn on the Luna Festival, or Draven will perish." Gemm hissed an animalistic sound, then continued. "The Golden One must Link, or she will never save his soul." Her tight grip finally dropped, and she sunk into Jadox's arms.

My heart pounded fast, beating a thousand questions. "What was that?"

"Gemm?" Jadox tapped her cheek slightly. "Gemm, wake up."

Her eyes squinted open, clear and lucid again. "Jadox? You're home? Once there was a boy lost in the mountains. He followed the stars to find home. It took years but finally, he followed the path of stones."

He sat her down on a rusty chair. "Yes, I'm here, Gemm. Are you okay?"

I hustled to the fridge, doing my best to ignore the flames coming from the stove, and grabbed her a glass of water.

Gemm sipped slowly. "Once, there was a leader named Elana Elidi. She had long brown hair and amber eyes, just like her daughter's son, Brent."

"Brent? Was that my father's name?" I quickly leaned forward, accidentally knocking over a pile of cookbooks.

"Once, there was a drummer girl with more passion in her soul than leaves in the forest."

Jadox rubbed her shoulders softly. "Gemm, you told of another prophecy."

"Once you two kissed, then lived happily ever after."

Jadox shook his head and said, "We're not a couple."

Gemm winked, then stood up as though nothing strange had happened and picked up her watering pail.

"Well, that was—"

"Intense," I finished Jadox's thoughts and blew out a big sigh. "I *must* Link? I don't think so."

While repeating her prophecy over and over in my mind, Jadox filled a glass of water from the sink.

She must Link before dawn at the Luna Festival, or Draven will perish. She must Link with the man who hunts her soul. The Golden One must Link, or she will never save his soul.

"What did Gemm's prophecy mean?" I asked Jadox. "I can't Link."

Silence.

"She said I have to Link with a man to save a soul?" Now I was just speaking out loud to myself. "What, man? Whose soul? And what is the Luna Festival?" I marched to Jadox's side and grabbed the glass from his hand, water slopping over the edge onto his shirt. "This is too much. I need more answers. There's too much being thrown at me! Do I have to Link with you no matter what?" My hands became clammy as I lifted the water to my mouth. "This is crazy!"

"I'm not your only option. There are other males still alive…Kyra, sit down; you're shaking."

"No, I need answers." I glanced out the window. "There aren't any males out there."

"Yes, all male Mystiers survived. It's not just me."

"Then why haven't I seen any?"

"They're on the annual hunting trip, a week-long tradition with males of all ages before the Lunar Festival. I'll try to explain more later." Jadox rubbed his stubbly chin. "But I'm going to try and convince Gemm to rest."

"Well, I'm sick of waiting for answers. I met your grandma like you asked, and I can't wait around here for a week to see if other guys show up, so I'm leaving for Hallie's now."

"Wait, not yet. Please wait." Jadox nodded toward the window where Alaska was watching from outside, concerned. "Alaska, can you please train Kyra how to center her Circle."

Alaska rolled her eyes. "Come on, Keyrah."

I sighed, letting her pronounce my name wrong, then reluctantly followed. If Jadox wasn't going to answer my questions, maybe his sister would. It wouldn't hurt to wait another hour to see what I could learn from her.

Outside, the sounds of a gushing waterfall poured into a lake in the distance.

"I have chores to get done, so let's do this quickly." Alaska took off her brown shirt, revealing a matching brown sports bra. The black ink designs under her clavicle were woven in intricate patterns.

"What do those shapes mean?" I pointed to her shoulder.

"They represent the four elements and necklaces lost during The Fall."

"Jay said they were all destroyed."

"Oh, you've given him a nickname, huh?" Alaska shook her head. "My brother doesn't know everything, as much as he pretends to.

I don't think any heirloom with that much power can be destroyed. I bet the other three are out there still." She stared at the ruby draped around my neck. "I'm only doing this because Jadox asked me to. Now, pay attention and imitate my movements." She drew a circle in the dirt with her bare toes and stood in the middle.

"I bet you a thousand of those little mushrooms over there that we'll be best friends soon." I let the sarcasm drip off my tongue, hoping that she couldn't read under the layers—how desperate I was for a friend.

"Those are poisonous."

"Oh, then our friendship could be full of sweet venom." I drew a lopsided circle in the dirt, taking twice as long as her. "So, what do you do for fun in this Magikal land of horizontal trees?"

"Is this your way of small talking? I'd rather not waste my breath on what doesn't matter."

I glanced at the women gardening. I had to get on their good side if any of them were going to help me with supplies for my journey to Hallie's. "What matters to you, then? What's worth your time?"

"At least there's one thing that's been realized during this catastrophe. The news announced that trans women are all still here." Alaska bent into a yoga pose. "My friend, Taylor, didn't disappear. That's proof that people truly are the gender they identify as. We need Ordull leadership to change laws to accept everyone."

"I agree, but I highly doubt that's what the president is focused on right now."

"You agree?" Alaska stretched one leg high like a circus performer. "Maybe you won't be the worst thing that's happened to my brother.

I tipped over, unable to keep my balance. "We're not together."

"I'm not blind, Key-ruh."

I cleared my throat. “Um, so, did you hear Gemm’s prophecy?”

Alaska nodded. “Yeah, I was at the window. Gemm’s prophecies don’t mean much anymore. She makes one every day; half the time, she speaks in riddles. Don’t even consider Linking. The Fall happened because Mystiers Linked. Repeating history would be stupid, dangerous, and selfish. And if you even think about involving my brother, I’ll cut you to pieces.”

“Gemm said I could save a soul. What if it’s Landon’s soul? What if that’s how I can save him?”

“Was he a Mystier?”

“No.”

“Only male Mystiers survived. The kid is gone. Accept it.”

I planted both feet firmly on the ground again and crossed my arms. “Accept it? That’s easy for you to say! You still have a male left that you care about.”

“No, I don’t.” She dropped her yoga pose too. “My relationship with Jadox changed years ago. I don’t have the same brother anymore. You don’t get to talk to me like you know my story. Everything has changed since Jadox erased my girlfriend’s memory years ago.”

“Why would Jay erase your girlfriend’s memory, and how?”

Alaska paused, and I could feel the gardener’s eyes on us. “Actually, he used a spell from the Unetlo Book. It’s in Vayu’s library. I bet you could bring Landon back if you find the right one in that book. You should go check it out, and maybe someone from that city will offer to Link with you.”

Something didn’t feel right. Why would she suddenly offer me advice?

“But what about meeting Hallie?” I asked.

“When you find your sister, you’ll have no way of bringing back Landon. But if you have the Unetlo Book with you, that could give you an advantage. Nothing here in Draven will help you, especially my brother.”

“Don’t worry. I don’t want anything to do with Jay.” A snort escaped in a half-laugh.

“Fine, so we’re in agreement? You’ll go to Vayu on your own and never come back.”

I studied her. “I’ll make you a deal. If you help me harness this firepower quickly, I’ll leave, and you’ll never see me again.”

She stuck out her hand. “I can’t work miracles, but I’ll try. You won't like my next move if you change your mind and mess with Jadox.”

“Why don’t you like me? You don’t even know me.”

She leaned forward and twisted impossibly, in complete control. “Jadox is still the most loyal, strong, and reliable man I’ve ever met. He’s my big brother, and I’d never want to see him get hurt, no matter how stupid he’s been in the past.”

“You think I’ll hurt him?”

Alaska rolled her eyes which was apparently her trademark move. “If you spend any time with him, yes, I know you will.”

“Why?”

She paused, glanced at Gemm’s den, then back to me. “Because everyone he ever cares for eventually hurts him.”

“He doesn’t care about me,” I said. “You’re awfully protective of someone who erased your girlfriend’s memory.”

“He’s my brother.” A statement as if nothing else needed to be said.

A flashback whipped me back in time with Hallie. I didn’t know what it was like to grow up with a brother, but I did have a sister, whether we were blood-related or not. Of course, we always stole each other’s jeans and held each other’s hair back when one of us drank too much at a party, but there was always one memory that I felt solidified what we meant to each other.

We stood in the lobby of a pro-choice women’s health clinic, waiting in line for Hallie to fill out her paperwork. She was only eighteen, and even though I had just received my driver’s license the week before, I was the one she chose to drive her home. Hallie trusted me to take care of her and counted on me to keep her secret. Waiting for her turn, the white shade of her face looked like a ghost, and her hands trembled wildly.

"Hallie?" I faked confidence. "It'll be okay. Dad won't find us."

A tear slid down her cheek. "That's not what I'm worried about. What if this is my only chance?"

I had no idea what she meant. "Only chance for what?"

"For a baby." Hallie wrung her hands together. "When I see my future, all I care about is being a mom." Her tears fell faster. "I don't care about college, where I live, or my job. Having a child is all that matters."

"You haven't told me that before."

She finally faced me, her cheeks red and eyes watering. "What if I never have this chance again? What if this is my only pregnancy? If I do this, I might regret it forever."

I inhaled deeply and stepped closer. "When you see a life for your baby, do you think you can give that to him or her right now?"

She sniffed. "I'd love them, no matter what. Isn't that enough?"

"I don't know, Hallie." I squeezed her shaking hands. "Do you want to go home? We can leave now and figure out what you need to—"

She rested her chin on my shoulder and cried harder. "No, no, I need to do this today. Blake won't help me, and you know Dad will kick me out."

I rubbed her back. "Okay, whatever you need."

"It'll happen again, right?" She hiccuped through choppy sobs. "I'll have another chance, right?"

"Yes, yes. Of course, you will. One day, you'll have seven kids running around."

"How about four?" She laughed and wiped her nose on her sleeve while backing away.

"Yes, four sounds great. And I'll be the world's best aunt." I forced a smile.

"Yeah, except you'll always buy them the annoying toys and get them into trouble."

"That's what cool aunts do."

"Okay, right, okay. I'll have my baby someday." She laughed and coughed at the same time.

Two short years later, Hallie got her wish, and along came Landon. But I was the reason Hallie lost her son, and I had to fix what I broke.

"Are you ready?" Alaska's glare could cut through Gemm's rock house, pulling me back into the moment.

"Yes, I'm ready."

Alaska's stone-cold expression and harsh bone structure mirrored Jadox's so closely that they could pass for twins, though she was probably closer to my age. She placed both palms flat against one another as if praying and balanced like a flamingo.

"You need to learn basic yoga and meditative breathing." Alaska rolled her eyes.

Jadox's tall silhouette casually walked out from the den across the clearing. Unaware of my gaze on him, he craned his neck to the thick treetops, and tears rained down his cheek. Despite the crying, his look encompassed pure joy while worshiping the view of his childhood home. The way he gazed at his Draven tribe with longing, wonder, and affection sparked a warmth in my soul.

Home. He was home, and I was lost.

Home meant belonging somewhere. No—belonging to someone. But who? All I had left was Hallie, and her grief was so raw that I wouldn't be able to lean on her for support, even when we reunited. I'd never even be able to tell her about my new confusing powers.

As if Jadox could feel my lingering gaze, his attention snapped to mine. My heart pitter-pattered, and I wished it to be slow and calm. But it kept thumping, even stronger than the passionate energy from my Circle. Some mysterious gravitational pull dragged me to Jadox, but I refused to accept the invitation. Gemm's prophecy echoed in my mind.

Must Link, or you'll never save his soul.

Whose soul? It didn't matter. Tomorrow, I'd journey to Vayu for the Unetlo Book and find someone there to Link with. I'd make my own future.

I turned to Alaska. "You're right about that Linking thing. It'd be stupid. But, hypothetically, what exactly does it involve if someone was interested?"

9

JADOX

Gemm's prophecy had scared the shit out of me. It was probably referring to me because I'd been searching for Kyra for a year. But maybe, just maybe, there was a small chance the Link would work with another Dravian. If I could convince Kyra to stay until the annual hunting trip was over, then Ryder, Alo, or Mato would be good options for her. But the thought of her connecting with someone else at such an intimate level gave me shivers. I had no choice, though: I had to convince her to Link if Draven's entire livelihood depended on her.

Draven's forest of emeralds and gold blanketed Chocolate and me. The lush scents of damp soil filled my nostrils. I never wanted to leave home again. Even the earthworms wiggling by my boots were a welcome sight. An apple fell from a branch above, gifting me a snack, and to my left, a birch welcomed me with open arms.

As I joyfully kicked at dried pine needles, the tips of the trees smiled down at me, reminding me of my youth with pebbles in my pocket and mud smeared across my cheeks.

But skipping over curved roots and dodging low-hanging branches still couldn't distract me from the fact that I had to figure out how to evade Nilson's threat. Why did he want Kyra? How did he know about her at all?

Ahead, Kyra gathered sticks for a campfire, determination set in her swift sweeps of the ground. I'd grown used to her fingers constantly tapping a mile a minute to a mystical drumming beat in her head. It was actually quite endearing. Holding back a smile at her constant intensity, I stole a moment, inhaling her scent from afar. Herbs from the den had latched onto her clothes, coating Kyra's every move with a crisp apple-cinnamon aroma. Delicious.

If only she wasn't so obstinate, maybe I'd kiss away every lingering smell of spice from her skin and replace it with my lips. Impossible—everything about her was temporary.

When she caught me staring, I raised my voice across the clearing, "Do you always have this much energy?"

She moved closer. "Are you always such a downer?"

"Are you always so infuriating?"

"What do you mean? I'm adorably delightful."

Soon, the Mystier males would return, and she'd hopefully accept one of them to Link and save our village. But that meant I needed to convince her to stay longer instead of meeting her sister. I sighed, thinking of the best way to convince her because, regrettably, I had already told Kyra too much about our world. There was no way to predict what information she might pass on to her sister about Mystiers. The Ordull army would torture her for intel if she was caught using Magik. Ordulls could never find out where we lived. In fact, it'd be better if Kyra stayed here indefinitely to learn how to protect herself.

Kyra's hips swayed when she moved closer. She pulled off her sweaty tee and threw it onto a pile of logs. A bright red sports bra matching the streaks in her hair covered the top portion of her hourglass form, and the black shorts alerted her curves. If I kept having these thoughts, I'd need to take a cold shower later or a frigid dip in the lake. My heartbeat accelerated, causing snapdragons to twist and ivy to grip the base of a picnic table so hard that it groaned in protest.

"Jay? Why do you look constipated?" Sometimes, when her wittier side shone through, I forgot how much trouble the woman caused.

"Like I said before, my face always looks like this."

"No, it doesn't. You're usually…."

I waited, interested in the last part of that sentence.

A little girl ran over and giggled. "Look, I make a cwown for a Pwincess." The girl held up her creation and smiled, missing half her teeth.

"Wow, that's so pretty." Kyra beamed.

Hmm– she was good with children. Interesting. Maybe she wasn't a heartless monster after all.

"Weally? You can have it." The girl handed it over to place it in Kyra's hand, and she bowed her chin.

"Thank you, my Queen." Kyra winked at the child.

She giggled in return. "We can go on an adventuh!"

"Yes! Where to, my lady?"

The girl's little nose scrunched up tight. "Hm, have you heawd about the Fowbidden Caves?"

Kyra stopped collecting firewood and gasped. "No, tell me all about them," she said, her voice turning as dramatic as a theater performer.

The little girl slowly crept her fingers along Kyra's forearm and scrunched her nose. "In the stowies, thewe's an evil demon who lives in the Fowbidden Caves in the shadows of Dwaven. She is one million yeaws old."

"Oh my!" Kyra pretended to faint.

"The demon answuhs a question for a pwice, but don't wowwy, she's twapped and can't get out of the caves."

"Oh, that's good. But why is she there?" Kyra leaned her chin on her hand, giving the kid all her attention.

"She's guawding something vewy special."

"What is it?"

I sighed, wondering how the same childhood stories were still circulating in the village.

"No one knows. But many Owdulls have twied to get it and died."

"Hmm, but why would they risk going into the cave?"

"I alweady told you, silly!" The little girl smiled even larger. "The demon has to answuh one question twuthfully to whoever finds the item. They want answuhs."

"Okay, that's enough story time." I rolled my eyes and said, "Go run along."

"She's cute. Landon wasn't really like that, though—he was always a quiet one." She sighed. "I miss him."

"How can I help?" I resisted laying my hand on hers.

"Distract me." Kyra leaned closer. "Are there any other campfire legends?"

"Of course."

"I'm all ears." Her look was ready to absorb any fantastical tale.

"You ready for this?" I stretched my arms behind my head, feeling the most confident I had in years now that I was back on my home turf.

"You've got the floor, Mister Griffin."

"For a thousand years, three divine nymph sisters reigned Lodesa." When I began the story, memories of sitting in front of Gemm by the campfire resurfaced. "Their names were Surh-Sig, Moroka, and Oniskel. They blessed one family in each Mystier tribe with enhancements to their Magik. Mystiers worshipped them like goddesses and were grateful for the blessings they bestowed on the next generation. Then one day, about eighty years ago, a greedy Mystier ruined it."

"Who?" Kyra's eyes widened.

"Your great-grandmother. Apparently, Elana Elidi was born with a wretched heart. The legends say that she sought destruction and power, even from a young age. The divine sisters tried to warn the elders about Elana, but they wouldn't listen. When Elana's tattoo formed, she was the only one in her family that the sisters did not bless with an enhancement.

"Elana was furious and vowed to seek revenge. As she aged, she created havoc and left her tribe. She hunted the Unetlo Book and translated an ancient spell that morphed the three sisters into despicable demons. Eventually, Surh-Sig became known as the Skin Scraper, Moroka as the Blood Maiden, and Oniskel became the Soul Stealer. After Elana cursed the elemental necklaces—emerald, crystal, and pearl—she confined the sisters to separate locations where they could never see each other again or use their powers. The end."

"Yeah, that's definitely a myth." Kyra giggled and messed with a stick in the dirt. "I bet that's the most you've talked in the last year." When she smiled, she had me drowning in treacherous waters, almost needing resuscitation.

The sunset was made to frame Kyra's face. I watched her, momentarily captivated by her raw beauty as she processed my story, then cleared my throat and glanced at the treetops.

"Wait, if there were three demons but four necklaces, why do I have the last one?"

"Well, if the stories are true, I bet Elana wouldn't want to get rid of her ruby."

She pushed some sticks with her foot. "Anyways, as *great* as you are at epic storytelling...."

"Hey, I *was* great."

"Sure, in your monotone soldier voice." She laughed. "What I still want to know about is Linking. Alaska wouldn't explain it to me. What exactly is it?" The curiosity on her face hinted at mischief.

After Gemm's prophecy, my plans changed. To save Draven now, I needed Kyra to Link. But before I gave her too much information, I needed to think of which Dravian would be the best match for her.

"Remind me to fill you in later. Let's practice summoning your fire."

Kyra stuck her hip out. "If Gemm is having visions about my future, then I deserve to know what this stuff means"

"Explaining Linking is...complicated."

Her eyes narrowed.

"Kyra. If you want me to teach you about Linking, you need to slow down and listen for once."

"I *am* listening."

"Fine," I groaned. "Mystiers stick to their own elements. Dravians partner with Dravians. Cydians marry Cydians. Get it?"

"Nope, this collegiate curriculum has my head *whirling*."

"Ugh, I can't even tell when you're being sarcastic because it's all the damn time." I rubbed a hand over my beard. "Okay, so most Mystiers are blessed with their Circle when they reach puberty, usually before sixteen. We're encouraged to train our Magik and stay within our village barrier until we turn eighteen. Then, as adults, we journey into the Ordull world. We can choose to stay out there or return. But honestly, most of us never want to leave our village in the first place or don't venture away for long. Here, we are safe and protected; we're a family."

"Did you want to leave?" She leaned forward as if straining to hear every syllable, but I knew her hearing was advanced now. So, why did she move closer? Could she be feeling the same tug that I was?

I rolled my lips and swallowed. Chocolate barked and stuck her head low with her butt up high, madly wagging her tail. Tossing her a treat, I ignored Kyra's previous question.

"Anyways, there are three rules Mystiers agree to follow when they leave their domed protection. One, never show an Ordull our Magik. Two, never reproduce with an Ordull. Three, never Link with a Mystier from another tribe."

She laughed again, her sweet smile reaching her eyes. "That's a lot of rules."

"Not really. They keep our people safe. Everyone knows it's for the best." I pushed a palm hard against my temple, trying to block out the stories Gemm had told me as a child. "The Fall happened because Elana Elidi Linked with a man from Cydon, your great-grandfather. That story definitely wasn't a myth. Their Magik doubled in strength but at great sacrifice. The borders of villages weakened, allowing the Ordull military to learn about their locations."

"So, what happened next?"

"Soldiers witnessed Magik and detained them. They were seen as an immediate threat. When the army raided the Mystier villages, the government kept the massacre a secret and disguised it with the lie that another country bombed Vuldow."

"I still can't believe it's been kept a secret for eighty years. More Ordulls must know about Mystiers."

"Probably the upper government. The Mystier population dropped to twenty percent of what it used to be. The places we picked to live still have strong shields in place, so it's easier to hide. We only have three original villages left, the strongest."

She slumped to the ground and placed both elbows on her knees. "So, then, what exactly is the Link?"

I stared at ants crawling along the dirt, then leaned back on both palms. Tiny pebbles pushed into my skin.

"Linking is a consensual pact. Two Mystiers must give each other permission to share power. Legend has it that the few who have Linked seem to lose a part of themselves and become...darker. Some even say that Elana had mastered ₾sμwi Magik."

"Can you tell me more about ₾sμwi?" Kyra asked, entranced by our history.

"Different Mystiers will have different answers. But I've been taught that ₾sμwi isn't natural; it's reserved for the creatures who have lost themselves to the shadows and deep dark."

"So, if my great-grandma was so powerful after she Linked, what happened to her?"

"We've been told that in order to break the Link, one of them had to kill the other."

A gasp flew from her lungs, and her eyes snapped to mine. "My great-grandma was murdered?"

I paused for a beat. "No, she was the one who drove a knife through your great-grandfather's heart."

"Holy Divinity," Kyra whispered.

I watched her shock evolve to strength and understanding.

"I never even knew Elana's child, who would've been my grandma or my own biological father either. He must not have been a better guy than my fake dad if he didn't stick around."

I gulped. "Kyra, about your fake dad—"

"I don't want to talk about him."

The only thought racing through my mind was the secret I was holding about what truly happened in The Crooked Chateau a year ago.

Surprisingly, she leaned her head on my shoulder, sending me into a spiral of confusion. Why was she moving closer to me if she didn't want a man to touch her? Her soft brown hair brushed against my neck. Unable to help myself, I sucked in the scent of her shampoo.

She sighed. "It's probably best I never knew my real dad; he'd be a disappointment too, just like all the other men. I mean, even *you* are a murderer." Quickly, she shifted and stared up at me through those long lashes. "After killing Quamir, and with everything else, there's probably some deep psychological shit you're processing."

It was the first time she had asked me how I was coping with everything after her wish had turned our world upside down.

"I'm a simple man. I just need Chocolate."

Under her breath, I caught her whisper, "Doubtful." Kyra buried her head in her hands and groaned, "I didn't make that wish thinking it'd actually happen." When she lifted her head, guilt was written across her face—an interesting shade on her. "You're the only one who knows what happened that night. Are you going to rat me out?"

"Depends. What are you willing to do to keep me quiet?"

"Seriously?" She nudged my side. "I hate you so much."

"I know."

"Linking with a man would be like resigning myself to a lifetime in a cage." Her arms curled over her chest. "But Gemm's prophecy said I could save *his* soul. It might mean Landon." Her tone turned as sharp as a dagger. "When are the other males returning? I guess I can see if any are interested."

I didn't want her to sacrifice that much of herself if she thought Linking was equivalent to prison. Scratching my stubble, I grazed a hand over my beard. I needed a shave. "We'd all owe you our lives if you save Draven. It's what I've always wanted, to protect my people."

"If I *don't* Link, I'll destroy another civilization. I can't be responsible for more deaths. But if I *do* Link, the protective shield around your village might vanish." Her gaze burned into my skin as if she was trying to pull the rest of my thoughts out of me.

"There's a chance Gemm's prophecy isn't what it seems."

"It's just like you: a confusing riddle."

I lit a match, the flicker igniting the sticks. "Nah, I'm an open book."

"If you're so open…" she said, the flame turning her gaze wild, then poisonous as the spark reflected in her iris. "…Then tell me about your parents."

"No."

Both her palms naturally lifted to the fire. "Right, you're such an open book. Tell me about your time in the army, then."

"Pass."

Silence enveloped us. It was my favorite time of day when the last moments of the sun faded beyond the horizon. The color of dusk matched Kyra's personality perfectly. If a moonflower were nearby, I'd pluck it and tuck it into her hair.

At that moment, a gorula poked its claw from the soil, reached one of its six arms to the sky, and then dug itself out.

Kyra screamed and pulled both drumsticks from what was left of her ponytail, pointing them at the creature. "What is *that*?"

A head followed, then its body slid out of the hole. I inhaled its shambling beauty as the gorula pranced to Kyra.

"Is it a monkey? A giant, furry spider? What is it?" She crawled closer to my side. "Will it hurt us?"

I sighed. "No, it's a gorula. She's as friendly as Chocolate. But remember what I told you."

"Don't accept its gifts."

I nodded.

"What will happen if I do?"

"Nothing good, trust me."

"*Should* I trust you?" She studied me with a look that made my cheeks warm.

"Yes, look." I placed my hand on the soft golden fur on the gorula's shoulder. Her broad shoulders and long arms resembled an ape, but those extra limbs reminded me of an arachnid.

I reached to help Kyra, remembering she didn't like being touched but hoping that someday, she'd accept my offered hand. Of course, like always, she ignored me and rose on her own.

"Come on, you can pet her," I said.

The gorula showed off her six muscular arms, and Kyra reached forward, slowly caressing her side. "Wow, can we name her?" At each pet, the pleasant smell of acorns, chestnuts, and hay ruffled off the gold fur.

"She probably already has one in her herd. Let's not offend her by trying to own her."

Fascination bloomed on Kyra's face and danced between her few freckles.

I stroked the spot between the creature's eyes, making the gorula purr. "Gorulas are known for never getting lost. If you're lost, they'll always know the way."

"Are you gonna quote some philosophical professor now?" She faked an ancient accent. "*Sometimes, the best way to find yourself is to get lost in a journey.*"

I smiled. Moments with gorulas were rare, and watching Kyra experience it for the first time was mesmerizing.

Suddenly, she smacked my thigh, making me jump. "Well, it'd be great if you'd stop flirting for a second, so I can start training."

"What? I'm not...you...you're absolutely enraging."

She moved closer to a camp fire, and I watched her, entranced by her connection with it. The energy engulfing us felt surreal—more power than anything I'd ever known lurked beneath her fingertips. Maybe that gold Circle meant that she really was special.

"Let's get to work. You need to be able to protect yourself in case an Ordull finds out who you really are."

"Maybe I should find out who I am first."

I already knew who she was. A creative musician who thrived on adventure, never backed down from a challenge, refused help, and prioritized family over anything else. Kyra possessed the fierce strength of an Elidian. I only hoped she'd never have to use it.

"Widen your stance and place both palms toward the sunset."

"Alaska already had me practice breathing for hours, so I'm definitely ready to defeat all the nonexistent cave demons."

"Safety isn't a joke. Pay attention. To master your power, I'll give you four challenges. First, light this stick."

Something shifted in her eyes, challenging my command.

"You want me to create fire?"

I truly wanted to slide a hand over the small of her back, but instead, I shimmied away and pointed to the pile of sticks. "That's exactly what I want."

"Right, super easy. And what are the other challenges? Maybe we should start with one of those instead."

"Patience, Kyra. When you find the need to respond immediately, try using the breathing techniques Alaska showed you."

"Do you practice your own advice? Your veins are popping like a madhouse." She tilted her head, following my swift glance to her chest, then eyeing me knowingly. "Oh, I get it now. So, when was the last time you got laid?"

I ground my teeth together. As the sun continued to lower, the hues of the evening sky cast an even more attractive golden shade on her skin.

"I can see your jaw twitching, Jay. Do you need to take a deep breath? Or should I put a shirt on?" Her mocking tone attacked from every angle.

I inhaled slowly, but her cinnamon scent hypnotized me. On the one hand, there was potential for the two most alluring breasts to be free and send me into a state of ecstasy. *No*. I didn't want her or her proud, persistent carelessness. Yet, accidentally straddling her on the floor of Gemm's den had been an intriguing perspective. I shook my head, erasing the memory of her hair pooled around her head when she was flat on her back.

"Uh, hello? Jay?" She snapped in front of my face.

An eerie gust of wind raced through the branches, raising the flame. Without warning, Kyra's eyes rolled to the back of her head, showing only the whites, and a cryptic sound thrummed from her lips.

"Ignis fervin calidum. Ignis fervin calidum." Her voice sounded like a phantom as it rose in volume and force. *"Ignis fervin calidum."*

How did she know a spell? What was happening? The fire stretched quickly over my height, blooming to the treetops. My heart battered with fear—the potential of Kyra demolishing all of Draven with her flames in the next minute clobbered me to pieces.

"Kyra!" Breaking my promise, I grasped her tight and shook her shoulders. "Kyra, snap out of it."

Her body seized violently as that foreign voice faded into a soft mumble, *"Ignis fervin cali—"*

I cradled her neck and pulled her to my chest, holding her limp body tight. "Shh, Kyra, shh."

Terror seized my bones, and I dropped us both to a kneel, needing to touch the soil for a greater source of support. Laying on our sides, the dirt coated my skin as I clutched her to my chest. Unsure if I could help, I called to my Circle to heal her mind. Mangled and distraught power felt wrong in my core as it was sucked from my tattoo.

"Heal her, damn it!"

The power swirled away from me, and I begged Divinity above that she'd stabilize. The fire went out, and Kyra's head slumped against my bicep, using me as a pillow.

"Kyra, wake up," I whispered.

Unconscious, she mirrored an exquisite angel. Softness wrote liquid poetry across her cheeks as her chest rose and fell like a calm wave. I brushed a long red strand of hair from her mouth, running my finger along her lower lip. Gemm's words rattled my mind while looking down at Kyra.

Must Link…or you'll never save his soul.

Whose soul? Mine? Maybe Kyra was here to save me. Maybe she wasn't meant to save Landon.

"Wh-what happened?" Immediately, her eyes fluttered open like silky butterfly wings and latched onto my gaze.

Concern inched its way into every fiber of my being. How did she know a spell? That wasn't normal, even for advanced Mystiers with years of practice.

"Have you ever seen the Unetlo Book?"

"No? Why?"

Kyra's Magik was strong—too strong—and she shouldn't know what power she had just shown. Maybe her gifted enhancement was a glossary of spells stacked up subconsciously. What kind of protection could she provide us with if that were the case?

"What happened?" she whispered.

"You said a spell."

"I did? How?"

"I'm not sure."

Groaning, she rolled away and hunched on all fours—eye to eye with Chocolate, who licked Kyra's nose. My watch chimed, and Nilson's face popped onto the screen. I twisted it so the screen was hidden and pushed my hands into my pocket.

"I'll be right back," I said, trying to keep my voice steady.

"Where are you going?"

I whirled around, and she slammed straight into my chest and ricocheted back.

"Woah! Ow!"

I almost reached out to catch her mid-spring, but I remembered how much she hated being touched.

"Why were you about to leave?"

"Nature calls."

"No, you're hiding something."

I'd have to tell her about Isaac hunting her soon. But since she'd immediately ask a million questions, first, I needed to figure out what he wanted with her. Hopefully, our barrier would hold against his threat, but my gut flared in warning.

Isaac Nilson was nearby. I could smell his presence in the air and feel him in the soil. How much longer did we have?

10

KYRA

The giant gorula grazing by a tree made a little purring sound. The fairytale creature was as unique as the songs I've written.

Jadox must have won the world's worst liar award in high school. Usually, his face showed me nothing but boredom on his flawless skin, yet he might've been hiding something. Why did he want privacy, and who kept messaging his s-watch?

Crickets stroked violins to my right, and owls hooted to my left. Sometimes, the music surrounding me was a comfort, yet, now, all I could focus on was Jadox's increased heartbeat.

"Tell me what's going on, Jay."

The statue planted his feet wider.

"Goddess, you're stubborn. Okay, this has been a lovely adventure. If you are done giving me any answers, then I'm leaving. Hallie's waiting."

"It's not safe yet." He worked his jaw.

"When will it be safe?"

"Soon." He turned toward Gemm's hut quickly and motioned for me to trail.

Against all rational thought, I followed. Chocolate frolicked close, choosing my side. Her soft fur grazed my ankle, and I petted her head. We passed another old elm with massive branches that tangled into braids. Gemm's prophecy repeated like a vintage audio pod.

Must Link before dawn at the Luna Festival, or Draven will perish. Must Link with the one who hunts her soul.

Jadox had been hunting me for a year. But I couldn't Link with him or anyone if it led to another Fall. But if I didn't Link, Draven might be destroyed. In frustration, I threw up both hands, knocking my knuckles against a branch. Wincing, I rubbed them. Jadox hovered his hand over mine, and in a single moment, my fear tripled.

"Please look at me." The deep rings of brown in his eyes reminded me of the rings in a felled tree trunk, as if he held the entirety of the woods in one meaningful look. "You can trust me. I'm not going to hurt you."

The sincerity of his words almost had me believing him. An inkling of hope tingled along the base of my neck and curled over my skin at the possibility of a man who might be safe–and also rugged, mysterious, centered. I shook the thoughts from my head. He probably held a whole bouquet of lies behind his back, full of worms, poison, and some side agenda. He even said other Mystier males would be in Draven, yet I hadn't seen one.

"Can I heal your scratch?"

"Fine, but I didn't ask for help."

"I noticed." A slight curve to his lip made me hold back a shiver.

Once he patched me up with an assumed silent spell, Jadox pushed open Gemm's door to a full kitchen of five women my age, all as gorgeous as Alaska with long, silky, raven hair. Great, all I needed was some competition. Not that I was competing for anything.

One woman scanned Jadox head to toe, then leaned back over her basket full of beans. Nostalgic memories wavered at the edge of my mind of Mom gardening in the summer, covered in dirt, asking me to help, then kissing my small nose—the times before things got tough.

"Gemm, may we use your oven?" Jadox asked. "Kyra needs to train."

"Shouldn't we ask them to leave?" I nodded to the women in the corner. "I might hurt someone."

Gemm smiled, showing loose dentures, then said, "Once there was a squirrel who ignited a campfire all on her own, and she brought her friends to boil cocoa, and no one burned their mouths."

"See, Gemm has confidence in you." Jadox nodded and flipped the knob to turn up the temperature. "Don't worry. We're used to practicing and training newbies."

"But this isn't my house. I shouldn't just—."

"Gemm likes you," Jadox whispered.

"Um, sorry to break up this riveting argument, but...." Alaska cleared her throat. "Jadox, do you remember Claire?" She pushed the thin, short woman to the front of the pack, her side-swept bangs covering half of one eye.

Jadox nodded, then reached to shake her hand. His forearm brushed against mine, creating a landmine of gooseflesh. I chose to ignore the comforting warmth of his skin.

Alaska pushed her close. "Claire, remember when we were kids? I enchanted all the doors to stay locked at night so Jadox wouldn't sleepwalk into the forest, but he climbed out the windows, and we'd find him sprawled on the forest floor, surrounded by foxes or wolves. Those were the good days before Mom and Dad...."

Jadox cleared his throat, cutting her off.

"Anyways, Claire likes fishing and camping, too. Maybe you two can meet up at the Luna Festival next week."

Apparently, Alaska fancied herself a matchmaker. At least she gave me an answer to one of the thousand questions I had. One week. I only had seven days to figure out what to do about Gemm's prophecy.

Jadox's throat bobbed. "I'll be...busy during the festival."

When he shifted an inch closer to me, a zap awoke my Circle and coiled deep into my gut. "Busy with what?" I turned the oven off.

"Training your Magik." He punched the buttons back on. "You can do this, Kyra. And I'm here to help."

"I won't be in Draven next week." Grunting, I turned the oven off again and blocked his access to it.

"Then I'll be where you are."

All the women slowed their projects and watched us. Claire sighed and turned back toward the table of vegetables.

"Who says you're invited to travel with me?"

Jay opened the oven door, and heat consumed the small den. Suddenly, everything felt right in the world. I welcomed the creature lurking beneath my skin, fueling me. I held out both hands and concentrated on my breathing. An image of a ring of fire zoomed in and out of focus.

"Uh, maybe we should step outside." Claire moved toward the door, but Gemm swatted a broomstick out, stopping her mid-stride.

"Once there was a woman with a wild heart who held all the crackles in her palm, but she bestowed a curse to the land."

"Sometimes your riddles terrify me, Gemm," Alaska said, but she sounded so far away.

Energy consumed me as I closed my eyes and reached out, imagining the sizzling sounds of a fire. Shadows crept through the den's window, cloaking us in darkness.

"When fear claimed the girl's heart," Gemm's voice dropped low. "She ran from the Link that could save her."

Puckering flames wrinkled and twisted in my Circle, roasting my stomach and consuming me with Magik. Hissing bursts splintered inside of me as I fell to my knees. My bones crashed against the stone floor. In the background, Jadox's muffled voice yelled something, maybe my name. The intensity of the heat devoured his voice. A high-pitched scream buzzed into my ears until I realized it was my own. A heavy hand pulled me back, but when I opened my eyes, a fire roared from the oven, nipping at the air like claws ready to take hold of me.

"I did it! I made that fire!" a smile bloomed on my face as I turned and jumped into Jadox's arms.

His eyes widened, but his solid hold on my waist squeezed reassuringly.

"Wait, let me go. You're the enemy." I backed away quickly and headed toward the door.

"Enemy?" Jadox asked. "Wait, just one second."

Gemm stuck out her broomstick to block my exit and proclaimed in front of the whole group, "Once there was a girl who held pain in her heart. And the pain lingered no matter what she tried, clutching her insides until she took a swim."

"Okay, thank you for that, Gemm." I sidestepped her slowly, but she grabbed my wrist.

"And once there was a man who scrubbed at his mistakes, trying to erase them all. But the scrubbing turned his skin raw until he kissed the girl under the Harvest Moon."

Unsure what to make of that, I glanced up at Jadox. A tightness formed in my chest when he lifted his gaze and locked onto mine. Fireworks were nothing compared to his eyes. Warmth crept up my neck and to my cheeks. Turning away fast, I switched off the oven and poured myself a mug of hot chocolate. The steam teased my nostrils in a flurry of ecstasy as I gulped it down. I could still feel Jay's attention on me. My skin tingled and a dangerous breath caught in my throat.

"When you're done with your little snack, you're going to make a fire outside," he said.

"I just mastered fire," I mumbled.

"I disagree."

Chest to chest, I rose on my tiptoes to try and stare him down. "Of course you would."

"You have two minutes. Don't burn your mouth."

After hours of rigorous training, a video call rang from my purse. I pulled out Quamir's old watch and walked into the dark forest to answer.

"Kyra?" Hallie whispered. "You're still coming here, right?"

"Yeah, why are you whispering?"

"It's not safe to call. But I forgot to tell you where we should meet. You won't be allowed into the president's headquarters." Her voice lowered as if she were talking to someone nearby. "No, Karen, almost every prison is empty now that all the males are…misplaced…."

I cringed as her eyes turned dead and empty. Hallie was in denial.

"Wait, that's a good point..." Hallie directed her attention to me again, "Syvonne Stirk might transfer witches to empty prisons. Let's meet at the closest prison. This one is still empty. Uh, hold on one second…It's at 2714 Crow Avenue here in the capital. Where are you?"

Based on the colder temperature, I guessed. "Uh…north."

"Well, only ten percent of hovercrafts are airborne, so you may need to take a hoverbus which is probably also delayed."

"I'll get there, don't worry."

"Great." Hallie's features clouded over again. "Did you hear about the new law passed an hour ago?"

"No, what happened?"

"All women aged twenty to thirty-five are required to fill out an application for pregnancy through the sperm banks, and trans women are required to make a donation if medically possible. A team of scientists has been formed to select the best genes and ensure the highest number of successful male births."

"That's…crazy. There's no way someone is going to force me to have a baby. I'm not filling out one of those."

"You won't have a choice unless you enlist. Plus, having a child is… it would forever change you." The beat of silence went on longer than it should've.

"I don't want to be changed. I'm fine just the way I am."

"Of course you are, but your only options are fighting in this army or potential motherhood. So, if you don't want a kid, come fight with me. A group called Aurum Orbis Society is already protesting against Stirk's orders. They want to stand with these witch bitches."

I ducked out of the way of a low branch as I walked further. "How do you know the witches are that bad?"

On the screen, her jaw dropped. "Are you serious? They took away Landon and half the world. Are you high right now? How could you defend them?"

"I'm not."

I stopped paying attention because behind me, I heard pieces of Jadox and Alaska's conversation. "Ryder, Alo, or Mato are all available for Kyra."

Wow, Jadox had the nerve to pawn me off onto one of his friends.

"Kyra? Did you hear me?" Hallie repeated into the phone.

An outrageous thud smacked into the forest floor outside. Chocolate growled. I jumped and whirled around. In the darkness, deafening booms thundered in all directions.

"I gotta go, Hallie." I regrettably hung up before she could ask more questions.

A giant crack split the hillside. Claire ran out of the den, followed by the others. They immediately formed a circle around Gemm in the clearing.

"He's trying to break through our barrier." Jadox dropped to a fighting stance.

"Who?" I asked.

All their arms were outstretched, summoning Magik and ready for whatever threat was coming.

"Is it Stirk's army?" Alaska's voice was sharp, angry, and fearless.

"No." Jadox glanced over, meeting my eyes. He checked his watch, then pointed to the forest. "Kyra, go find a gorula. It'll take you to safety."

"What? No, I can help."

"You're too weak, and this isn't Elidian territory. You may do more harm than good. Now, leave."

I moved toward him. "I can still fight."

"No!" Jadox's voice boomed. "You're a liability and will put us all in more danger. They don't want you here—go!"

"No!"

He glared and paused, "I don't want you here."

My heart stopped. Why did that sentence rip me to shreds?

I held his gaze for a full minute, making sure to only show rage rather than hurt in my eyes. "Fine, I don't want to be here anyway. Goodbye, soldier."

Another invisible crash shook the very air like a trembling spirit. With only the moon as guidance, I stomped further into the lush peppery green. Once out of sight, I'd leave Draven's world of secrets through their stupid Magikal veil and never have to see Jadox Griffin again.

After only a few minutes, it felt like I was already in the heart of the forest. I circled around, and the trail that was behind me had vanished. The trees looked like they were moving, resituating like a maze with each of my steps. Eerie silence sent intimidating beats from the roots underground up through my legs, communicating a message to return to Jadox's side, but I refused. Never–I never wanted to see him again.

A loud screech called out from the high branches. I froze and dared to squint up. My heart sped as I crouched behind a bush, holding my breath and trying not to move my sneaker against the twigs.

A heavy thump landed in the leaves behind me, and I could hear its breathing. I slowly pivoted, crouching my body into the smallest ball possible until I met a sweet gorula's eyes. It bowed and danced on its six legs like a toddler awaiting sugar. My body relaxed, and I smiled, holding out a dog treat I had kept for Chocolate in my pack.

"Here ya go. I know Jay says I can't name you, but can I call you Goldie?"

It purred and rubbed its ape-like paw against my forehead.

I swept a hand through their soft golden fur. "Okay, Goldie, I've heard you're good with directions. Can you take me where I need to go?"

Immediately, Goldie lowered flat on the ground on her stomach and spread all six arms out like a starfish.

I jumped on her back and wrapped my hands around her neck. "Okay, I'm ready."

Expecting her to run forward, I gasped when she jumped straight up to the trees. She climbed higher. Higher still. Then she swung from branch to branch. I clutched her neck tighter, and a gleeful chirping sound vibrated in her throat. The wind whipped my face, and there was no way I could contain my shock; even though we were high above safe ground, I smiled.

Freedom.

Goldie swooped to a lower branch, taking me with her. The flying sensation almost blocked out the distant whispers in the darkness ahead. Almost.

Sensing a change in the atmosphere, Goldie slowed and scaled down a tree branch slowly. The trees shimmied to the right and left, forming a perfect aisle on the path. Goldie slid me off her back to the long weeds. After exchanging a quick glance with my new best friend, she nudged my side into the darkness.

"Wait, this is not where I needed to go." Shivers crept up my spine, and frustration crushed my vertebrate. "You were supposed to take me to Hallie."

Whispers taunted my ears again in an ancient-sounding language that resonated deep in my soul. I tip-toed forward down the path. Goldie took my hand, dwarfing mine in her large paw. A tiny whine came from her when the Harvest Moon shone through the treetops, dimly lighting a cave entrance.

The whispers grew louder. *"Ignis fervin calidum."*

I didn't dare respond, but questions soared in my mind. Why had Goldie brought me to a cave? A small flash of orange erupted from within the cave, calling to me. I walked forward, entranced by the heat, the flames.

"Come, Elidi," the same snake-like voice whispered.

Goldie lurched forward, ripped my necklace off me, and sprinted away, stranding me in front of the cave.

"Hey!" I spun after her to follow. "Give that back!" When would this nightmare end?

"Come, Kyra."

The voice knew me. The vibe was wrong, toxic, as if a pianist made the slightest switch to a minor key. All the hairs on my arm spiked up, and a chilling tingle crept up my back. I stepped forward into the unknown.

11

JADOX

I could smell the sweat of the intruders through the barrier, spiced with rage and resentment. The sandstone wall and walnut trees cornered us. If we didn't win this fight, all of my people would be exposed. There was no fucking way I'd let harm come to a single Dravian.

I didn't know where Kyra had fled to, but at least she was fooled by my false anger and harsh words. I needed her to stay hidden. A zing flared my Circle, and Magik coursed through my veins, racing to my fingertips. I inhaled deeply and commanded the rocks to rise. They floated; sharp ends pointed directly to the barrier's entrance.

Alaska commanded the soil, and a hole immediately appeared. A tunnel formed, and she led some children to the opening. "Gemm, keep them walking through the tunnel. It will lead you to safety and close it behind you as you move."

Gemm shook her head and grabbed a sturdy stick leaning against the trunk. "Once, there was a warrior who never backed down from a good fight."

With a stern look, Gemm flicked her wrist in the air like she was orchestrating the grandest symphony. Hundreds of sticks hovered near my floating rocks, jutting their pointed ends toward the threat. Well, I guessed she was staying.

"Come on. I dare you!" Alaska yelled at the invisible booms shuddering our air.

It felt like toxins seeped through cracks in our shield and were poisoning our energy by the second.

I stepped forward. "I'm going out…alone."

Completely disregarding my command, my sister ran forward and jumped through the shield.

"Alaska!" I darted after her like a missile. The zap squeezed my muscles tight, and I rolled in a somersault onto a pile of dirt on the other side. Wind whirled and spiraled the scene out of control. Scrambling up, I dashed in front of my sister.

"It took you long enough." Nilson stood between a pair of oaks. He lowered his hands, and the wind died, settling the leaves of the forest back in their resting place. The thunderous booming ceased, and in just one moment, peace returned to the woods.

"Leave." I pointed west, in the direction of Vayu.

Seething darkness clouded Nilson's gray eyes, competing with the nocturnal gleam in every animal witnessing our exchange. "No. You have to pay for the pain you've caused."

"Nothing you do will bring Wes back."

He clicked his tongue and casually ran a hand over his high bun—much too confidently for a man this outnumbered.

"A storybook in our library tells a legend of a girl with a Golden Circle. Tell me, Griffin. What color is Kyra's tattoo?"

I paused.

"I know more than you think." His smile slithered high. "Linking with Kyra will change the course of history and bring the males back. The only obstacle in my way is you and your sister here. So, I'll only say this once more…move."

A fast wisp of wind pushed Alaska into my side, rocking me as I caught her.

"You're not allowed in Draven, and you know that."

"The treaties were void when you took away my son!" Nilson screamed.

To gain the upper hand, I had to say something to set Nilson off balance and surprise him. "Maybe I'll take away all the Ordull women next. They cause just as much trouble for us." I forced a rude chuckle. "Actually, why would you care? Rajitha is already dead."

In a heartbeat, Nilson launched himself at me. Mid-leap, he swiped something long from his back pocket. A whip. *Shit.* It sped forward, about to crack against my shoulder, just as Alaska zoomed in front of me. The whip slashed her side, and she screamed out, dropping.

"Alaska!"

"I'm fine," she growled from the ground.

Fury boiled inside me like bubbling lava and my fists clenched with the power of dynamite. Pebbles underfoot tremored. A seething roar exploded from my chest as I slammed my hand into the soil. Birds flew off the nearby trees, escaping the danger. My Circle scorched stronger than ever before, and the ground split between Nilson and us, creating a deep trench. The soil continued to shift, quaking apart, and the hole deepened, turning into a ravine. I used every ounce of power to separate Draven's walls from Nilson. Now, he'd have to fly to join us.

Nilson grunted in frustration far on the other side. Watching him lift both hands to the stars, I knew this battle was only the beginning.

"We don't have much time." Panting, I crouched next to Alaska and asked, "You okay?" My voice sounded hoarse, weak—but I had also never created a quake this large before.

When Alaska lifted the edge of her shirt, a giant angry welt was spread across her skin. My muscles felt like Jell-O as I hovered my hand over her injury. Gritting my teeth in concentration, I tried to heal her skin and absorb her pain. Nothing.

"It's okay, Jadox. I'll finish him. Go check on Gemm."

"Not a chance."

The smell of manure wafted through the new wind frenzy, followed by the scent of fur. A gorula was traveling closer, swinging above at top speed.

"Something's wrong. Please go back inside, Draven. Please, Alaska," I begged her, and thankfully, she nodded.

She crawled behind me and disappeared through the border. I turned to fight Nilson, but he wasn't on the other side of the ravine. The smell of the gorula grew closer, spiking alarm through my system. Out of nowhere, a gorula dropped from a branch directly in front of me. She held the Elidian necklace between her claws, then dropped it at my feet. *Fuck.*

"What happened to Kyra?" I searched the creature's face for any blood or sign of battle.

The gorula lay flat on the ground, belly down, and spread out her arms, inviting me for a lift. I couldn't pick up the necklace since it'd burn me.

"Take me to Kyra," Nilson's voice commanded from somewhere above.

My gaze darted up. He was already on a different gorula, his arms wrapped around its golden fur.

"Stop!" I jumped on my ride and clung on tightly.

"Too bad these creatures don't choose sides, huh?" He smiled and saluted as they jumped away.

The rest of the pack swung after, from branches to vines, with the ease of giant monkeys. My gorula moved so fast that the breath was sucked from my lungs. I could barely see through the chaos of darkness and whirl of branches we soared by, but my nose never deceived me. She was taking me directly to Draven's Forbidden Caves. My head pounded with adrenaline, and I prayed that my energy would return by the time we arrived.

I could feel my gorula's muscles working below my thighs, pulsing with strength. She reminded me of Chocolate—wanting to race. If I didn't have so much at stake, so much to lose, this could've been a moment of true bliss. I might have even smiled. Then a high-pitched scream struck the quiet night air.

"Kyra," I whispered.

My gorula slammed to a stop on a branch. Fifty feet high, the gorula holding Nilson rolled him off his back.

"*Shit!*" Nilson screamed as he tumbled through the air and smacked his arm into three branches on the way to the forest floor. He landed hard and stayed as still as death.

I stared, waiting for any sign of movement. There was no way I'd get so lucky for Nilson to die from an accident. But he lay still as a stone.

A soft groan came from below, then, "Help." Nilson's voice was wet like he was choking on his own blood.

Ignoring him, I braced myself to use Magik inside the caves.

"Please," a slushy sound begged from below.

Nilson's arm was bent at a sickening angle, and blood streaked his lips. He coughed, and more blood spat out. I buried my head in my hands quickly, cursed myself for having Gemm's heart, and then scaled down the trunk fast.

"Your rib probably punctured your lung."

He wheezed and tried to roll to his side but was unable. Fear etched deep into his irises when he locked onto my eyes.

"Heal me."

"Why?" I knew I would if my Magik was recharged enough, but I wanted to hear his bargain first.

"I'll…leave your…." He gasped. "…family alone."

I placed both palms on his chest and imagined dirt coating a ring of roots below me. "And you'll stay away from Draven."

He tried to speak, but only blood poured out, so a slight nod would have to do.

"*Terra angakok. Terra angakok.*"

My biceps burned with fatigue and my temples throbbed—completely spent. A wolf-like growl ushered from my mouth as I used every bit of Magik left to heal him.

His cheeks slowly turned pink again, and his eyes opened wider. Nilson's breath turned steadier, and his arm swayed back into a normal angle. He gasped and sat up, leaning against a tree trunk, patting his chest frantically.

"I can't believe you actually helped me." His lopsided smile had already returned as if this were only a game.

Quickly, I grabbed the whip sticking out of his back pocket, tied his wrists together, and then wrapped him securely to a tree. "You're alive, but now you may die from whatever creature decides to eat you tonight."

Leaving him behind, I ran toward the cave opening. I had already wasted too much time. The entrance was bare. No gate. No door. No protective shield. But, of course, no one sane would ever enter inside willingly—not after all the rumors of what lurked within. A layer of fog masked the delicious darkness unraveling in that cave.

I could smell Kyra's lotion on every surface. Why did she come here, of all places? Her cinnamon breath from the cocoa earlier lingered against the flat limestone walls. The faint smell of her drops of sweat stained the gravel underfoot, leading me.

"Kyra?" Stupidly, I whispered into the darkness as I trekked forward, tip-toeing into the silence.

The unforgiving darkness had a texture that crept over my skin. I shined my watch's light, unable to see more than five feet at a time. I weaved between stalagmites, their jagged teeth ready to gnaw straight to my bones. The further I ventured, the colder the air grew. Kyra's pheromones were quickly covered by the stink of rot, something festering and rancid. Soft, slow drops of water plinked from the cave's ceiling onto my forehead. An unsettling sensation haunted me, hovering between real and fake, life and death, truth and lies.

After a few minutes, more smells made me gag. Burnt flesh. Blood. Rotting organs. I plugged my nose and moved to the cave wall to brush my hand along the side. But the wall changed surfaces from hard to rubbery. I needed the rock's strength to maintain my focus. Pure revulsion crept into my gut.

Hoping I was wrong, I hesitantly shone the light on the cave's walls. At the disgusting sight, sour bile rose in my throat, but I swallowed it back down. On the walls, flesh was flattened and plastered like tapestries. It stretched as fast as I could shine my light. On both sides of the cave, there was beige flesh. Brown flesh. New flesh. And rotten flesh all hung on display. Dizziness rushed through my head, and I gulped.

"Kyra?" I glanced across the cave, my heart growing heavier with every passing moment.

"Like my décor, boy?" A voice not made of this world echoed softly from the darkness.

So, the legends were true. Something dark lived in here. I tried to summon my Magik, but no spark lit inside my Circle. Damn, Nilson and his wounds took every bit left.

"Where is she?" My heart pounded.

The voice slithered closer, tickling my neck with whispers. "I gave Elana's descendant a task. Your petite amour wants me to answer a question. She must earn that gift by first doing something for me."

I felt ultimate respect for Kyra's bravery. If only I possessed half her strength, I could always keep her and my family safe.

Mind whirling, I glanced around for any other exits. "Tell me where she is."

"Why do you care? She will break your heart one day," the mysterious voice hissed. "Don't you want to know my name?"

"No, with names comes power."

"Right you are. I know you, Jadox Griffin. You are in my own book of legends. Don't you want to know how your story will end?" A disfigured skeleton's hands with crooked, boney fingers stuck out from the shadows.

A pressure clamped down on my shoulders like an invisible weight was trying to suffocate me.

"Ask me my name, and your dear Kyra will not drown today."

"Where is she?"

"Ask me my name!" she screeched, her voice scraping the walls of my skull.

I swallowed hard, still tasting the foul vomit. "What is your name?"

"Surh-Sig." She lunged forward into my beam of light, showing obsidian eyes as sharp as death.

A flash of long, bright fangs sliced close. I bolted back, ramming my back against the wall of skin.

"Where is Kyra?" My voice boomed off the cave walls.

"Smell her fear for yourself."

Kyra's wet hair scent met my nostrils. Behind Surh-Sig, a splashing sound was followed by gasping. There was no way of telling what kind of sea creatures haunted the dark grotto. My arms ached to find Kyra and shield her from pain, but Surh-Sig pinned me to the wall. A slimy tongue licked the side of my face.

"I've never added skin as luscious as yours to my collection." Her silky fingers grazed over my abs. "We could have some fun first, you and I."

"Not interested," I gritted out, swallowing the bile that idea brought.

"Since The Fall eighty years ago, I have been cursed with an appetite for skin. Because Elana Elidi imprisoned me here, I am rarely given a way to satiate my constant hunger. But if you please me, Draven boy, then you will be rewarded with your life."

There was only one thing that mattered. And I had made my choice.

12

KYRA

I was treading water in the middle of a boiling lagoon. Hot waves splattered into my mouth and spurted water inside my throat. Miraculously, the heat didn't hurt, but some creature swarmed the depths below.

"Help!" I yelled.

I inhaled, holding in as much oxygen as possible. Seaweed wrapped around my ankles again and tugged me under. My arms paddled harder. Kicking with all my might, I freed myself from the weeds' clutches. Jumping into this death pool was the worst decision of my life.

Midnight indigo surrounded me in the crescendoing chaos, with only a speck of bright aqua deep in the center. Every muscle prickled with surrender, but I hadn't found what Surh-Sig demanded. And that treasure was my only ticket to receiving an answer from her.

Boiling bubbles splashed into my eyes, blinding my limited vision in the murky cave. My body tensed, longing for a break. Flashes of memories melted what was left of my energy–Hallie throwing a pillow at me, Landon teaching me how to activate his robot toy, and Jadox's smoldering eyes locked on mine. A dreamy sensation of his hand caressing my spine distracted me from the strong current sweeping me under, challenging my last breath.

Panting and thrashing, I struggled to keep my head above water. I visualized a ring of fire. Nothing. Weakness cascaded over me.

"Kyra!"

My heart battered faster than a pair of drumsticks in a presto song at the sound of his voice. I tried waving my arms, but scalding water drenched my face.

"Kyra!"

I knew exactly how far away Jadox stood from the acoustics of the cave bouncing his voice off the walls covered in disgusting flesh.

"Jay!" I screamed between gasps while trying to scoop and swim closer to the shore.

"I'm coming!" Jadox yelled, followed by Surh-Sig's hysterical laughter.

I was usually a great swimmer, but this lagoon held layers of traps under the current. I needed his help, but the heat of the water would probably burn anyone who wasn't Elidian. A flicker of a shadow swam below. Something or someone still guarded what I needed.

The loud battering of water rammed in my ears. I sucked in more air, fighting against the inescapable. A sea creature reached up and ran a scaly finger over my thigh. I kicked and spun, but it made no difference. Stunning navy eyes popped above the surface and snatched my attention as the wicked siren sang a hypnotic lullaby.

Love the demons of the sea,
Sleep, my child, eternity.
Elidi flames come to me,
Sleep, my child, eternity.

Let my voice lead your way,
Time to follow the blue ray.
Never need the light of day,
Time to follow the blue ray.

Love the demons of the sea,
Sleep, my child, eternity.
Elidi flames come to me,
Sleep, my child, eternity.

The siren pulled my leg hard, and a scream soared from my lips. She dragged me under the surface. Deeper. Deeper. Swirls of her long, flowy cyan hair danced in the water like streamers, but I could sense the poison lining each strand.

The depths reflected an aqua-marine light reflecting off diamonds and sapphires. In the middle, I spotted what Surh-Sig requested—Draven's ancient necklace. The giant emerald shone with obvious Magik, emitting a rippling signal from its core. My lungs ignited with need. Dazed, I tried to twist from the siren's sturdy grasp. *Oxygen. Please*!

Suddenly, the pulling stopped. *Air.* I needed up! Out of the corner of my eye, Jay wrestled with a siren. I stroked to the surface. The further I rose, the hotter the temperatures escalated. At the top, I gulped a sack of air, then treaded water until Jadox finally burst through the surface. He swam to the bank and crawled out, panting.

"Why did you follow me?" I hollered, my voice echoing.

"You're welcome." He held out a solid arm for me to grasp. "Come out. Your skin will burn."

"No! I've got this."

"You'll get yourself killed!" he grunted forcefully, his skin newly rashy. He hissed in pain.

"Jay, your skin is—"

"I know…"

"I'll be right back. Heal yourself, and don't follow me."

"This is suicide!" he yelled.

I still needed the necklace for Surh-Sig to answer a question. I took a deep breath, my conviction renewed with the much-needed oxygen, and kicking as hard as possible, I dipped into the murky depths toward the beating pulse of the Draven emerald. The piles of other gems surrounding it formed together into a mirror.

My reflection stared back at me, but instead of the usual red streaks in my long hair, golden streaks parted my locks. The illusion version of me lifted her shirt and showed me the Möbius Circle tattoo. However, it was not sitting there alone. Another Circle looped through it, connected like a chain.

My chest seized, and my vision blurred. I snatched the emerald and thrust it into my pocket. The melodic song ceased. A herd of sirens lurched out from the shadowy waters and chased me. *Need. Air.* I kicked. Swam. Stroked. Up. Higher. *Need oxygen!* I reached up and broke the surface, gasping.

Hideous laughter erupted from the cave's corner. Swimming toward the shore, I glanced around for Jadox in the darkness. Exhaustion beat into my arms, legs, and every inch of my being. I opened my mouth to shout his name, but only a whimper came out. Finally, I groped the edge of the bank, water washing up the side.

"Give me the necklace, mortal!" Surh-Sig screeched. Claws protruded from the shadows and scraped the rocky ground. When she turned her palm over, dangling skin made of nightmares reached for the emerald.

"Don't...give...." Jadox's weak voice mumbled from the darkness, then he coughed.

"The soldier dies if you don't hand it over!" Desperation laced every one of her haunted syllables.

I crawled, spitting water out with each clamber forward. My knees raked against the hard cave floor.

"Jay?" I whispered. "Where are you?"

"I'm...here." His voice shook, obvious pain layering his sounds and sending a raw strip of agony through me.

"The necklace, girl."

A violent razor-sharp claw attacked my calf, slicing my skin open with one smooth tear. I cried out and grabbed my leg, accidentally releasing my grasp on the emerald. It clattered to the ground and rolled with the chain in its wake. Blood trickled out of my leg and trailed into the black lagoon. A siren's song echoed louder with each second.

"Jay?"

A large heap lay behind a boulder to my right, shifting slowly and groaning.

"Jay?" I dragged myself closer to his mound of a body, stopping when I saw his face.

Red blisters spotted his skin. I jerked away in shock. His gorgeous bone structure had transferred to a minefield of irate sores, popping and gushing steam like an eruptive volcano. Jadox writhed and moaned, clutching his stomach. Shaking, I lifted his shirt. Boils covered his entire body, gushing head to toe.

"Fuckin' Abyss," I whispered. He'd die within minutes.

A harsh cackle burst like a firecracker from Surh-Sig. Time stopped, and Jadox's squirming stiffened. All around us, onyx jewels floated impossibly, shimmering in the air like an omen.

"Thank you, child." Surh-Sig hissed only to me as she emerged from the cave's shadows. She glided ghost-like above me. Her figure was one of story-book monsters sprinkled with doom and death. Wide, round black eyes peered through me, into my soul, sending a shudder up my spine. Over her exposed bones, chunks of mismatched skin were draped like scarves, slippery and sleek, flowing in a nonexistent wind. The emerald's chain dangled from her skeletal finger.

"Now that I have my necklace, you may ask one question, Elidi child."

I stared at Jadox, knowing I could ask how to save his life. "How can I bring my nephew, Landon, back?"

Her silky skin wrinkled when her eyebrows rose.

"How can I save Landon?"

What might be the equivalent of a smile wormed up her glossy cheeks, showing those sharp fangs. "You must Link with the one who hunts you. He knows you better than you think. Drop your wall and let him in. It is the only way. But all choices come at a heavy cost. Be warned of *who* you choose." She turned and fled.

"Wait! You never told me what you needed the Draven emerald for."

Surprisingly, she stopped and turned. The arch of her back straightened as she reached the wall and ripped off a piece of flesh. "You foolish mortal. I've been trapped in the forbidden caves for eighty years. I have enchanted wanderers inside these caves in the hope they could free me. The only way to escape was by receiving my necklace. Each prisoner refused or failed, sacrificing themselves as a trophy on my wall." She threw her head back with a laugh. "But you… I didn't even have to charm you, girl…you stupidly volunteered."

Guilt crushed me from all sides, and I tried to connect with the Magik in my tattoo, but some force blocked my access. When she sped away, time restarted. Jadox's frozen state blasted back to life. He gasped and cried out in pain.

"Come on!" I tried to lift him, guilt gnawing at me for my question choice. "Gemm will have herbs to heal you." Pulling on his arm, I tried to drag him.

He pawed at the air, completely delirious, mumbling for his sister repetitively. My heart was breaking for him.

"Jay, you're too heavy. Try to stand."

His eyes rolled to the back of his head.

"Shit!" I dropped his hand, ran through the cave into the night air, and screamed as loud as possible. "*Help*!"

Leaves rustled by my ankles, and the water droplets from my clothes pitter-pattered against the sticks and my bare feet.

"Help!"

Something shuffled behind a tree, and a little squeak huffed out.

"Who's there?" I peeked around the trunk.

Goldie sat with two large hands covering her eyes and the other four supporting her position.

"Goldie, I need help! Can you take Jadox to Gemm?"

She reached for a wad of berries hanging from a bush and handed it over while bowing her head. A gift.

I backed up. "I can't accept a gift from you."

She stuck it out farther, but I only retracted more. Goldie sprinted past me into the cave.

"Yes, he's in there. Please carry him back to his home."

Still clutching the fruit, Goldie leaped ahead from paw to paw, splashing in the shallow puddles of the cave. Limping, I raced to where Jadox lay. His back was arched, his skin flaming rose-red like death over every section, and sweat dripped down his neck. With eyes closed, he gnashed his teeth together and grimaced in agony. Each sound he croaked sounded like nails on a chalkboard.

Goldie handed the berries over to me again.

"Kill me," Jadox mumbled.

My gaze frantically darted between him and the berries. Unsure what it would do, I swiped the berries from Goldie and shoved a few of them in Jay's mouth. Clamping his jaw shut, I ordered, "Swallow, Jay!"

I cradled his head in my lap, his raven hair spilling over my thigh. Goldie smeared the rest of the berries over his cheeks and blistered shoulders. The steam rising from his body tapered and disappeared.

His groaning died and only soft hums vibrated from his throat. The light brown shade of his skin slowly returned, erasing the boils. Those bushy eyebrows, always full of his stern expressions, softened, and the lines carved into his painful grimace turned to putty. He finally opened his eyes. I let myself drown in the intensity of his gaze for a moment.

"Never thought you'd cry over me, Petal."

"I'm not." I sniffed and brought a hand to my cheek, wet with tears.

"You're so beautiful." Then Jadox's eyes shut, and he instantly fell asleep, smooth snores thrumming from his chest.

Watching his chest rise and fall slowly sent a wave of peace through me. Comfort. No, I couldn't lower my walls for him. Now that he was safe, I needed to leave. When Jadox awoke later, he'd be healed from the berries, and I'd be halfway to Hallie's.

I tucked a strand of his sopping hair away from his closed eyes and caressed the side of his face. He'd never have to know about this strange urge I had to touch him. Since I was leaving, I'd never have to admit how scared I was of losing him. Caressing his face while he slept felt like…home.

We sat like that for hours, his head in my lap, and I almost fell asleep until—

"You're touching me," he mumbled.

I jumped.

"Did the sirens put a spell on you?" His eyes were still closed, a tiny smirk rising at the corner of his lips.

I jerked my hand away from his hair and dropped his head from my leg. Jadox slowly rolled over, lifting himself to a seated position with obvious struggle. He leaned against the cave wall, his head craned to the dark ceiling. Despite hating him for thinking he knew better, for following me to the cave, for playing a stupid hero, I couldn't take my eyes off him.

"Of all places, why in the Abyss did you come *here*?" Jadox weakly staggered to his feet.

I followed as he began limping toward the exit of the tunnel. I'd let him lean on me if I were a good person.

"Goldie led me here," I said, "you told me they always know where to go."

He shook his head, frustration written in his wrinkles.

"You could've warned me, like, *hey, Kyra, don't go to the creepy cave that whispers your name.*"

Jadox groaned as he used the cave walls for balance. "It was only an ancient legend. We knew something was wrong over here, but I never expected *that*. This cave is on one of the borders of Draven. We're technically not inside Draven or outside of it right now. When Ordulls accidentally cross this area, we didn't have to worry about them finding our shield entrances because they'd always disappear without a trace."

I snorted and immediately regretted it from the terrible, rank smell in the cave. "Convenient."

"You gave that monster our strongest heirloom." Exhaustion spewed out of his look. "We gained *nothing* from coming here." His voice grew defeated. "Actually, we lost two necklaces during this escapade."

"Two?" I paused. "Oh, yeah, Goldie took mine." I stole a moment of bravery and magnetized my side to his, pulling one of his arms over my shoulder so he could lean on me. "But you can't technically blame me. You're the mighty savior who commanded me to leave Draven. What even happened back there?"

His nose briefly twitched in that way I had noticed when he was keeping something from me. "Everyone in Draven is safe."

"Well, look on the bright side. It's not like *you* almost died or anything."

What I really wanted to ask was why he came after me. Why did he care enough to track me? Why did he put himself in danger for my sake? It didn't make sense. But I held my tongue.

Once outside the cave entrance, he tilted his head, staring at me with such intensity that all I wanted was to wrap my hands around his neck and calm his pretty pout. "Wait a second, how *exactly* did you save me from the boils?"

I felt my cheeks flush. "Uh, I didn't. You healed yourself."

Goldie poked her furry head from behind an oak tree and purred.

"Kyra! What did you do?" Jadox's lips rolled into a straight line.

Defying physics, a gust of inexplicable force moved our bodies and clasped our wrists together. A vine flew through the air and wrapped around both our hands. I tried to rip it apart, but the draw was too strong. We pulled and tugged. It was unbreakable.

Jadox's thicker eyebrow of the two, rose, forming a picturesque mountain peak on his face. "I'm definitely going to hate this."

13

JADOX

Kyra tried to pull her wrist from mine, but we were Magikaly bound.

"Is this vine going to handcuff us together forever?" she hissed, so close to my ear that I almost couldn't hear the owl wildly hooting above.

I rotated our wrists, searching for any key to unlock the hold between us. "Answer my question, Kyra. How did you save me?"

Her eyes dropped—for once—and the few ruby strands in her hair covered her face when she mumbled, "I accepted healing berries from Goldie."

"Who's Goldie?"

"The gorula."

Despite the weakness barreling through me, I raised both hands to my temple, accidentally pulling Kyra's wrist along with me.

"Ouch!" Her whole body leaned into me.

"The gorula cursed us, Kyra!" I stomped toward Draven's village, tugging her along behind.

She wrenched her wrist back, almost popping my shoulder out of its socket.

I swiveled, getting tangled in our connected arms. "You should've left me to die. Now we are *literally* stuck together."

Rage devoured her sweet fuckin' perfect face. She raised both our wrists, inspecting our skin. "Can we cut through the bind?"

"We can try, but it's sealed with Magik."

Her chest rose and fell fast, mirroring my own feelings. "I'll fix this. I will."

We passed black cherry trees in silence, and I could smell hibiscus plants ahead, leading the way back home. At least I could still track. Thankfully, she stepped in sync with me as I squinted into the night's inky artwork. Wait, the stars were in the wrong spots. My palms turned clammy, and it felt like needles covered my body.

"Jeez, Jay! I can hear your heartbeat." Her big, unique eyes widened. "Why are you freaking out?"

"Time has passed." I swallowed the terror. How much time had passed in that cave? I punched buttons on my s-watch and brought up the local news station. Six days? Fuck!

"We lost six days." I tried to keep my voice calm. "Six days passed while we were in there."

"That's impossible. It was only an hour or two."

I sunk into a pit of disbelief. Storybook fairytales of demons and time warps weren't supposed to come true. We just lost days of important time—time I needed to convince Kyra to Link. Now, we had one day until the Lunar Festival. Unless Gemm canceled the festival after Nilson's attack. I'd have to remind everyone not to tell Kyra about him. I should've crushed his windpipe when I had the chance. Hopefully, he was still tied to that tree where I had left him, or some bear had devoured him already. Either way, he should be dead. Not even a Mystier could survive six days without water.

Braided canopies of willow trees dangled their branches, swaying in rhythm to our steps.

As I started my meditative breathing, Kyra demanded, "We're going to Hallie's now."

"Well, you're literally stuck with me, so we're going where I decide." I wanted to fold my arms across my chest but couldn't with her connected to me. Stomping away was also out of the question so I wouldn't dislocate her shoulder.

"Who put you in charge?" she fired.

"You make terrible decisions."

"Excuse me?"

"Kyra, you volunteered to enlist in an army whose focus is to capture Mystiers like you. What else...let me see, you walked into the forbidden caves alone and handed over one of the strongest Magikal tools to a dangerous demon. Oh, and you accepted a gift from a gorula!"

"You were going to die if I didn't."

"Why do you care? You clearly don't want a man in your life."

She froze and rolled her lips.

Staring at her treacherous lips, I imagined brushing mine to hers or nibbling her ear–either would suffice. Too bad I didn't hate her as much as she despised me.

Kyra pulled me in the opposite direction and walked faster. "Hallie's waiting for me."

I lagged, so she'd have to tow my weight. "Right, and once we're out of Draven, how do you think you'll explain that our wrists are glued together by a plant?"

"I'll figure it out."

"Let me guess...alone, you'll figure it out alone."

"I don't see any other way," Kyra spat.

"Of course not."

"What's that supposed to mean?"

"Why don't you ask me for help?"

"I have!" Anyone living on the other side of the country could've heard her at this point. "I've asked you to help me get to Hallie, and you keep holding me back. Why exactly? It's not like you want me around either."

She had a point.

I sighed. "Can we sit for a minute, please? My skin still burns when we move fast."

"Oh." She immediately slowed.

We struggled to sit at the same time to avoid anyone's elbow or shoulder popping out from fast movements. Quietly, she traced circles in the dirt with a twig, then tapped it on her bare foot, covered in scratches.

Far off, I could smell burning leaves. It drifted closer, easing my mind into a memory from my teen years, shooting off fireworks around a campfire with my buddies. It was too bad fireworks only reminded me of gunshots now.

Kyra rubbed two sticks together fast. "If I can't start a fire with my Magik, maybe this will work."

"I can help train you."

"Why can't an Elidian teach me?"

I pulled a lighter from a pocket and lit the end of her twig. "Elidians are the rarest form of Mystiers, especially after The Fall. Our guess is that Elidians are nomads, living in solitude."

Mesmerized by the flame's flicker, she waved a hand through the heat. I felt her body shudder next to mine and smelled her aroused scent due to the new fire. "Okay, wise one," she said with a spellbound look in her eyes. "Teach me. The fire calls to me. I already tried imagining a ring like you said, but it didn't work."

"What were you thinking about when you imagined it?"

She licked her lips as she tilted her head, riveted by the dancing flame. "Probably not dying."

Concern tightened around my Circle at her entranced gaze. Some Mystiers turned dark when their powers were too strong. Kyra was an anomaly with her Golden tattoo, so maybe the legend of cursed Ꮳsμwi really did exist too. I didn't know what to expect from her Magik.

"You need to focus on living instead of not dying." I studied her, trying to keep her focused. "What does living mean to you?"

"What?" An adorable giggle crept out of her throat, snapping her back to reality. "Are you a psychotherapist?"

"Just answer the question. What would your ideal life look like?"

"Probably winning the lottery."

"Nope, if you want your Magik to work, you've got to dig deeper. What matters to you more than anything else?"

"Freedom from men and your cruelty." Her fierce eyebrows knitted together. "That's as deep as it gets."

I leaned my head against the scratchy bark of a tree and stared up at the stars, mentally labeling the constellations. "You shouldn't have accepted the gift. We could be stuck like this forever."

"One of us will eventually kill the other to get free." Her head slanted on my shoulder, a single moment of vulnerability at the most confusing time.

Wondering where she was going with this conversation, I tried not to move a muscle.

She smiled. "How long do you think we'd last? I think you'll be the first to break. I bet you'll try to kill me in my sleep tonight."

"Give me more credit than that." I smiled back. "I'll bet we both last four nights, but you'll be the one to snap first."

Kyra rolled her eyes. "No, I'll outlast you."

"Then I guess we're stuck together."

"And why is that?"

"Because I'll never hurt you, Kyra."

Her gaze dropped to my mouth before saying, "You look positively thrilled to be tied to a woman for eternity."

"It's always been a hope." My voice softened as I confessed, wondering if she'd think I was joking still.

Kyra slowly met my gaze. "Do you wish you never entered the cave after me?" There was a chilling edge to her voice.

"No, best hot-tub accommodations. Five-star service and the décor were one of a kind."

She snorted in laughter, making my heart patter fast.

"We could post a review, but finish it with, a *deathly smell, couldn't find the source*."

A deep chuckle spurted from my chest. "I disagree. You still smell like…."

A dream. She smelled perfect.

"I've been running and sweating in the woods, then swam in a death lagoon with evil sea creatures. I probably reek."

"Is this your way of telling me that I stink?"

"Well, we're gonna be stuck together, so how is this going to work? At some point, I'll have to bathe...."

"And at some point, I'll have to...."

She glanced at my crotch. "Oh, we should establish ground rules until we figure out how to undo this."

"No sex," I mumbled.

She snorted again absolutely adorably. Why the Flames were her annoying habits also endearing? "Sex was the first thing you thought of?" Her laugh sounded like a witch and angel mixed. "Of course, no sex. Not now or ever." Kyra looked around at our surroundings. "But I do want to wash off. Can you smell any lakes?"

"You knew I had enhanced scent?"

"I'm not an idiot, Jay."

I nodded south. "There's a lake half a mile this way with a waterfall."

"Great, I'll hold my breath until then because you smell like Surh-Sig."

"I'm not *that* bad."

"Rule number two, you can't touch me without my permission."

I lifted our locked wrists. "Uh, how is that possible?" Shaking my head, I let a grin claim my cheeks. "There's no way any of this will work."

"Rule number three, we head straight to Hallie after our bath."

"No, we need Gemm's knowledge to undo this curse. Draven is first. Plus, I need to say goodbye to Chocolate."

"Chocolate is a high priority, true," she said, and I caught another half-hidden smirk blessing her cheeks. "Fine, but I'm leaving the second Gemm unhooks us from this curse."

I sighed, counting how many hours I could prolong the walk back to Draven to spend more time with her. I might as well learn a thing or two until we broke the curse.

"Deal, but let's play the question game again," I said.

"Seriously?"

"Do I look like I'm joking?"

I focused on the nearest pine before her eyes could swallow me whole. As we moved toward the scent of the lake, I caught whiffs of fish. Fresh water. Woods. Lingering soot from campfires weeks ago. I could smell a herd of deer a few clicks to the east. Autumn leaves crunched underfoot as fatigue from the night rolled in.

"I can hear it." Sincere awe struck a chord in her voice.

When we passed the next oak tree, a towering waterfall cascaded into white foam ahead. Fish sparkled like diamonds at the base of the pool, shimmering through the clear water.

"I'm surprised you'd ever want to go in the water again after that cave," I said to her.

"Fear doesn't control me."

"Everyone gets scared sometimes."

"I don't. What I *will* admit is that was some freaky shit back there. Did you see the mermaid-siren creature?"

"No, I was too busy burning to death."

"Right, too bad it wasn't made of lava. That could've been fun." Kyra tore off her shirt, then realized the sleeve would be stuck hanging at our joined wrists. "Uh, how is this gonna work? I don't really want to take a dip with all my clothes on again."

Trying my best not to check out her cleavage, I swiped out a knife and cut the fabric so it'd fall off.

When she shimmied the hem of her bra, my heart shuttered. "Do you want me to turn around?"

"I don't care, Jay. You're ancient. You've seen all this before."

"Ancient?" As I tore off my shirt, laughter flowed, releasing so much tension. "I'm not even thirty."

She raised one brow at my bare chest. "Twenty-eight, right? You're super old, dude."

"Three years older than you. Maybe you're too young."

And with that, Kyra wiggled out of her bra. I froze. Holy shit. Entranced. Her breasts were glorious, suckable, and edible. My breath hitched in my chest, and I bit my lip, averting my gaze to an immensely captivating squirrel. Before I could steady my heart rate, she shimmied out of her shorts and kicked them aside. Fuck. Her curvy form jolted a ping in my tattoo.

Steadying my breathing, I turned away.

"Your turn. Pants off, soldier."

I squeezed my eyes shut so tight that I might've popped a vein. "Nope, these are staying on. That's rule number one now. The only one that matters."

"Whatever, let's go." She lurched forward, lugging me behind.

I kept my eyes squeezed shut for my own sanity.

"It's fun to see the little vein in your forehead throb when you're angry."

Anger was the last feeling rushing through my blood. Ankle deep, I used every bit of energy to keep my focus on the scents of the swaying trees, branches, and leaves. But when she accidentally splashed me, my eye flew open to her small waist and bare, round ass.

Don't turn around. Don't turn around.

She did. The Hunter's Moonlight brightened her skin, sweeping dreams from her shoulders all the way to her belly button. Just below her golden tattoo was a thin pathway to glorious bliss.

I suddenly hated rules.

"Still have your knife?" Playfulness lingered at the corners of her lips.

I tapped my back pocket, finding it difficult to breathe. "Uh…um, yeah."

"If you drown, I'm gonna need you to cut your hand off, so I can get to the surface."

Laughter had never felt so good. "Roger that."

"Roger? Hm, tell me about your time in the army."

"There's nothing to tell."

Curious, she eyed me, "I'll get you drunk at the Luna Festival, and you'll pour your soul out to me."

"I thought you weren't staying in Draven that long."

Her eyes flickered, and I wished I could translate the meaning. "Right, I'll be with Hallie, destroying one evil witch at a time." She shook her head, erasing the smile I wished I could keep on her face forever.

Wading into the shallow end together, I tried to keep my gaze on the crashing waterfall. That didn't matter. Kyra's confidence absolutely hypnotized me.

"Do you embarrass easily, soldier?" She grinned and splashed a little water on me. We waded deeper until the shallow ramp angled low, then we both were treading water. Because of our bond, our bodies kept touching, and sparks of desire shot up my core.

"Question number one." I gulped. "When did you start playing drums?"

"When I couldn't stand being home after school, so probably twelve."

I longed to hear her elaborate, but instead, she took a turn.

"Question number two, have you ever done *this* before?" She licked her lips.

Damn. Why did she have to be naked?

"Have I ever been cursed and glued to an annoying woman? I can't say that I have."

She ducked under the water for a moment, and when she came up, it looked like little beads of diamonds clung to her collarbone. I was dying inside. Dead. A heart attack had taken my soul to the spirits.

Kyra floated, putting her hardened nipple directly in my sightline. I could take her in my arms, kiss her, run my tongue over that bottom lip, or caress her neck. Instead, I cleared my throat and sucked in a breath.

"I meant have you swam here in this lake before?" she asked.

"All the time as a kid. Do you see that tree over there by the waterfall? Some friends and I used to tie a rope to the top branch and swing through the waterfall. I always pretended the other side of the falls was the entrance to Ordull."

She turned upright, releasing the tension on my shoulder from helping her float while paired together.

"We're not supposed to leave Draven until we turn eighteen."

"But you wanted to leave."

"My parents…never mind."

She moved closer, not that it took much effort. I could feel the warmth of her breath on my neck. "I have a bottle full of secrets, Jay. There's room for one of yours."

"My bottle is all darkness, full of thick, black ink." My voice felt stuck in my throat.

"Then open the top and spill some out."

My chest tightened, and I wasn't sure if it was because of the genuineness in her eyes or the thought of my parents' murderer—or maybe it was just that a hideously gorgeous woman was inches from touching my skin. The last thing she wanted was my hands anywhere near her.

"Okay, soldier, I'll spill my secrets first." The muscles in her neck tensed and pulsed. "When I was five and Hallie was eight, we had a three-year-old brother. He was our everything." Kyra's eyes dazed out of focus as if she had wandered back in time. "We were on vacation at the beach, and I was holding his hand as the waves crashed onto my knees." Her words quieted and were twisted with torture. "Our father called me to our tent for help."

I clenched my jaw together. Watching the raw ache in her features twinged a deep torment through my Circle.

"When I turned around to the shoreline, my little brother was gone." Her shoulders trembled. "I tried to dive after him. I kicked until my legs gave out and swam deep until my lungs were on fire, but he was just…gone. And I was only five. After that, my father, well, my fake dad, never looked at me the same way again. He blamed me, and each year, he increased his harsh insults. And then I managed to date Quamir, an asshole who mirrored him."

My stomach coiled with fury toward those men in her life. Guilt had weighed on me for the past year for murdering Kyra's stepdad. But now, it seemed like he was put in my path to help her be free of him. I was glad I had killed her stepdad. At least she'd never have to suffer at the hands of the man who raised her again. At some point, I needed to tell her the truth.

She wiped away a single tear. "I don't blame myself for my brother's death. Maybe that makes me a terrible person."

I pressed my lips together, guessing where she was going with this. Now, things made a bit more sense.

"Other people blamed me for my brother being lost to the ocean, though. But it was my stepdad's fault. I was only five. That day was the beginning of the end."

We waded in silence until I could tell she wanted to change the topic, so I offered, "You should stay for the Luna Festival. The food is one of a kind."

A contagious yawn ping-ponged between us. "No way, Jay."

"Chocolate needs you."

"Hallie needs me. I'm her rock."

"Who's *your* rock?"

Kyra opened her mouth to answer, then closed it slowly.

"Let's get dry," I said.

She nodded, so I swam us back to the bank, helping her follow with each slow movement. Leading her to a patch of soft grass, I used every bit of effort not to touch her wet skin, but each movement of her arm carried my wrist with her when she dried herself off with her shirt.

"Here." I looped the hole of my dry, ripped shirt over Kyra's head. "You'll be warmer."

She accidentally bumped my chest, then sat, pulling me down with her. Kyra's gaze held a violent vow. Not in any world would I have been able to resist her if she made a move. But instead, with wrists awkwardly entangled, she leaned her head on my chest. I didn't dare move. Why did she feel comfortable touching me now? Did she realize what she was doing? Water droplets dripped from her hair down my bare skin.

"I have another secret, Jay."

Almost too terrified to speak in case it'd break the moment, I whispered, "What's that?"

"Sometimes, you're not totally awful." Her fingertips played a light rhythm on my chest.

I realized that with our wrists connected and her nearly naked body next to mine, we were already linked in our own way—prophecy or not.

"Goodnight, soldier."

I tried not to watch her fall asleep but couldn't help myself from my angle. Goddess, she was breathtaking. Irritating as Flames, but worth the agony. I caught myself in a smile, then clenched my lips together. After she was humming soft snores, I held up my free hand and slid my watch off carefully. Using one hand, I muted it and checked for messages from Nilson. None. Good, maybe a bear ate him whole. Or Surh-Sig. I shuddered at the potential massacre of his ripped flesh.

A news broadcast interrupted my thoughts, silently flashing across the bottom of the screen. On a stage, Syvonne Stirk sat in her hoverchair in a white and lavender suit next to two women strapped to electric chairs. Fear strangled one's eyes while a hollow shade owned the others. They both wore rags, cut short to reveal the Möbius Circle tattoo on their abdomen. *Cydians*. I held my breath. A banner transcribing her speech was scrawled along the bottom:

We will not tolerate terrorists. This is the first of many executions of our witch prisoners. We will conduct two a day until their leader meets with President Stirk.

Syvonne nodded to someone off-camera, and the two women were electrocuted in front of all of Lodesa. These were live deaths for the world to suffer through. We were living in a new age. This Ordull president had declared war on all Mystiers. Now, there were even more reasons to Link than just saving Draven—we needed the increased power to fight against an army. I'd have to convince Kyra to Link.

14

KYRA

I awoke flat on the ground, nuzzled into Jadox's neck. My limbs were sprawled all around his torso. Despite my shivering, I scooted away, definitely not taking notice that he was only wearing briefs. Miraculously, spending the night bound to him hadn't been complete torture. My dreams had inspired lyrics about murdering mermaids and fantastical demons, but maybe the reality of being with him wasn't totally worse than those nightmares. In a small way, Jadox was…tolerable.

When I tried to roll away, the tug against my wrist reminded me once again of our curse. Connected. This was torture, except for the many moments when it wasn't, such as when he slept so soundly that his face was finally the image of calm and peace.

Sometimes, I wished I didn't despise him in every way. Times like when he offered me his shirt. Disgusting. And how he followed me to the cave. Despicable. And how his arm was probably numb all night from letting me use it as a pillow. Absolutely heinous. I needed his help out of this mess I created; if Linking was the only way forward, I'd do it. I didn't want Ryder, Alo, or Mato, as Jadox mentioned.

Surh-Sig's words repeated in my mind, "*You must Link with the one who hunts you. Drop your wall and let him in. It is the only way. But all choices come at a heavy cost."*

Jay told me he had been tracking me all through Lodesa for a year. A bit creepy, but he was my only option. I'd never lower my guard against him—Linked or not. I stared at Jadox's sleeping form and his nauseatingly strong jawline that framed his parted lips. Once we returned to Draven and asked Gemm how to cut our curse loose, I'd have a moment to see his grotesquely adorable, terrible smile again in his sleep, Jay. He groaned and hugged me close.

I nudged his bare shoulder, *not* glancing at his firm, exposed chest. "Jay, wake up."

"Yes, Petal?" Running a hand through his messy hair, he cuddled me even closer. He was so warm that I could melt into his skin.

"Jay...hey, mister drool." Pushing him, I questioned how professional of a soldier he had been if he always awoke so lazily.

"Just take a second and listen to the birds." Without opening his eyes, he curled into me closer.

I had almost forgotten one of my own rules–*don't touch me*. Well, maybe one more moment of peace would be okay. I nestled into the crook of his arm, cussing to myself at how idiotic I was behaving. Though Jadox's arm and chest ratio made for the perfect pillow, I hated that touching him no longer sparked a deep desire to rip him apart. What had changed?

He yawned and mumbled, "If this were any other morning, I'd bring you breakfast in bed."

"Haha, so funny. Get your ass up. Let's go."

A breeze blew my hair in a whirl, but a strange, soft whisper in the wind made me straighten.

He's not the one for you.

Prickling nerves slithered up my skin. "Did you hear that?"

Jadox wiped the dirt off his chest and side, then looked around, only semi-alarmed and still half-asleep. "Hear what?"

He's not the one.

The magical voice was male. If Jay couldn't hear it, then maybe the voice came from my enhanced hearing. Jadox bounced up and walked, pulling me along with him while I checked over my shoulder. Then it hissed again like a phantom:

He's not for you, Kyra.

The voice knew my name, just like Surh-Sig. I jolted to a halt and scanned the treetops. Putting one finger to my lips, I gestured to Jadox, who mouthed, *"what are you doing?"* with a mocking grin. I carefully peeked around a tree trunk. The forest was silent. After meeting a demon yesterday, anything seemed possible.

"How much farther is Draven?"

With irritatingly sexy eyes, Jadox pointed to the peak of the mountain in the distance. "That way. Here, wear my shoes." Jadox knelt in front of me and double-knotted his extra-large sneakers on my feet. He opted to walk over the twigs barefoot, not seeming to be phased in the slightest. The deeper we treaded, the calmer his posture looked. Along the mountainside, Jadox labeled dozens of types of trees, handed over the edible berries, and tried to teach me how to track. It must not be close if Jadox didn't smell whatever being was whispering to me in the wind. We'd be safe.

He lies, Kyra.

I stopped and whirled around. "Who are you?"

"What? Who are you talking to?" Jadox's features turned concerned for the first time on our walk as he glanced at the rustling branches.

"Nothing."

Jadox scanned the area apprehensively, then turned to me. "Kyra, we need to talk. The Luna Festival is soon."

I stumbled over a rock, but he caught me mid-fall.

"Have you considered Linking? There are three guys I think you'd like: Ryder, Alto, and Mato."

"No, Jay, I'm not on some dating show. Plus, it seems like you've forgotten that I'm the one who wished away all males. The last thing I want is to connect with one."

What I refused to say was that the only man I'd consider was him.

A tightness formed in my chest as I reheard Gemm's words, "M*ust Link with the one who hunts her soul.*"

"Fine, be stubborn. I'll let you camp out in your little world of denial for a bit longer, but they're all good men, and you'd save our entire village."

"I'll figure it out."

"No! You're always challenging me, so now it's *my* turn to push back, Kyra. If you don't Link, how else do you expect to return Landon?" Leading, he zig-zagged us around thorny bushes. "Together, you and Ryder will be stronger. And Alto is an amazing contractor. He can build anything. Don't even get me started on Mato; he—"

"Jay!" I screamed into the trees. "Please, stop! I don't want them. I'll never want them. Just drop it."

"There's about to be a war. Last night, Syvonne Stirk made a speech declaring Magik outlawed. She offered rewards to anyone who brought in a Mystier. If you go into Ordull territory, it'll be chaos. People will turn in innocents left and right, then those who work together will fight against a common threat—us."

When we hit a patch of mud, I stepped in his large footprints, doing my best not to fall in the slick, squishy heap. "Mystiers will be safe if they stay within their barrier, right?"

"Ideally, yes, but electricity is our weakness. Ordulls might discover how to break through the seals, especially since government officials have inside knowledge about what truly happened at The Fall. This is their chance to destroy us all for good." He stopped and made us face each other. "You'll be in danger, and lots of people will die. You *have* to Link."

"Then why don't you volunteer yourself?" I pushed at his chest. "Is the thought of connecting with me so entirely loathsome to you?"

His jaw dropped open. "Me?" His puppy dog eyes reminded me of Chocolate with that sincere look.

Another whip of wind carried the male's whisper.

Don't trust him, Kyra.

All the hairs on my arms stood on end. If I told Jadox, he might assume I had lost my mind.

"Forget it." Adding a sliver of space between our bodies, I kept my gaze on the mud. "There has to be another way to save Landon."

"I thought you didn't trust me, Kyra," he said slowly.

"You're…different than other men."

He paused; an obvious struggle battled in his eyes. "I'm just as monstrous, Kyra." He sucked in a deep breath, his eyes portraying an internal battle he was fighting, then finally said, "I killed your stepdad, the man who raised you."

"What?" I stopped and forced myself to lock with those deep brown eyes. "What did you just say?"

"I killed your stepdad."

"H-how? That's impossible. Wh-what are you talking about?"

"It was me. That's why you recognized Chocolate when we first met in the elevator. You saw her a year ago."

His admission was so sudden and concrete that it stole my breath. And all the puzzle pieces suddenly fit into place. That night in The Crooked Chateau, I searched for my grandma's ruby necklace, unaware that it contained Magik. My stepdaddy had tried to stop me, and…yes, there was a chocolate lab there too.

"You're telling the truth," I whispered.

Jay nodded.

I opened the locked box in my mind of savage memories from my stepdad. Numerous smacks from the back of his hand across my cheek. The sound of his horrid voice bellowing insults through the house. Regardless of the flurry of shocking emotions flooding in, the one at the forefront of my mind was gratitude to Jadox for ridding me of that villain.

"Last year, I was hunting for your necklace," he said.

I was about to interrupt, but he held up a hand and continued, "I finally found you in Andersonville." Jadox's voice turned soft. "I knew you'd be at The Crooked Chateau for your family event. So, I was going to introduce myself and try to convince you to travel to Draven with me. Whether you like it or not, we all need you. All of this is happening for a reason, and you're at the center of it. You're the only one with a Golden tattoo and this prophecy…Kyra, you have to understand. Something big is going to happen."

"*Why* did you kill my stepdad that night?"

Jadox stepped over a broken branch with a look on his face that I couldn't decipher. "I witnessed him raping a woman in the ladies' bathroom a few minutes before. I had heard her calling out." He cleared his throat. "I didn't know he was your stepdad at the time."

I nodded, believing every word. After dropping this bomb, I should have felt grief, confusion, anything, but honestly, I just wanted to move on and forget that man existed.

"Are you holding any other secrets from me?" I asked.

There was a long pause. "No…"

Continuing over the log, the mud underfoot hardened. Relief washed away my nerves. If he confessed to the murder of my own family, I doubted Jadox hid any bigger secrets than that.

"Kyra, if your dad ever…ever *hurt* you, it's safe to tell me."

I stared back at him.

"I'd listen, no judgment."

"I…I don't have anything to say." Hot tears pooled behind my eyes, but I held them back.

"Okay, can I hug you?" he asked.

I huffed out an awkward laugh. "Yeah, okay, not too tight, though."

Slowly, his arms wrapped around my frame, holding me close. I should move away, but I didn't want to.

"Thank you, Jay. For telling the truth. You just proved yourself wrong. You're not like other men. You're good and honest."

He sighed, and his shoulders sagged.

Wanting to drop the subject, I glanced around, wondering when the voice would whisper in the wind again. Jadox had proven the mystery voice wrong by telling me the truth.

I matched his pace up the hill as the sun rose higher, racing us to the top of the sky. The trail turned steeper with each step, and my breath became heavier. Beams of light shone through the gaps where autumn had left holes.

"Can you teach me more about Magik?"

"Really?" His face lit up, and he jumped right in when I nodded, saying, "Okay, the components of Magik are manipulation, generation, harboring, and elemental combat. A few of us have some extras, like my geokinetic regeneration."

"Those are big words, Jay. Slow down."

"Regeneration is how I heal others, and I think if you have an enhancement, it has to do with knowing ancient spells. For now, all you need to learn is how to control fire and heat and use it to protect yourself. Later, we can—"

Sweat dripped down my hairline. "Let's do it all now before I go to Hallie."

He frowned. "Self-defense is the most important. If someone attacks you, you need to centralize your Magik to create a bubble around yourself."

"Like Draven's invisible dome?"

"Similar, yes."

"Won't my necklace do that?" I reached for it, forgetting Goldie had snatched the ruby from my neck at the cave's entrance.

He wants to use you, Kyra.

Shit, the whispering returned. I didn't look around this time, hoping it'd simply leave me alone.

Jadox stopped our ascent. "Show me your wrists."

"Uh, you're connected to one of them, genius."

He tried to hold back a smile and flipped our joined wrists over. The trail of veins crawling up his forearm showed me the path to his heart. A journey I'd rather run from.

"Can I touch you?" he asked softly.

Swallowing the feeling of rocks lodged in my throat, I nodded slowly. Gently, Jadox traced my own river of veins from the base of one wrist, carefully, up to my elbow, then shoulder, and held his finger still at my neck. I used all my effort not to lean into his touch.

"The Magik runs through your veins. To connect with it, you must feel it, become a part of the fire, and accept yourself as Elidian. Your strength will come from knowing yourself…" his fingers brushed to my heart, "knowing yourself in here."

Hoping he couldn't feel my heart clamor like a spastic drum, I rolled in both lips and stepped back. "Okay, cool, cool. So, try something on me, then. I'll block you."

"Kyra, it's not that easy."

"Do it."

A frustrated animalistic growl vibrated in his throat. I felt a sudden urge to kiss his large Adam's apple and show him what it felt like to have a fingertip skim him like a tickling feather. Instead, I blew out a breath and concentrated on my Magik, racing through my body. With a flick of his hand, Jadox beckoned the trees to shake above.

Pumpkins, sweet potatoes, and carrots impossibly plummeted from the unknown above, raining and smashing all around my feet. At least none rammed into my head. Then thousands of leaves attacked head-on, soaring like arrows straight to my temple.

I thought of meditation. Deep breaths. A calming center. Nothing happened. All the sharp edges of the leaves scraped into my skin in a thousand mini cuts.

"Ow!"

Jadox hovered a hand over my head, and each scratch instantly healed shut.

"Your skill is really impressive, Jay. You're very valuable to everyone in Draven."

"If that was true, they wouldn't have shunned me years ago," he grumbled. "Try again."

I craned my head up to the robin-egg sky. "Maybe the Golden tattoo means I have some defect."

"You can do it. What's your gut telling you?"

"That the meditation thing won't work. It's not who I am."

He leaned in with a twinkle in his eye. "Who are you, Kyra?"

Memories ambushed my mind. Pranking Hallie, high-school friends daring me to jump off a roof, creating havoc in kickboxing class, and drumming with my bands until two in the morning.

The answer became obvious. I was chaos. Ruckus. Energy. Wild at heart.

I smiled up at Jadox. "Do it again."

He widened his stance, and his face turned so sexy and serious that I could have climbed him right there. At Jadox's whispered command, a loud crash split through the rock next to us. A giant root sprung to life, twirling and twisting in a frenzy. It flung itself toward my ankle.

I let the beast inside my soul take over. Drumming pounded in my blood. Harder. Faster. Stronger. Holding out both hands, I imagined the beat slamming to life in my fingertips.

The crazed root stopped mid-air as if it had slammed into an invisible shield.

"I did it!"

Something strong wrapped around my ankle and threw me to the ground. Jadox fell too, and the root dragged us a few feet before letting up. Laughter exploded from deep within his belly as he rolled over.

"Never let your guard down." Panting, he lay flat on the ground, his face beaming with pride. "You're strong, oh precious Golden One."

My laughter matched his. "Don't call me that. It sounds like a stripper's name."

"What should I call you?"

A deep tingle zapped my tattoo. "What do you want to call me?"

"Petal has slipped out a few times." His eyes were set on my lips. "I think Petal is a good nickname."

I licked them and could've sworn I heard a little groan sneak out of Jadox's destructive mouth. "Why Petal?"

Remembering how comfortable it felt to wake up in his arms earlier, I hovered my lips directly over his.

"Because the petal makes the flower what it is. No one buys a flower for the stem or the leaf. The reason why it's so inspiring and desired is because of the petal."

All words escaped me.

He's not the one for you.

I gulped and moved away from Jay.

"Don't move a muscle." His eyes widened. "We have a few spies directly above."

Disregarding his exact warning, I immediately looked up and recognized the set of trees to our right. I heard the giggles of the Draven children up in the treehouses and immediately relaxed.

"We're back already?" I asked.

"We're home." His heartbeat became crazed as I moved our bodies closer and dropped my gaze to his lips again.

"What's next, soldier?"

15
JADOX

Kyra's eyes held a thousand promises—all guaranteed to be broken. When she smiled, stars filled the cavities of my chest where no light had touched for years. I staggered up from the soil, away from her treacherous lips, and pulled her straight toward Gemm's den.

"Jay?" Her voice held a hint of doubt for the first time. "Your face goes all crooked when you're thinking too hard. What are you thinking, and why are you walking so fast?"

My love for Draven's village was fossilized in every nook and cranny of rock and stone from here to the quarry. But what she said earlier was wrong. I wasn't suited to Link with her or better than any other man. Alaska had made it perfectly clear to me over the years that I only created harm to those I cared about. Risking the same mistake wasn't an option. Maybe Gemm would be lucid enough to give us another option, a way around the prophecy, so Kyra didn't need to suffer an attachment to someone she hated.

Chocolate ran to us, tail wagging and tongue drooping.

"Hey, girl." Kyra leaned over and stroked her back, taking me down with her.

"Can you not yank out my elbow, please?"

"You're tough. Deal with it."

The smell of fried dough and melted sugar wafted through the autumn leaves. Marching through the pine-soaked woods, we passed the garden and ancient fountain wrapped in ivy with a faded Möbius Circle engraved in the stone. Tents were hoisted high, decorated with roses of every shade. Only then did I notice the tables set up with a banquet of food. I stopped short.

Kyra tugged me in a chaotic circle. "Look! There are decorations everywhere. It's tonight," she said. "That Luna Festival is tonight."

"Yeah, I know. Remember, our hour in the cave for us was actually six days for them."

I busted through Gemm's front door, desperate for a solution. She sat braiding Alaska's hair in a thick, intricate crown above her head. They both wore flowing swan dresses with moss attached to form the train—a festival tradition. At least Kyra calmed down in their presence.

Gemm smiled. "Once there was a chain of locks, and the boy didn't know that the key to unlocking it was already in his pocket."

Refraining from checking my pockets, I shook my head and lifted our joined wrists high. "Gemm, can you unbind us?"

"Did you get the Unetlo Book, Key-rah?" Alaska interrupted.

Kyra glared at a crack in the floor, frustration radiating from her.

I glanced between the ladies, tension drenching the room. "What do you mean? Kyra was never going to Vayu."

"Right," Alaska narrowed her eyes, "just like *you* never hid a little prize in the forest." Alaska tilted her head.

Shit. My sister had found Nilson tied to the tree. Did she find him alive or dead? Where was he now? I gave Alaska a warning glare. Kyra shouldn't know about Isaac yet. I didn't want to scare her. Seconds ticked away at a fast pace.

Gemm stood and leaned on her walking stick and ushered us forward. For once, Kyra remained silent. I held my breath as Gemm inspected our wrists and flipped our forearms back and forth, inspecting the invisible bond.

A humored laugh blessed her lips. "Once there was a destiny that would change the world, but a goddess gifted the Mystier with choices."

Words rang from a fuzzy memory, but where had I heard them before? *"All gifts come at a heavy choice. Be warned."*

"Please untie us," Kyra begged. "That's my choice."

Gemm nodded and hobbled to her counter of apothecary bottles. She grabbed two, swirled the contents inside, and handed them over.

"Drink this elixir."

One tiny whiff had me gagging at the potent stench rotting from inside the mixed tonics. "Are you sure?" I pinched my nose.

Gemm simply turned her back and sat behind Alaska again, twisting her braid.

Kyra tapped her bottle against mine, said, "Cheers," and threw her head back, choking on the liquid as she gulped it. Her face would've been entertaining if I didn't have to do the same.

I took it like a shot. Grainy, warm, thick liquid full of chunks stuck in my throat. Coughing, I bent over on my knees and sealed my lips shut, holding it in so I wouldn't vomit.

A vine snaked in from the door, up my leg, and wrapped around our wrists. It cleaved our bind in half, exposing the green inside, which automatically turned black. The curse connecting us broke.

"I'm free!" Kyra pulled away and leaped across the den, then straight outside.

I placed my hand on my chest and belched. "What in the blaze was in that?"

Gemm hummed to herself, not taking her eyes off Alaska's braid.

I rolled my wrist, grateful to be free of Kyra's constant pulling. But then suddenly missed her presence.

"Where the Flames have you two been for six days?" Alaska asked.

"I already sent you a message." I sighed. "Don't act like you don't know."

"What I *do* know is that you're thinking about the prophecy." Alaska studied me. "You two can't Link. We can't repeat history and risk another Fall. Plus, the only way out of the Link is if one of you kills the other."

"I won't want out," I said, unsure if it was the truth or not.

"She will. That girl will murder you."

I leaned over the sink, sucking in water from the faucet, then said, "I disagree."

"Bring her to the Vayu guy. What's his name, Isaac Nilson?"

"So he's alive?"

Alaska smiled. "Yup. And pissed."

"Where'd you put him?"

"He's locked in the cabin, and I hexed the doors so he couldn't escape. If Key-rah leaves with him and Links, her prophecy is fulfilled, and Draven will stay safe."

"No." I spat the lingering taste into the sink. "It can't be him."

"Why?"

"Because."

"Because why?" My sister shot me a look of daggers.

I stared at Gemm's cookbooks and the ancient penmanship scrolling the pages.

"You *like* her!" Alaska darted to her feet, ripping her hair from Gemm's clutches. "You *like* Key-rah?"

"It's *Ky*-ra."

I moved toward the window. A shade of eggplant twisted into plums and lavenders as the sun kissed the horizon. Kyra was yelping for joy outside, already changed into a fresh, flowy white dress. Who had given Kyra a traditional Luna dress so quickly? And why did she accept it if she planned to leave? At least someone had also lent her a pair of boots to cover the blisters that kept ripping open at her heels during our hikes. Why did I immediately want to peel those boots off and kiss her from ankle to knee to—fuck, I shook out my hands.

Kyra whirled in the clearing, yelling, "I'm free!"

I laughed out loud and felt Alaska's glare burn into my back. I admired that Kyra didn't always calculate everything as I did. What would it feel like to live spontaneously for once and follow my heart from moment to moment instead of rationalizing every little detail? The woman was my opposite in so many ways.

"You're happy with her," Alaska scolded.

"No, I'm not."

"You like her."

"No, I don't."

Gemm silently appeared beside us. "Once there was a family with enough love to make a line of dominos wrap around the planet, but when one knocked over, they all fell."

"See, Gemm thinks it's a terrible idea to Link," Alaska huffed.

I looked deep into Gemm's eyes, understanding a different interpretation of her domino riddle.

"Thanks for your advice, sis. But I think I've got this covered."

Gemm dipped her finger in an overturned, empty turtle shell full of a green and brown mixture and swiped the paint over my cheeks and forehead. I was used to the custom from childhood, yet I didn't think she'd allow me to participate after being shunned by Draven. My grandma pulled out the traditional male wardrobe, a simple pair of loose, brown pants with vines stitchwork decorating the side. No shirt, of course. Gemm slathered her hand in the paint and stuck a handprint on one side of my chest.

"Thank you for the outfit, Gemm." I tucked the clothes under my arm.

"Once a boy fell in love under Hunter's Moon."

Alaska jumped in front of the door. "You were gone almost a week. There was a mass breakout of the Cydian prisoners from the president's headquarters. At least half escaped." Her eyes lit with adventure. "But the wild part is, Ordulls are the ones that freed them, a group called the Aurum Orbis Society standing with us against Stirk's orders. So, I got an idea."

Straddling the threshold, half-inside, half-out, I froze. "Alaska? What did you do?"

Music began playing beside the tents. Flutes and other instruments I didn't know the names of chirped and whistled along with the birds. Half-naked women in lizard headdresses danced by the campfire, stomping hard enough to crack the ground. Squinting, I scanned their bodies. No Möbius tattoos.

I bolted back inside the den, raging toward Alaska. "What. Did. You. Do?"

With a smile on her face, she raised both hands. "I brought some Ordulls from that Society to give us information about Syvonne's army. They could be our spies."

"That's a terrible idea. You're putting us at risk. We can't trust any Ordull."

"They're not *all* bad, Jadox!"

"How do you know? You weren't there when they killed our parents!"

Gemm laid a soft hand on my heaving chest. "Once, a shard of glass wedged in a boy's heart. All he had to do was pull it out, but he let it sit and slice open his soul."

Turning on my heels, I swept out past Alaska and jogged outside.

Resentment coated Alaska's voice when she called out, "If you convince Key-rah to Link with Nilson, I'll send the Ordulls away for you and never invite them back."

Why did my sister hate Kyra so much? Protectiveness? In the end, it didn't really matter. I'd always love Alaska with everything I had. Love was like dirt. When held onto too tightly, it sifted through fingertips, falling out of grasp, yet some people left a mark and stained our hearts. Memories were also supposed to be permanent. I never should've erased Alaska's girlfriend's memories. She still hadn't forgiven me for taking away her ex, Paola. But some days, I wished someone had used that same spell on me to erase the memories of the night my parents were murdered.

Drums thumped near the dancing women, and I met Kyra's fiery gaze as she hunched over, beating her own wild rhythm. The sunset framed her face, casting a golden hue over her skin. Her energy infected the very air I breathed. Though our curse was broken, my wrist itched for her skin.

Was Alaska right that I cared about her? No. And even if I did, I'd have to shut it down. She'd be Linking with someone else. Mato was probably the best option. Once he returned, I'd talk to him about the prophecy.

When Kyra waved me over, her lips parted, newly stained the color of berries in winter. She was divine. I glanced behind her at the grand display of fruit baskets and bread. While weaving between the dancers, I focused on Kyra's talented hands. *Tap. Tap. Tap.*

I sat beside her, hovered my fingertips near her blistered feet, and chanted a silent healing spell. Once she felt it, Kyra's eyes snapped up and sent a token of gratitude in their golden shimmer. I leaned back, absorbing the beat. We still had a few hours before Mato returned, so maybe this was my last chance to relax before entering a war of Ordulls versus Mystiers.

Trees bent toward the music in a trance for a delicious moment. Peppers and garlic scents snapped to life, and my mouth salivated in anticipation of the upcoming feast. Little girls ran around giggling, playing with stick swords and flowers in their hair. A few petals showered on the ground. *Petal.*

Sometimes, petals clung to their stem for so long that being plucked off was the only option for release. Instead of enjoying the fluttering drop to the soil, the petal succumbed to being trampled on by dancing feet. *Petal.* Why was something so valuable and delicate created with the possibility of being ripped to shreds? *My Petal.* I wouldn't let anyone hurt Kyra again.

Alaska guided Claire over, another match-making attempt doomed to fail. Claire was smart and beautiful, yet she ignited no spark within me. She brought over a bottle of cranberry wine and rested the rim on my lips, but I scooted a bit closer. Kyra pretended she hadn't noticed, but every place her skin brushed against mine felt ablaze.

Dancing bodies glided between the campfire and garden, around fruit bowls, and through smoke. With arms raised and heads angled to the navy sky, peace surrounded our people. Chocolate frolicked between bare feet, springing and leaping. For once, the joy bouncing from Kyra's face eased my racing mind. At that moment, I fell in love with the Hunter's Moon all over again. The festival took me back in time to my roots. When the scent of sweet molasses and soil mixed with the clashing of cymbals, memories flashed from years ago.

. . .

My mother danced in a tulip-white gown, lifting Alaska on her shoulders. Both their raven hair fell to their waists and twirled with the wind. My father threw sticks into the campfire, handprints on his chest. He looks over at me with a stern face and nods. I take the invitation and run over, helping him bring the flames to life. Once the fire roars and Alaska cheers, we all dance together under the moon without a care in the world. The last Luna Festival as a full family.

Before I knew it, the heat of Kyra's skin radiated at my side. I pressed my lips together, wanting to kiss her. What a bad idea. Terrible. Awful, but how she looked at me made me question if I might have a chance after all. Kyra winked at me, still rapping her drums happily.

I checked my watch, the screen lighting up in the darkness. All the Dravian men would return soon from the hunting expedition to roast the midnight feast. Time was running out. Soon, she wouldn't be available.

"Come with me," I offered and held out a hand. "I want to show you something."

Kyra tucked the two drumsticks back into her ponytail. Together, we moved past a haunted willow with charms and sorcery embedded in its core toward my old treehouse. The music and cheers faded, but my senses were in overdrive, with Kyra's forearm brushing against mine. In the dark, she tripped over a root, and I caught her mid-fall. Again. I'd catch her a thousand times over. Her amber eyes lit up like a campfire, igniting all of my senses.

Behind a line of trees, a waterfall ferociously crashed into the calm lake, creating a white foamy spray. I imagined each individual droplet, a force to be reckoned with, like Kyra—possessing the intensity and vigor of all those water droplets combined. But she was made of fire—the strongest of us all.

"Climb." I nodded toward a tree ladder.

"No way, the last time you made me climb, I had to jump out of a tree."

"I thought you liked spontaneity."

"Touché."

Mouth-watering smells of roasted nuts wafted up from the festival. I followed Kyra up the tree, gripping the thin boards with my fingertips, ready to catch her if she slipped. Moss swooped low from the train of her dress, blinding me when it swept side to side.

At the top, my heart jittered uncontrollably at the sight of my old bedroom. The planks of the treehouse were warped and cracked, but almost everything else was as I had left it—in shambles.

"Wait, did you live here?" Kyra overturned my old bow and arrow, split in half from when I had cracked it over my knee in rage and grief.

"Until I was twelve, then I came back at eighteen."

"Where were you in between those years?"

"Nowhere special."

I sat on the edge of my high-rise treehouse, dangling my feet over the edge. She examined the dust-filled blanket draped over the swinging hammock. Chocolate sat far below, rolling over onto her back in the leaves. Kyra laughed at her and sat next to me. She laid a hand on my thigh with her fingers, and I forced a gulp.

"Tell me what happened when you were younger." The softness of her face couldn't be feigned.

"Mystiers don't usually leave their village until they're eighteen, but I begged my parents to visit outside the barrier. Finally, they agreed, and we went shopping." I sucked in a breath, taking a moment to realize the enormity of telling someone this for the first time. "The world of Ordulls mesmerized me with all those skyscrapers, hoverboards, and holograms. I thought it was magical in its own way. Just the variety of food in one grocery store was mind-blowing."

Kyra stayed quiet and drummed a slow beat on my leg.

"When we left the store, it was already night, and my parents had forgotten where they parked their hoverboard. They didn't travel often and must have gotten confused. We were walking down a deserted alley when three men in suits blocked our way. They asked my folks questions and wanted to take us to some science facility, but all I can remember is staring at their guns."

"My parents refused and fought back, protecting me." As the wind blew through the treehouse, I paused and dropped my head. "I watched them bleed out, unable to heal yet. If I had been more patient to wait until my enhancement had come, I would've been able to save them."

Kyra rubbed my back slowly.

"I had no way of knowing where Draven was located, and I hadn't received my tattoo yet, so I couldn't summon any Magik. I found a forest and lived off the land as long as I could. Gemm and Alaska didn't know what happened until I returned at age eighteen, six years later. They assumed I had died too."

She covered her mouth with one hand, and her eyes enlarged twice their size. "Oh, Jay. What did you do for six years?"

"The foster system picked me up. I lived with ten families. They always knew I was different. Unexplainable, little events would happen around me, and the foster families never wanted to keep me around." I turned to her, our knees touching.

She ran her fingertips over the brown paint smudged on my chest.

"You have to understand Draven is everything to me. I have to protect my people from Ordulls. If they already found Cydon, they will find us too. But your Magik paired with Mato's will make us stronger."

"They found Cydon? Goddess…You want to save your tribe as much as I want to bring Landon back." Kyra stared up at the moon. "Did I tell you he's autistic? Landon loves music, and our rhythm is the same, so we understand each other most of the time. But otherwise, he communicates with pictures and pointing. He is as sweet as an angel but doesn't like being touched."

"Sounds familiar."

"All children with autism are different. He is curious and playful in his own way." Another tear slid down her cheek, and she dropped her head. "I miss him so much. I made such a mess of things." She wiped away her tears. "Gemm's prophecy said the Linking has to be done before dawn. I guess I don't really have a choice anymore, do I?"

"We always have a choice."

I lifted her chin slowly. "When the world is at its darkest, that's when a single ray of light is most noticeable and bright. You hold that light at your fingertips, Kyra."

Her eyes locked onto mine, searching, digging for the lie behind those words, but there weren't any. She was the fire, the core of this world.

"I'll do it. I'll Link."

Quickly, I faced her completely. "I need you to be sure, Kyra, because if you hate all men so much…."

"…I don't hate *all* men." She gulped and wiped away a tear.

"Okay, I'll talk to Mato when they return."

"No, Jay. I want it to be you. You're the one good man left."

A tightness formed in my chest. Something in my gut felt right like it was meant to be. I couldn't push a strange man onto Kyra after her past. If sealing my fate to hers was the way to give her what she needed, then I'd figure out a way to work through it. Instead of arguing back or spending precious time going over the reasons why it was a terrible idea, I just nodded.

"Okay," I whispered. "And, I promise, I'll do everything in my power to bring Landon back."

"But we do need rules. First…" She held up one finger. "We need to make big decisions together. Second, we never lie to each other—what else?"

I nodded, not wanting to say anything about Nilson to change her mind, but I added, "We don't use our Magik against each other."

"Good one." She pointed at me, then scanned my chest, her spunk returning. "Oh, and this is a professional alliance only. Once we Link, there's nothing between us. I'm not making any Magikal babies."

The moon slid out from behind its shield, and the clouds stilled, gifting me the most perfect moment. My heart skittered faster, and blood rushed to my crotch at the sight of the moonbeams painting her skin. If I was going to respect her rules, I had to at least take one shot.

"If professionalism is required once we're Linked...." I inched closer. "Can I kiss you now? Just once?"

"Kiss me?" Her face colored to a shade I'd never seen on her before and wouldn't even try to decipher.

"Yeah, Petal, a kiss. It's when two people put their lips together and...."

She rolled a devious smile, but her eyes dropped to my mouth. "Just once? To get it out of the way, right?"

"Of course. I'm merely mortal, but maybe it won't be too bad."

She scrunched up her nose in a way that obliterated my self-control. "Let's just get it over with. Then we'll know there's no chemistry and eliminate any distractions."

"Exactly."

"One time won't hurt anything." She leaned back against the trunk in the center of the treehouse and curled one finger as an invitation. "Well, what are you waiting for? Come get me, soldier."

I memorized the hunger in her eyes and how her lips slowly parted into a soft O-shape. Her chest rose and fell faster, shifting the neckline of her drooping white dress. She embodied a goddess, and I'd happily devour her for as long as she'd let me. I leaned over, hovering my mouth above hers. Her raging pheromones spread a message of raw desire and sent my senses into a frenzy. She wanted this just as much as I did.

My lips swept over hers. Softly. Gently. Our kiss started as a temptation of the night but quickly evolved. The slip of her tongue over mine sent my head spinning and the rest of me into a free fall of thick desire. She tasted like starlight as midnight swallowed us whole. I couldn't get enough and never wanted to stop. Her hand found the back of my neck and tugged me closer. Her breath hitched.

"Kyra..." I whispered, but her soft moan cut off my train of thought and sent me into overdrive.

She scooted atop my lap, straddling me. An unexpected groan escaped my lips, and she sucked in my air, translating it into another soft moan. Intoxicating. The kiss suspended time, coiling with heat. My tattoo pulsed with intensity, forces deep within, clawing for more pleasure. I wrapped my arms around her waist, holding her tight. Those lips. Never had I experienced a kiss that sent me into such a crazed spiral.

Kyra's fingertips roamed my bare chest, exploring and claiming. Moving lower and lower over my abs. Lower. I gasped and lurched away. Her eyes were wide, pupils dilated, and lips were swollen. Green paint covered the front of her white dress.

Her mouth dropped open. "I…um…right, yes, we got that out of the way. Never again."

Those words crushed me. I was speechless. Dumbfounded. And my cock was rock-hard, throbbing for her. I wanted to kiss her again. Needed to.

She tucked her wild hair behind her ears and nodded. "Actually, let's just do that one more time."

I gulped, knowing that if I did this, it was the beginning of the end.

16

KYRA

I kissed Jay again and again—unable to hold back. His lips enchanted me into a moaning mess. I shivered under the pressure of his hands against the small of my back. His bulging cock was hard for my taking. I wanted Jay to forever kiss ancient Draven words against my throat and run my hand through his mass of wavy hair. When had I started to like him?

In the distance, wolves howled a song of the stars, not holding anything back. I'd do the same; I'd become the animal—wild and free. Jay looked to be in a trance as I stood up, placing his line of vision level with my belly button. I looped one strap of my dress over my shoulder. The fabric fell off me into a puddle of desire. My soul reached for him as if he called to my essence, deep in my bones.

"Kyra, wait," his voice croaked. "You're right. We need boundaries." His eyes were eating me alive, but worry lines etched themselves into his face that weren't there a moment before.

I scooped up my dress, feeling my cheeks flush. "Right, yes, you're absolutely right. Plus, that was the world's most atrocious kiss anyways."

"Agreed." He resituated his crotch.

After I covered myself again, I followed his gaze to the broken picture frame on the treehouse planks shattered down the middle. Four people stood with arms wrapped around each other, blessed with the same smile. Because of his earlier story, I didn't dare ask if they were his parents, already knowing with certainty since they shared his features.

"Okay, so, um, do you still want to Link?" He cleared his throat. "Because the other Dravian men will be here soon. Maybe Mato—"

"I want it to be you."

He nodded, holding my gaze. "Okay, then. We need to touch to Link and say a spell at the same time."

"That's it?"

"Yes. Are you sure you want to do this? We can't change our minds after."

The drumming at the festival in the distance intensified and sped faster, reminding me of what was at stake. Landon. My sister. Everything that mattered to me. "Yes, what do we say?"

"*Atuyasdodi promitto.*" He held both palms up, outstretched to me, and I laid mine in his when he whispered, "On the count of three?"

I nodded and felt his hands tremble underneath mine.

"One."

I sucked in a deep breath.

"Two."

Jay's eyes reassured me it would be okay. He wouldn't be like other men. Linking with him would be safe.

"Three."

"*Atuyasdodi promitto,*" we spoke in unison.

Immediately, my tattoo flared with a blazing scorch in my abdomen. Jay threw his head back and screamed. His tendons flexed in his neck, and his entire body convulsed. I tried to pull my hands away, but strong magnetic energy locked us tightly together. Pain seared through my tattoo, and I dropped to the treehouse planks on my side. I felt needles slicing from the inside like another Circle was being drawn onto my skin. Magik claimed me, possessed me.

Another scream. Was it mine or his?

"Stop fighting it, Kyra!" he yelled, though I could barely hear him.

Sweat dripped down my temple, and the entire treehouse shook. Pressure suffocated me, and I locked eyes with Jay when I finally managed a breath. A whirl of his emotions cascaded into me, crushing me from every angle.

"Let me in!" he screamed, desperate and afraid. "Let go of your fear!"

It felt like a train speeding straight into my temple. Every negative memory, nightmare, and fear flooded my consciousness, drowning me, shredding all ounce of sense and obliterating reality.

Blinding white light sent me staggering into nothingness.

"Kyra! You're gonna kill us!"

I didn't even know what I was doing wrong. All the air was stolen from my chest. Jadox pulled me closer. But something inside me fought against whatever was happening. The impact was too strong, too soon. But then a snippet of Jay's pain snuck in the cracks between our souls and settled on my heart. Feeling the intensity of his struggle, I lowered my wall.

Immediately, my body ceased to exist. No wooden planks rubbed against my skin. No wind tossed my hair. No festival sounds.

Images flashed, but not my own. Jay's memories unraveled in my mind like loose stitches. I saw his past in spurts.

Jay skipping rocks along a river, holding a younger Alaska's hand.

Planting seeds with Gemm.

Climbing a cliff wall after Alaska.

In an alleyway, a bullet soaring into a man's chest. Blood. Dead.

Terror. Rage. Confusion.

A woman acting as a shield. A bullet piercing her head. She stumbles. Dead.

Shock. Pain. Pain. Pain.

Seeing a girl on stage playing drums.

Intrigued. Captivated. Protective.

. . .

Screaming.

"Kyra! Kyra, stop screaming."

I violently shook in Jay's arms, staring up at his brown eyes, full of concern, worry, and something else, something new.

I lurched back, clutching my heart. "What happened? Was I in your head?"

You're okay, Kyra.

Jay's mouth hadn't moved.

"What? How can I hear you?" I asked. "You didn't speak."

We did it. We Linked. Take a breath, Petal.

My body trembled out of my control. "Stop it. Are you in my head?"

"I think so," he said aloud and ran a panicked, shaky hand through his thick hair. "Try to send a message to me."

"No!" Panting, I crawled away, despite not wanting to. Everything in my heart told me to move closer, let him hold me, and ask him how he felt. But, somehow, I already knew how he felt. He liked me—way too much. His feelings bombarded me, caging me with an intensity so strong that it would drown me. I didn't sign up for this.

"Make it stop!" I whimpered.

Kyra, I'm here for you. We're okay.

"This is too much. I don't want you in my head!" I scooted further away, and flames flicked at my fingertips.

His healing Magik rolled over me in vast waves, calming the neurotic panic racing in my mind. With a soothing breath, I studied him. Somehow, his muscles looked even more defined now. His eyes had an extra sharpness that wasn't there before. I glanced at his painted chest. The top curve of his original tattoo was lit with a brown glow, and it was obvious that a new red tattoo was on his stomach, attached to the first in a loop. Elidi red. So, why was mine Golden?

A deep understanding of his soul resonated in every fiber of my being. I could feel his wants, needs, desires, and fears. Jay cared for me. Somehow, against all odds, this man truly cared. That couldn't be true. This must be some mistake, some joke.

Jay reached a hesitant hand to my face. "Your hair, Kyra, it's golden."

"Huh?" Overwhelmed, I grabbed a lock and held it in front of my face. Sure enough, every strand was bright gold. I lifted my dress, exposing my lacy underwear, but Jay didn't even bother to look away. A brownish-green Circle, glowing intensely, looped with my original gold tattoo.

"What now?" Jay asked.

He looked as lost as I felt, though I didn't even have to rely on his facial expressions. It was like I had my own direct translation of his feelings flowing straight into my heart. The intensity rattled my senses.

Gathering myself, I squeezed my eyes shut. "I need to wish for Landon. That's what's next." I gulped and balled my hands into fists, focusing on my Circles. The power entwining them felt too strong to bear as if any wrong move would make my body explode. "Please, I wish for Landon to return. Please, bring Landon back."

Nothing.

Jay sighed loudly, and Chocolate barked below. And then, in the distance, a scream penetrated the night air. Followed by another. Then another.

"Can you hear that?"

"No." His eyes glittered in a way that didn't seem natural. "But something smells weird. What did you hear?"

A breeze tickled my neck.

Kyra, come to me.

The same male voice that had whispered in the wind had returned.

"Something's happening at the festival," Jay said.

We launched toward the treehouse ladder and scurried down as fast as possible. I landed on the ground hard. At the bottom of the ladder, I broke into a run. Jay sprinted past me. More screams, then a loud bang, followed by a boom echoing off the trees. Chocolate sped ahead toward the campfires, leading the way. Jay's fear catapulted through our bond, terrifying me. His protectiveness, confidence, and alarm all mixed into a soup of feelings, dripping to my heart as if they were my own. Could he feel my emotions too?

Concentrating, I tried to form a wall, denying him access to that part of me. It was too much, too soon, too intense. I couldn't think with him swirling in my mind, in my heart.

I pumped my arms faster toward the noise. Loud threats grew in strength. The wind accelerated to a whipping speed, thrashing at my face. Leaves slashed across my shins, and my flowing dress acted like a parachute behind me. As I reached the clearing, a shocking sight stopped my movements so fast it felt like I had run into a brick wall.

Two sets of men. I had been used to seeing only Jay. But he had been telling me the truth all along. There were others still left. I hadn't completely destroyed the future of our species. A dozen bare-chested men stood by a campfire, painted in green and brown, some holding weapons, and others with arms out, Magik at their fingertips. The Dravian women I had danced with earlier stood by their sides. They all faced five men wearing gray suits who were positioned in the same stance, ready for a fight.

"Nice to meet you, love." A blond man from the pack of gray suits walked forward, claiming the mysterious voice I had heard whispering before.

"It's you," I hissed to the stranger.

Jadox's side was suddenly glued to mine. "Have you two met?"

"No," the blond and I said at the same time.

His riveting eyes were as stormy as a thundercloud as he glided like a ghost. "My name's Isaac Nilson."

"I don't care."

His windblown hair flew in front of his face. With a flip of his wrist, the tornado winds died to a calm breeze. His shoulders were made of corners. Without a care that half of Draven's force had their Magik trained on him, he tied his sandy locks back into a high bun, making his razor-edged nose look more pronounced. But all I could focus on were his unnatural gray eyes, as if they could see right through me.

Isaac tsked with a smug expression, "Now, love, I know you'll warm up to me on our journey." It felt like a shard of ice scraped against my spine when he spoke.

Energy swirled in my tattoos, making me drunk on power. The natural protectiveness Jay harbored in every cell transferred through our bond. At that moment, all I cared about was keeping his village safe.

"Leave!" I commanded this Isaac guy and his intruders. "I don't care who you are. Get out."

Isaac circled me like a predator stalking its prey. Through our tether, I could feel Jadox tense.

"Why would I leave? It was so sweet of you all to lower your shields and invite us to your..." he gestured mockingly, "...raging party."

"Enough!" I crouched, slamming my hand into the earth. Flames from the campfire rolled to me over the dirt. Crackling fire rose in a circle around the men in suits. They cowered and formed a tighter knot, bodies scrunched together.

Jadox waved his hand in the air, extinguishing my fire to ashes with dirt. We exchanged a quick look, a silent message, and when I turned back around, Isaac's jaw dropped.

"*No*." Isaac's voice took on a completely different tone. "I'm too late." His gaze darted between Jadox and me. "You two already Linked?"

"Tell me you didn't." Alaska moved away from her brother but kept her Magik at the ready. "You Linked? *You're* the reason our barrier has been breached. You weakened our shield!"

A Dravian man glared at Jadox and yelled, "How could you? You brought enemies here!"

Jadox shook his head with wide eyes. "No, Gemm had a prophecy about her, I—"

"Leave." The man pointed through the forest. "Never step foot on Draven soil. We were fools to trust you again."

Jadox's torment and heartbreak ripped through the Link, but I was done with all the theatrics. Revenge boiled in my blood with the intense need to shield Jadox from his wishy-washy villagers. For the next two minutes, it'd be just Jay and me. Two against the world.

Isaac raised his hands to the sky, and the wind picked up again. It crashed into the tents, food, and trees, snapping branches in two. Dravians used every forest element at their disposal as a weapon.

"Break the Link!" one Dravian male hollered at Jadox through the fierce tornado. "Kill the girl!"

Glancing over, Jay's thoughts weren't apparent on his face, but I heard his promise through our bond.

I'll never let anyone hurt you, Kyra. Never.

A different man summoned a sharp branch, thrusting the pointed end straight at my chest.

Jadox jumped between me and the weapon and stopped it with an armor of branches. "Stop! We'll leave."

Isaac crossed his arms and smiled. "This is cute, but Kyra will be leaving with me."

Gemm popped out from behind a tree, leaning on her cane. "Once there was the end of our world—"

"Just kill the girl now!" Another Dravian yelled.

Run, Kyra!

My boots crunched over sticks as I fled, squinting through the blinding wind. My eyes teared up from its resistance, but I pushed through, Chocolate at my heels. Which could only mean one thing—Jadox was close.

Linking was supposed to save Draven, not hurt them. But I couldn't comfort him now. His misery and guilt for putting his village at risk wrestled in competition along our tether. We sprinted, running from the fight. Risking a glance behind, I saw a flurry of chaotic wind knocking away each attempt the Dravians thrust at the men in suits.

Jadox cast his hand toward the threat, creating a tower of dirt straight up, forming a wall between us and the battle.

"Keep going!" He was panting as he jumped, more dirt caking his delicious skin. "Look, gorulas!" Jadox pointed to the treetops.

I whistled loudly, and Goldie dropped from a branch. Quickly, she sprawled flat on her stomach and purred. Hopping on, I quickly wrapped my arms around her neck, and Chocolate leaped up behind me. I held her collar tight. "Wait, Goldie, hold on!"

But she rose just as Jadox reached out. He was too late.

Goldie scaled the trunk with all six limbs, then swung from branch to branch, squawking as she climbed higher. Up. Up. How could I steer her back to Jay?

A rustling sound to my right made me jump. "I'm so glad you joined me on our venture." Isaac rode another gorula next to me, swinging from branch to branch in unison.

"Leave me alone."

Isaac's snakelike smile crept higher on his wind-blown cheeks. "I've been looking for you for a long time and can give you what you need. We can get your nephew back together and my son. We can Link and both get what we want."

The gorulas slowed to a calmer pace, heading west. Chocolate whined but somehow stayed atop Goldie's strong back.

"The Dravian you're Linked to is a murderer, a liar." Isaac lifted his square chin. "He abandoned his fellow soldiers, his family, his tribe, and he will do the same to you. Griffin stole everything that mattered to me." Isaac's eyebrows knitted together. "You and I both want to return a boy. Griffin doesn't care about children, so Linking with him was useless. We both have the same goal. Only us together will bring them back. We could even try tonight after we get rid of Griffin. I need to repay him for that little stunt he pulled outside the forbidden caves."

"What?" If I had reins, I would've jerked Goldie to a stop.

"Oh, he didn't tell you?" Isaac smiled, his perfectly straight teeth shining in the darkness. "We've been chatting about you ever since our hunt began."

The night stilled like I was in the twilight zone.

"Hunt?"

"Yeah, we've both been searching for you for the last year. Didn't he tell you?"

Jay had kept a secret from me. Gemm's prophecy repeated in my mind, driving me insane. My chest clamped tight. Goldie must've sensed my frazzled heart because she slowed without a command, balancing on a high branch and breathing hard.

When Isaac signaled, Goldie and the other gorula stopped close by. He held out his hand as an offer, a gift, an invitation. I stared at Isaac's hands and knew what I had to do.

17
JADOX

Linking was a huge mistake. An irreversible, terrible, all-consuming mistake. Kyra's feelings and memories poured into my soul with so much force that I couldn't help but immediately fall for her—hard. How was it possible to love someone so intensely? So fully? So unconditionally? It must be an error, a glitch. This wasn't real life.

I understood her at a level that wasn't even explicable. Her essence wrapped around me, and we undeniably became one, even though I could already feel her fighting against the bond. She needed my support. On the other side of her mask of fearlessness, Kyra was just scared after being beaten down by men in the past. I had done the same thing by keeping Nilson's threats from her, but from now on, I swore to be someone she could rely on. Someone she'd be proud of.

I sucked in a steadying breath, but instead of welcoming a wave of calm, the smell of ventus creatures wafted through the wild wind. Fast hooves thundered behind, then the loud flaps from their giant wings sent a shudder up my spine. Wind accelerated and thrashed against my skin as I continued to chase Kyra. Why hadn't she turned Goldie around for me yet?

My heart slammed against my ribs. Vayu men were mounted on

their half-horse-half-eagle ventus rides, close on our tail. The sunrise light cast a glow on the twelve-foot white-feathered wings of the venti, looming closer. Goosebumps prickled my skin. We had no time.

"Kyra!" I shouted, then commanded the dirt to lift me straight to the treetops like an elevator of soil.

"Watch out!" Kyra warned me, motioning to Nilson, hidden in the branches.

Fire exploded from her fingertips. It singed Nilson's forearms as he blocked his face, then a gust of wind thrust me back. I almost toppled off the platform of soil.

"I don't want to hurt you, love, but it's time to come to your senses! I'm your only hope," Nilson bellowed.

Surprisingly, Kyra angled her gorula toward me, reached for my hand, and yanked me onto its back.

"Go, Goldie!" She gave it a little nudge, and the gorula swung forward, its six limbs flinging us from branch to branch at top speed. "Don't fall!" Kyra reached back and tugged one of my arms around her waist, but I kept the other on Chocolate's collar as she whined.

I could feel Kyra's sheer determination flowing through her veins, straight to where my hand latched onto her waist. Our connection surged to my tattoo. Divinity, she was so powerful. I'd vow to protect her until my dying day.

"Kyra!" Nilson's shout was quickly drained out by the beating wings of several ventus growing closer.

My eyes watered from Nilson's wind slamming into us from all angles.

Where are we going?

I sent the question through our thread, but Kyra's mental wall blocked me from diving into her mind.

Wait, was she pissed at me? Why?

"We're going to Vayu for the Unetlo Book," she said with an edge to her tone. "Since I couldn't return Landon, the book of spells might have answers." When she glanced over her shoulder at our chasers, her fear groped at my heart, clawing and shredding it to pieces.

It'll be okay. I'm right here.

Her muscles tightened for a moment. Why? Then Goldie quickly dropped five feet to lower branches, making us both grasp her neck, the gorula's golden fur blending in with Kyra's flowing hair.

I sniffed the heavy cologne of the Vayu men. We couldn't outrun them. Our weight was too heavy. Too slow. Goldie couldn't swing fast enough.

Maybe I'll have to jump off.

"No, Jay. You're not leaving." She reached for my hand again.

Sucking in a deep breath, I clenched my jaw and focused on the power radiating through our tattoos. Not just mine but Kyra's too. Silently, I commanded a branch to break, but it caught fire by mistake. Damn it, our Magik was twisted together.

With a sweep of Kyra's arm, the blazing branch soared like a spear. Straight into a venti's chest. The creature shrieked. Flailed its wings and rammed into a tree, tumbling to the ground. Its rider crashed, too, pinned underneath. He lay deadly still, blood draining from his head.

"Shit!" Kyra yelled.

In unison, the remaining ventus called out a vicious, vengeful scream and dove. Massive feathers and wings surrounded us. Goldie jolted to a stop on a high branch. The poor gorula whimpered and cowered into a ball. With our hearts pounding, we slid off her back.

"Surrender." Nilson jumped off his hovering venti, fury written on his face. The branch shook from his weight, but he kept his balance. "How sweet, you're trying to protect each other." Nilson pulled out a Taser and pointed it at us. "It's too bad we have to resort to violence after so many years of Mystier peace."

"What is th—"

A crippling electric shock obliterated my senses, but as I tried to register what was happening to me, I realized Isaac had shocked Kyra, not me. Her body jolted in agony, but I felt part of her pain.

"Kyra?" I swept an arm out to keep her from falling off the gorula.

Her face screwed up, and I held her tight to my chest. I frantically kicked Goldie to rise. Higher. Higher we flew. Kyra's anguish tore through me, and then her memories followed.

Her brother's empty seat at the kitchen table. Kyra's drums in a child's bedroom. Skipping school. Meaningless flirtations from guys too old for her. Taking the blame for Hallie's mistakes. Her stepfather raising fists to her face. Quamir forcing himself into her.

I didn't know which was worse, her physical pain from the Taser or the emotional pain from her past. The spurts of Kyra's story cleaved my heart in two.

I held Kyra close to my chest until her seizing finally stopped, and drool dripped from the corner of her lip. Goldie swooped further away, and I used the rest of my energy to ease Kyra's pain. But she stayed asleep, leaning on my chest for support. At least the creature had some sort of trick to keep Chocolate from falling off her back. Treetops zoomed above as the gorula swung rhythmically. Isaac's men slowed, carrying two dead bodies; the soldier and the venti that perished.

Once we covered more distance, I finally let my muscles loosen. I stared down at Kyra's face, so serene in slumber. It didn't even matter where we were headed. If she was with me, I'd be okay.

A gentle hand ran through my hair. A dream zoomed in and out of focus of me touching Kyra and running my lips over her collarbone.

"Wake up, Jay," a sing-song voice, with a dash of sass, cooed in my ear.

I opened my eyes to puffy afternoon clouds shifting from cotton balls to long streaks of white. Long grass tickled my bare back. Groaning, I squinted against the bright sun. Where were we? Amid tall stalks, Kyra sat on flattened wheat in a new outfit. Tight black workout pants were painted onto her toned legs, and a loose tank top fluttered in the breeze, revealing a new ladybug-red bra underneath.

What is with this girl and red lingerie?

I scanned the prairie wheat. If "clear" had a smell, this would be it.

We had traveled straight west, obvious by the mountainous terrain in the distance.

"I think we're close to Vayu's border. While you were getting your beauty rest, I walked to a little shop down that road and stole clothes and food." Kyra pulled at the backpack again. "I'm assuming you had your knight-in-shining-armor moment last night when I passed out from the Taser gun?"

"Are you…okay?" I asked.

"I'm fine."

My tattoo sent a twinge of need through my core, wanting to hold her and comfort her unease while also feeling desperate to ask her a hundred questions. No matter how hard I tried, I couldn't take my gaze off her amber eyes. She hypnotized me into a trance, but the armor around her heart was as hard as stone and covered in thorns.

"So, what were those white-winged creatures?" she asked.

"Venti. They live in Vayu."

"They're…"

Majestic.

"Exactly." Her nose scrunched up.

I pushed off my palms and squinted through the dancing wheat, wildflowers, and weeds into a vast field. In the distance, a ramshackle barn sat by a rusty fence. Eagles flew in circles in the other direction over an obvious cliff drop-off. Sniffing in the pollen, I breathed in the new air.

"I didn't think the Link would feel like…this." She handed me a canteen, freezing to the touch with little beads of condensation clinging to the outside. "You told me we'd be stronger if we Linked together. But we lost the battle with those Vayuians." She threw leftover scraps to Goldie and Chocolate, curled together in the tall wheat.

We have to practice. It's not automatic, I said through our Link, testing how it works. I gulped the water, letting it glide down my throat.

Kyra reached into a new backpack I had never seen and pulled out a granola bar, handing it over. "I still need your help to return, Landon. After that, you're a goner." She mimed, slitting her throat.

Your jokes aren't funny.

"I'm hilarious."

It wasn't fair that she could hear most of my thoughts, but she somehow blocked me from her mind. "If you lower your wall, we could understand each other, and this would be much easier." I bit the chewy granola mixed with chocolate that melted over my tongue.

I could faintly feel her considering the options, even if it was just a mild tingle across the bond. While waiting for her to process, I surveyed the foreign land, a never-ending sky encompassing us like a snow globe.

"Thanks for the food."

"Don't thank me," she grumbled, pulling a drumstick from her newly golden hair and tapping a beat on my shoulder playfully. "Thank the poor clerk I stole from." Kyra finally chuckled, pink smoldering her flushed cheeks.

She laid a hand on my chest with a forest-green t-shirt crumpled in her palm. Just the simple act of her touching me sent a jolt of excitement to my crotch.

"Quit picturing me naked," she snarled and threw over some combat boots.

"You stole *all* of this? They could've arrested you."

"First, they'd have to catch me." She wouldn't meet my eye. "So, I have a plan on how we can steal the Unetlo Book."

I sighed, willing to let her change the subject. At this point, I'd be the last to push her into something. "I saw the book once in Vayu. Last time, it was underground in a vault, protected by a bunch of charms."

"I can sense you don't want to go in there." Her chin nodded to the turquoise and white swirling clouds that stretched on for infinity.

I nodded. "Nilson will have it more heavily guarded now that he knows we're Linked. If something happens to me, promise me you won't listen to him. I can't tolerate the thought of him trying to control you." A shiver trembled my shoulders when Kyra's memories flooded back. Men had abused her–over and over—all of her life. She must really love Landon to sacrifice staying by my side.

"Stop trying to force yourself in my mind," she whispered, "it happened once, but as long as I can help it, I won't let you in my mind again. So, don't ask."

"Understood. You can have full access to my mind; what's mine is yours."

She wiggled uncomfortably atop the wheat. Chocolate sniffed around Goldie, who pranced in circles, giddy on all six limbs.

"So, this field obviously leads to a cliff's edge." I pointed in the distance where the wheat pasture abruptly ended.

"Yeah, that's where the ventus flew off the cliff earlier. Just *poof,* gone. I didn't want to jump after them without some sort of plan."

"I bet you were tempted, though." Every ounce of my energy went to resisting brushing my fingers across her cheek and pulling her in for a kiss.

We sat side by side, hypnotized by the blue sky and hawks circling above. The freeing way it dove and hovered reminded me of the woman sitting next to me. The same feeling came over me when she played drums last night at the festival. She was a free spirit meant for soaring.

"Hey, Kyra?"

"Yes, Mister Jadox?"

"That night we were in your apartment in Andersonville, I saw sheet music everywhere."

"Wow, you're great at random thoughts, soldier."

"Have you ever written a song?"

She froze for only a second. "I've…dabbled in writing."

"Do you remember any?"

"Wouldn't you like to know." A divine smirk quivered at the corner of her lips.

An engine roared and sputtered behind us. "Oh, she's here already!" Kyra shoved my head below the surface of the wheat. "Be good for once, and don't move."

I peeked around her to the sight of a vintage aero glider flying above, gas-fueled from a century ago. "There's no way any pilot can land that old thing."

"Quiet, she'll land fine. It's flat here, the perfect landing strip." But as she said it, Kyra cracked her knuckles, then thumbed a quick beat on her thigh.

My heart raced, speeding faster than the aero glider.

Who is meeting us?

She ignored my question. As the glider zoomed lower, it showed a large, tangled net hanging from the base. Not a good sign. I gulped down any hesitation, but Kyra's nerves were stuttering with a chaotic rhythm evident by her fingertips, *tap tap tapping.*

"Lay flat. Stay here, and whatever happens, don't use Magik," her voice was bordering on frantic.

The pilot landed ahead, just shy of the cliff's edge. Kyra ran toward the old craft, boots kicking up loose wheat along the way.

"Chocolate, come," I whispered and held her collar low to the ground. She licked my face and placed her brown paw over my cheek.

Above, Goldie's drool dripped and splattered on my neck. I tried to tug her lower too, but she was too massive to maneuver. Hopefully, whoever Kyra had invited to help us knew about the gorula's friendly nature.

"I made it," an unfamiliar, high-pitched voice projected.

The stranger smelled of lavender soap and guns, but I couldn't smell a hint of Magik. Was she from Elidi? How did Kyra manage to contact one of her kind? Where had they met?

Quit with the questions, Jay. You're distracting me.

I smiled. Finally, Kyra communicated through our tether, even if it was only to scold me. Unable to control myself, I peeked my head above the surface of dancing wheat.

A woman with a shaved head, wearing a silver and purple jumpsuit, held Kyra's hand. Bits and pieces of their conversation floated over in the breeze.

"Knock down the barrier…" the stranger said.

"…better way…" Kyra angled the stranger away from where I hid.

Why couldn't this woman know I was here?

"...Hallie, no..."

Hallie? Her sister. Kyra had somehow called her Ordull sister. No, no, no, no. Nothing good could come of this. My mind raced, and I pressed against the shield in Kyra's mind, needing answers.

Let me in.

In the distance, Kyra pressed both hands to her temples and bent over. Pain thrashed through my own tattoo, and I screamed out.

"What was that sound?" Hallie turned, aiming a gun where I hid, and stomped closer. I scooted Chocolate behind me quickly and held my breath.

"Nothing, come here. Let's talk about this." Still in obvious pain, Kyra begged and twisted her sister's shoulder toward her.

"Someone's out there. Go hide in the jet."

"No, everything is fine. Listen, Hallie, you can't send a shockwave like that over this area."

Acute understanding quickly evolved to anger, and my Circle warmed, sending prickles through my stomach to my fingertips. I swept a hand at the ground, and the dirt rippled like a wave. The wheels of the aero glider tilted, and the entire machine toppled to the side.

"Show yourself, witch!" Hallie squeezed the trigger.

Bullets zinged above my head. I flattened my body completely over Chocolate.

"Stop, Hallie!" Kyra jumped on her sister's back.

"Chocolate, stay." I bolted upright and dashed toward my girl.

I lifted one hand toward the wheat. At my command, it bundled, weaving together into an elaborate rope. It surrounded Hallie, twisting around her body.

But the Ordull pilot jumped from the cockpit and began shooting.

"Is that..." Hallie's eyes widened, flailing both arms against the wheat rope. "It's a man! He's a witch!"

Another shot—but it missed me by a mile. Though, a terrible howl gouged my eardrums from behind. I was too terrified to turn. If she killed Chocolate, I'd tear her body to pieces. Kyra's jaw dropped in horror, and I followed her gaze. Blood gushed out of Goldie's chest, and she collapsed to the ground. I hurried to her side, hovering my hands over the creature, then dropped them to her golden fur. She was already gone.

In a rage, I sent another wheat rope to restrain the pilot. The Ordulls struggled against their binds, furious marks scratching into their skin.

"You killed Goldie!" I charged the pilot. But when I glanced over at Kyra, kneeling in defeat, I only felt her heartbreak, no revenge layered behind her tears.

Jay, I need you.

And just like that, my rage evaporated. I moved to her side. Kyra sucked in a deep breath and took my hand in hers.

Hallie gasped. "Back away from my sister, witch!" She fumbled her restrained wrist, digging in her pocket.

"Listen, I can explain. We're trying to bring Landon back. Jay is powerful, and together, we—"

"We?" Disgust curled into a grotesque cringe. "Are you…no…you can't be working with *him*? With the witches? No…" Hallie's voice faded.

"I can explain. Let me show you." Kyra rolled her pants to her belly button, exposing her glowing tattoos.

"*No*!" The word ripped out of Hallie's throat, and Kyra jerked, startled next to me. "You're one of *them*?"

I hovered my hand over Kyra's shoulder, wanting to ease the pain rattling through our thread. Unfortunately, my healing powers didn't take away emotional turmoil in the same manner, no matter how much I tried.

"It's okay to be scared, Hallie, but I'll fix this." Kyra's jaw clenched tight. "I'll get Landon back."

"I'm not scared." An oddly curved, near-insane grin warped Hallie's porcelain face. "All the witches will die." Her words sliced a wound of betrayal so deep through Kyra's heart that it felt like a dagger stabbing my own chest. Hallie's finger twitched inside her pocket, and a loud creak groaned near the aero glider.

Kyra dropped to the ground again and covered her ears,

screaming. Her pain shocked my gut, bending me in half. Straining against whatever force was hurting her, I crawled to her side again.

"Kyra!"

She rolled to a fetal position, writhing with eyes clenched tight and fingers jammed into her ears.

"Stop! Stop it. You're hurting her."

"Good. I was a fool to come to her aid. She's no longer my sister."

"Please!" I screamed, realizing it must be a high-pitch sound hurting Kyra, something only she could hear.

Chords and wires shot out of the glider in all directions like manic tentacles. Tiny lights flashed from one end of the chords, then straight up. All I could hear were Kyra's endless screams.

All power in my Circle disappeared. "Stop this!" Agonizing pain ripped through me, but I screamed at Hallie again. "Stop!"

She was no longer tied up. Without my powers, my wheat had dropped uselessly to the ground. Seemingly out of nowhere, an enormous spark exploded in the sky like fireworks. Pops and sizzles rained hard, and the air quivered like a wave of illusions.

I kneeled near Kyra, opening my arms to her. She crawled to me and shoved her head against my chest. Together, we watched Vayu's shield shatter before our eyes. The entire city became crystal-clear, towering on the other side of the cliff. Skyscrapers sat atop a mountain peak like they were sitting on a throne of clouds. Sleek, sharp buildings ranged from blueberry shades to cyan to navy. My jaw dropped. I had seen Vayu once from its streets, but never from this angle. It was a city exclusively meant for Magik, for Mystiers. Yet, an Ordull had just destroyed the last chance of keeping them all safe.

In shock, Kyra trembled in my arms as both of our powers were stripped away. I held her tight as I watched her sister push a button on her watch.

"It's done," Hallie said into her watch. "Send the rest."

A dozen other aero gliders appeared from afar and zoomed overhead toward the city. They crossed the cliff's abyss and straight into Vayu's territory. My Magik didn't answer my calls with the electricity still caging us. At least I still felt Kyra's presence through the Link. Even if she led me to my death, I'd help carry the weight of her burdens.

Kyra clung to me for a second more, then sucked in a breath and stood, brushing off the dirt from her clothes. Something changed in her eyes with the wicked understanding that her sister had just betrayed her. Kyra sprinted after Hallie with full force. This woman was my everything, and I'd fight any battle with her by my side, no matter what. But, instead of waiting, she ran ahead, darting away from me.

Kyra, wait...

Hurry up and help me, soldier.

18

KYRA

"Hallie! Slow down," I screamed at my sister.

She ran fast toward the old glider machine. Vayu's skyline of azul-striped buildings stole my breath away. We were so close, but the deep, wide ravine separating us from the city was one monstrous obstacle.

I couldn't let Hallie's backup team fly in there. Somehow, I'd have to convince her to trust I'd find a way to bring Landon back.

I sprinted faster. My lungs burned, and my muscles flared. I tried to summon my Magik, but its absence was clear: no pulsing force, no pull of heat from my Circle. The only constant was Jadox's strong determination pushing through our thread as he chased after me. I blocked that beautiful man out.

Ahead, Hallie reached inside the door of the tilted plane and pulled out a hoverboard.

"Hallie, wait!"

She finally turned, the sunlight gleaming off her newly bald head. At first, her new look shocked me, but it suited her, making her eyes pop. But the way she used to smile at me was replaced with a venomous glare.

"I'll give you one chance. Give me information about your witch kind. It's President Stirk's orders, and there's no way to escape it. If you cooperate, I'll try to convince her not to electrocute you."

"That's such a generous offer, sis."

"You're no longer my sister."

"Hallie..."

Nostalgia flared achingly as I took in her angry face—the expression she saved for fake dad when she stood up to him on my behalf. But it had never been directed at me before. She jumped on the hoverboard.

"Jay and I can try to bring Landon back right now. Turn off the electricity, and we can use our Link—"

"I always knew you were...different...the way Dad looked at you."

Her words slapped me across the cheek. I staggered back, straight into Jadox's chest.

"You two won't live through the next month. All your kind will be destroyed."

As she pivoted to take off on her hoverboard, the pilot tossed me a wad of paper, then steadied her balance on her own board and said, "I'm sorry about your pet. I didn't mean to shoot it."

They rose over the cliff's edge and zoomed toward Vayu, a powdery city made of crushed diamond that glittered in every spec of the air.

"That went well," I sighed and unrolled the note.

radio station- channel 102.5

Not all of us agree with President Stirk. Meet me in library in 48 hours.

-Fiozee - A.O.S.

"A.O.S.? What's that?" I asked while his warm body tickled my skin.

"The Aurum Orbis Society. But it could be a trap."

I shook my head. "Hallie will eventually understand, and she'll explain what this means. She's my best friend. I just need to give her a few days to process."

"I don't think that's a good idea. Hallie caused all of this." His arms spread wide. "We can't trust her anymore, and that pilot is working with her."

Jadox was insane for thinking Hallie would turn against me. My heart battled that thought with an intensity that physically hurt my chest.

"What now?" I groaned and spun in a defeated circle. "This is a hopeless situation."

He leaned against the plane. "We can go find a nearby forest to live in. The trees like us, right, Chocolate?"

"No, I'm getting in that damn city."

"Of course we are. Lead the way."

The dog wagged her tail and weaved between Jadox's knees. I refused to glance at Goldie laying in a heap in the meadow. For now, I had to ignore the layers of pain building higher and just focus on the finish line. Hopping inside the rickety plane, it creaked under my weight. Through the door, Jadox hovered his hand near my elbow. At least he was trying to stand by the rule to not touch me without asking.

I twisted the rusted dial, and a recording played on repeat. I turned it up. It was a directive from President Stirk with some phrases cut off by static.

"...Anonymous source...Electricity will harm the witches...Stay in urban...Plug in old devices...Do not use guns. I repeat, no guns. Witch powers can kill. They aim to eliminate all of us who don't possess powers...."

"That's not true!" I slammed my hand against the dashboard.

"...You've probably seen the video footage on the news of the felon, Kyra Kozelski. The bounty on her head is still ten thousand, and one thousand for all the other witches you can turn in."

"I guess I'm famous now." I shoved my palm against my temple. "And worth ten thousand."

You're worth everything.

I rolled my lips at Jay's silent admission.

Syvonne continued, "Remember, they did this to us. The witches took away everything; our loved ones, our families, our everything. In a week's time, all our agony will be avenged. Now that we have discovered another witch city, the next step of our plan is underway."

After the speech looped back to the beginning, I twisted the dial off. "I guess a world of only women isn't as ideal as I had hoped."

Jadox rolled his eyes at my sarcasm. He rubbed the stubble framing his sharp jaw. "I'm worried about how they discovered that electricity is our weakness. That means a Mystier broke under torture." He held out a hand for me to exit the plane. I grasped it and thudded to the ground, crushing wheat underfoot. "We need to free the prisoners they've captured."

"Yeah, but it's not goal number one."

"Of course, it's not," he said, "after that announcement, everything has changed. Goal number one is hiding you. Syvonne knows you're valuable, so now Mystiers might also turn you in."

"No, goal number one is returning, Landon." I walked toward the cliff's edge and peeked over. There was no way to the other side. Clouds floated below into an abyss. "I guess I can't trust anyone now if the whole world is hunting me for bounty."

"You can trust me…." Jadox whispered from behind me, his voice like silk against the back of my neck.

Every bit of me wanted to believe him, to lean into him. I blindly reached behind me and let my fingertips brush against his inner wrist, giving myself just one moment of comfort.

"I'm not hiding from all of this, Jay, and you have no right to ask me to."

He sighed and ran his calloused fingers up my forearm. I didn't mind. In fact, it felt like a slice of the Divine. I refused to look at him. If I met his deep brown eyes, I'd lose all control over the urges longing to pretzel around him. Dropping my hand from his, I felt his disappointment.

Kyra, let me in. You can't deny this connection.

My jaw clenched, and I finally succumbed to his gorgeous gaze.

Passion poured from the depths of his eyes, overflowing like lava from a volcano. He didn't move a muscle, but I could feel through the Link how much he wanted to wrap his arms around the small of my back.

"You need to stop thinking about us like that, Jay. This isn't a game," I said.

His throat bobbed. "I didn't say it was."

I bit my lip. Still a few feet apart, the sensation of his hands on my skin sent a shiver up my spine. His craving hunger burst through our bond, carrying the memory of his feelings when we swam in the lake under the stars, tied together by our wrists. Somehow, that felt like years ago. Because of this Link, I understood Jadox's soul better than any other person in my lifetime.

I swallowed my feelings. "Do you think Isaac knows we're out here?"

The corner of his lip curled up deviously. "I'd rather you not mention another man's name when sex is on your mind."

I gently slapped his chest, but instead of pulling away, my fingers paused, trailed up his firm pecs, and wrapped them around his neck.

His breathing turned heavy, his woodsy scent tickling my face, and his lips inches from mine. A breeze ruffled his wavy hair and made the wheat brush against my ankles.

I rose on my tiptoes, bringing him closer, and whispered with the fierceness of a goddess, "I can sense how much you want to kiss me right now. But if you do, I guarantee we will *never* be an option. So, soldier, here's a test. Can you control yourself?"

Jay's lips parted, and his nostrils flared. That strong chest heaved against my body. "But if *you* kiss me now, I promise I'll get you the Unetlo Book before midnight."

A frustrated grunt rose deep in my belly, and my head spun with dizziness. Jadox's watch chirped an alert, and he jerked away. Another second away from his mouth was torture. The moment vanished.

"It's Nilson. He spotted us," Jadox said.

"How?"

"Probably with his enhanced eyesight."

"Oh, great, so he's special too."

Jadox clicked a few buttons as I turned and paced in front of the edge. "He's offering us safety in Vayu for a day if we help him capture and kill the Ordulls hiding in their city. Maybe they have an ally helping them."

"Probably, but who? I don't know your people. And I'm not going to kill my sister."

"I know, but we could lie to him, make Nilson believe we would help."

"Right, men are expert liars. I should've guessed that'd be your plan."

"Kyra, stay still and look at me." Jadox crossed his arms, teasing me with the bulge of his biceps. "I'm sorry for keeping Nilson from you. What more do you want from me?"

"Nothing, I want *nothing* from you. I want Hallie and Landon back and you to leave me alone. Forever."

I cleared my throat. "Fine. But I'm not the only liar here. We need to figure out how to get to the other side of the canyon. Maybe somehow, we can turn off this electricity, then our Magik will return. Or we can steal a hoverboard from a nearby town, but they might recognize me."

I rushed back to the plane and hammered my fist on random buttons. Little meters on the dashboard lit up and twitched back and forth.

"Please get out of there," Jay begged, "you might hurt yourself."

I yanked on random chords, and sparks crackled in yellow spurts. "At least then, I wouldn't have to deal with you anymore."

Why was I still pushing him away when all I wanted was to ease the inner turmoil raging inside us both? Memories of how his lips felt on mine made me want to explore what else he was capable of.

His angular jaw jutted out, and a growl rumbled from his chest. "Stop pretending like you're heartless."

I paused, spun on my heels, and faced him. The entire plane shifted. "Excuse me?"

"You're in denial, pretending you don't feel this..."

Chocolate sat on his combat boots, her dopey eyes watching Jay's motions back and forth between our chests.

"...This thing between us," he continued, "This depth, the intensity, the realness. Look me in my eyes and swear you don't feel this."

"It's called Magik, Jay. Get over yourself. The night I met you, I thought you were the last man alive, and I didn't wanna fuck you then, and I still don't now."

"See. I knew you were thinking about us together. Just admit it. I can smell your arousal."

I pointed at his nose. "Because you...you ..."

He leaned through the door, close enough to kiss. Close enough to wrap my legs around his waist and bury my hands in his hair. Close enough to...Goddess, I wanted him.

A sudden alarm beeped wildly on the plane's computer screen and flashed large numbers with a robotic voice counting down.

My gaze darted to Jay's.

"Jump!"

He caught me mid-air and dropped me into the wheat. We bolted away, Chocolate at our heels, barking.

"Four," the robotic voice continued.

A humming sound quickly turned into a loud drilling noise.

Wheat crumpled underfoot, and I sprinted as fast as possible. Jadox stayed right by my side, even though he could run faster.

"One."

He grabbed my shoulder and shoved me to the ground, throwing his body on mine.

A low, rapid boom exploded behind us. Jadox cradled my head in his hand, serving as a buffer between me and the ground.

"Are you okay?" His words came out between pants. His eyes were wide and alert.

I peeked over his shoulder. Tangerine flames crackled from the plane, and thick smoke rose, blocking the view of Vayu. But then the fire swiftly traveled up the tentacle chords suctioned to Vayu's shield, burning the wires. The air itself flickered, and the entire city disappeared.

"We did it!"

Glancing up at Jay's face, a mass of feelings scorched through my stomach. Deep within my core, energy swirled and torched my Circle. He grunted at the same time power streamed into my tattoo. The energy didn't travel to my fingertips this time but went straight between my legs. My thighs warmed with desire. The view of him on top of me turned me as wet as a river. Damn it, Jay.

"Our Magik…it's back," I stuttered.

"I know. Are you hurt anywhere?" He searched my arms for any sign of injury.

As his body was pinning me on the flattened wheat, all I could think about was our future potential. A shared treehouse in Draven. Sparring lessons near a crashing waterfall. Gemm teaching me her potions. Chocolate playing fetch. A future with him was terrifying. This Link was playing dangerous mind games.

"I can smell your fear. Are you *this* scared of me?" Despair stripped his voice raw.

I tried to slow my racing heart, unable to speak. He was right. This bond was other-worldly, breathtaking, and uniquely ours.

He rolled off, a frown claiming his face. But I couldn't explain my thoughts, my feelings, not now, maybe not ever. Jadox stood and moved away, and sadness rained through the tether. I'd cut off my arm to not feel his emotions so vividly.

He ran a hand over his neck and surveyed the land. A fire consumed half the wide prairie toward the cliff edge, begging me to absorb it into my power, but I let the fire blaze. He closed his eyes, allowing me ample opportunity to scan his body again. This was the last time I'd allow myself to be distracted by his sincerity, his kindness, and his protective soul.

Arms extended, Jadox summoned the wheat together, and it braided into a long rope. Then a loud crash thunked behind me, and bits of earth rolled to us from afar: sticks, twigs, hay, and dozens of plants I didn't know the names of. With a whirl of his arm, the materials formed a giant bridge. Jay thrust a finger toward the cliff, forming a tightrope across the ravine to Vayu's invisible seal. The end on our side planted itself deep within the ground. I closed my mouth as he turned so he couldn't witness my amazement.

"Uh, how do we know the other side is connected to something strong enough?" I gawked down at the clouds.

"We don't." The severe seriousness etched into the lines on his face confirmed that I had finally gotten through to him, that this was all we'll ever be. "I'll go first," he said.

"No."

He raised both massive hands in surrender, giving me a picturesque view of corded muscles worthy of masterful art.

"You don't even have to come. You should take Chocolate home."

"Shit, Chocolate..." He crouched.

"You forgot about her?"

"No, I...yeah, I forgot about her." He kissed the pup's forehead, right between the eyes. "I'll be back soon. You find some squirrels to eat, okay?"

Her tongue flopped out, and she danced in a circle.

"Jay, she needs you."

"You need me more. Chocolate survived weeks alone once. She should be fine."

I sucked in my lips and took a hesitant step forward. The rope creaked and sagged under my weight. "Woah, this is...we're really high. Please, distract me."

"You're afraid of heights?"

"Um, no, definitely not."

"Who's the liar now?"

"Shut up, Jay." But his banter was working, distracting me. "Tell me something I don't know about you."

"Hmm, I got kicked out of the army for breaking the rules." When Jadox followed, the rope drooped lower, croaking in protest.

"What'd you do?" My hands trembled.

"I got in a fistfight with a commanding officer."

"He must've deserved it."

Why was I taking Jadox's side without even knowing what happened? An image seared my mind through our Link: a man in uniform forcibly stripping a young woman. I cringed and gripped the railing of the bridge. Why were so many men the devil in disguise?

"Sorry, I wasn't trying to show you that," he said.

"My fake dad gave me a black eye when I was twelve. Then, one night, when I was sixteen…."

He inhaled sharply. "Kyra…you don't have to."

"Just…listen."

"Okay. I'm here."

At the sincerity of his voice, hot tears suddenly pooled behind my eyes as I continued across the bridge. I'd never told someone this story before.

"When I was sixteen, I snuck my boyfriend into my room after midnight. Tyrique was my first love, and it was my first time. Honestly, the sex couldn't have gone better, but my fake dad must've heard us because he stormed in with a bat and beat Tyrique." I sucked in a deep breath. "I can still hear the cracking of Tyrique's skull. My father killed him, in my bed, right in front of me."

I wouldn't let a tear fall and concentrated on putting one foot in front of the other. "My father wrestled me, keeping a hand on my mouth to silence me. He yanked off my clothes, and…."

"Kyra…"

"Just listen, Jay…I thought he was going to…but he took naked pictures of me next to Tyrique's body. He said that if I told anyone about the murder, he'd plaster the pictures everywhere. And he said I couldn't touch another boy as long as I lived in that house, or I'd have the same fate."

Jay paused for so long that I wasn't sure he'd ever reply. "Did you tell your sister?"

"No, Hallie was always his favorite."

"Kyra, what he did was—"

"I'm not weak. There's nothing else to say about it. If you want to do something to support me, then I need you to learn how to put up a mental wall against me."

"Why? Maybe I want to give you all of myself." His words were as soft as a feather.

I tapped my foot ahead and took another hesitant step on the bridge. Holding my breath, I continued the balance-beam death walk.

"Jay, maybe I *want* you to put up a wall against me. You're a man, just like the rest. I never said I wanted inside your heart and mind."

Silence.

And then an ear-piercing caw shrieked above. A venti dove, close and fast.

"What the?" I froze.

"Go!" He nudged my back. "Hurry."

I clutched the railings as hard as possible. Sweat dripped. My hands slipped. Ankle twisted. Then the rope disappeared from under me. I fell. And fast. Jay's sudden absence gutted me. The wind whipped around me. A final descent.

"*Kyra*!" Jay screamed above.

His voice drummed a beat my body finally understood. The further I separated from him, the more everything clicked into place. Away from Jadox, I felt starved, shriveled to nothing. He was mine, and I was his. We were one and always would be. I never wanted to be separated. But I kept falling. Air rushed by.

I was leaving him.

Wind and air. I was falling faster. A force tore the oxygen out of my chest. I couldn't breathe—in more ways than one.

19

JADOX

I awoke from a dream that painted a canvas of honey-gold eyes burning with passion, a fire lit so deep that no one could extinguish her flame. I longed for the edgy arch to Kyra's eyebrow and how my hand dwarfed hers. Sinister shadows of emptiness consumed me. How did she survive the fall off the bridge? Kyra was still alive somewhere—although weak and distant, her energy zipped through the tether in spurts.

A rare piece of trash in Vayu's pristine city rolled by the gutter and stopped at my foot. My muscles groaned as I stretched out of the curled position behind a dumpster in a dark alleyway. The smell here was different, sweet, and wholesome, like cotton candy. Magik blew through the air like a never-ending streamer, flailing and rippling. It was like the city was lying to itself, feigning a whimsical atmosphere when Hallie and the troops were somewhere close, preparing to attack.

I squinted up at the sunset. After searching for Kyra, I wasted too much time passing out from exhaustion. I knew she was still alive. Was the rescuer helping or trapping her? Why wouldn't she respond through our Link?

At least no one had caught me. Yet.

While growing up in Draven, gardeners had studied their precious plants and learned over time what each one needed to thrive—the most observant workers cherished the plant last to bloom. But instead of becoming a gardener, I joined the army, clueless about being a nurturer. How was I supposed to know if Kyra needed to be watered, pruned, or dug out of bad soil?

"Hey, you!" A Vayuian in a military outfit pointed a rod at me. "No one's allowed outside their home. Go back inside."

"Yes, sir." I snuck around the corner to the next alley, shadowed by the azure and indigo towers stabbing the clouds.

Stirk's soldiers could be hiding around any corner. But I wasn't going to try and save a city when Kyra's fate swayed on a seesaw just out of my reach. Did Hallie have her trapped somewhere? Would her sister stoop that low?

Empty streets made my movements less conspicuous but also gave me fewer threats to pass. Most of the building walls were made entirely out of glass, so dozens of people would catch me sneaking around by looking out their kitchen windows.

"Where would Kyra be, girl?" I whispered and looked down at Chocolate, forgetting that I had left her on the other side of the bridge. So stupid. My pup might try to cross it herself.

I tried to focus by testing my Magik, but my muscles only twitched. There weren't many elements nearby at my disposal outside anyways. Various plants stood inside apartments, but their windows would shatter if I tried to retrieve them. Concrete paved the roads, and the high-tech metal framing the skyscrapers required significant energy to manipulate. Sniffing the air, there were barely any scents of soil, plants, roots, dirt, or sand nearby.

Following my instincts, I crept from shadow to shadow, peering around corners until I reached the center of the city. I had been in the library before, but nothing good came from it. A massive gray stone statue of a windmill stood in front of the library. Despite the statue being made of stone, the Magik of the city circulated its mighty blades.

The corners of the kite-shaped building uniquely tipped at a slant, reflected the setting sun to nearby buildings, bouncing off the light like a trick. I set my sights on the front doors, knowing some of the secrets that lay buried within.

A figure streaked between buildings across the road and crouched, her midnight skin blending in with the shadows. I sucked in a deep whiff. The pilot—Fiozee. She scanned the area and stared at the library doors, reminding me of her note to meet in the library.

Trusting an Ordull with anything sounded like the worst plan possible. I scanned right and left, searching for cops, then bolted across the empty clearing of the city square straight toward her. Fiozee's eyes widened, but she didn't move a muscle. I flattened my back against the cold steel. After a quick nod, I waved her over.

Silently, Fiozee grabbed a hoverboard leaning on the side of the building. It hummed as she rode to me, staying low. Once at my side, she flipped it to her hip, holding it comfortably like a surfboard.

"We're surrounded," she spat out with a strong, unplaceable accent.

My gaze darted to the rooftops, looking for shooters. "Where?"

"I meant surrounded by blue." She gestured in a wide circle. "Everywhere: denim, berry, indigo. You'd think they'd use at least one other color."

My shoulders loosened from her attempt at a joke until two Vayuian police officers marched past on a nearby street, their swirling Möbius tattoos glowing a robin egg's color through their flapping shirts.

"Where's Kyra?" Fiozee whispered.

Going against every moral Kyra stood for, I pinned Fiozee to the wall, making the beads in her long black braids dangle against the metal. "Why do you want her?"

She struggled against me. "We're on the same side, dude. I have information for her."

I increased the pressure on her shoulders. "Give me one reason to trust you."

"Didn't you listen to the radio broadcast?"

"Yes, that doesn't prove anything."

"Of course, it does. I gave you secrets. Syvonne Stirk has the entire army searching for Kyra. She also has men from Cydon imprisoned."

I released my grasp on her and leaned against the shiny wall.

"Stirk wants Kyra captured and brought to her new office." Fiozee rested the hoverboard against the side of the building.

"Why? Kyra doesn't have anything that Syvonne wants."

"The president knows more than she's telling us. I heard every remaining Mystier currently in custody will be tortured by electric shock until they give her the whereabouts of Kyra. The ones who won't talk will be killed." Fiozee blew out a heavy breath.

I ran my hand through the fuzz of a new beard and inhaled the fresh aroma of chicken cooking from an apartment above. "Why would you help me?" I asked Fiozee.

"I'm a member of the Aurum Orbis Society. We were a secret organization for years. Our leaders speculated about people with magic, and *The Scorch* confirmed it." She peered around me to the city square and tugged my shoulder closer, away from the moving sun that stretched along my sleeve.

"What do you mean '*The Scorch*'?"

"That's what everyone called the event when all the males disappeared. Didn't you see it? When every human male vanished, they lit up in an abrupt flame."

"How do I know if you're just saying all this but have plans to turn us into Stirk?"

"I can't force you to believe anything. You'll have to trust that our worlds are merging." She smiled, her tomato-red lips popping against her brown cheeks. "Aurum Orbis takes a stand for equal rights. Mystiers shouldn't have to live in hiding, shouldn't be outcast, and should feel free to partner with anyone they love, whether they have magic or not."

"You haven't called us 'witches' once."

She laid a soft hand on my shoulder. "That's because you're not."

Memories flashed of my childhood in foster homes, surrounded by bullies who made my life a living Abyss, who treated me like vermin for years because they had an inkling I was *different*. "Okay, I'll work with you, but we're doing this my way."

Fiozee nodded. "What's the plan?"

A sharp shock jolted my Circle, and a message invaded my thoughts.

Meet me at the vault under the library. Hurry.

My heart ricocheted within my chest from Kyra's mental message, and I stumbled to the side, falling off the curb.

Kyra?

Silence.

"Kyra?"

"Ssh! You'll get us killed." Fiozee glanced around. "Do you see her?"

"No, I'm going to the library." Adrenaline spurted through my veins at the knowledge that Kyra was okay.

"Okay, I'll find a way for us to travel. Once you find her, we need something stronger than a hoverboard to carry all three of us. You look like two hundred pounds of muscle, so this won't hold all our weight."

"Try finding a stable holding some venti. Meet here at midnight. It'll be the safest time."

She glanced at my bare wrist. "You don't have any comms."

"My watch broke."

She unhooked her watch and wrapped the band around my wrist. "I know my number, so I'll figure out a way to contact you. If I'm not here by midnight, leave without me. No matter what, don't let the soldiers get ahold of Kyra. Stirk is planning something."

"Thank you, Fiozee."

She darted in the opposite direction down an alleyway. Quickly, I used all my energy to shoot a message through our Link.

I'm coming to the vault. Are you hurt?

Silence.

Tightness snaked in my chest at the possibility of Kyra's injuries from her fall, but all I said was, "*Dehano huc.*"

A ball of dust rolled from the alley, growing larger with each second, soon taller than me. I shoved it toward the spot the police had been marching and sprinted toward the back of the library. Completely exposed in the city square, I smelled a buffet of dinners wafting from the open windows. My stomach rumbled, but I kept running through the stinging wind. Straight ahead, the library towered above most other skyscrapers.

"Mommy, what's he doing?" Above, on a high-rise balcony, a little girl whose long hair blew in the breeze pointed at me. Fluttering scarves that draped over doorways tore from their tacks.

"Get inside!" The door slammed shut, but the mother stood, hands outstretched like a butcher holding two knives. With a flick of her wrist, all the fabric flew toward me at impossible speeds.

Vayu flags hanging from windows ripped from their posts. I darted past the first flag, but a scarf wrapped around my wrist and pulled me back, slowing my momentum. Another flag and scarf coiled around my other wrist, wrenching me to a metal hoverboard stand. I stretched my chest forward, straining against the fabric, but the first scarf tied itself to the post. Locked. My other wrist, bound firmly, attached to the cold metal.

I kicked at the ground and writhed against the restraints. My biceps bulged, and I grunted. Heaving. More Vayuians appeared at their windows, pointing, then drawing their shades. The sunset's rays bounced off the sapphire buildings, mocking me with its cheery hue.

"What's going on here?" The sweaty smell of the same military man sprinkled the air from behind.

Almost spent, I finally ripped apart the tough fabric and was free. Then, just ahead, a metal grate scraped loudly across the pavement. Golden hair emerged from the base of the windmill statue. Kyra shifted a section of the sidewalk over. The power inside me immediately tripled.

"Jay!" Her eyes widened as she spotted me and then noticed the military man approaching fast.

Before she could climb out of a hole in the pavement, I borrowed Kyra's fire through our bond and shot flames at the guard. It formed a massive wall. I dashed to Kyra's side. We jumped into the stale tunnel, then, quickly, she pushed me to all fours.

Don't move.

I immediately understood her intentions. Kyra used my back as a step ladder. The strong smell of gunpowder came closer from above. She slid the barrier closed fast and sealed the trap door shut with a lock.

Rough hammering started on the other end of the metal door. Darkness surrounded us, but I knew exactly where she stood from her fresh, fruity scent.

"Are you hurt?" I asked.

"I'm fine."

"Good, then I can pester you for smelling so good." I licked my lips, wishing I could taste that delicious scent. "When were you able to shower?"

"Wish you could've joined me."

I froze. "What?"

"You heard me, soldier," she said teasingly, almost playfully.

"Really?" My eyes adjusted, and I tried to read her expression. "I thought you hated m—"

Kyra roughly pinned me against the wall with her hips, and her hands slid around the back of my neck, pulling my face low to meet hers.

Shock seized my bones as I leaned into her. "Wh—what are you doing?"

Her mouth met mine. Eager. Greedy. Impatient. Kyra invited my hands to her waist and placed them under her shirt. Such soft skin. She moved them up. Up. Up. Fuckin Abyss, no bra.

Her tongue claimed mine with the assertive glide of liquid gold. I couldn't breathe. Her lips pressed against mine, shoving my back harder into the stone wall. Ecstasy. While palming two handfuls of her breasts, I grunted into her mouth. They were smooth and sized to fit my hands perfectly, like a missing puzzle piece. Both nipples pointed so hard that I couldn't help but squeeze each a little.

She yelped softly into my lips and climbed my body, latching her legs around my waist. I held her ass up, gripping the plump, full, roundness, and let her devour me. Sinking into her tongue's rhythm, I relished each soft pulse of her hips against my pants. My cock was ready for her, caged by the fabric, begging to be set free.

"Kyra..." I rasped, panting between kisses.

"Shh, kiss me." She sank her hands back into my hair, wrecking my control.

Separating for just a moment, she pulled her shirt high. Then a flicker of flame danced on her fingertips. She moved the torch closer, showing me the curves of her breasts.

"Did you just growl?" Her smile grew in the faint shadow. "I missed you."

My heart soared from her words. Her lips found mine again—home. My heart needed nothing else. No one else. But, for some reason, I couldn't believe this was real.

"Where is this coming from? Did someone put you under a spell? Are you being manipulated?"

"No, Jay. I'm done fighting you. When I fell off that bridge and fell further and further from you, I wasn't thinking about if it'd hurt when I smacked the ground, or Hallie, or my past life. The only sensation that mattered was that every movement away from you felt like a rip in my sanity. I need you like I need air."

"Are you drunk?"

"Stop teasing me."

"Well, give me some time to process this. It's not like you've enjoyed me so far."

"I accept us and this thing, this Link. Our bond is non-negotiable. Didn't you feel the desperate pull toward me when I fell?"

"Yes," I said. My breath became heavy as she licked my neck.

"Then you know exactly what I'm talking about. This isn't something I can put into words, so stop overthinking it and kiss me."

A loud grinding sound and the smell of a gasoline motor erupted above. They were sawing through the trap door.

Crap!

Kyra leaped from my waist and dropped to the ground, fumbling with her shirt.

"Too bad we need to run now." The surprising excitement

threading through her voice showed that she was not only safe but thriving on this adrenaline, and she cherished it, swam in it.

"Where you go, I follow," I said.

Her finger flashlight burned steadily again like a mini torch as she jogged down a tunnel. Somehow, it smelled meticulously clean. What was the tunnel there for? Where did it lead to? Did other Vayuians know about it?

Quiet, Jay. You're thinking too much. Let us focus on this maze.

I held back a smile but matched her steps. Light poured a slight beam from behind, and four smacks echoed down the tunnel walls. Thwack. Thwack. Thwack.

"Stop, you're under arrest!"

Faster!

Her adrenaline unraveled like a ribbon through our joined thread, spiraling into a frenzy. The tunnel split into two ways. Right and left. She stopped abruptly and surveyed both options. I knew where to go this time.

This way, Petal. The Unetlo Book is in the lower vault.

We descended a ramp, moving further into the ground. My Magik grew stronger the deeper we ran, and the intensity of our connection was about to burst me into pieces.

"Can you feel it?" Exhilaration laced her voice. "I can feel the energy of the book. It's calling to me."

I failed to understand the sensation she described about the Unetlo Book because all my energy revolved around her. She owned my entire heart and soul, and I'd give her the world.

"Here. There's a door!" She shone her flame on a locked wooden door made centuries ago with a couple of different bolts and locks.

"How do we open it?"

20

KYRA

"I have an idea." Jadox held both palms out, an invitation, without laying a hand on me. "Can I touch you?"

"You don't need to ask that anymore." I bit my lip and met his gaze.

I placed both of mine in his large, calloused hands. His warmth eased into my skin. With a roar, the door's wood split down the middle, and splintered pieces shot forward like a missile.

Holy goddess, he is so hot. That was the first time our joined Magik had worked the way we intended.

Bright light almost blinded me, and we stepped through the threshold together into a circular room encased in marble walls. An empty, single podium stood in the center.

"Is this the vault?" I asked him.

Jadox stormed forward. "Damn it, damn it!"

"What's wrong?"

"The Unetlo Book is gone. This is where they kept it."

I hunched over the podium and pressed my palms onto the wood. "No, no, no. If we don't have that, I don't know what else to try."

"It's okay, we'll look upstairs in the library. Maybe they moved it to a different floor in the archives or restricted section."

I rubbed my temple, a headache forming. "Wait, Fiozee is going to meet us soon."

"Plans have changed. I met up with her in an alley, and we agreed to meet there at midnight after she finds a venti."

"In what world did you agree to work with an Ordull? I thought you hated them all."

"Some people are worth changing for." He gave me an obvious look.

"I never asked you to change, Jay."

"Fine, then some people are worth growing for."

"If you grow any longer, I won't be able to handle you."

One of his eyebrows shot to his hairline, and a slow smirk rose.

I flushed and turned my back to him, running my fingertip over the swirling pattern in the marble wall. "There's a lever or something in the wall here."

"Don't touch—"

But I'd already pulled it. Part of the wall slid into itself, exposing pitch-blackness beyond.

"Come on." I laced my fingers between Jay's, and we walked into the darkness together. Each time we stepped forward, a faint, automatic light on the ceiling turned on, brightening only a little more of the tunnel at a time.

"I've been here before. There are traps hidden in the walls and a wind-powered machine. We have to hurry."

His heartbeat drummed at a rapid rate as we hastened. The confined quarters of the tunnel amplified every sound, and an eerie sensation washed over me. A quiet hiss sounded as if it were blowing through a vent.

"Don't look back." He squeezed my hand.

I dug my heels into the smooth concrete underfoot as the hissing grew closer and louder. It felt like a drug, hypnotizing my thoughts.

Dizziness took over as I grappled for air. "I'm gonna pass out."

Jadox turned quickly to check on me and his gaze locked on something behind my head. Terror filled his face. "Run, Kyra."

I stumbled into his chest, and he scooped me up, holding me like a damn fool. Rushing forward, Jay stopped at an elevator door and slammed his finger into a button.

"Come on! Come on!"

My lungs were on fire, and I gulped for air, choking on nothing. In my fuzzy vision, Jay's lips were slowly turning blue, and he staggered to the side. His body leaned against the wall, almost dropping me. I twisted in his hold, peeking behind me for the threat. A pair of giant gray eyes that filled the entire tunnel glared at me—Isaac's eyes—an illusion. The faceless eyes rushed forward, death in their stare.

Curse words soured my tongue, but I couldn't breathe. The elevator doors finally closed, and we both collapsed to the ground. My lungs filled with relief. Jay reached up and pushed the second-floor button. The elevator didn't stop on any of the floors and went straight up. Three. Four. Five. Six. Seven. Rising to the roof.

"Great! The last time I was on a rooftop, Quamir was shooting at me."

I'll keep you safe, Petal.

The doors opened to the phenomenal view of the city with outrageous skyscrapers laid before us. I had never seen anything like it. The artistry of the building's shapes teased me about turning my head sideways and inspecting at a better angle. Vayu must have twenty times the population as Draven and a hundred times the resources. Everything below felt so fresh and clean.

Holding Jay's hand, I weaved through flapping sheets and tablecloths hanging from clothespins on the neighboring rooftop.

"Well, we can't look for the Unetlo Book up here."

"The elevator was rigged not to stop on any other floor." Out of breath, I asked, "Do you think anyone will know we're here?"

"I'll smell them first, and you'll hear them from far off."

"True…okay, so, now what?"

He stood beside me, confident and poised. "We need to meet Fiozee at midnight, but if we go there too early, someone will see us."

"So, we wait a few hours."

"Yes, we wait." He raised my hand and kissed my knuckles. "Then figure out a plan."

The space where his lips found my skin tingled with desire.

He turned, his deep brown eyes studying me. "I'm sorry I let you fall from the bridge."

"It's not your fault. I tripped."

"How did you survive? What happened?"

I slid to the stone ground of the roof and leaned my head back. The stars twinkled with a dare, but I had already made one wish that I regretted. Jay scooted by my side, giving me a few inches of space. Not only did I want him to touch me now, but I also needed him to. It felt like my very life depended on him being near me.

"When I fell off the bridge, a venti caught me. Maybe the creatures of our lands aren't loyal to only one type of Mystier. It flew me to a Vayuian apartment, and the family helped me. They fed me and let me bathe too. It was so sweet. I accidentally fell asleep for a few hours and then set out to find you."

"I'm glad you're okay." His energy turned nervous, but I also realized I couldn't feel his thoughts and emotions as much as before.

"Uh, Jay, did you put a wall up against me?"

"Yes…you asked me to." His voice was soft, vulnerable as a puppy, and a little broken.

His sweetness created a tightness in my chest, and I laid my hand on his thigh. "I was wrong. I wouldn't mind you letting me in…if you want."

In a simple second, his shields lowered. A cacophony of his feelings rattled in my mind: the sounds of his memories. Harmonies of his devotion. Beats of his heart. Chords of his desires. I had to concentrate on resisting the temptation of kissing him to death right then.

He gulped audibly. "So, if we can't access the Unetlo Book, what's next?"

"Surh-Sig will have answers." I blew out a deep breath, wanting to stop the conversation and straddle him.

"You want to find that *demon*?"

"It's our last option. We can't actually search through thousands of books on random shelves. That'll take too long."

He paused, taking a moment to consider it. "Then I'll be by your side."

"You...you've been loyal, reliable, and supportive...why?" I slowly turned to him and softly positioned his hand on my inner thigh.

"Maybe men aren't all inherently bad." His voice deepened and turned more ragged. "And maybe I want to be someone you're proud to be with."

"Because we're Linked?"

"I cared for you before that, and I always will."

My heart struck against my ribcage fast and hard. I braved the possible pain of the future and straddled him. "Maybe women aren't all inherently good. Maybe I have my own dark secrets."

His eyes darkened with yearning, and he massaged little circles on my thighs. "Tell me one."

"You first."

"Fine, I love ear massages."

I laughed, then clamped my hand over my mouth so no one below could hear. "Wow, you're a complete demon for admitting that terrible sin."

"I know. If you rub my earlobes or my neck right *here* behind my ears, I'm yours forever."

"Got it. I'll avoid your ears because we wouldn't want to be trapped in an eternally binding agreement."

A chuckle mixed with a grunt sounded from his lips as I leaned forward and kissed his neck. "Your turn," he coaxed me with the movement of his mouth on my skin. "Tell me your deepest, darkest secret."

"I'm afraid...all the time," I whispered.

He leaned away and lowered his chin, watching me patiently.

"I'm afraid I've lived so long protecting myself that I won't ever know how to feel true freedom again. Over the years, my walls have grown taller and thicker, creating this mass shield against men, against the world…I'm so scared that I'll never be able to lower it. What if my fear controls me?"

He wrapped his hands around my back and rubbed softly up and down my spine. I arched into him, longing to give him all of myself.

I'll always be here.

You can't promise that, Jay.

"I'm probably the only one who can let myself out of this cage," I said aloud, "but I don't know how."

"Well, I could take a sledgehammer and shatter all the bricks and stones of the wall to pieces…or …." His fingertips deepened, massaging my back. "When you eventually find the key to unlock that stubborn door, I'll always be close, waiting."

A little moan fled my lips from his perfect touch, exactly where I wanted his hands. "What if I…mmm, that feels good…what if I want to sneak through a crack in the mortar of my cell for just one night."

His hands froze, and I could hear his heartbeat slam chaotically. "One night?"

"Just once."

"Hmm…that depends on the ear-lobe negotiations."

Slowly, I eased away from his chest, letting his gaze absorb my fears. "I don't want to hurt you. Most people can't touch fire; I hurt, scorch, and kill. I make people vanish. I don't want to be your end."

"Be my fire. Burn me to the ground," Jay said.

"Kiss me."

And he did. His thick lips bewitched me. Tender but firm. Fast but teasing. Hard but knowing. The stars blessed us, igniting celestial Magik between us. My Circle pulsed with raw passion.

"Kyra." His voice came out scratchy like sandpaper. "Do I have your permission to…"

"Yes, Jay, yes, do it all. Touch me everywhere. Please."

Jay's restraint untangled into a beast. He tore off my shirt. "Holy Shit, Kyra. You're so—"

I tasted his woodsy skin, cutting off his words, and became delirious from his deep, guttural groans.

"Tell me what you want."

"I want to see all of you," I whispered.

Straddling him, I slid my finger under his shirt and slowly, so slowly, rolled it higher until it hugged his chest and ended up tossing his wavy hair in a mess as he helped tug it over his head.

"Tonight, you're mine," I purred.

In response, his catastrophic gaze ruined me. I ran my hand over his toned abs, and my fingertips traced his pecs.

Wiggling on his lap, his hard length twitched under me, I glided off his pants in a moment of delightful anticipation. His chuckle rumbled softly, but his eyes rippled with boiling fascination.

I pushed down his briefs. His cock sprang free, and I palmed him. Skin to skin. Shit, his groans would unravel me to pieces. His erection rubbed between my legs while I, still somewhat clothed, relished the control. I gently ground against him, savoring each sound of pleasure puffing out from his perfect lips. I gasped as his tongue swirled around my nipple, tormenting me.

"More?" I asked.

"Never stop."

Jay turned my wrist over and kissed the path of veins up my forearms. In a low voice, he growled, "These veins are the roots to your heart. Kyra, you are *my* roots, gnarled, twisted, and rough, my very source of life."

He licked and sucked my breasts with flawless pressure. Arching, I leaned and gaped at the stars. His hands held my bare waist tight, egging me closer.

"Oh...oh!" My nails dug into his shoulders. "Woah!"

Craving everything that was Jadox, my lips explored his smooth skin. My hands slid up and over his strong back. He shivered and groaned. His cock flicked again below me, rubbing against my thigh. We were in treacherous territory. Everything was closer. More intense. Hunger clutched at my soul as I eyed his crotch. Jay's breaths sped up, reading my mind. His Möbius tattoos glowed and showed a surge of energy. Dominance.

I wanted to be filled with him. Possessed and claimed by him. And I hoped he could hear every. Single. Thought.

"Fuck, Kyra!"

I gasped. "Take these off." My hands groped at the fabric of my pants, wrestling them off so hard that he toppled over, and we both landed on our sides.

"Ooof."

His smile and the joy in his eyes could've stopped the planet's rotation. My heart skipped a beat as I pulled him to my lips. He tasted like Magik, like the woods and berries. I wanted him only to myself. My hands found his massive bulge again. Hard. Thick. Long. My body tingled. Wrapping two hands around his base, I realized I'd need a third hand to cover it all.

"Go on," he said with eyes monstrous, wild, and made for my dreams.

"Is that a dare?" I licked my lips.

"Double dare."

With a quick reach, he grabbed all the flapping sheets and tablecloths made of silk and cotton from the clothesline. Jay bundled them together into a soft bed. He flipped me onto my back, and I prayed the soft layers would be needed to clutch onto soon.

I gulped. His fingertips skated between my thong's fabric and my hip, and he swept it toward my ankles. As I bent my legs, he kissed each of my knees slowly. My heart was about to explode, and I couldn't believe how much I truly trusted him.

Naked. Both of us.

"Damn, you're…." He blew out a deep breath.

I reached up and stroked his cock again. "Ravage me, Jay."

A wolf's growl followed his smirk as he positioned himself over me on all fours, his muscles flexing, and biceps swelling. His cock rubbed between my thighs.

"I know a spell for protection," he whispered.

"Seriously? Yes, yes. Everyone should have access to that."

"*Venereae ostaguyelu,*" he mumbled.

There was no turning back now.

We can always stop if you want, Petal.

I mean my heart, Jay. I'm giving you everything.

Are you sure you want to?

Yes. I'm yours.

The vibration of his powers hummed through me, enhancing my own, and fire ran through my veins.

"Ready?" He positioned his tip between my wet folds, right at the opening.

"Please don't make me wait any longer."

"You're mine, Petal," Jadox said as he eased inside me.

I gasped. So thick. So hard. Filling me. Opening me up. Deeper. Pushing farther into me. Slowly. A little bit at a time. Fuck, we fit so perfectly.

"Mmm, damn, Kyra."

He moved deeper until I melded with him entirely. A soft moan parted my lips, and a strangled grunt escaped him at the same time. He held my waist with certainty, holding me down as he tortured me slowly, easing in and out. So slow. Damn him.

Jay...

I've got you, Petal.

Our connection made every sense sharpen to a telescopic feeling. His lips pushed against mine as he moved his hips in a roll, making my entire body clench and beg for more. He pumped. And I watched, entranced by his body disappearing inside mine. Nothing had ever felt so good. He moved, giving me an exquisite view of his chest above me, glistening in sweat, muscles carved out of ecstasy.

"Harder, Jay," I whispered between strokes.

"Not yet." His tongue swirled mine. "You're gonna finally feel how badly I've wanted you."

The heat between us was scorching hotter than a fuckin' oven. Blazing like the fire coursing through my veins. I needed to be even closer to him, to combine our two souls into one. He read my mind and eased his full weight onto my chest, sliding his hands under me and cupping my ass. My eyes rolled to the back of my head. So good. My breath ran rough, and my cheeks flushed.

I love being with you, Kyra.

His words sunk deep, rooting me into reality.

He brushed his lips against mine while shifting in and out, a torturous, blissful rhythm.

"Come for me, sweet Petal."

I dug my nails into his biceps.

"Drop your walls once, just for this. Just for me," he demanded.

A fiery inferno lit within and ran through my veins like lava rushing through a volcanic stream. Embers spurred through my system, and my blood boiled. Bubbling. Ready to burst.

"That's it," he groaned, thrusting his cock inside me, deeper, skin on skin. I bit my lip and met his gaze. So close.

He grunted into me, then pulled almost all the way out and stilled.

"You." Jay thrust back inside. Deep. So deep. Then he pulled all the way out again.

"Are."

Thrust.

"My."

Thrust.

"Home."

Thrust.

I grasped his muscles so tight that I was afraid I'd break him.

"Fuck, yes, Kyra, do it. Drop your walls. Now. Now."

A euphoric scream fractured me in two as I curled forward and up, shoving my hips into him and releasing the fear. I let go. My orgasm shook me into a rattling mess. I clutched his back and grabbed his hair. Heat blitzed through my tattoo, and delirium took over.

Jay pounded hard as my legs became weak. His cock slid in and out with such an intense, slippery fever. My moans might have never stopped. He planted his lips on mine as his tongue performed Magik of its own. Those huge pillars of arms trembled above, strong as stone in my grasp.

His whole body tightened and stiffened. A wild grunt seized his movements, and his eyes squeezed shut.

I'm coming, fuck. Fuck. FUCK!

His warmth flowed through me, and he finally slowed, holding himself steady over me, panting. A droplet of sweat dropped from his forehead to my breast. He licked it up and smiled.

"I'm in such trouble with you, Petal."

I reached for his ear lobe, slowly caressing the part connected to his skull.

"Oh, oh…" His eyes sealed shut, and his jaw dropped as he leaned his head onto my arm, using me as a pillow.

I didn't want the clock to strike midnight; I wanted to extend this moment for eternity. Sighing, I continued to stroke behind his ear as he hummed whispers of promises under his breath.

"What are you thinking?" he asked, words finally breaking through his nonsense sounds.

"I'm thinking we may need to do that again sometime."

His howled laughter rippled free, and he smacked another kiss on my lips. "I agree." His eyes sparked with the promise of more time together.

I snuggled into his chest, listening to his steady rhythm from within. I showed him flashes of pictures and my feelings. I sent him my perception of him from our encounters. How, on the first night we met, he was protective and strong against Quamir. I showed him my hidden joy during our sarcasm battles. How I appreciated his caring nature toward Chocolate. And how his presence was a healing factor, even without his Magik.

Jay's brown eyes watered as he locked onto my gaze. "You care."

"Of course I care." I continued to show him how I felt, how impressed I was on learning he would die fighting for Draven's safety. And that I admired how he confronted his commanding officer in the army for a woman's safety. I showed him how his determination, understanding, and patience won me over.

"Thank you, Kyra." He tucked a strand of my hair behind my ear, then kissed my nose. "Now, will you tell me about the song you wrote once?"

"Fine. I'm only singing this once." I crossed my arms in a pout.

You ignore my soul that could've shined so bright.

Behind the mask of this minnow is a deadly shark.
You've swallowed me whole and stolen all my light.
But no matter what you do, I'll find my violent spark.
So, watch your damn back, cuz one day I'll ignite.
And not one single man can keep me trapped in the dark.

He waited a moment, then started to ask, "Was it about…."

The wind abruptly flung the corners of the sheets below me up into a parachute mess. Then, a ruckus of stomps echoed in the stairwell exit at least four stories below, climbing fast. I jerked up.

"What do you hear?" He quickly reached for his pants.

I grabbed my clothes, fast threading my body through the pant legs and sleeves. "Soldiers. Do you smell them?"

He sniffed while bolting upright. "Shit. At least ten."

"Crap." I ran to the elevator, pushing the button. "I think it's jammed. We have to get off the roof."

Jadox rushed to the edge of the roof with me on his trail. Below, someone whistled, then waved their arms.

Squinting, I asked, "Who is that, and what is next to her?"

"Fiozee." He scanned the side of the library exterior, but the kite-shaped building was at a diamond slant and had no fire escape ladder. "We have to get down!"

The footsteps thundered closer. Before I could warn Jadox, a door slammed open, and a solid body knocked straight into him.

A voice I had already learned to despise mocked me, "I've been looking for you, love."

A dozen Vayuian militia marched up the stairwell and burst through the threshold. One carried a rope, another a lasso, each with their own unique weapon enhanced by their power. Wind captured me in a soundless cyclone, swirling around me in a frenzy.

With a flick of his wrist, Isaac shouted something. Then Jay rose from his feet, floated mid-air, and turned on his back. Isaac flipped Jay's body, rotating him in the air, spinning him like a broken doll.

"Let him go!" I shouted and pounded against the wall of wind trapping me.

Isaac's lips moved, but somehow, I couldn't hear him. He pointed to the side of the roof, and Jay's body floated over the edge, suspended over six stories high.

Kyra, if I die, just remember...

Don't, Jay, don't. I won't let him drop you.

I raised both hands in the air and glared at Isaac. "What do you want, asshole?"

21

JADOX

Nilson dangled my body over the edge of the rooftop. His nasty cologne bombarded me, making me nauseous. My heartbeat rammed in my chest, and my stomach lodged in my throat. The air between me and the sidewalk far below was full of nothingness, emptiness, absence. All Nilson had to do was say the word, and I'd be dead.

Kyra lunged for Nilson. "I said, what do you want, Isaac?" Her nostrils flared wildly, breathing fire at him, unfortunately not literal fire—yet.

The fact that Nilson had interrupted our cuddling session made him worthy of a limb-ripping death. I glanced at Kyra's stomach, where my lips had kissed promises onto her skin only moments before. But her Circle wasn't glowing either. Something was wrong. Did Nilson have electronic currents nearby?

"Bring back my son. Now!" Nilson's usual snarky voice was replaced with a menacing bellow. "Use your Link, do anything. I don't care. Just bring him back, then I'll let you and Griffin leave unharmed."

Kyra tried to step in my direction, but the whirling wind blocked her and tossed her already sex-tousled hair.

Nilson lifted one hand, and I dropped slightly.

"Put Jay back on the roof, and I'll do what you say. We can't concentrate on our Link if he's suspended like that."

I hoped the desperation in the edge of her voice was genuine and not just for show.

"Bring Jadox to safety, and we'll try to return your kid."

With a whoosh, Nilson dropped me to safety on the rooftop floor.

The wind wall around Kyra also disappeared. Nilson nodded, and his group of men circled Kyra. Her worst nightmare. Fuck! I seethed, and every one of my muscles pulsed in response. I pushed against our thread to send her a word of comfort. Two men grabbed her by the waist mid-jump and held her wrists behind her back. A cry of rage started deep in my chest and soared its way up, but when my mouth opened, no sound came out.

Nilson chuckled, "I control air, Griffin. Sounds move through airwaves."

I didn't have the capacity to consider science or Magik logic. I shoved up from the concrete.

Nilson pulled out the Elidi necklace from his pocket, the ruby gem swinging like a shiny pendulum. "This ruby is so strong that it probably has a power we still haven't discovered."

Her eyes narrowed. "Where did you get my necklace?"

"Your boyfriend told me where to find it."

Nilson twirled his finger around the ruby's chain.

"And because I'm so brilliant, I found a nifty spell to make sure the heat can't hurt me. But the first time I picked it up, wowza. That was a shocker." He flashed a red burn on his finger and thumb. "So, Golden Girl—that's what they're calling you, by the way—this soldier thought he could pull a fast one. He's been lying to you all along, love. Griffin found this necklace and handed its power over to me. You probably don't know that he and I have a history. I was the one who told him the Unetlo Book was locked in the vault. And you should know, love," Nilson addressed Kyra, "Your soldier boy and my Zeph had a *moment* last year."

Kyra stopped struggling against the guards, and her face flickered with insecurity for a beat as her eyes shifted to mine.

Truth or lie?

Um, some truth, some lie, but—

I pressed my plea against her wall again—futile. Furious, she immediately raised her mental shield against me, breaking my heart.

"Once you return my son, you can get revenge against Griffin. He can't hurt you when I have this too." He pulled out the Draven necklace from his other pocket, the emerald from Surh-Sig's demonic cave.

"That's not yours," I grumbled fiercely.

"Oh, yes, it is. A new friend swapped me this for a tiny favor."

Fear twisted my gut that Surh-Sig could be close by. I strained against the blanket of power controlling my movements.

We have to get out of here, Kyra.

Absence. Her eyes flickered to mine again, but her lips were pulled taut. Did our time together on the roof not solidify anything between us?

The watch pinged on my wrist, and the president's voice began playing aloud, "Attention all units, the fugitive, Kyra Kozelski, has been identified and confirmed to be at coordinates 68R-980N. All troops in the Northwest Sector will report to that location immediately. Immobilize her on sight, but keep her alive. Repeat: do not kill."

Nilson's gray eyes turned to stone. "Apparently, Griffin gave the president your location."

"No," I growled. "You have a traitor among your kind who'd give up your city for a reward."

"Zeph, babe, go sound the alarm and come back." Nilson blew a kiss to a woman with an azure powder dusting her cheeks—a woman I happened to kiss last year— something I had failed to mention to Kyra, but maybe that wasn't why she was furious. Zeph pushed her glasses higher on her nose, then Nilson continued, "The rest of you, keep every ounce of your Magik focused on these two."

The three soldiers, containing Kyra's beastly writhing, twisted her closer to me. An infestation of rotting roaches swirled in her amber eyes when she glared at me.

"You lied." Her tone could slash through a block of ice.

An automated female voice rang from Fiozee's solar watch on my wrist. "Received orders, Ms. President. Unit twenty-two is the closest unit, forty hours from Vayu."

"Where did you get that watch?" The tender Kyra from only minutes before was gone.

"Think about it, love," Nilson snarled. "Why would the president send him a message? It was him. He ratted you out. He fooled you into Linking to increase his power and then plans to hand you over to the government."

She shook her head in shock, registering each word. "Did you?" The pain on her face was like sharp nails slicing my neck. "How will I ever know the truth? You lied to me already."

"Kyra, why would you believe a stranger? I didn't give Nilson that necklace. I didn't set you up or trick you."

Even with her mental wall up, the brutality of her fear shoved through the bond, shattering my insides. Then she continued, "I never should've trusted a man. I never should've let you touch me."

She didn't mean it. Our connection was too strong. Nilson folded his arms and leaned against the edge of the rooftop. "As entertaining as this is, we have to prepare our city for war. So, bring my son back, now." He nodded a command to a soldier who reached into the darkened stairwell and tugged someone into the moonlight.

A bald woman stumbled next to us.

"Hallie?" Kyra ran over and ripped the cloth from her sister's mouth. "Are you okay?"

"Do what they say, witch." Hallie's voice cut sharp.

A thin line of liquid ink streaked from the charcoal makeup framing Kyra's eyes. She wiped it away quickly and sniffed.

Let me in. Lower your walls, Kyra. I'll show you my memories.

Nilson nodded at a colleague, then a loud zing echoed across the building. It must have turned off the forcefield because power started sizzling from deep within.

"Bring back Wes, or your sister dies." He jabbed a finger straight into Hallie's forehead.

My power came rushing back in a whirl, and I reached out to Hallie to heal her, but Kyra shook her head. "No, I need all of your energy for this." She hesitantly held out her hands, hot to the touch.

Despite Kyra's reluctance, our connection pinged strong. Images flickered between us of her body under me, my body inside hers, both of us surging together.

As her walls lowered, Kyra's confusion about me felt like a silent scream. I could feel her tears and heart jerk with the devastation from mistrust and hesitancy, but our Circles still beamed brightly. She chanted silently, teaching me what to say. Now, I was certain she had an enhancement involving spells.

Reditus atsutsa.

Then out loud, she said, "*Reditus atsutsa.*"

"*Reditus atsutsa,*" I joined in unison.

The rooftop gradually faded away. Midnight transitioned to bright light. Her Magik overwhelmed me, consumed me, and devoured me. Scents vanished. Kyra's eyes burned bright, straight in front of me, calling me. Deep within. Our fingers tightened their hold on each other—Kyra, so terrified of latching on too tightly, and me afraid to ever let go.

"*Reditus atsutsa.*" The chant became a prayer, life in itself.

A crippling charge coursed between us as a violent compression melded us. Magnetized. Glued. Linked.

All the air was sucked from my lungs. Gravity ceased to exist. Seconds passed. A lifetime flew by. Every beat of the earth's bubbling lava under the crest thrummed with hope to Kyra's heart, then straight to my own. Love.

Realization struck. Kyra was so hurt by Nilson's words because she truly cared about me.

"*Reditus atsutsa,*" we both hummed, but she added, "Landon," in a whisper at the end.

A pulse bombed within my center, rupturing my spirit and molding something brand new. Unlike anything I had ever felt, power gushed through my blood in a heap of drowning waves. The only constant keeping me breathing was Kyra's eyes.

Hold on, Jay! I can feel him in the Abyss. He's there!

I gripped onto nothing and everything at the same time, ready to vaporize at any moment from the unfathomable stream of breathtaking hope and overwhelming yearning.

Breathe. Just breathe.

Then Magik emptied me into a shell of nothing, draining the source of life from my every pore. Sharp, stinging screams crashed through our realm, snapping us back into reality. I collapsed, my tattoo throbbing. My entire body shook with exhaustion. More shouts. Clatters. The smell of someone new, different, wafted from nearby.

Wait, my eyes were closed. I pried them open and saw midnight darkness again. Blue, indigo, and gray chaos stared back. Heat. Something was on fire.

"Kyra?" I blocked my eyes from the whipping wind that ripped tears from my eyes.

Kyra, where are you?

Crawling, groping the ground. A body. Still. I reached for the neck. No pulse. Someone kicked my back.

"Umph." My face collided with the concrete.

A punch socketed into my stomach. The smell of burning flesh assaulted my nostrils. I held back a gag.

"Grab her!" Nilson shouted from the other side of a tornado wall.

Kyra?

A venti screeched, and wings flapped somewhere nearby. Dragging my exhausted worm legs behind me, I tried to calm my trembling hands with every forward attempt.

The wind died to nothing. My jaw dropped, and my pulse pounded at the sudden sight in front of me. One remaining male guard held a gun to Hallie's head. The rest were sprawled dead on the rooftop.

Panting, Kyra cast a ball of flames that surrounded Nilson.

And between them all, a little boy with a mop of curls crunched his shoulders together and crouched into a ball.

That's not Wes Nilson. That's not Isaac's son.

I glanced back and forth between the boy and Hallie. The boy and Hallie. He was Hallie's spitting image. Kyra did it. We saved Landon—together. Her nephew was back.

"Mommy?" Landon rose, eyes widening with each passing second. "Mommy?"

"Landon!" She reached out, but the guard pushed the gun barrel into Hallie's temple. Hallie's half-sob, half-scream shredded the stars, splitting the sky in two.

"Let her go!" Kyra increased the closeness of her fireball to Nilson.

He yelled nonsense, fighting his way out with his wind pushing back. Kyra's face fumed cherry red, and veins bulged in her forehead. Every part of her neck was strained as she corralled him in treacherous flames.

"Kyra! Drop it. The power is going to kill you!" I slithered helplessly toward her, unable to summon an ounce of Magik. So weak.

She moaned, sweat dripping down the side of her face. Her fire lowered a little.

"Mommy."

"It's okay, Landon; we're going home soon," Hallie said.

"Don't you move," the guard commanded and hovered his finger over the trigger, "not until the Golden One releases Isaac."

"Kyra, please, let him go," Hallie cried out. "You did it. You brought Landon back. You saved him."

Kyra's firewall around Nilson lowered further, succumbing to the weakness.

Through the chaos, a familiar vanilla scent wafted like an omen from the stairwell, making my skin crawl. Zeph burst through the door.

Kyra's strength faded, and she toppled to the ground, her fire disappearing. I reached her side and spooned her into my body.

Zeph squinted at Nilson's unconscious state and staggered back. "What did you do to him?" she screamed.

Zeph pulled a gun from her holster.

She pointed it at Hallie and squeezed the trigger.

A bullet pierced Hallie's forehead.

Again.

Another. Hallie sagged into the guard's arms, blood trickling down her nose from three holes in her skull.

"*No*!" Kyra screamed until her voice cracked.

Landon covered his ears and squeezed his eyes shut. "Mommy! Mommy! Mommy!"

Through our cosmic connection, I felt every crack as Kyra's soul fractured into pieces. She let out a whimper and wedged her back closer to my chest, curling into me. Defeated. Shivering. Completely broken.

I cradled her, pledging to make this right somehow.

The guard gently laid Hallie flat on the rooftop and gestured at Zeph. "Why'd you kill her? She couldn't hurt us. She's just an Ordull."

"She was holding a gun…I thought."

Nilson grumbled within the blackened circle and rose off the ground. He dusted off his gray suit and stretched his neck to both sides like he had finished a workout.

I gritted my teeth and concentrated on soil, rocks, dirt, anything, but no Magik hummed—I was utterly spent. I kissed Kyra's too-warm forehead gently and tucked her quaking body into the shadows, then pushed up off unsteady fists. After barely reaching all fours, Nilson strutted over and grabbed a fistful of my hair. He snapped my neck back, and all I saw were stars and his gray eyes—demonic eyes.

"You brought back the wrong kid," he spat. "Do it again, but this time, bring back Wes."

Whining from the corner, Kyra whispered, "Hallie, Hallie, Hallie," over and over in between Landon's desperate calls for "Mommy, Mommy, Mommy."

The little boy rocked back and forth, head ducked, clamped into a ball.

"Heal her. Use your power to heal Hallie," Kyra begged. "Bring her back, please, Jay, please."

"Kyra, I'm sorry. She's gone. I can't."

Kyra's pain charred me from the inside out as if I could actually feel a demon's jagged teeth scraping my flesh off my bones piece by piece.

You did this. You couldn't keep your own parents safe. You failed them, and you'll fail me. All your friends and family relied on you, and you abandoned them, just like every other man in this world.

You don't really mean that.

Yes, I do.

"Bring back Wes!" Nilson screamed. "This is the wrong boy!"

My neck twinged in his grip, but I managed to squeak out, "We don't…have any…power…left."

Nilson threw me to the ground and waved over the last guard and Zeph. "Bring them to the Vorso room. After the demon has her way with the boy, maybe then they'll quit messing around and listen to me."

22

KYRA

Captured. I was so cold. Freezing. I shivered in the corner of a dark, glass cube, trying to distance myself from the giant fan spinning frigid air in this cage. Goosebumps freckled my skin, so I wrapped my arms around my knees and blew my breath on my hands. If only I could summon heat, fire, anything. But my Magik was gone again. Damn you, Isaac Nilson. Everything felt empty without my power. When had I become so accustomed to the fire living inside me?

Two identical cells for the other prisoners, my friends, and my family, were through the glass. Even though we shared a wall, none of them could see or hear me. No matter how much I pounded on the glass, none glanced my way. Jay and Fiozee shared a cell. Jadox, trembling, had pulled off his shirt and wrapped it around Fiozee's thin frame. Next came his pants. He threaded each of her legs through the fabric, then sat next to her again. My heart clenched with love. He hated Ordulls, yet he was risking his life to save a stranger.

They didn't talk, but the way they pressed against each other, entangled in an embrace for essential body warmth, sent jealousy through my veins. At least he had someone for body heat. That gave him a better chance of survival. I could see him, but he hadn't acknowledged me through the glass.

The other cell showed Landon with blue lips and a shaking body. He lay in the fetal position in the corner furthest from the winding fan, tears turning to icicles on his cheeks. I stared. He was *alive*. I brought my nephew back against all odds. My heart should be pitter-pattering with glee, but fatigue and pain shrouded my chest. I was wrong– bringing him back didn't fix everything but only put him in danger. Landon's breath was visible in the air with every exhale.

Thick, suffocating agony wound tight around me. The terror creating havoc on my soul would destroy me. There was no way out. No escape. My fate was set, and any chance of change or freedom had cracked and splintered. Everything I attempted failed.

There were no clocks, no watches, and no windows. Minutes dragged. It had been a couple hours already since Jay stopped trying to communicate through our thread. How many, though?

Everything was cold. A soft scratch clawed at the last wall in my glass cube where a grand white venti stood proud next to the guard outside the door—Zeph—the woman who killed Hallie. I wanted to rip her precious glasses off her face, snap those lenses in half, and then gouge out her eyes with the shards. Or break her ribs with my bare hands, crush her skull, everything, all of it. Tears pooled behind my eyes.

Hallie was dead, so only darkness remained. It was suffocating. Smothering. I became exactly what I had feared. Caged by a man—Isaac Nilson and his minions.

Loss crushed me beneath its heavy weight. It swept me away into nothing, holding me in the depths. Messy tears ran down my face as I choked on stones of despair.

"My sister was murdered," I spoke to the whirling turbine.

I imagined the ditch they'd dump her body into, and a shudder sped up my spine again. Shaking my head, I wiped away the last of the tears. I should be the one to dig her final resting place. Families were supposed to lower their loved ones deep in the earth. But I was stuck in an ice tomb, unable to fulfill that role.

"You're just…gone. Hallie, I need you."

Whispers haunted me, but maybe my mind was finally lost to delirium. I focused on my stomach cramping from hunger. As my teeth clattered together, my molars clashing echoed back. Wishing my sorrow would turn as numb as my body, I tried to block out the fact that I'd never be able to argue with Hallie again or ask her to braid my hair. She'd never invite me over for pizza, and I'd never be able to play her a new song.

After our brother died so long ago, Hallie was the glue that kept me together. She always put a positive spin on any situation, shining a light on the darkness surrounding me. My heart clenched tight with grief. How could she be gone? Nothing felt real. Wishing Chocolate was by my side to ease the pain, I whispered to her from afar, "If things were different…I'd…if I could turn back time, I'd…."

Sobs corrupted my thoughts and muddled them into a mess. Unable to hold back, my body racked, and tears blurred my vision. I felt wrecked with the shock. This was impossible. Hallie couldn't be dead. This couldn't be happening.

More tortuous hours dragged by. Hunger eventually turned to further numbness, matching the rest of my slowly freezing body. The door slid open, and Isaac stepped inside leisurely. No longer in his gray suit, he wore flexible clothes, ready for combat. Holding a book bound by some sort of animal hide, he trailed a fingertip down the symbol, then opened it, turning the page as if it were a fragile leaf. He sat next to me, then stopped the turning fan with a snap.

"It's a little chilly in here." But his usual arrogance was gone, the joke dying flat on his tongue.

Asshole.

"Can you decipher the language of this spell?"

He turned the Unetlo Book toward me, and symbols I had never seen covered the page, yet I somehow understood them all immediately. The ancient words glowed on the old papyrus and popped out like notes on sheet music.

Fitus menday lapisu.

Shaking my head, I closed the book, knowing what it meant but unwilling to enlighten Isaac. "There's nothing special about me. If you can't read the spell, why do you expect me to?"

He petted the book's front cover, which was slightly ripped in the corner. "I'm sorry for your loss."

"No, you're not."

"Yes, I am. Zeph shouldn't have shot your sister. I know what it's like to lose someone you care about more than anything." He ran a hand through his long blond hair. "What would you do to get her back?"

My body twitched from the cold, but I wouldn't humor him with a response.

"I'd do anything to get Wes back." Lines creased his tanned face. "Anything. Just like you'd do for your sister."

"Don't talk about Hallie."

"Well, I discovered that your sister is actually the one who gave up your location to President Stirk. She betrayed you, not Griffin."

"*Leave*. I'm not going to help you, Isaac."

He put an arm around me, and under any other circumstance, I'd smack him, but my fingertips and toes were numb. "Yes, you are because you don't want one of *them* to suffer." He nodded to Jay and Landon's cells.

"Do you…" My head was pierced with sharp glacier edges pushing into my temples. "Do you…enjoy this? You keep threatening me with anything you can think of. Do you like torturing me? Being the bad guy?"

He sighed and hugged me closer. "I promise I'm not the bad guy, Kyra. I just need my son back. I need you to Link with me, love. It doesn't have to be this hard. Just say yes. Together, our energy would be focused on what I love most, Wes, and there won't be any more mistakes."

"Landon isn't a mistake or the problem—*you* are," I said, yet I longed for the warmth of his skin to blanket me completely and defrost the crisp, cold, cropping holes out of my heart.

Isaac rubbed his warm hands along my forearms. "We are the same, you and me. We've been at the mercy of Griffin."

"Shut up."

"Griffin isn't on your side. Sever the Link with him, then you and I can fix what you broke. We can bring everyone back. I won't betray you."

A snort lodged in my throat, frozen in my mucus. "I don't want to Link with you. Link with any other M-M-Mystier." My legs shook as I pushed off the ground to stand. "I'm not s-s-strong. I haven't mastered my M-M-Magik. It'll work better with someone else."

"I don't have time for this. The Ordulls are flying closer by the minute. You're the only one with the Golden Circle. It has to be you; it's why I've been searching for you."

Hunting. Gemm's prophecy said to Link with the man who hunted me. "If my life can't go on without Wes, so then, neither can his." He rose fast and marched to the door.

My neck craned to meet his gray eyes. "Wh-whose?"

"Say goodbye to your soldier, love. I'm giving him to Surh-Sig. Then maybe you'll understand how serious I am."

"No. Jay doesn't deserve to suffer for my mistakes."

"It looks like I finally found something that will break you."

Isaac froze under the doorframe, stuck between my cubed cage and freedom. "You determine how long you stay trapped. You're the only one who can decide to let yourself out of here. Links are a voluntary promise. I can't force this on you, but I can still make you regret waiting. Choose wisely." The door clanked shut behind him, and icy temperatures bit at my blood again.

There was no use anymore. I had tried to master my Magik and failed. Diving for the Draven necklace in the caves led to disaster. My actions got Goldie killed. Vayu was under attack because of me. Now that Hallie had been murdered, I had no one left. Landon would have to grow up without a parent. I never should have brought him back at all. Death sounded a lot better than this life. Nothing could get worse.

I pressed both hands against the glass wall between Jay's cube and mine. He sat shaking with his arm around Fiozee's ebony skin, her head curled into his neck, her fingers tucked into his pockets. His own fingers were blue-tipped. I clung to what fuzzy connection was left of the tether like a game of tug of war, grappling fist by fist to move closer to Jay. But our Link felt snipped, shredded, like something blocked my access to him. If only I had answered when he was trying earlier, we could have come up with an escape plan.

I kicked the wall. Slammed it, punched it. Screamed. My knuckles split, blood coated the ice wall, dripping down, and Magikly froze before hitting the floor.

Isaac hadn't even needed to lock me up because I caged myself. Bars, thick as titanium, indestructible to any fire or Magik, surrounded my heart and trapped me inside a web of mistrust. Isaac made me question Jay and throw off our connection. I was so stupid to have believed him and needed to do something about it.

But there were no other options, no path forward. According to legend, the only way to sever the Link with Jay was to murder him myself. But the only way to save Jay from Surh-Sig's nasty bite was to Link with Isaac. There was no way to win. I sank to the floor again, dropping my head into my hands.

I don't know what to do.

A faint light flickered on in the last cell, connected to the last wall of my cube. Obsidian eyes, sharp as death, peered through the foggy wall. A flash of long fangs gnashed the air. I bolted back, ramming my back against the turbine. Claws scraped the length of the icy wall.

"It's only me, child," Surh-Sig's unhinged voice hissed. "Come to me, little Elidi."

Pieces of borrowed skin flapped over her exposed bones like a cloak of nightmares.

"W-w-what are you doing here?"

"I'm here to answer another question, child. Then you can reclaim my emerald again."

I folded my arms tightly over my chest. "I d-d-don't want any answers."

Her cackle crept up my spine. "Of course not, how silly of me. Fear has kept you alive. Stick close to fear. That's the only way."

"Fear has held me back from living."

"What did you say, child? Speak up. I'm quite ancient."

"I'm n-n-not afraid of you."

"Of course you aren't. Let's make a deal, child." When she raised both hands, a golden gleam glittered from the seams where the skin was sewn together on her cloak.

"That is golden hair." I brushed my locks dangling across my chest behind my shoulders fast.

"Maybe there was one like you with a Golden tattoo before with similar golden hair. Is that the question you wish to ask?"

"No, I'm not b-b-bargaining with you again. Leave my f-f-friends alone." My teeth chattered. "I won't dive into any more d-d-depths for you."

"But will you dive into the depths for *him*?" Her razor-sharp claw pointed to Jay's frame, huddled in the next cell. "You could save his life from the Vayu prince. Ask me a question, child. I'll tell you any truth. We could make a deal."

"I already know the truth."

After saying it aloud, something thawed within me for a moment, giving me a clear picture. I blamed my father, then every male, for hurting me, trapping me, caging me. But Jadox was good, and Landon was good, and so many others were good. Ever since my brother disappeared into the sea and my father changed for the worse, I have lived in fear, protecting myself. Power thrummed like a drum beat in my center.

"You can't save me, demon."

Jadox also couldn't save me. I had to free myself. I'm the one that needed to change.

An ironic smile snailed up my freezing face. "The depths *are* the answer. Sledgehammers won't shatter any of these glass walls, but maybe all I need is to dig deeper under the walls," I whispered to myself. "Jay can't save me, but he could be the key to unlocking the door."

Surh-Sig walked straight through the solid glass barrier into my cell. "Tick-tock, child, The Vayu puppet has promised me a meal." The flesh patched over half of her face smiled, exposing those immortal fangs, but maybe I was hallucinating.

An idea sparked, so I asked the demon, "You wanted to make a deal?"

Surh-Sig crept closer, silent as a cat. "Yes, my child, a game."

I held out my arm. "I'll give you one bite now if you help me in a time of need. I don't want an answer but an oath that you'll return a favor I ask of you later."

"Perhaps." She licked her yellow bones. "How big of a slice?"

"One bite. One swallow." I gulped.

"Deal."

Bracing myself, I turned my head away. Stale smells like maggots and worms wafted from the decaying flesh pasted to her face like a pinned-on rubbed mask. Suddenly, she bit off a chunk of my shoulder. Howling out in pain, I crouched to the floor, shaking as blood slid down my arm.

"Watch me chew your flesh, child."

Forced to watch, I gaped at my flesh bouncing between her jaw made of only bones, down her rib bones, through her skeleton until it fell lower, latching into a piece of the cloak near her ankle.

"Now we are bound in our own way, child. You gave a piece of yourself, so in time, I'll give you something in return."

"You can't back out. I need you to get me out of here." I pressed on the blood gushing from my shoulder.

"You risk wicked games, child. I never said if I'd honor your first request, just *one* request."

"But I need your help *now*."

Bleeding and barely able to move, I watched Surh-Sig walk through the ice wall like a ghost and disappear into the shadows. Teetering on the cliff of death, I wondered if a spec of hope was left anywhere.

Exhaustion overcame me. My eyelids dropped, and my head bobbed heavily to the side. Pain radiated in my shoulder. The side of my cheek slid down the glass barrier between Jay and me. He was so close, yet so far—my solid ground that planted me steady, but I was away from nature, from him, and from my heart. Guilt hollowed me until I was an empty vase.

Jay, I need you.

Silence.

I glanced at Landon in the other cell, his chest still rising and falling so slowly. If he died from hypothermia right after I rescued him, Isaac would feel more pain from my hand than he'd ever imagined. All males weren't the problem, just a few of them, those like Isaac. A pattern of ancient spells whispered through my Magik—power drumming stronger from my ancestors. Answers lay in the center of my Möbius tattoo. Now, I only had to believe.

Opus amare.

Balling my fists hard, I strained to reach Jay through the bond, repeating my sacred chant with more desperation each time.

Opus amare. Opus amare.

A simmer of hope quivered in my Circle.

"Come on! *Opus amare*."

Drowsiness rushed in, fogging my consciousness. My breathing turned shallow, and my limbs went slack. Weakness was boring down on me, frosting my thoughts, my plan.

"*Opus amare*!" I screamed, but it didn't sound louder than a whisper. "*Opus amare*. I need you, Jay! Hear me. I trust you!"

I'm here.

My eyes snapped open at the warmth and sincerity of Jadox's response, and I grappled against the slippery wall. My heart swelled so largely that there wasn't enough room in my chest any longer. "Jay, can you hear me? Can you feel me?"

Jay?

I'm...here...I...love...

Waiting a moment too long for him to finish, I gasped. He was dying.

Stay awake. I'm coming. Stay awake.

Dizzy, I crawled to the blades of the rotating fan and pulled. Heaved it but couldn't even feel the metal in my blue fingers. My heart slowed further. I was too weak. I jerked. Twisted. Useless.

Slumping to the ground, I sent another message.

Jay, focus on your tattoo. We need to heal you.

Love...you...

His thoughts cut me in half, and his weakness was apparent, his voice fading like a ghost into oblivion.

No, Jay. Focus. You're a soldier. You survive. Feel that power. I'm sending it to you. Feel that? Concentrate on your Magik. Your hands in the dirt. Your feet in the mud. Your skin against the bark. Your hair brushing against leaves. Cover yourself in the earth, Jay. Go deep. Deeper than you ever have. Dig to where it's so hot that you can feel my lava from the core. Kiss me once more.

What was the healing spell? My body shook with exhaustion, and I slumped to my side again, eyes sliding closed. Broken images flickered of Jay healing himself in the stairwell after stealing my Elidi necklace when we first met.

Terra angakok, Terra angakok. Say it with me, Jay. Terra angakok, Terra angakok.

My tattoo singed with my energy. I just had to control it.

Please, Jay. Stay awake. Terra angakok, Terra angakok.

Suddenly, my turbine fan switched back on, whipping my golden hair everywhere. My body succumbed to the cold, the darkness—completely.

23

JADOX

Numb. Every part of my body was frozen. If someone straightened my elbow, it'd probably crack in half like an icicle. My body was impossibly stiff. No longer trembling, no longer shivering. If only my heart was as cold and hardened, I wouldn't have to care about Kyra's pleas through our tether. But where was she? I only saw this revolving fan spinning in our cube to solidify my hypothermia. The only indicator of seconds ticking by was the defeating whoosh of the giant turbine blades twirling. At least Kyra wouldn't have to witness my last few minutes—wouldn't have to watch my death.

Jay, answer me!

Using every bit of effort I tried, really, I did. But weakness won. Kyra deserved so much not to be captured. How had so much changed in such little time?

Escape wasn't an option anymore. Even if someone had managed to rescue us, I wouldn't be able to walk or crawl. A whimper sounded from somewhere close. I pried open one eye crusted shut from ice and spotted an arm as dark as midnight resting on my skin. *Fiozee*. Were we frozen together? Memories blacked into the confusion of the last few hours. Nothing made sense anymore, and the world blurred.

Curled, mostly naked, with frostbitten toes and fingertips, I was cursed to die in the arms of an Ordull—my enemy. Ever since Mom and Dad's murder, since all those foster families destroyed my spirit, since the Ordull army kicked me out of their service, I thought they were all my enemy. I was wrong. A strange sharpness pierced my chest—it felt a lot like regret.

You can forgive them, Jay. Let the pain go. Choose love.

Shock struck me, but I couldn't move. How was Kyra still strong enough to feel my thoughts? She must be close, but where?

Fiozee slumped. Her chest no longer rose or fell. Wishing I could check her pulse or warm her with more of my clothes was pointless. I was frozen. There was nothing left for me to give. Empty. Desolate. Bare. Alone.

Stop being so dramatic, Jay. I'm right here. You'll be fine. We'll be okay.

But any response to match Kyra's wit stayed lodged in my mind, tangled in a web of weakness. I squirmed against the ice wall on my back, my skin tearing off. My muscles tightened. Maybe, I wasn't sure. A sharp tightness pierced my chest when I glanced over at little Landon's cell. His eyes were sealed shut, and his face was pressed against the ice wall, but no breath marks showed his exhalation.

My blue-tipped fingers melded against the gray-fogged wall. If I had another chance, I'd do life differently, tell Kyra I loved her, make peace with Ordulls, and....

A loud crash banged outside the door, and the walls cracked, splintering all the way up. One wall shattered, exploding ice and glass in all directions. A woman fluttered toward Landon. Perhaps I was hallucinating because Gemm stood before me, using a walking stick to poke my side. Then a dozen women walked in behind her.

"Once there was a man and a woman who changed life for all Mystiers and Ordulls."

The last thing I saw was Alaska running in, grabbing Fiozee, and them both teleporting away. Gemm raised her staff, and everything turned black.

I awoke to the comforting scent of chestnuts roasting on a fire and cinnamon sprinkled with cocoa steaming above the flames. Wiggling my fingers and toes, I quickly checked inside my pants, then sighed with relief—the most vital of appendages was still attached.

With much effort, I pushed off the floor and glanced around the unfamiliar dim room. One blanket away, Landon's sherbet cheeks turned even rosier when he shuffled under his fur blankets and sighed. I crept over his tiny frame. Next to him, Fiozee snored softly, her chest rising and falling.

Then, to my relief, Kyra slept tucked into layers of fleece, with her golden hair spread over the pillow like an angel. A rock lodged in my throat at the overwhelming desire to hold her, kiss her.

"Jadox is awake," Alaska spoke to a cluster of Ordull women in the corner wearing sleek, soft blue and white swirled spandex jumpsuits.

Shadows flickered on the wall, bouncing off a wall of books. From a couch covered in novels, Gemm peeked her eyes out from behind a page, winked at me, and bowed her head in acknowledgment.

Alaska tiptoed across the creaky floorboards and sat with me against the stone fireplace. Flickers danced against her skin, reminding me of our childhood campouts in Draven.

"Where are we?" I whispered to my little sister, keeping my eyes on Kyra the whole time.

"An underground sanctuary in Vayu. We can't stay long."

I rubbed my temple. "Did I…did I heal us somehow?"

"No, I think Kyra borrowed your power and healed everyone right before she passed out."

Glancing at Kyra, I resisted the constant urge to cradle her close. "Is she okay?"

Alaska nodded. "Yeah, but Fiozee almost died. We don't have much time to make a plan before Stirk's army arrives."

"How much time?"

"An hour." She pointed to the shadowy corner by the shelves. "The women here are deserters. They have insider info to help us from the Aurum Orbis Society. I know you don't trust Ordulls, but—"

"It's fine." I scanned Fiozee's sleeping face. "Not every Ordull intends to hurt us. I need to move on from the past."

She took a moment and looked me over, searching my eyes. "You've changed." Alaska squinted, studying me further.

"Alaska. I'm sorry. I never should've erased Paola's memory. I was only trying to protect you from Ordulls hurting you, but it wasn't my place, and I took away your future. I had no right to do that."

"Maybe Kyra isn't the worst influence on you."

"Who says Kyra has anything to do with it?"

She ruffled my wavy hair and smiled. "I'm glad you're feeling better, but eat up and change quickly."

"Why aren't those Ordulls in custom army gear?"

"These jumpsuits change colors depending on the environment. These blue shades will blend into the buildings downtown. Others are preparing on street level, but we will be vastly outnumbered. President Stirk's orders are to capture us. We think she wants scientists to study our DNA to make sure no other baby will be accidentally born with powers."

"And then she will electrocute all Mystiers?"

Alaska rubbed my shoulder. "We won't let that happen. We also can't hide here while an entire Mystier city is in jeopardy. She passed over an old camo uniform I had once worn to war years ago.

Flashes of memories eroded my mind. Exploding bodies. Bloodied limbs. The smell of burned flesh. Snapped bones. Screaming. The screaming. The screaming was the worst.

"You know Nilson and his minions want me dead, right?" I asked. "Fighting alongside Vayuians may be complicated."

Under the blankets, I quickly changed into an old-school military uniform, wishing I had a bulletproof vest, just in case. My Magik would have to be enough.

A large sigh and yawn behind me stifled my thoughts.

"Jay?"

My heart fluttered at the sound of Kyra's voice. Through our bond, I could feel her fear and pain from her sister's death.

"I'm here." I held out my arms, and she nuzzled in close, burying her head in my chest.

"Are you okay?" she asked quietly.

"I am because of you." I stroked her golden hair.

"She's gone, Jay. I'll never see Hallie again." Staring at the fire, she held back tears, tension building up through our tether. "And what about Landon?"

"Landon's alive, and I'm here."

Her shoulders quivered in my embrace, shaking as she tried to control her sobs silently. Slowly, I massaged little circles on her back, envisioning the healing waterfalls in Draven. When she finally steadied and wiped tears away from her eyes, she looked up at me through thick, long lashes.

"Are you…are you sure you're okay?"

"I am now." I kissed her forehead. "Let's not get separated again."

A tiny smile lit her face for a moment. I knew she loved me, even if she wasn't aware of it herself yet. Her lips met mine and swept me into a kiss so deep that I'd never need to question her feelings about me. The power of her love radiated through her mind, and heat swarmed inside my tattoo, even though she hadn't proclaimed the words yet.

"When we were in those ice cages, Isaac said I must Link with him," she said.

My mouth opened to protest in every way possible, but her lips pressed against mine harder and with urgency. I was so grateful she survived. Without her, I'd be nothing.

"You scared me, Jay. You almost froze to death." She leaned her forehead against mine. "These…feelings are…terrifying."

"Good, be scared with me."

"You challenge everything I believed."

"I love you," I said to her.

She stared, doe-eyed, and sucked in a breath. "Even if I'm a poisonous petal?"

"You'll never be poisonous to me." A second passed. Then two more.

Her gaze barreled into mine. "Say it again. I couldn't hear you."

"Doubtful, you have the most superb hearing." I kissed her neck, moving to her collarbone. "I love you, Kyra."

"I…I don't know if I can say that yet."

"It's okay."

Alaska cleared her throat across the room. "Excuse me, you two, there are children present."

Kyra spun in a circle. Seeing Landon on the floor near the fireplace for the first time, she rushed to him. My heart tightened watching her exchange a few signs with him and point around the room. Landon never looked at her eyes but focused on a random spot on the wall.

Kyra followed his finger when she asked, "What is it?"

"It," Landon repeated, then dug in his pocket and pulled out a keychain of pictures. He flipped through his dozens of cards and pointed to a dog.

"No, bud. There's no dog here, but maybe we can get you one someday."

"Someday," he repeated, then turned and pointed to the shadows behind a bookshelf.

Kyra cringed, then whispered to me, "Hallie would have usually helped me translate. I don't always understand what he's trying to tell me."

Landon repetitively poked the dog picture until he rocked back and forth, side to side.

And then I smelled Chocolate, and it all made sense. A door nudged open, and my pup's coal-black nose was followed by her brown fur. Instead of running straight into my arms, Chocolate leaped into Landon's lap and licked his face. I couldn't hold back my smile if my life depended on it.

"Guess you have a new favorite." Kyra giggled and petted her head.

Sighing, she stood, eyeing the fireplace with a greedy gaze.

"Here, fuel up." An Ordull soldier handed over sandwiches and water bottles.

We gobbled them while Alaska pointed to maps of Vayu's city projected from her watch onto the wall.

"So, listen up. Getting the necklaces is the top priority."

"Isaac has them both." Kyra leaned against my chest, so I looped my arms around her stomach, feeling the heat sizzle from her tattoo.

"And Kyra is the only one who can grab it without getting burned," Alaska said, "So she has to go."

I didn't like where this plan was headed. "Where's Nilson now?"

"Our Ordull spy last saw him headed here." Alaska pointed to an image of a half-crumbled castle structure at the rear of Vayu, between the base of a mountainside and a row of skyscrapers blocking it from view. "The Aurella Fortress."

"They're probably hidden in the highest tower of this ancient castle."

"Stupid storybook tropes." Kyra chuckled, her back bouncing against my stomach. "So, I guess that's my mission. What about all of you? Where will you be?"

"I'll be with you," I said.

"I want a team protecting Landon here," Kyra said.

Fiozee spoke up from the fireplace mantle with a groggy voice, "I'll stay with him, and Gemm will be here too."

Kyra nodded gratefully. "So, how will we invade this Aurella Fortress before the army arrives?"

Alaska pointed to herself and rolled her eyes.

"Oh right, teleporting."

"But I can only get you so far. Gemm says there are enchantments protecting the exterior."

"Of course, and I bet I won't be able to manipulate fire." Sarcasm laced Kyra's voice, but I felt her racing nerves and rapid heart rate accelerating with each passing moment.

Alaska glanced at the clock on the wall. "We can't lose this battle. That emerald will help protect us. Failing isn't an option."

"Right, no pressure." Kyra's thumb played a steady drumbeat against my wrist.

Silently, I kissed the top of her head again and sent a message.

It'll be okay. We've got this.

Alaska threw Kyra a spandex uniform too. "The soldiers had some extra."

She stripped in front of the whole group. Clearing my throat, I tried to peel my eyes away from Kyra's form, but her curves magnetized me. The color of her camo spandex matched my green cargo pants.

"Uh, Jay? Hello?" She snapped in front of my face.

"What? Huh? Oh, sorry." My eyes shot to Kyra's entertained gaze.

The Ordull women laughed.

"Don't worry, ladies, he's not just checking out my fine ass. That monster loves me, isn't that right?"

A moment of her uncertainty coiled through our Link.

"Forever and always." I reached over and crushed her to my chest. "I'll be your monstrous beast."

Her smile tugged at my heart, melting me like candle wax. Kyra rose on her tiptoes and grazed her lips against my neck, trailing higher to the back of my ear. A shiver skittered up my groin and into my core.

"Woah," I said, pushing her down and releasing a low exhale. "...We can't start that now. Hold it for me until after."

She licked her lips. "After...after we get the necklaces and save the city."

Alaska's map flashed off, darkening the room. "Alright, team, everyone knows their assignments. We don't know all of President Stirk's orders, so be prepared for surprises."

The women checked their guns, a rare weapon since The Fall, and handed over knives to both of us. Kyra stared at the sharp Ordull-created blade reflecting the flames off its point and sheathed it.

"I think it's safer if I focus on my Magik as my weapon," I said.

Alaska noticed my tension and patted my back. "We need to rely on Ordulls and their weapons too, Jadox."

The team silently marched out a back door, and I sniffed what lay on the other side. Besides the strong scent of dusty books and the fire, only the smell of mold was recognizable from the hallway.

Kyra turned toward me, meeting my eyes. "Jay, we don't have just one enemy out there but two. Isaac *and* Stirk's army. I haven't mastered my Magik, and we haven't practiced our Link enough. If we get caught, I need you to—"

I pulled her closer, her chest pushing against me. "Look at me."

She tilted her head in that sassy way. "I already am, Jay."

"We can do this."

Kyra held her breath, her every muscle stiff as she searched my eyes. She slowly nodded. "Okay, we can fight anyone together. Our Link will protect us, right?"

"We always have a chance if I have you on my side." I lifted her chin. "You are the light in my darkness. As long as we have each other, there will always be hope."

She kissed my nose. Smiling, Kyra wiggled free, twisting out of my hold. "Don't look at me like *that* again until...after. Especially in that uniform, soldier." Her smirk knocked me senseless.

I saluted and straightened my shoulders. "Yes, ma'am."

"What's that sound?" Her eyes widened in fear.

Instantly, the smell of decaying flesh assaulted my nostrils, and my heart slammed in my chest. A secret door slid open from the bookcase, and books fell to the floor. Surh-Sig's grotesque form jumped out, bones jangling together. She cackled loudly and grabbed Landon in a millisecond. He screamed, piercing my ears, and my heart stopped. The demon jerked him back through the opening.

"Landon!" Kyra screamed. She bolted forward just as the opening sealed shut. Locked. Her fists pounded against the wall. "Landon!"

The gravity of what had just happened, and Kyra's fear, tackled me through our tether. Without communicating, Kyra absorbed my power, glanced at the fireplace, and summoned the fire to relocate. Flames burnt the door fiercely.

"We have to split up!" Her eyes were wild, crazed. "I'll get Landon, and you get the necklace."

Alaska sprinted to us from across the room. "No, Kyra, you're the only one who can touch the Elidi necklace; it has to be you."

She glanced at the dark tunnel leading to who knows where, then back at me, back and forth for what could've been a second or a lifetime. Resolution set in her eyes, and I knew her choice without asking through our bond.

24

KYRA

Wild-eyed, Jadox clutched my wrist harder and commanded Alaska, "Take her to the Aurella Fortress. Now!"

I thrust a knee into his thigh, then jerked out from his strong grasp. "Let go! I have to find Landon."

Alaska nodded to her brother, cast me a quick apologetic look, then laid her hand on my shoulder. I lunged toward the tunnel, but the entire world turned upside down. Spinning through a vortex of fog, I felt air speed past, bristling against my skin. We rolled into a pile of golden leaves with a heavy thunk, half attaching to my hair.

I whirled around on hands and knees and chucked a stick at Alaska's boot. "Take me back!"

"No, we're already here, so let's hurry up; then we can help find Landon. My brother won't give up until the kid is safe."

Behind us, pale skyscrapers kissed the sky. The setting sun cast hues of purple, creating violet-streaked bridges from rooftop to rooftop. But, in front of us, it felt like we had gone back in time a few centuries. An old stone castle loomed at the base of a mountain cliff. Vines and trees formed a barricade around the crumbling walls, disguising them as part of the rough mountainside.

"The Aurella Fortress," Alaska whispered in awe.

Relying on my enhanced hearing, I focused on every soft movement. Animals scurried high on the steep cliff. Worried conversations murmured through the apartment walls behind me—families hiding from the battle. But what worried me was the sound of strong Magik, a steady beat pulsing from within the Aurella Fortress. Alaska craned her neck higher to the arrow-slit holes at the top of the castle, but I knew the sound was coming from underground.

"Someone powerful is close." I led Alaska to the arched doorway to find it locked and sealed from the inside. We both pulled, pushed, kicked, and heaved. *Useless*. My muscles shook from the failed attempts.

"Can you teleport us to the tower?" I asked.

"No, there are barriers in place stopping me, but try your Magik."

"Can fire burn through stone?"

"I doubt it'll burn through this type of Magik. It feels like ₾sμwi. Some call it unnatural. Some call it darkness, a difference.

"I think I have something different too."

"What is it?"

"Knowing spells."

"Really?" She looked impressed. "Try that."

The wind accelerated, tossing me into the stone exterior.

"I...I don't know how to choose one. Normally, spells come to me randomly like they're sent to me from the divine as a message."

"Okay, let's keep pounding this door and wasting time."

She was right; I had to try. I closed my eyes and inhaled deeply. The wind rustled the leaves at my feet, and I focused on what the Unetlo Book looked like when Isaac carried it into my cell. Imagining my fingers grazing the animal hide, I imagined opening it, searching the ancient symbols for a spell that could work.

"This isn't working!" My eyes snapped open to the sight of Alaska trying to scale the stone, rock-climbing-style.

"Then try...something else." She panted between words, reaching higher. I stood below, ready to catch her, just in case.

"Don't fall."

"I won't."

Her boot slipped, and her whole body skidded, her front side scraping against the hard stone. She landed on her ass, thin lines of blood leaking from her forearms.

"Damn it!" She glanced at her watch. "We have to hurry."

My heart pounded in agreement, increasing to match the faster beat of the Magik drumming within the fortress. The tempo teased me, called to me. I tapped my fingers nervously against my thigh. On cue, words etched in my mind like lyrics, a song etched in my heart.

Monile volare. Monile volare.

What spell is that for? Are you okay?

Jadox questioned me through the tether. I immediately felt his adrenaline and rapid heart rate, but I shut him out so I could concentrate.

Monile volare. Monile volare.

Energy rippled through my core even stronger than the wind billowing against my face. I steadied myself against the side of the fortress, bracing myself. Heat spiraled through my tattoos, and suddenly, I levitated off the ground, hovering a bit above the leaves, tornadoeing at my heels.

"You're floating!" Alaska gasped. "Keep doing whatever you're doing!"

"*Monile volare*!" I screamed. "*Monile volare*!"

Suddenly, my body soared upward and over the entrance wall to the inside. My boots clunked hard on the rough cobblestone that was snarled with weeds.

"You okay?" Alaska yelled.

"Yeah." I tugged at the door's lock, but the wood was warped shut. "I can't open it."

"Magik, Kyra, use your fire."

I stood back and pointed a finger at the wood, sparking a little flame from the tip. A flame shot out and coated the wood, but nothing burnt.

"It's not working."

"Just go get the necklace. I'll meet you soon."

Hesitating, I laid one hand on the door, knowing Jadox wouldn't want me to leave his sister alone or for me to venture inside without backup, but the setting sun cast its last beam onto the door, reminding me that time was ticking. I turned, scanning an open square with a deteriorating well at the center. Leaves scattered the cobblestone, and a cat's meow called from somewhere out of sight.

"Hello, love..." Isaac's whisper echoed from the depths of the well, the same voice that had taunted me in the forest before. "Come play with me."

"Bring me the necklaces."

"Play hide and seek, love." His low voice vibrating against the well's stone walls should've sent shivers up my spine. Instead, my tattoo blazed and strengthened, and I followed the voice, walking hesitantly.

Gritting my teeth, I braced my back against one curved side of the well and my boots along the other. Slowly, I lowered, bit by bit, into the darkness. The roar of the wind above faded, and a soft plinking of water dripped, adding to the percussive beats, their tempo accelerating with each passing minute.

With my heart pounding, I ignited my finger like a flashlight and shone it on the well's floor. Halfway through the descent, my legs shook, and sweat trickled over my temple. My loud groans rang from the well. I dropped further and suddenly hit a clear buffer.

I swiped at it and felt an invisible platform below me resisting my entry. I huffed, straining to hold myself up, not trusting whatever layer suspended there to hold my weight fully. With my stomach in my throat, fear slinked in further, deeper. I was running out of time.

Images fluttered over my vision of Jay's sweet smile. He had told me he loved me. I should've said it back. Cursing aloud for separating without a proper goodbye, I swore I'd make it up to him. For now, I had to focus. I called upon ancient words mysteriously written in my soul.

Lahkee plico relie. Lahkee plico relie. Lahkee plico relie.

The spell caused the enchanted shimmer shield under me to

disappear, and I quickly descended the rest of the way to the base. Shivering, I rubbed my hands over my arms.

A puddle of water glided at my feet like a living, breathing creature. My reflection showed gold hair and amber eyes, but another woman stared back at me instead of my other features. She looked both strange and familiar, my face from another time. The image transformed into another woman with similar features, then finally, a man's face replaced her. Despite having no recollection of ever meeting him, I knew without a doubt who this man was: my real father. A droplet of water landed on his nose, disfiguring the image, so only my face gaped back.

"I'm waiting," Isaac's voice called from the cryptic tunnel.

I stepped forward, one hesitant foot at a time. His quiet breathing ahead was the only sound crawling along the shadowed walls. Cold slithered along my skin, reminding me of the caged cubes and that it was Isaac who had trapped us there. I'd kill this son of a bitch.

The tunnel narrowed, and Isaac's breathing grew louder. I tapped a nervous beat on my thigh. Soon, Isaac's heartbeat was as loud as the Magik drum. A small door creaked open.

"Hello, love."

I spun to my right and expanded a flame directly into Isaac's striking face, but he dodged it. His gray eyes entranced me in a hypnotic state, layered with knowledge as if my intentions were clear to him. With an inviting smirk, he ran a hand through his blond hair.

"Come." He turned, disappearing into the darkness. "Now, I can speak to you without having to manipulate sound waves and whisper through the air, just to you."

"I knew it was your voice in the forest."

"Get used to my voice, love. You'll be hearing it a lot."

Unwilling to show weakness to any man, I followed, allowing my fire to guide me. The unsteady feeling of walking into a trap made my gut twist into knots.

Isaac led me to a small room surrounded by stone walls. Half a dozen tables were spread around, different sizes and shapes, all covered with framed feathers of all types. Ostrich feathers. Cardinal feathers. Feathers of every shape, size, and texture were proudly displayed. Isaac pointed to a table holding four glass cases. Two were empty, but the others held the Elidi Ruby and Draven Emerald.

"Welcome to my man cave." Isaac held out both hands with a chuckle. "Don't touch anything in here."

"I was told Vayuians like wide-open spaces and vast skies."

"You're right, but we're all cursed with the fear of dealing with our shadow. We avoid basements, the darkness, the gloom, the demons lurking in our hearts, and that inevitable pull to jump into the abyss."

"How poetic. So, I take it that you welcome all that?"

The door behind me slammed shut from an impossible gust of underground wind. I resisted the urge to turn away, unwilling to show my fear. Trapped. Stuck. Caged—again.

"Ancient holy nuts," I faked calm coolness. "…If you wanted me alone so badly, all you had to do was ask me out."

"Ancient holy nuts? Wow, that's a good one. I'll have to write that down." Isaac sat in a stone chair shaped like a throne near a couple of lit candles.

"Just hand over our necklaces." I walked toward the table but slammed face-first into an invisible screen.

Isaac crossed one leg over the other casually. "Listen to my story first, then I'll give them to you."

"I don't have time for this."

A gust of power flattened me against the wall, stone scratching into my back. He stormed close, his handsomely rotten smile quickly replaced with stern lines. "And I don't have time for your attitude, Miss Kozelski, so listen to my story." Isaac leaned in, placed a hand on the wall behind me, and tucked a tendril of hair behind my ear. "Hmm, interesting."

"What?" I growled.

"I'm thinking, one day, you'll beg for me to kiss you."

I leaned in closer, slowly. "Like this?"

His breath hitched. I reached up and slapped his cheek—hard.

Isaac didn't even flinch. "You'll want me soon enough."

He was the epitome of everything that was wrong with the male sex. Why were the attractive ones always the most dangerous?

"Shut up, Isaac."

"Actually, I think I'll do the opposite." He backed away to sit on his stupid throne again. "So, like I was saying, before I was rudely interrupted, is that Vayuians are…."

"…Afraid of the dark, yeah, I get it. I don't care."

"My unique darkness is that…my son, Wes, is a hybrid. He is half-Mystier and half-Ordull."

I felt my jaw literally drop since I was the same. How many more hybrids were in Lodesa? How many of my friends or classmates grew up with their Ordull parent, not knowing the other was Magikal?

"Are hybrids common?" I asked.

"No, very rare. We're not supposed to mix our kinds, but Wes is the most perfect kid. I had to keep my life and powers secret from his mother. Even with our joint custody, she never knew where I lived. Rajitha had never seen or heard of Vayu. It was ten years of…lies. I'm an expert liar, Kyra. Deceit is my darkness."

I struggled against the hold of his invisible wall of pressure, pushing me to the wall. "Loosen this pressure. I…can't breathe."

The force of the wind shoving me against the wall was released. "Better?"

Now that I was free, I glanced at the red ruby that glowed brightly. Its presence increased my strength, and fire surged through my veins. Maybe this power could reach Jay. He needed every bit of strength to fight against Surh-Sig. So, I lowered my shield against him and sent Jay a message.

Jay, I have an idea.

Are you coming back? Did you steal the necklaces yet?

Almost, Jay, listen. Surh-Sig owes me. Tell her I'm collecting her debt, and she's not allowed to touch Landon.

A twinkle of hope zapped through, sending me warm vibes. But then the Magikal beating intensified, captivating all my attention with its fast pace.

"What is that drumming sound?" I asked Isaac.

"You can *hear* them?" He jumped off his throne, a devious look spreading over his face. "Excellent! After we Link, you can help me search for Vayu's necklace."

"I'm not Linking with you."

He circled around me like a jaguar, ready to pounce. "We have to, to return Wes. Plus, your nephew is at the frontlines, in danger. Together, we'll be stronger and can defeat all of Ordull's army."

"What? Why is Landon out there? If you know where he is, that means you're responsible for his capture. Again!"

Unable to hold back any further, I sucked in the energy from the flickering candles, turned it into a raging wall of fire, and hurled it at Isaac. My flames pinned him to the wall but didn't burn his skin. Apparently, another enchantment protected him. He writhed against the hold, trying to break free.

"It doesn't feel too good to be trapped now, does it?" I pushed it further, watching his face redden from the heat.

"Bring back Wes with me, then Landon can go free! Deep in here..." he struggled to point to his chest, "I know we won't fail."

"If we Link, I don't know what happens to Jay!" The fire crackled, roaring and growing, almost blocking my view of Isaac's pale face.

"Please..." he gasped in pain. "Listen, you need me because of the prophecy. You *need* me. You picked the wrong guy."

Curiosity crowded me, shoving away my rage. How did he even know about the prophecy? I dropped the flames, and Isaac collapsed to the ground.

"I didn't pick wrong!"

"The prophecy wasn't about Griffin, love. It was about *me*. You are my future. Gemm said you must Link with the one who hunts your soul."

"How do you know about that?"

"I'm the library keeper of Vayu. My job is information."

Panic coursed through my blood. "How is the prophecy about *you?*"

"I was hunting the one who was responsible for taking away Wes. I thought Griffin did it, but I was after the wrong person. Without knowing it, I was hunting for you. It was *you* all along. We don't have to be enemies."

"My sister is dead because of your people! You stole my necklace! You put us in an ice cage and almost let us all freeze to death! You threatened Jay?"

"Link with me, and I'll show you that I'm good."

Jay's sudden, desperate message relayed through our bond, broken and defeated.

I wish we had more time together.

What do you mean? What's wrong, Jay?

Stay away. Surh-Sig is here. The only way to save Landon is...

Shocks of pain and agony darted through the tether with such a strong force that I fell to the ground in a heap, fists tight.

Jay! Answer me! Jay?

25
KYRA

A sharp gash dug into my thigh, and my skin ripped and tore away. Screaming in pain, I looked down in surprise, but my leg remained healthy and strong. Untouched.

Another tormenting sensation stabbed higher up my thigh, then to my stomach. I collapsed, my back flat against the cold stone in Isaac's man cave. Agony slid its way into my body. Phantom fangs slashed into my tattoo, burying deep in my organs and slicing me to pieces. Torturous pain ripped me apart. A blinding light crashed into me. It was complete torture. I clutched my stomach—I was still unharmed. How? Jay.

Jay!?

Understanding snapped me to attention. Jay was dying. Pangs of anguish drowned me, covering me in heartbreak. Despair hacked at my insides in a deep gash of unending terror.

Gripping the stone wall, I fought against the miserable weakness and forced myself upright.

"What's going on?" Isaac stared, wide-eyed and speechless.

"Something attacked Jay. He's too weak to heal himself." Panting, I barely managed the words. "I have to go to him!"

"Not until we Link."

The little I knew about Magik wasn't enough to make this decision. I had been given the bare minimum of information about their world. Yet, a strange gut feeling tugged at me to agree with Isaac. Some little unknown voice whispered in my head to take the leap of faith, and it would all be okay in the end. The universe must know what it was doing because I had already hurt enough people. Maybe this time, I'd choose to help others the right way. Maybe Linking with Isaac would end up saving Jay.

"Fine. Fine!" I rushed out the words in a panic. "Fine. I'll do it." I stumbled closer to Isaac, knocking into the tables on the way. "But then you have to help me too. After we Link, we will go to Jay." Phantom pain shredded through every inch of me, sending me stumbling into Isaac's arms.

"I've got you, love." He lowered me to the ground, sat, and held me tight. "Repeat this spell: *Atuyasdodi promitto."*

Stinging sensations spread up my leg and stomach. Fatigue suffocated me as I closed my eyes, succumbing to the weakness.

"Kyra, stay awake." Isaac patted my face. "You can do it. Say it with me."

"Atuyasdodi promitto," I whispered. *"Atuyasdodi promitto."*

Isaac's smooth voice joined mine like we were meant to harmonize and walk-through life together. A sudden jolt pierced my stomach, and terror bombarded me that Surh-Sig had completed her final strike on Jay.

But a new power within my Circle called out to me. A cutting edge cleaved my stomach, connecting the other two. I didn't even have to look to know a new tattoo was there.

Fresh Vayuian Magik rushed through my veins, immediately wiping away my suffering. Wind. Air. Still in Isaac's stronghold, I glanced up, locking gazes with stunning gray eyes and a whole palette of his feelings, thoughts, and memories smashed into my heart and soul.

. . .

I'm holding a newborn baby in a blanket, rocking him back and forth. My love for Baby Wes is stronger than the force of gravity. Looking up at his momma napping in bed, the same warmth for this woman cocoons me in a dream world of eternal love. Images flicker, spanning through time to an afternoon painting a country house on a sunny day, a toddler's bare feet making prints on the patio floor. I sweep Wes up in my arms, swinging him through the air. His laugh makes the world turn. The power of wind, air, and clouds all bow at my feet as I create a pile of leaves for him to land in. Smiles. Laughter. So much laughter that my chest tightens with need.

"Kyra…your Magik is…unbelievably strong," Isaac croaked, astonished.

I snapped my eyes open, gasping. Isaac's exquisite face lit everything afire for a moment until he leaned down and hovered his lips over mine. Slowly. Tenderly. Sweetly. A part of me wanted to let him kiss me, a magnetic pull drawing me toward him with raw desire. What the Flames was going on?

"Holy fuck," Isaac's soft voice purred. "This feeling is insane, all-consuming."

"Back off, Isaac!"

After he moved away, his eyes were bright and yearning while he breathed heavily.

More of his cloudy memories puffed by.

Anguish. Wes isn't in his bed–nowhere to be found. The news relays that all males have evaporated into thin air. A government official calls. Over the phone, she tells me Rajitha's plane crashed mid-flight. My world implodes into nothingness. A cyclone reels from my fingertips. Destruction. My house—no, Isaac's house—obliterates into a pile of dust.

A wave of fresh nausea catapulted me into reality. It didn't matter that Isaac's haunting ache was justified; he was still the villain in my story.

I needed to help Jay. I focused, but my new powers wouldn't allow me to feel his wounds anymore. Panic soared in. Did I sever our bond? Did I kill Jay by Linking with Isaac?

Jay? Answer me.

Silence.

"Fuck!" Tears started to cascade down my cheeks. I reached out through the tether.

Jay? Please, answer me. Please.

Help...

Jadox's response was so soft, low, and weak. But relief ravished me. He was alive, and our Link was still intact–for now.

Hold on, Jay.

He was fading fast. Much too fast.

"We did it. Now, let's bring Wes back." Isaac lifted me from the cold ground in one swoop. Everything about his demeanor had transformed as if I were viewing him from a different angle. But I didn't want to see this silky side of him. Concentrating on my Magik, I blocked Isaac out of my mind.

Exhaustion and dizziness took over, but I fumbled to the door. "Not until we...heal Jay." I struggled to speak with the weight of Jay's death moments away.

"He's too far away."

Isaac blocked my exit to the door, and my gaze stupidly ran over his sculpted arms. How did I not notice his muscles before? Confusion washed through me when he brushed a fingertip over my cheek.

"Listen, love, we won't get there in time. It's over. Now, it's just you and me. Lower your walls, and we can save my son."

"Move out of my way! Alaska is outside the fortress walls. She can teleport us. I did what you said by Linking. Now, uphold your side of our bargain."

Flames exploded from my fingers, but Isaac blocked them with a wall of heavy mist. Glaring at each other through the chaos, I could sense his soul, his deepest desires, and everything that mattered to him, and I felt a heart of gold buried deep under the turmoil. Impossible. He was supposed to be the bad guy. His eyes softened.

"Kyra, please, you can't hate me. You can sense it too, how deep our bond goes. We're teammates now, so I'll prove it to you. You're right. I'll help you save Griffin."

I dropped the fire and nodded, relief almost overcoming me. "Let's go."

After cracking the glass sheltering the Draven and Elidi necklaces, I grabbed them and draped them around my neck. A steady drum pulsed from the ruby and synced with the energy from the emerald. The gold chains both glowed intensely, making Isaac gasp.

"They're too powerful for you; let me hold one," he said.

"Not a chance."

He swung the door open with a smirk. I ran down the dark tunnel, and he chased after me. While grappling with the intensity of Isaac's feelings, I tried to sort them out to gain some control. I felt his loathing for Jay. His revulsion that I was the cause of Wes's disappearance. His powerless feeling that Ordulls were already attacking Vayu. His confidence that he'd fuck me one day.

Arrogant prick.

At the base of the well, stars freckled the circle opening above. Out of breath, Isaac wrapped his arm around my waist. I didn't even flinch. Why? I needed to hate him. I did. I hated him.

No, you don't, love.

"Hold on tight." His words held a layer of sinful seduction. Isaac shot us straight up like an engine had exploded from the heels of our boots.

Instead of setting us in the shadowy courtyard, he grunted and flew us straight over the wall. We landed softly next to Alaska, whose face was smeared with dirt and muck.

"What is *he* doing here?" Alaska snapped.

The drumming beat of the necklaces sped up, sensing the urgency.

"We don't have time. Jay is hurt. Take us to the front lines. Now!"

"I can't take you both. I'm not strong enough."

"This should make you stronger." I looped the Draven necklace over her uniform. "There's no other option!"

Nodding, she hovered her hand over both of our shoulders and swallowed. "What if?"

"Now!"

In a moment, the ground flipped. We churned, swooshed, and twirled through space and time. Isaac's powerful strength consumed me, lifting me higher and higher. But I didn't want to follow. I needed to be grounded. I needed Jay.

In unison, we landed in the middle of the pandemonium of battle. Bullets soared. Bombs exploded. Arrows flew. Soldiers screamed.

"Where's Jay?" I swiveled in each direction, my head spinning as I squinted through the darkness.

Ventus creatures dove from rooftops, snatching Ordull women from atop tanks. Gorulas charged ahead and smashed hoverboards with their multiple fists. Bodies lined the street, streaming the pavement in crimson. The night's menacing glare threatened to strike every enemy when a lightning bolt cracked the sky. No clouds, no rain. But strikes continued to flash, burning the tops of the skyscrapers.

"Who in Vayu is powerful enough to control the weather like that?" I screeched to Isaac.

His mouth hung wide open. "Only me. And I'm not doing it. It's that machine!" He pointed to the Ordull battle line, where a massive electrical device manifested sparks and currents. A giant net that looked like a charged metal spider-web encompassed the exterior, shielding the machine from attack.

"Save my stupid brother." Alaska draped the Draven necklace over my head and turned, "I have to go help my friends." She darted off to the frontlines, summoning boulders as weapons and hurling them through the air.

Exhaustion bore down on my limbs as I ran, hunting for Jay, straining my ears for any sound resembling his familiar heartbeat. There was no point without him. My life was merged with his.

Where are you, Jay?

Isaac stayed close on my heels, thumping behind me. We had no armor, only our joint Magik. It had to be enough. A missile sound hissed from afar, quickly growing louder.

"Watch out!" I turned and rammed Isaac into an alleyway, landing atop him in a straddle position.

"I could get used to this view," he said.

"Ugh, you're a pig." I jumped off, ignoring the excited feeling of touching him.

We darted between explosions and wind rising into cyclones at every step. Running. Sprinting. The necklace's drumming accelerated. *Thump thump*. Faster. Harder. Stronger.

Jay?

I heard him before I saw him. Jay's wheezing and gurgling were razor-sharp to my ears despite the popping and banging from every angle. Horror sucked out my last ounce of calm. I sped to Jay's side and dropped to my knees.

Hovering my hands over his broken body as he lay in a pool of blood, there was no way of telling what organs were still inside and which were spilling out of him. His leg was ripped off above the knee. Bone jutted out from his thigh like a nightmare. Unable to hold back, I turned to the side and vomited sour chunks. I felt a fraction of Jay's injuries, but it must have been nothing compared to his torment.

"Oh, Divinity above," I rasped, my whole body shaking as I took Jay's cold hand in mine. "Is he already—"

"No, no, he's alive, look." Isaac dropped to his knees next to me, brows furrowed. "Take a deep breath, love. We can do this."

Trembling, I held Isaac's hand. He quickly clasped his other one into Jadox's limp hand on the ground, crusted in dirt and blood.

"Terra angakok. Terra angakok," I pleaded, leaning over his body. Gagging, I tried to ignore the wretched smell of flesh and guts. "Please, Jay."

Power scorched through my three tattoo rings, boiling with energy. Isaac squeezed my hand in encouragement as he continually repeated the same spell.

"*Terra angakok. Terra angakok,*" I chanted, tears dripping onto Jay's forehead. "Please, don't leave me."

"It's not working." Isaac dropped my hand and placed it on my back. "Kyra, he's—"

"No. I won't give up! He's my...he's...we can't stop."

Desperate energy coursed through me, stronger than any power my Magik had ever shown. I needed a final leap of faith. Without a plan or backup, I didn't care. It didn't matter. Trying was the only option. I dug deep within, placed my hands on the bloodied street, and pressed my forehead to the ground, calling up all the strength from any soil below the pavement. Jay's source of power.

Suddenly, the street cracked and parted. Soldiers in the background hollered, and engines boomed and croaked from falling into the crevice. Roots crawled up fast from the depths and wrapped around Jadox's mangled body. A painful grunt wisped from Jay's lips, and his eyes fluttered for a beat.

A budding flower blasted from the ground straight up, growing thicker and taller by the moment.

The stem wrapped around Jay. Thick and strong, it twisted around his entire body, covering him. The plant turned into a trunk, then a full-grown oak tree in front of our eyes. Its root dragged him underground.

"No!" I screamed.

Buried. Jay had been buried by a tree.

"Jay!" The loaded force pressing on my chest wasn't tolerable any longer.

"Jay!" I tripped while lunging to my feet but was caught again by Isaac. Leaning against him for support, I cried a river of longing. "He can't breathe underground!"

Isaac brushed his lips along my forehead softly. "I'm sorry, love."

"No! He can't breathe. I can't breathe."

"You're safe."

Pulling away from Isaac's embrace, I summoned fire. Heat spiraled from my hands and engulfed the tree in flames. Then as fast as the branches caught fire, a roaring wind extinguished it.

"Stop it, Isaac! I need to save him."

"That wasn't me. I didn't do anything," Isaac said.

From our Link, I knew Isaac was telling the truth.

"He's gone, love."

The tree continued to grow over Jadox, higher to the skies. Branches spiked out, followed by scarlet and golden leaves. I had never known this level of pain. First Hallie, and now Jay. Sobs racked my chest. Pounding my fists against the tree, I kicked it over and over with the small amount of energy left.

"Let him go! Let my Jay go!"

Isaac brought me to his chest, embracing me tightly. "Shh, I'm here."

My face rested against his chest, and my tears stained his shirt. With a subtle movement, the Elidi necklace brushed between our bodies, glowing brighter than before.

Your necklace. Use your necklace.

The voice was unfamiliar, but I needed to trust it. I grabbed the ruby, stuck it inside the bark, and twisted it deeper like a key until the tree almost swallowed it. Still attached around my neck, it pulled me closer. Dragging me.

"Wait!" Isaac's vice-like hold tried to pull me back. "You can't leave me like Wes left me. Not now."

I started to hit the tree again and again. I screamed and clawed at the trunk. "*Take me instead*! I'm the monster. I caused the pain. Let Jay live!"

The air stilled. Sounds disappeared.

Maybe Jay would still be here if I had gone with him before instead of splitting up. Or if I had brought him with me to the fortress. Maybe if I never Linked with him, he'd still be alive. Maybe if the stars were aligned differently, he'd still be breathing. If only I could go back in time and never meet him, then his rare smile would never have changed my life for the better. I'd never have known this agony if I had never met him.

On a high branch, Gemm stood, ferociously shooting tree limbs at our enemy.

"Gemm! Jay is under there."

Despite having to use a walking stick all the times I had seen her, she surfed down a moving branch and landed on the ground right in front of me. Gemm held my shoulders under her palms and looked me square in the eye.

"Once upon a time, there didn't need to be an end."

"Gemm! Just tell me what to do."

"You know the spell." Words were meaningless. I didn't know how to conjure a spell in the time I needed. She kissed one of my cheeks and stepped toward the fight.

Sometimes, they'd randomly pop into my head, and others, my power seemed to abandon me completely. Gemm was wrong. I couldn't save him.

"I can't do it."

"You know the spell, Kyra," Gemm encouraged me. "You can still save him."

I closed my eyes, focused on the shape of the Möbius, and imagined a drumbeat slamming harder and faster. I pictured Jay's face when we swam in the lake and how his lips felt during our first kiss. Suddenly, a spell materialized in my mind like a miracle. I chanted until my voice echoed in the night air, sounding like someone else, "*Hostia donadagohvi. Hostia donadagohvi.*"

The tree shifted, stepping back little by little. I held my breath. The limbs unraveled, and Jay lay flat on a blanket of vines. Healed. Whole. But heart-wrenchingly still.

As the roots fully untangled from him, there wasn't a scratch anywhere on his body. I ran forward, and the vines laid Jay straight into my arms, but his chest wasn't moving. Panic-stricken, I leaned my ear over his face. No breath.

"I don't want you to go." I hugged him closely. "I need you to stay with me, Jay, please."

I waited for his smirk and could almost hear the ghost of his voice make a joke on my behalf, calling me out for being sentimental. But his body was still. Lifeless. I choked out a sob.

"Okay. If you have to go…if it hurts too much to stay…I'll forgive you for leaving. If you can't stay here...I'll try to understand." I brushed a kiss over his lips. "But only you know my heart, Jay. Please come back."

Isaac laid a hand on his shoulder. Jay immediately sucked in a breath and rolled to his side. My heart burst with relief, and tears flowed.

Jay's eyes shuttered open, showing me that dark brown shade I could swim in forever. "Landon." He pointed to my nephew, out of harm's way, tucked behind crates by the side of a building.

A half-laugh, half-sob choked me as I brushed a lock of Jay's thick, wavy hair from his face. My lips found his again, molding together, and I never wanted to let him go. But the tree creaked and groaned. Wide-eyed, Jay pushed up, resting against my chest.

Gemm hobbled closer. "Once, there was a boy who changed the world," but when I looked at her, she was staring at Isaac.

We all glanced around at the continual explosions across the street.

Isaac stepped forward with a stern look and leaned close, "I need to tell you something."

Then whispered into my ear as I sucked in an astonished breath.

Isaac's revelation wrapped tight around my gut and strangled me. I tried to push away what he'd said and buried it deep. There was no time to ask questions. For now, I'd have to cling to hope for dear life.

"It's time," he said.

"Time for what?" Jay swayed as he rose, then helped me up too.

"Can't you feel it, Griffin?" Isaac danced around our secret, taunting him with his wicked grin. "Can't you feel the difference?"

"What?" Jay's confusion covered his features.

"Your Link with Kyra is broken." Isaac lifted his shirt, showing his blue tattoo entwined with a new red one. "You'll eventually understand and accept it, Griffin. She was always meant to be mine."

"No." Jay's body slackened. He looked at me with such a look of betrayal and hurt that my heart shattered in two.

You didn't Link with him. Tell me you didn't, Petal.

I had to do it to save you.

I can't. I can't lose you to him!

My hands found his chest, and I continued to speak through the bond. *I'm right here. You didn't lose me. We can still communicate, Jay. Our Link is still intact.*

Unaware of our telepathic conversation, Isaac pulled at the back of my shirt, separating me from Jay. "You made me a promise. Let's do this now."

In a daze, Jay finally noticed the giant electricity generator. I followed his gaze to the menacing destruction growing closer. Only a shallow sizzle of my power crackled in my Circle. My energy was depleted from the spell to save him. There was no way I'd have enough strength.

"I can't bring Wes back yet," I mumbled.

Isaac's eyes narrowed.

"Leave her alone." Jay staggered between us, his chest out and fists clenched. I felt his Circle light with energy and become soaked in power.

"We need time to rest, Isaac. We need to find a safe place away from the fighting, then when I have more energy—"

"No!" He released a gust of wind straight at the little haven hiding Landon. "You will bring Wes back right now, or Landon dies. I'm fuckin' tired of waiting and having to threaten you. I don't want to hurt the kid, you know that! Don't make me."

If I hadn't linked with Isaac, I wouldn't have known the love behind his words and the truth that he had no intention of hurting my nephew. Or me.

I locked eyes with Jadox, sent a message through our bond, and he nodded his response.

26

JADOX

Our Link felt jumbled, strained, and corrupted. I sensed Nilson's toxic energy through Kyra, and I needed him gone. The fact that she sacrificed herself by Linking with him made me want to fight for her even harder. Bits and pieces of her heart were already fading each time Nilson tugged her attention away. But she wasn't mine to control. She made her choice. I'd stay by her side, regardless.

Wind sped in a flurry, pushing me sideways like a wall of pure force. From the battlefield, an announcement echoed from a loudspeaker in President Stirk's voice, "Detain criminal Kyra Kozelski. Capture as many as possible. Kyra is the focus. Find her!"

Thankfully, we weren't in plain sight of their battle zone but were hidden in an alleyway. Ordull soldiers still fought against Mystiers with Tasers and electric whips. My war stood directly in front of us: a six-foot-two Mystier with a blond bun and sneering smirk. Nilson needed to leave, and Landon had to stay safe—or Kyra would never be the same.

When I glanced at Kyra, communicating silently again, realization sparked on Nilson's face. He looked back and forth between us.

"Wait a second," he growled. "Show me your tattoo."

Her hands covered her stomach over the army uniform. "No."

Nilson stormed closer, and fear surged through her Link.

"Don't touch her!" I pounced forward.

But Nilson flipped up her shirt and pulled her hemline down a bit, despite her struggling against his strength. Three tattoos Linked together, a greenish-brown Draven on one side, the unique Golden loop in the middle, and the new blueish-white swirled Möbius on the other. My heart sank at the proof. She was truly Linked to us both.

"I can't believe it. How are you still Linked with Griffin? I thought I felt a snap, a separation between you two." Shock lined his face in every wrinkle. "Linking with you was supposed to sever your connection with him. This wasn't supposed to happen."

"I don't know. Legend also says the Link only severs if one of us kills the other," Kyra said calmly, despite the chaos encircling us. "I guess it was a myth."

"I can't bring Wes back if you're still Linked with Griffin! It'll never work."

"Why? We can try when I have more energy."

"Kill him! Now, or your nephew dies." He pointed to Landon, who sat terrified on the sidewalk.

"No." She stayed calm, calmer than I'd ever seen her. "You won't follow through." She smiled; confidence spread across her face. Obviously, she had a plan, but our connection was muddled with a third member added in. I didn't have time to sort out her web of thoughts.

Kyra threw her hands forward and a small, weak flame connected to the giant tree. It caught fire and grew, crackling. Each limb was devoured in flames. As Nilson stared, I knew she had used it as a distraction.

Kyra threw both necklaces to where Landon sat, curled against the wall, and two strong orbs encircled him like a bubble. How did she know they'd do that? Did she silently cast a spell? Draven's forest colors swirled with Elidi's flames in a shield, protecting the boy from harm.

Nilson fumed in a mighty scream, then he whistled loud. A venti screeched above and dropped, white wings outstretched. When it swept near the ground, Nilson jumped atop. With his face darkened and stern, he pointed to the sky. Clouds submitted to his control and piled in heaps of black and gray. Thick rain splattered fast, turning to hail. The heavy balls smacked our heads.

Kyra shielded her head with both arms and ran for cover under an awning. I followed, leaping over trenches. In a quick moment, guns popped like fireworks as havoc and mayhem continued. We didn't have much time to stop this battle before they were all dead.

"We need to merge our powers. We're stronger when touching each other." Kyra moved so we were side to side, arms brushing against each other's skin, both of our other hands outstretched and ready.

A blast of Nilson's wind hit us head-on, but I dug my heels in. My eyes watered from the blow, adding to the showers streaming and drenching my cheeks. I commanded a giant oak tree ahead. Its limbs whipped crazily just as Nilson's venti plunged closer. The animal dodged, swooping around the flailing branches. Bark and twigs broke off, forming spears and tridents. The weapons shot toward Nilson. He swerved at the last second, gliding higher, then lower. Up and then down.

"Damn it! They're fast!" Kyra chucked a sphere of fire at them, singeing one wing. The venti cried out and dropped fast, shaking Nilson off its back onto the ground.

"You two will eventually turn on each other!" Nilson yelled.

"You're wrong."

Relief washed over me so strongly. My own people, including Alaska, took years to forgive me for erasing that Ordull woman's memory, yet Kyra blessed me with that gift so quickly.

Kyra hurled more cannonballs of fire at Nilson. He blocked, then raised his hands again and flexed every muscle. Veins bulged, and his skin turned red under the streetlights. He screamed out in strain and moved the sky impossibly closer. The clouds grew larger, nearer. Huge. They engulfed us, thick and heavy with the scent of rainfall smelling poisonous. Sweat poured down my temple from the strong humidity.

The air turned so foggy that I couldn't see Kyra next to me; I only felt her arm brush against mine.

Hold onto me, Kyra.

Magik clustered in my Circle, stronger than before. With a mighty yell, I stomped, and the entire ground shifted underfoot. The ground rolled up in a hill, then swished back in a forceful wave. Undulating again and again.

"Ugh!" Nilson barked in frustration. "Griffin, stop!"

"Never. I love her."

"She'll turn on you, abandon you, just like every other person in your life."

Wind stronger than dynamite shoved us both hard against a building's edge. Kyra crashed through a glass window, landing inside. The sudden pain of her scrapes mirrored onto my arm, and I gasped in shock.

Reaching through the threshold, I lifted her up. "Are you okay?"

"I'm fine." But turmoil twisted on her face.

"This motherfucker needs to die!" I roared.

She nodded softly, but her doubt flared through the bond. Flames exploded from her hands, burning up the thick fog. "Show yourself, Isaac."

He appeared only an arm's length away with a devilish smirk. "I don't want to hurt you, love."

With a flick of his wrist, Kyra fell to the ground, clutching her throat. Her sweet amber eyes locked on mine. Choking. She couldn't breathe.

"Let her go!" I charged like a tiger but only made it halfway before I dropped to my knees, breathless.

No oxygen. Suffocating. Kyra fell completely on her side, twitching on the pavement. Panic swept in. Neither of us had air. He'd kill us both.

But then Nilson dropped too, his face turning red with wide eyes bulging out. He released the power over us, and we all gasped for breath, sucking in air.

Realization struck.

Nilson couldn't hurt Kyra without hurting himself, and he also couldn't hurt me without injuring Kyra. The three-way Link must have changed the rules. We were stuck in a circle, connected for eternity. Rage consumed me that he had forced Kyra into this position. The last thing she wanted was to be controlled by a man.

Stretching my arm out, I commanded shrapnel nearby to trap Nilson. I couldn't hurt him without hurting the woman I loved. Sweat drenched my shirt as it screeched closer. A sharp pinch throbbed in my head from the exertion. It exhausted me. Finally, metal surrounded him, pinning him to the side of the building.

"Let me out, asshole!" He squirmed and thrashed.

I reached for the tentacle from the electric machine. I just needed a little time to cage Nilson's powers. Unfortunately, it was much heavier than I'd thought. Grunting in earnest, I focused harder and could sense the location of the button to turn on the electricity.

"If you turn that on, it'll eliminate yours too." Nilson basically read my mind as he begged desperately.

Kyra marched to where Nilson was restrained against the building and slapped his face. "Isaac, give up. It's over. I will *never* choose you."

Through the Link, all I could feel was her devotion to me.

"I never want to see you again," she said to Nilson. "Never step foot in Draven. Never seek us out. Do you understand?"

He licked his lips. "How about we try that kiss before you go?"

Kyra's memory flashed in my mind of Nilson's lips hovering over hers. Fury seethed my spirit, and without hesitation, I flipped the switch on the giant machine. Sparks erupted throughout the city, and I dropped to the ground. None of us had Magik, but Kyra's essence surrounded me in a bubble of determining protection. She chose me. No matter what Nilson threatened, I'd protect her until my dying day. But a blast catapulted me to the ground, and everything went black.

Dawn's early light cast a cautious beam of warmth on my face. Soreness crept up my back. I rolled over on the pavement to see Kyra chewing on a sandwich on the curb, sitting next to Landon. She whispered something in his ear. The metal cage that had pinned Nilson to the building wall had melted, and he was gone. The air was quiet. There was no fighting, no screaming. Unfortunately, the smells weren't as calm.

The sky's refreshing colors of carnations, dandelions, and goldenrod shades didn't mask the blood that coated the quiet city. Bodies littered the streets, including Fiozee, straight ahead, dead in a pool of her own blood.

How long was I unconscious?

Five hours, soldier.

Kyra faintly smiled, warming me more efficiently than the sunrise. I crawled over with a sigh and sat next to her. The smell of death eliminated any desire to accept the sandwich Kyra handed over.

"No, thanks," I mumbled. "Have you seen Alaska?"

Kyra pointed ahead while chewing, at a couple of figures in the distance, bending over and dragging bodies. My sister paused above Fiozee, and her shoulders drooped low.

Does anyone have the power to erase Landon's memories of last night?

I know a spell, but I won't use it again.

Kyra exhaled deeply and rested one hand on my leg.

You almost died, Jay.

"We'll be okay." I took her hand and, with a tired smile, kissed her inner wrist. I wrapped an arm around her waist and asked, "What happened to Nilson?"

"He's gone." She stared at the ground, not elaborating.

"He'll come back. Then what? I can't hurt him without hurting you."

"I noticed," she groaned. "I'll just help him bring back Wes. I agreed to it, and that's all he wants. I was willing to last night, be he wasn't patient enough to wait."

"And then we'll never have to see him again."

She swallowed hard and nodded, but hesitancy shot through the tether. I was too afraid to ask why, and since she kept her walls up a bit, I couldn't sense the source of her nerves.

I brushed her golden hair behind her ear. "We need to talk about this three-way Link, Petal."

Her tired grin lit my entire world on fire. "The last time you called me that, it was after a different kind of invasion." Her wink made me laugh.

I kissed her cheek softly, glad she was next to me.

Alaska strolled over with a frown painted on her skin. "Our allies from the Society lost ten members, but Vayuians lost fifty-eight in total, and Ordull soldiers suffered hundreds of losses. We think they captured five Mystiers for their science project. When you turned that electric machine back on, it surged and created a power outage, so they finally retreated. But this isn't over. President Stirk didn't get what she ultimately wanted."

"Me. She wants me." Kyra brushed the dirt off her uniform and stood. "But why?" Her hands brushed against the spot where her unique tattoo was etched into her skin.

I bolted upright. "We need a plan."

Kyra nodded. "I can't let more innocent people die because of me. I'm already the cause of the males disappearing. I have to fix this, not make it worse."

"We'll figure something out."

She leaned her head on my shoulder. "Do you think President Stirk will attack again right away?"

"No, they lost hundreds. They'll need to regroup."

Landon tugged on my pant leg. "Dog."

When I looked, he scrunched his nose and pointed at a picture of a dog on his keychain.

"That's a good idea, bud. You play with Chocolate until we leave for Draven."

It'd be the first time I'd welcome an Ordull into my village. Maybe my rules have changed. Or I had changed.

Kyra smiled, raised on her tiptoes, and swiped her lips over mine. Her delicious tongue promised me a night of stress release and comfort. I leaned into her, thanking the goddess above that she was safe—and she chose me. Kyra chose me. Relief swarmed my core when she laid a hand over my chest.

"I can hear your heart, soldier," she snuck out the words between kisses.

"Could you trust a man with your heart?"

She gulped and leaned away. Studying me, Kyra tapped my nose. "You're not any man, Jay. You're *mine*."

Joy latched onto my exhausted muscles as we linked hands along the brightening street, along the pathway forward.

27

KYRA

One Week Later

I patted Chocolate's head and tossed her a treat as a bluster of wind flung a piece of my golden hair across my face. Sunrays beamed through the naked branches above, spotting the Draven Forest floor with little circles of light. A fluster of sounds all blended into an orchestra of the woods—cardinal songs, a rushing river, footsteps of friends in the distance, Gemm stirring her potions in her den.

"Chocolate." Landon giggled and rubbed the dog's belly as she rolled over. "Chocolate!" His smile was beaming as he repeated the new word he had achieved while he threw a stick and raced her, zig-zagging between Draven's bare trees.

Jay stood before me silently with a posture as straight as a soldier. Those near-black eyes entranced me, so full of love and depth. There were endless sparks in them, springing life in his eyes. He'd always remind me of an oak: supportive, protective, strong, and very climbable—in every way imaginable. He would always be where I belonged.

What are you thinking about?

He sent the message through our thread and smirked. But, sometimes, I preferred to hear him speak just to feel the thrilling chills his baritone voice zapped through my veins.

Thinking about tearing off your clothes, soldier.

I scanned his cargo pants, military boots, and tight brown tee that hugged his sculpted chest and shoulders. Those dark eyes were boyfriend-worthy, with abilities to convince me to lower my wall bit by bit, day by day. Leaning closer, he pulled the chords of the oversized hoodie so my face was smushed inside. Temperatures had been dropping, and the village was preparing for winter, requiring warmer clothes.

"Hey. I can't see!" Laughing, I jumped up and wrapped my arms around his neck.

With only the tip of my nose and mouth protruding from the fleece, he laid his lips on mine. Hypnotic. He mesmerized me with his skill, my bones turned to water, and both knees went wobbly.

"I like this." His tongue teased mine, sending warmth through my body despite the nippy wind. "We should try a blindfold next time."

I fixed the sweater and winked at him. "How about we move *next time* to right now?" I reached for the first rung of our treehouse ladder, but it was broken.

"Hey now, Petal, Be careful. Do you need some help?"

"No." Grunting, I reached again, slipping and sliding down no matter which angle I tried.

Jadox crossed his arms and kept that smug grin plastered on his face.

"Fine, help me up, but only because I asked you. This is *my* idea."

He rubbed his dark stubble as if considering the option of denying me. "Okay, and when we're up there, there's something I need you to...do to you."

"Is that a promise?" I whispered in his ear, then let my tongue trail over his ear lobe.

The deep vibration rumbling from within him gave me goosebumps.

"Hurry up. I can't wait any longer."

Jadox laced his calloused fingers together, and I placed one boot in the center. With the ease of an athlete, he projected me straight up. As I climbed, melodies of children's laughter harmonized in the distance as Landon waved to a knot of girls in the garden. I smiled and sighed. This could eventually be our home.

But Jay didn't know that when he was unconscious, I had freed Isaac by melting the metal that had caged him to the building. Knowing about Isaac's past, intentions, and son, I couldn't leave him there. Now that I had seen inside his soul, killing Isaac Nilson was out of the question. He held a piece of me—no matter how much I hated him. Hated him. Completely. Because there was no other option. But no matter how hard I fought against Isaac, the unnatural pull toward him was undeniable.

Our bond's strength still couldn't compare to my connection with Jadox, but staying here in Draven might endanger the tribe. There was no way I'd risk Gemm, Alaska, or Landon's life again. Jadox would follow me to the ends of the earth, so I'd eventually have to talk to him about leaving.

For now, at the top of the ladder, I snuggled into our newly decorated treehouse. I cast an invisible, heated wall around us that kept us warm from the brisk wind, yet a shiver ran up my spine when I heard Isaac's voice in my head again.

I'll see you soon, love.

As always, I ignored him. Maybe he'd eventually give up. But what did he mean by *soon*?

"You okay?" Jadox tugged me closer on the mattress in the treehouse. "You've felt a little distant in the last hour."

Smiling, I straddled him and pressed my hands to his strong chest. "I'm fine as long as you're with me."

He studied me intently, searching my eyes. "I've been thinking we should research the effects of Linking with more than one person. I'm worried that—"

"That I've split my soul?" I drummed a little rhythm under his shirt on his bare stomach, circling his tattoo, slowly moving one hand to his chest, and one to his inner thigh.

His brows knit together as his eyes turned to liquid night, fierce and longing. Those large hands found my waist and gripped tight—I adored it, wanting him to touch me every second of every day.

"Jay, I'm okay. My soul is intact, and I'm all yours for the taking."

He smoothly moved my hands out of his pants. "Let's talk about what happens if there isn't a happily ever after, just in case."

"It won't be an option. You and me forever, sugar cakes."

"Sugar cakes?"

"Terrible nickname?" I laughed.

I grabbed a little pebble and chucked it into the river below, hearing the splash so clearly it was as if I stood right next to where the rock hit the water.

"Stop looking at me like I'm about to shatter, Jay. I'm okay."

Jadox massaged the top of my thighs. "Do you want to talk about Hallie again?"

"There's nothing more to say. She's gone, and I'll always miss her, but what's done is done. I loved her, the end."

"She betrayed you."

I sighed, letting the rest of the tension out. "She was trying to save Landon, so I understand. I made that wish which caused this mess, and now I plan to fix it."

"What are you going to fix?"

"First, I'm going to stop the president from capturing the Mystiers."

"You aren't invincible, Petal." He tucked a strand of my hair behind my ear and tilted his head.

"Wanna bet?" I rested my head against his chest and watched the children run below. "At least all these Dravians are hidden again. These necklaces are supposed to protect them, right?"

"Well, they're supposed to."

"Now that we have two, hopefully, everyone should be safe from President Stirk."

I reached under my stack of pillows and pulled out a little wooden box. I twisted the top open and dug inside. The Elidi Ruby and Draven Emerald lay sparkling and glowing next to each other.

Jay ran his hand over the ruby. "It's so strange that the heat is gone. It's like the Magik was sucked out of it."

A new fear bubbled to the surface. "What if it's broken? Do you think it'll still protect us?"

He tilted his head, inspecting Draven's Emerald. "I hope so."

I tried to block out the curiosity about where Vayu's crystal was. Would Isaac know where it was?

"Kyra!" Alaska shouted jokingly from below. "Give me a beat!"

A group clustered by the garden, cheering and waving their arms, reminding me of the Lunar Festival. Until Stirk regrouped her army, we had some time to take a breath in our sanctuary. We were safe, for now. I grabbed two broken sticks by my feet and pounded them hard and fast, creating the hypnotic rhythm all the dancers below craved. My heart ballooned to the size of a drum as Jadox jigged his shoulders ridiculously—something he'd only show to me. A hint of a smirk quivered at the corner of his lip until it turned into his genuine smile.

That smile—beautiful and dangerous, breathtaking and mine. I literally inhaled sharply at the perfection of the curved arch of his thick lips. I wanted to stop drumming for just a moment and devour his stupid, kissable face. Desire to know everything else about this confident, stubborn, protective man shot through my chest and ripped out any decent sense that remained. We were two bodies, but together, we were one soul.

"I love you," Jadox said unbelievably sweetly. "No matter what."

"Even if I turn into a dragon? Oh, maybe that's a spell! How cool would it be to breathe fire?"

"Hurry up and bring those lips over here." He waved me closer.

A mighty force, like magnetic energy, pulled me straight to him. I'd never tire of the sensation. My entire being gravitated toward him—like we were one. Our mouths met, hungry for one another, an appetite that was never filled. Jay's tongue swirled with mine, making me moan. I gulped in courage, deciding to finally tell him how I felt.

He flipped my wrist over, kissing the blue trail of veins. "Kyra, you are my roots, gnarled, twisted—"

"And rough…" I finished for him. "My very source of life."

Suddenly, Jadox's s-watch binged. His mouth tightened into a line as he pressed the button and projected a news update onto the tree trunk.

Syvonne Stirk sat in her high-tech hoverchair on the top step of The Crooked Chateau, of all places. Her long hair fell flat and straight against the traditional silver and lavender presidential robe, covering her missing legs.

"Our capital has been bombed. We have received an update that this is the work of an organization called the Aurum Orbis Society. They are people without powers who stand for a merged society with the witches. They demand freedom for the witches who are currently imprisoned. We have declared war against these terrorists."

She raised her chin. "Anyone who aids this society, or the witches, will be tried for treason. We must work together to eliminate the remaining threats and keep our country safe. Rewards for your cooperation in providing knowledge regarding other witch villages or Kyra Kozelski's location have increased."

President Stirk nodded to someone off-screen, then three female army soldiers with black silk gloves dragged a man on stage.

Several gasps from the audience were projected through the camera's microphone. I had forgotten that most Ordulls weren't aware that Mystier males had survived *The Scorch*.

The prisoner's body was wrapped in electrical cords, shooting out sparks every few seconds. He held his head high and glared into the camera. Something about his eyes looked familiar, but I couldn't place him. When I leaned into the projection, his eyes shifted from navy to green, resembling the color of the ocean floor depths sprinkled with flickers of white sand.

"Who is that?" I pointed to the screen, my finger tracing a long scar stretching from his temple, across his cheek, and down to his chin.

Jadox shrugged. "I hope they're not doing a live execution again; I should turn this off."

"Hold on one second."

On-screen, a soldier moved the man's tunic, and the camera zoomed into his aqua-marine Möbius Circle on his stomach—a Cydian.

"As you can see for yourselves, witch males survived *The Scorch*. This tattoo is the symbol you all need to check for to confirm their status as a witch." Stirk continued, "There are four different color combinations: those with red-orange have fire powers, those with green tattoos can manipulate the earth elements, blue and white swirls indicate the witches who control the air, and finally, those with this aqua shade hold water power in their hands." Stirk pointed like a dagger at the camera. "Do not be fooled by their tricks. They are all highly dangerous and are not to be trusted." She shoved the prisoner. "Go ahead, tell the world what we agreed on."

The Cydian prisoner continued to glare into the camera. The lights accentuated his long scar. "I need to speak with Kyra Kozelski."

His rare island accent was thick and unexpected. He spoke as clearly as ocean water shining in the morning sun.

Jadox snorted. "Like we're that stupid to walk into a trap."

"Kyra, I have something you need to know about your family." The prisoner's eyes twinkled with confidence. "Meet me here at The Crooked Chateau in one week."

My family. Did it have to do with the secret Isaac passed on to me? I knew what I had to do.

About Cassie Swindon

Cassie's next writing idea includes fairy-tale retellings. She's very interested in turning the tables to show stories with gender reversal from other perspectives. Of course, she finds the best place for brainstorming ends up being in the shower or while trying to fall asleep, which isn't convenient in the least for taking notes. In her spare time, she collects bookmarks, stickers, washi tape, and cats.

Sign up for my newsletter here:
https://cassieswindon.com/

facebook.com/cassie.swindon.3
twitter.com/CassieSwindon
instagram.com/cassie_swindon_author
bookbub.com/profile/cassie-swindon
amazon.com/stores/author/B091N72414
goodreads.com/cassieswindonauthor
tiktok.com/@cassieswindon

GLOSSARY OF TERMS

(alphabetical)

Circle - the branding Möbius circle tattoo that a Mystier obtains when coming of age. There are four coloring shades of the tattoo depending on which tribe the Mystier originates from.

Elements - fire, earth, air, water.

Hybrid - this term has not been formalized since it is rare that a Mystier and Ordull mate produce offspring. A hybrid would have Magik of some sort but may not fit within the typical rules.

Magik - sacred elemental powers that only Mystiers possess, not to be confused with witchcraft or the mythical sorcery found in Ordull fairytale books.

Mystier - a being who can harness Magik, part-human.

Ordull - a human not possessing Magik.

₾sμwi - cursed dark Magik where little information and history is known.

CHARACTERS

(alphabetical)

Alaska Griffin - Jadox's little sister. Enhancement - teleportation. From Draven.

Chocolate - Jadox's brown lab based in Draven.

Fiozee – Aurum Orbis Society member as a spy in the Ordull army.

Gemm Griffin - Jadox's grandmother. Enhancement - prophecies. From Draven.

Goldie - gorula creature based in Draven.

Hallie Kozelski - Kyra's step-sister. Ordull. From Andersonville.

Isaac Nilson - Librarian of Vayu. Enhancement - eyesight and weather.

Jadox Griffin - Past soldier for the Ordull army. From Draven. Enhancement - smell and healing.

Kyra Kozelski - The Golden One. Enhancement - hearing and knowing ancient spells.

Landon Kozelski - Hallie's son. Ordull.

Paola Perez - Alaska's Ordull ex-girlfriend/soldier in the army. From Andersonville.

Quamir - Kyra's Ordull band manager/ex-boyfriend. From Andersonville.

Rajitha - Isaac's Ordull ex-girlfriend and Wes's mother.

Surh-Sig - The Skin Scraper/earth nymph. Harnessed by the emerald.

Syvonne Stirk - President of Lodesa.

Wes - Isaac's (and Rajitha's) son - hybrid. From Vayu.

Zeph - Isaac's Mystier ex-girlfriend. From Vayu.

CREATURES

(alphabetical)

Gorula – (Goldie) A mammal with six long arms that end in sharp claws and fur that ranges from peach to gold, beige, brown, and tan. Five feet tall and four hundred pounds of mostly muscle. Omnivore. Likes to dig in the dirt and swing from trees like a monkey. Usually lives in/near Draven. If a Mystier accepts a gift from a gorula, there will be a price to pay.

Venti/Ventus - Flying creature. A mixture of an eagle and a horse. Beak mouth. Omnivore. Covered in feathers of white, beige, powder blue, or gray. Nine hundred pounds. Twelve-foot wingspan on average. Gallops on four legs with hooves or flies. Usually lives in Vayu.

For drawings of the four fantastical beasts, check their images at www.cassieswindon.com

MYSTIER TRIBES

(alphabetical)

The locations of the village tribes are named after the most powerful ancestors in their tribe. Before The Fall, about eighty years ago, there were over fifty Mystier clans. Now, only four remain.

Cydon - Cydians possess water power. With training, they control elements involving water, ponds, rivers, lakes, oceans, and waves. Their Circle tattoo is a blue/green/aqua swirl. The strongest family of this element, blessed with enhancements, is unknown.

Draven - This village is on the northeastern coast, full of dens and treehouses deep in the forest. Dravians possess earth power. With training, they control and manipulate elements such as soil, rocks, and plants. Their Circle tattoo is a green/brown swirl. The strongest family of this element, blessed with enhancements, are the Griffins.

Elidi - Elidians possess firepower and are wild at heart. With training, they control elements involving heat and flames. Their Circle tattoo is a red/orange swirl. Mystiers with this Magik are rumored to be rare and nomadic in nature.

Vayu - This Mystier city is on the northwestern coast with a population ten times that of the other villages. Vayu's skyscrapers look like they are floating when viewed from across the ravine that separates the city from the Ordull world. Vayuians possess air power. With training, they control elements involving wind and oxygen. Their Circle tattoo is a white/blue/gray swirl. The strongest family of this element, blessed with enhancements, are the Nilsons'.

LOCATIONS

(alphabetical)

Andersonville - the capital city of Lodesa (where Kyra grew up).

Aurella Fortress - an ancient, crumbling castle on the edge of Vayu's border.

Crooked Chateau - originally an art museum and community center with a ballroom, has a shifting purpose in the novel's progression.

Forbidden Caves - on Draven's border, the setting for many legends.

Lodesa – the main country.

Vuldow - The Shadow Land in the south is miles of dystopian-like terrain, not due to a nuclear bombing like the Ordulls assume, but because of the massacre during The Fall, eighty-two years ago, that wiped out hundreds of cities.

See the full epic map at the beginning of this book or online at www.cassieswindon.com

Necklaces

(alphabetical)

All four elemental necklaces have the power for enhanced protection and power when used.

Crystal - necklace from Vayu.

Emerald - necklace from Draven that bound Surh-Sig to the forbidden caves.

Pearl - necklace from Cydon.

Ruby - necklace from Elidi that burns when touched by someone without a protective spell.

UNETLO BOOK

The strongest and oldest spell book belonging to the Mystier race, residing in the Vayuian Library from year 05G-present day. Spells are listed alphabetically.

Atuyasdodi promitto - I vow to Link to you.
Dehano huc – come here
Digati impetu – attack.
Hostia donadagohvi - let go.
Monile volare – levitate.
Opus amare – open love.
Reditus atsutsa - return to me.
Terra angakok – heal.
Vand zalit – release.
Venereae ostaguyelu - protection against pregnancy and STDs.

ENHANCEMENTS

(alphabetical)

Healing – Jadox.
Hearing – Kyra.
Prophecies – Gemm.
Scent – Jadox.
Sight – Isaac.
Spells – Kyra.
Teleportation – Alaska.
Weather – Isaac.

CHRONOLOGICAL ORDER OF THE LINKED TRILOGY

Isaac's Curse
Jadox's Spell
Kyra's Ruin
Scorched
Caspian's Demise
Severed
Syvonne's Sting
Shattered

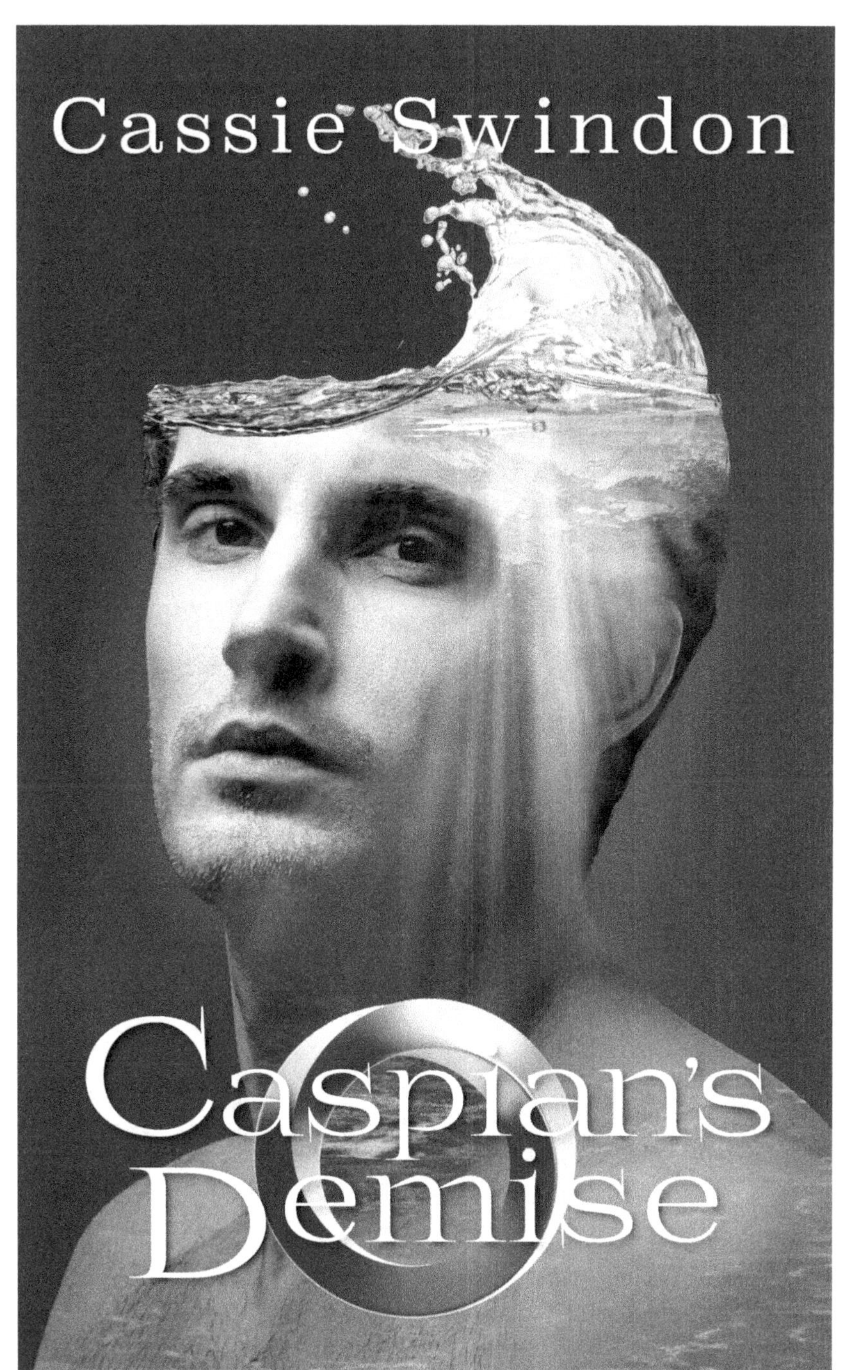
Cassie Swindon
Caspian's
Demise

Cover Design by Anna Cackler

CASPIAN

If I could access my Magik right now, I'd drown Stirk in a heartbeat, right where she stood. A beam from the Frost Moon lit her silky, fake white hair as she spoke into a microphone in front of a dozen cameras. Female soldiers wearing gloves tightened the electrical cords around my chest, strapping me to this chair for all of Lodesa to witness.

One of the women winked as she bit the end of one glove and slid her hand out. She skimmed her soft hand between the lethal chords and pulled open my tunic. The sensation of her skin on mine sent a bolt of energy straight to my Möbius Circle, zapping me with renewed strength. A wave of water Magik gushed through my veins for a split second, fighting against the electricity choking my powers from all angles. "You like that, pretty water boy?" She licked her lips.

"Fuck off."

"Oh, and your accent is a certified panty-dropper." Her hot breath warmed my neck as she smiled and whispered, "Caspian, sit still for the president, and smile for the cameras. It's show time."

The cold wind tickled my bare skin, sending goosebumps up my chest. Even the bottom of the ocean wasn't as dark as President Stirk's stare when she turned toward me.

"This is the symbol you all need to check for to confirm their status as a witch." Every news camera fixated on me as Syvonne pointed her finger toward my tattoo like a dagger. "Do not be fooled by their tricks. They are all highly dangerous and not to be trusted." She shoved my chair with her boot. "Go ahead, tell the world what we agreed on."

My fists tightened into balls on the side of the chair, and I strained against the electrical ropes binding me.

"Go on, witch," one guard whispered, "we wouldn't want to do another live electrocution now, would we?"

I gritted my teeth and glared into the camera. "I need to speak with Kyra Kozelski."

I hated that Syvonne had control over me. There was only one reason I'd agree to follow her little threats and games; unfortunately, she had my balls under her command. Putting another Mystier at risk was against the Cydon code, but I had to do as I was told. Hopefully, this Kyra girl was as smart and strong as she needed to be. But why did the president want her—of all Mystiers? What did she do, and why was she so important?

"Kyra, I have something you need to know…." I stated the memorized script. "Something about your family. Meet me here at The Crooked Chateau in one week."

I hoped she'd never show up—because it could be that girl's last day alive. Regardless, I needed a solution to free my people from Stirk's wrath. Plans whirled through my mind as snow fluttered and hit the road, cast in shadows between the streetlights. I glanced at the hoverboards leaning against The Crooked Chateau's proud stairway.

The heaviness of the electricity humming from the thousands of apartments and shops suffocated me. If I wiggled out of these cords somehow, there was a chance I could reach a hoverboard and ride through that graveyard and into the forest. It was a better plan than navigating through all the other buildings surrounding us.

"That's a wrap," a camera man said.

Darkness cast a comforting cloak again as the camera lights finally turned off, reminding me of the ocean's depths and the deepest underwater caves of my secret home—my home with Narelle. Longing tore through my bones, and an unfathomable ache for coral reefs and saltwater made me itch for the sea.

The pathetic Ordull newscasters congregating outside the castle dispersed slowly. I scanned each of their hoverboards, all too far away.

"Don't even think about running." The soldier aimed her gun at my chest.

"I need water." I pledged to myself weeks ago that I wouldn't show weakness or beg, but everyone had their limits. "Please bring me water."

"No way, fish-man."

"My name is Caspian."

"No one here cares."

I groaned, deprived of the source that kept my heart beating. Water. My tattoo cried for liquid, an inlet, a stream, a cup of ice, anything. Desperation strangled my throat, and my vision turned blurry again. How long had it been since I last saw the ocean? A week? Two? I wouldn't last much longer without access to water.

"Drag the prisoner inside," Syvonne Stirk spat out to her guards, the only Ordulls remaining around the chateau. She guided her hoverchair inside the building.

Energy failed me, and I was unable to protest again. My gaze climbed the flame-like structure, wide at the base with a slick, curved, sloping exterior that reached for the moon with its pointed tip. The sleek red metal of The Crooked Chateau matched the fiery threats layered in Syvonne's eyes. Dizziness claimed my sight, and the castle door swayed before me. My eyelids dropped shut, and my chin knocked into my chest.

"Stay awake, witch!" a guard yelled.

Staring up at the inky sky speckled with stars, I imagined it was the ocean floor with glistening treasures shining from their hiding places in the sand.

Suddenly, the soldier straddled me as I was tied to the chair. A swarm of power jerked from my tattoo to my fingertips. Magik tried to spiral within me, first into a ripple of water, then a deadly current crashing through my body. But there was no water nearby to pull from. Every muscle tensed. The connection of our touch wasn't strong enough to break free like in the past. I needed water.

"Get off of me!" I growled.

She laughed, writhing her crotch over mine, dry humping me on the chateau's front stoop. I cursed my dick for hardening from the friction.

"Enough, Paola." Her friend laughed. "You'll have to pick one of the other witches. You know these men are off limits." One of her teammates pulled her off my lap, then clicked buttons on her s-watch. As she moved, I caught her last name on the soldier's badge: Perez.

Paola Perez huffed dramatically. "You know President Stirk won't let any of us fuck them…because, goddess forbid, any of us got pregnant with a witch spawn." Bitterness oozed from her disgusting lips. "But all our men were taken away. How are we supposed to play?"

"I thought you were bi," her comrade said.

"I am, but now those remaining males are off limits, it enhances the draw, don't ya think?"

The first rolled her eyes. "Not really. That should be the least of your worries with everything happening right now." She gripped the leg of my chair. "Now, help me lug him inside. I can't haul two hundred pounds of muscle by myself."

"I have an idea of what I can do with all that muscle." Paola snorted mid-cackle, then helped her comrade tow me from the unnaturally bitter temperature into the chateau's main lobby.

I wanted to close my eyes and fade into a dream involving dolphins and sea turtles, but each thud and bump of the chair jerked my neck. Plus, the sights of the castle's décor were distracting. It once served as an art museum. Blasts of aqua-marine abstract paintings were framed and hung, each at a crooked angle. I tilted my head, interpreting the shape of one as a starfish.

The legs of the chair scratched against the hardwood floors, leaving long streaks in our wake as they yanked me past the spiral staircase in the middle of the lobby. Instead of scaling the stairs, the soldier pulled a necklace from under her uniform, a key dangling from the chain. My tattoo overflowed with a hunger for a different gem—the precious Cydian pearl that someone stole from our treasure chest.

The soldiers grabbed more wires and tangled them around my chest, tying my entire chair to the staircase railing.

"What are you doing?" I asked.

"You didn't think we'd let you rejoin the other witches, did you?" The revolting one ran her hand through my hair and trailed her fingertips down the back of my neck.

"Perez, you have first watch. I'll be back in three hours to switch." Her teammate lowered her chin. "And please don't fuck him."

"But he's too delicious. Feel his abs for yourself. Come here."

"No, thanks."

"Swimmers aren't your type? What, is he too tall, too strong?" Paola laughed, sarcasm lacing each word. "His shoulders are just too big?"

"Perez, if you even think about…."

"What you don't know won't hurt you." Her wicked smile reached her eyes, sparking a nauseating sickness in my gut.

"Fine…" Her friend waved her off. "I warned you." As she strutted away, the soldier flicked a switch near the door, and wires lining the walls flickered on.

Electricity smothered me. If Paola wanted her way with me, I had no capacity to stop her. Just as I anticipated, hunger filled her eyes as she dropped to her knees and ran a hand up my thigh.

"Is your tentacle as long as an octopus'? You'll enjoy me and be begging for more tomorrow."

"I have a wife."

She licked her lips. "I don't give a damn. If the scientists got what they needed from her, she's probably dead by now."

I struggled against the firm hold, but the wires dug further into my skin. There was no way I'd tell this lunatic that Narelle hadn't been captured and imprisoned in the basement of this chateau with the many others.

"Let me out of here."

"Not till I get what I want."

Sucking in a deep breath, I counted to five, then changed tactics.

"Fine. Get me just one glass of water, and I'll give you the best night of your life. I'll bend you over on this stairway like you want and give it to you harder than you've ever had."

"Finally, you see reason, Mister Poseidon." She licked her lips, considering. "I know you're being sarcastic, but I'm oh-so curious."

I tried to think of anything that would trigger my rage, maybe that would overpower the electric restraints. Memories flashed.

Death. Blood. All Cydians being dragged from our home. Children screaming. Guns blasting. Taser guns knocking everyone unconscious. Ordulls using our fishing nets to drag us away. But the Ordull soldiers were too fast, already flying away with the innocent children on their hoverboards. Narelle's face turning red from horror.

Rage pounded through my temples, and my heartbeat sped wildly. I tried squirming and lashing against the chords binding me.

I screamed until my throat turned raw. "Let me go!"

Wide-eyed, Paola scrambled away, her back plastered against the wall of the chateau's lobby. "Shh, quiet down."

I tried to scream again, just to get her in trouble. Impossible. Parched. The dryness of my mouth and my throat begged to be moistened. "Bring me water." The sounds came out like a frog croaking on his dying breath.

"I'll give you another hydration injection." She reached into her pack and pulled out a syringe.

"No, not again. Quit stabbing me and give me something to drink for once." I wrestled against the ropes until a shadow swooped by a window behind Paola. My heart stuttered a beat. Who was there at this late hour?

"You know it doesn't hurt, so sit still. It will make you feel better, then maybe you'll get in the mood." She staggered closer, the needle pointing straight at my arm.

In the window, a face made from Divinities popped up. Narelle.

My wife. I held my breath so I wouldn't give my shock away just as Paola stabbed the injection into my arm. She was right. My veins were already soaked in the fluids meant to rehydrate me. I sighed deeply, and my shoulders relaxed.

"See, I told you."

Not daring to lose sight of Narelle, I locked my eyes on hers through the window as she raised one finger to her lips.

"This is your last warning, soldier. Untie me."

I shot a pleading look at my wife standing outside in the darkness. Narelle nodded and ducked out of sight, then a deafening crack split my eardrums. Windows shattered into pieces from a storm of water bursting through the glass.

"What the?" Paola jumped up and trained her weapon on one window, then the next. "What did you do, witch?" she snarled and tapped her s-watch for backup.

My heart pounded in my chest as Narelle surfed on a hoverboard through one window straight to me. She turned the switch off on the wall, draping us all in darkness. Chaos cycloned as water spiraled around Paola, trapping her in the corner. She screamed, but an Ordull was no match for my wife. Narelle pulled a knife from her boot and slashed through the electric cords imprisoning me. Magik surged through my veins, empowering me with the strength of floods and hurricanes at my fingertips. The ocean blue-green of Narelle's tattoo flared bright through her wet, white tunic.

"Caspian, are you okay?" Her murderous gaze darted to the wall of water. "Do I need to kill that bitch?"

"She's not worth it. Come on, we need to free the others in the basement."

Right as I turned toward the trap door, Narelle grabbed my hand. "There's not enough time."

"What do you mean? They're right below us!" Adrenaline drenched my senses at her touch, the only touch I ever wanted and needed to feel whole.

"I know where the children are being kept. They're not in this basement. We have to choose the adults or children."

I glanced at the basement entrance again, knowing the tortures the Cydians had endured for the last month, but I lunged toward the hoverboard anyways. "Take me to the kids."

Narelle hopped on, and I jumped after her, latching my hands around her thin waist as she steered.

"Thank you for coming, babe."

"Always. Our love is…."

"Richer than the treasure of Vodagua's Cove and…."

"More powerful than a whale," Narelle finished our saying.

We flew out of the chateau and soared higher into the snowfall. Buildings zoomed by as we sped through alleyways by moonlight. The streets had never sounded so quiet. Maybe because over sixty percent of the population was dead and gone. I couldn't believe it. How did someone wish away all Ordull males? And why?

My Magik hummed with water, begging to break free, especially when in such close proximity to Narelle. Our touch magnified my strength. I had no family until Narelle, but despite this, the Cydon villagers nominated me as their leader. Everyone knew I had an enhancement only passed down through the strongest of the Mystier families.

Narelle whispered over her shoulder through the whipping winds, "The children were taken to one of the empty prisons outside the city."

"Do we have anyone helping?"

"Just four of us. The others went under the sea. Cydon isn't safe anymore."

"Do you know what Syvonne's doing with the children?"

"No. What did she do to you?" Narelle guided the hoverboard toward the city limits, where the lights were fainter, and treetops swayed in the breeze below.

"Her scientists abstracted our DNA. They're trying to gain as much information about Mystiers as possible through questioning and genetic research. She wants to figure out if reproducing with us remaining males would result in children with Magik."

"I heard the Ordull woman are being forced by law to apply to get pregnant, and they're selected by a strict panel."

"Yeah, Syvonne wants to hand-select the genes of the babies that will be born."

"But why?" Narelle shook her head. "What does she get out of it?"

"Control, maybe. I don't know yet."

"Why would she keep all Mystier women alive?"

"Maybe to use your powers? I don't know." I clenched my grip around her, grateful my wife was still alive and free. "I missed you."

"I missed you more." Her voice shook. "What if…what if the children are…."

"They'll be fine. We'll get them out."

"No, it has to be you alone." And in the next second, I understood why. Our hoverboard glided across the border of the trees and lingered over an enormous lake. Half a mile away, a gray fortress towered on a tiny island. Skylights shone down over the grounds, creating dancing circled beams that changed direction, igniting the obvious electrical wires cloaking the entire building.

With a heavy sigh, Narelle eased the hoverboard behind a tree. After we both slid off, she pointed to the dark waters. "We found maps. There's one underwater entrance on the south side. The code is 11-27-14, but I don't know if…." She bit her lip and both brows furrowed in a line.

I gently cupped her cheeks. "Don't worry, I'll get all the children out." Kissing her cheek, I prayed to the Divinities above that my promise would ring true.

"I know you will, babe." Shaking, she pointed to the various points in the tree line and specified where the other members of our team awaited, out of view. "You only have six hours until sunrise. You need to hurry. They could be separated, chained, or …" Her breath turned ragged.

"Narelle, look at me. They'll be okay."

She rose on her tiptoes and brushed her lips against mine, a pact made with her urgent movements. "Caspian, I need you to come out of there alive."

Stepping away, I stared at the lake. "The children come first."

Before letting her respond, I tossed off my shoes and sprinted across the sand. Cold water splashed my ankles, sending immediate relief up my legs and into my core. I sucked in a giant breath and dove headfirst through a patch of water-lilies straight into my glorious haven. Sublime beauty painted a picturesque view in the murky depths. It didn't compare to the ocean but still jolted my Circle with the power I had desperately longed for in captivity.

Coontail plants tickled my skin as I swam deeper, further away from Narelle, and closer to the enemy. The moonlight highlighted golden rocks at the bottom of the lake, and a memory flashed in my mind, crippling me motionless.

A golden seashell sparkling in a small hand. A petite smile matching mine. Child's laughter and a high-pitched singing voice that rang from somewhere deep, etched in my soul. Waves crashing at my ankles. Confusion. Water. Waves. Darkness.

I gasped for clarity, unsure why the string of images felt so important. Shaking my head, I stroked harder, faster, toward the island. My hands acted like paddles, and my feet kicked like fins. Water rushed into my lungs like it always had as a young boy, comforting me with the strength it provided my tattoo. Just because I could inhale water didn't mean I'd last without oxygen forever. I had about ten minutes left until I'd need to resurface. For now, energy still swirled below my stomach, ready to burst.

Fifty more strokes away. So close. A school of fish parted for me as I barreled through, completely accepting me as one of them, a creature of the deep. Instead of fatiguing, my muscles raged with life, anticipating the upcoming fight. Forty more strokes away. I could basically feel Narelle's warm hug wrapped around my neck already. Thirty strokes away. The entrance was right where Narelle described, a round door under a latch. Nearly there. Everything would be okay.

Suddenly, a net latched around my ankle and tugged me back. It wrenched me lower, lower, anchoring me to the lake bottom. Frantic,

I fought against the tangled web. I reached up, but the weight held me as solid as a stone statue sunk from a shipwreck.

Stealing a moment, I calmed my racing heart and chanted a spell in my mind, one my mentor taught me years ago as a teenager. *Vand zalit. Vand zalit.*

No help arrived. Seconds ticked by, robbing my last few minutes of breath. "Come on!" I shouted into the water, bubbles rising from my mouth.

Struggling again, I bit at the netting, tried tearing it apart, and patted my pockets for anything sharp. Once more, I begged for assistance.

Vand zalit. Vand zalit.

Finally, a high-pitched, eerie call crooned from the depths of the pool. Stunning navy eyes popped up and snatched my attention as the wicked siren sang her hypnotic lullaby.

Love the demons of the lake.
Let me help you, child, trust in me.
Cydon boy, why do you ache?
Let me help you, child, trust in me.

Let my voice lead your way.
Time to follow the blue ray.
Never need the light of day.
Time to follow the blue ray.

Love the demons of the lake.
Let me help you, child, trust in me.
Cydon boy, why do you ache?
Let me help you, child, trust in me.

Swirls of her long, flowy cyan hair danced in the water like streamers, but I could sense the sugar-sweet algae lining each strand. She set me free, kissed my cheek, and swam into the shadows.

Rushing, I swam hard to the entrance. The door swung open,

sucking me inside the chamber designed for water entry, then shut. Water collected at my knees, and my clothes dripped heavily. After shaking out my hair, I took a step forward. A red laser beam strobed against the wall, and a loud alarm ripped through the air.

"Shit!" I lunged into a dim tunnel, hearing the plink of water from inside the walls. My bare feet slapped against the wet floor as I ran in the only direction possible, straight to my captors.

Panting, I summoned my Magik, letting a fistful of water roar in a typhoon in my hand. Stomps and thuds grew louder, echoing off the tunnel walls. There were no other options. I bulldozed through the first soldier since she was only half my weight. But the second one lodged a bullet straight into my shoulder. And the third shocked me with a Taser gun, electrocuting me into a heap on the floor.

"Well, well..." Syvonne's voice was rigged with anger. "How did you manage this?"

I grunted, still trembling from the residual electrical zap numbing every limb.

"Maybe this situation could work to my advantage. Bring him to the littles."

"Yes, President." The soldiers chanted in unison, then bent down and latched a pair of electric cuffs onto my wrists.

After the sensation in my limbs returned, I stood on my own. I didn't need to be dragged this time but followed her willingly to the children. The tunnel eventually split into three, then five, then seven passageways, becoming more of a maze as we marched along. I wouldn't be able to keep track of how we entered.

Unphased by the puddles under her hoverchair, Syvonne flew over confidently, leading the team until the light finally shone in the distance. An opening grew wider the closer we walked until a massive underground room, surrounded by walls as thick as an underwater tank, came into view. Nothing could burst through that concrete. In a giant circle, dozens of cages hung from the ceiling, all wrapped with electrical cords and wires, zapping little bursts of light through the grayed wires every few seconds.

Sounds of soft sniffling and whimpering set a fire inside me, and I lunged for Stirk, ready to snap her neck with or without Magik.

A soldier sidestepped me and shoved the barrel of her gun into my stomach. I doubled over in pain, falling to my knees.

"It's over for your kind," a soldier hissed. "A witch like you destroyed us, obliterated our families, and took away all the men. Now all of the children will pay."

"I didn't take away your people, and neither did these children. Let them go."

"Daddy?"

In that single instant, my heart shattered into a million pieces. A child thought I was her father. I craned my neck from my knees, determined to know which cage housed the girl. Her little hand stuck out from the wires in her cage, but I was unable to see her face. A ton of bricks stacked on my chest when her fingers curled around the bars.

"It'll be okay, sweetie." But my hands were still strapped behind my back.

Syvonne leaned closer with a smirk. "It's not nice to give her false hope."

I rammed my skull into hers, sending President Stirk stumbling into a puddle.

"Tie him up!" She hollered while rubbing her forehead.

"Wait!" I cringed, unsure if my plan would work. "What's something you'd exchange for them?"

"Even if there was something I wanted, I can't trust you to follow through." President Stirk laughed as if she never knew what laughter was, then wiped the water from her skin and stood again. "But what exactly did you have in mind?"

"You want that Kyra girl."

"You're definitely a certified genius."

"I'll find Kyra and bring her to you if you free all these kids and give them immunity."

Syvonne crossed her arms. "That's not enough. Kyra is the one responsible for all the males' disappearance."

With this new piece of information, it felt like a rock was lodged in my throat. How could I hand over the most powerful Mystier our kind had ever known? It went against everything we believed in. But, if *The Scorch* was her fault, then she was also to blame for the attack on Cydon.

Syvonne tapped her foot, then checked her s-watch. "I need to test these littles again." She pointed to a soldier. "You, bring my equipment."

"No! Wait!" I stepped forward. "What else do you want for their freedom?"

Syvonne flew around me in a circle. "Hmm, no one has ever been so willing before. I have so many desires. Which should I choose?"

Tension coiled right in my chest, threatening to explode.

"I need you to bring me the one she's Linked with, alive."

Panic twisted into a torturous knot in my heart. "She Linked?"

She tapped my nose like petting a dog. "This is my offer. Take it or leave it."

Warnings flared like an impending shark attack. Syvonne could annihilate our kind.

"Where's my Daddy?" The girl's angelic voice sliced open everything.

I had to make Syvonne believe that she had won. I swallowed hard, relishing my last moment of freedom, but at least the children would be safe and free. "Okay, deal, you will guarantee all these kids will remain unharmed and free to be returned to their families."

"Deal." Syvonne tilted her head and raised both brows. "And, Caspian, once you find out who Kyra truly is, you can't take this back. Capturing her is part of the deal."

"Who is she?"

"Time will tell."

I knew what I had to do.

CONTINUED...

The Linked Trilogy continues in Severed and Shattered. Order your copy today!

CASSIE SWINDON

SEVERED

THE LINKED TRILOGY

BOOK TWO

CASSIE SWINDON

SHATTERED

THE LINKED TRILOGY
BOOK THREE

GOLDEN CHAINS

Cassie Swindon

New Adult Romantic Suspense

www.ingramcontent.com/pod-product-compliance
Lightning Source LLC
Chambersburg PA
CBHW060543310726
48982CB00009B/1361/J

9781737346920